black roses

samantha christy

Saint Augustine, FL 32092

Copyright © 2016 by Samantha Christy

All rights reserved, including the rights to reproduce this book or any portions thereof in any form whatsoever.

This is a work of fiction. Names, characters, places and incidents are either the product of the author's imagination or are used fictitiously, and any resemblance to actual persons, living or dead, business establishments, events or locales is entirely coincidental.

Cover design © Sarah Hansen, Okay Creations

ISBN-13: 978-1530601578
ISBN-10: 1530601576

For my mom and dad.
I will never be too old to need parents.
Thanks for doing such a great job being mine.

Books by Samantha Christy

Be My Reason
Abstract Love
Finding Mikayla
Purple Orchids (The Mitchell Sisters Book One)
White Lilies (The Mitchell Sisters Book Two)
Black Roses (The Mitchell Sisters Book Three)

black roses

chapter one

piper

I squeeze my eyes tightly shut. I turn up the already blaring music in my ears, hoping it will drown out the sound of the plane engines catapulting me closer to the one place I don't want to go.

Home.

Can I even call it that anymore after all this time? What is home anyway? According to Google, it's *'the place where one lives permanently, especially as a member of a family or household.'*

So by definition, I'm homeless. A wanderer. A gypsy.

And that's exactly how I like it.

Why did I make that stupid promise to Skylar last year? To come back for her wedding; plan it even. What the hell was I thinking?

I re-read the conversation Charlie and I had during my London layover.

Charlie: You okay?

I smile, thinking how it hadn't even been three hours since I left her at the airport in Barcelona. She flew there with me from Istanbul. She was going to shack up with a guy we met there earlier this year. I begged her to come with me, even though I knew she wouldn't.

She hates home even more than I do.

Me: Yeah. Wish you were with me.

Charlie: You know I can't go back.

Me: I know. I still wish you were with me.

Charlie: I am in spirit. We'll talk every day—every hour if that's what you need.

Me: Gotta go. They're calling my flight. Love you.

Charlie: I love you, too. You can do this, Piper. I know you can. Six weeks will fly by.

Six weeks. The words bounce around in my head like a pinball. I know I've gone back before. But it was a day here and a day there—manageable mostly by large quantities of alcohol, something I tend to stay away from normally. Baylor's wedding was the last time I dared to cross the Atlantic. But six whole weeks back home? Away from Charlie. Away from my comfortable life. Away from the possibility of—

I startle when someone touches my shoulder. I look up to see the flight attendant handing me my drink. I turn the music down so I can hear her.

black roses

"Would you like some pretzels with this?" The statuesque brunette with a pasted-on smile hands me a tiny bottle of Jack and a plastic glass filled with ice and Coke.

Ignoring her question, I stare at the glass as she places it on the tray table in front of me. I reach for it clumsily, toppling it over the side of the tray knowing it will probably stain my new white shoes. "Oh my gosh, I'm so sorry!" I lean over and pick up the glass as she pulls a towel from her apron, looking slightly irritated, but still managing to keep the fake smile on her face.

"No problem." She wipes up my tray. "This happens all the time. I'll just run and get you another."

"Maybe you should just bring me the can this time." I shrug and smile sheepishly. "Less likely to spill."

"Of course." She hands a couple bottles of water to the people sitting next to me.

A few minutes later, she returns with a can of Coke and glass of ice, placing them carefully on my tray. She raises a brow as if to say *'you'll be more careful this time, right?'*

"Thanks." A sigh of relief exits my lungs when I hear the sweet *'phsst'* sound of the can opening. I then break the seal on the tiny bottle and proceed to pour them both over the ice. I catch the flight attendant before she's out of earshot. "When you have a chance, I'd like another," I say, waving the empty bottle of Jack in the air.

She nods as she walks away. I turn the music up again and wait for the liquor to calm my nerves.

Four hours and three drinks later, the plane makes its descent into JFK. The whiskey has dulled my anxiety, making me brave enough to collect my things and be herded into the airport along with the hundreds of other travelers; people who are happy to be returning home or going on vacation; people who are complete strangers to me. People whose faces are unfamiliar, yet I wonder if I know any of them. Or if maybe they know me.

My eyes catch those of a man. He appraises me seductively from head to toe, causing bile to rise in my throat. I quicken my steps, rudely bypassing many of the other people heading to customs. I look back over my shoulder to see that his attention has turned to another pretty face and I take a breath. Maybe I didn't have enough liquor after all.

As I stand and wait for the carousel to start delivering suitcases, I peruse the crowd gathering beyond customs. I see women jumping into the arms of men. Children being scooped up and plastered with kisses. Businessmen and women scurrying to car-rental booths, and sign-carrying limo drivers waiting on their assigned fares.

I don't, however, see my big sister.

I quickly send Baylor a text telling her I'm waiting on my luggage. No doubt, she's running late as usual.

Once I have my bag, I rest against a pole, stretching my legs while I await my ride. A few other people have done the same thing, most of them pulling out their phones, oblivious to the world. Not me. I'm a people-watcher. I like to know what's going on around me.

It makes my stomach turn when I watch some of the men come through customs. They stare at beautiful women, undressing them with their eyes. Ogling their breasts and asses. Even following them to try and arrange a hookup or a date. Whenever one of them looks in my direction, I give them my look. My look that says *'fuck off.'* The look I've perfected over the years.

I check the time and text Baylor again, contemplating getting a cab to take me to Mom and Dad's on Long Island. Baylor invited me to stay at her house in Maple Creek, which also happens to be the house we grew up in. My other big sister, Skylar, offered me a room at her and Griffin's townhouse in the city. But both of my sisters have new babies. Not exactly my idea of a fun vacation. Not that any of this will be fun. More like six weeks of torture.

God, I wish Charlie were here. She gets me. I think she's the only one who does.

I look across the arrivals terminal and see a guy who's people-watching like me. He's leaning casually on the wall, a foot pressed up against it behind him. He's wearing a ball cap that's covering what I think is blonde hair, but it's not pulled low enough to hide his recklessly handsome features. He's very tall, crick-in-your-neck tall. His chiseled good looks lean towards rugged and unruly, and the broad chest beneath his crossed muscular arms exemplifies power and strength. The short beard on his face is so light, it's easy to miss if you don't look closely.

Why am I looking closely?

Unlike a lot of other men, he's not ogling women. He's simply regarding each person he sees as if he's trying to figure out their story—why are they here and where are they going?

I see a woman with super-model looks walk by him. I watch intently as they make brief eye contact. He acknowledges her with a lift of his chin and then moves his attention to the next person who walks by. I don't miss the fact that the model turns her head and gives a longing look to the people-watching stranger. I snicker inwardly. I'll bet she's used to a lot more attention than he gave her.

A moment later, he springs off the wall and sprints over to a crying child. I gather from the boy's hysterical demeanor that he's lost his parents. The stranger gets down on his knees and within seconds, has the boy calm—smiling even. Shortly after, a woman runs up and scoops the child into her arms. It looks like she thanks the man as the boy whispers in her ear. She gets something out of her bag and the man scribbles on it. He gives it to the boy, and I'm not exactly sure why, but the boy is very excited about his mom getting this dude's phone number for a hookup. The boy and the stranger high-five before he walks away.

Then something peculiar happens.

He looks at me. He looks at me and my knees go weak. They actually almost fail to hold me up. My heart thunders and my breath catches. My skin heats up and the hair on my arms stands on end. Good God—why am I having this reaction to a total stranger? Why am I having this reaction period? In all of my twenty-one, almost twenty-two years, this has never happened. I sit down on the nearest bench, wondering if maybe I picked up a flu bug on the plane.

I mean, he could be an axe-murderer. An axe-murderer who hangs around airports and gives his number to single mothers of scared little boys. Maybe he's a pedophile who sits around looking for kids—that's why he doesn't pay much attention to women.

For some inexplicable reason, I can't pull my eyes away. He doesn't look at my boobs. His eyes don't even stray from my face. He tilts his head to the side like he's trying to figure out *my* story as he'd done with all the others. Then a slow, smug smile full of masculine arrogance creeps up his face.

I avert my eyes and send an all-caps text to Baylor asking where the hell she is. The tension of the flight and the toxins from the alcohol are getting to me. My head hurts. I reach up and free my hair from its constraints in the hair tie. I rub my temples and stretch my neck. Then I hear it.

His voice. The voice that slices into my skin like a knife through butter, permeating my entire being against every ounce of my will.

"Piper, right?"

Despite the smooth yet rugged sexiness of his voice, I start to panic. *Oh, God. Who is he?* How does he know me and what the hell does he want?

I can't speak. Along with my wits, I try to gather my things as I contemplate running. But with my luggage, it's not really an option. He must think I'm crazy.

He briefly removes his cap, running his fingers through his hair before putting it back on. "I'm your ride."

samantha christy

chapter two

mason

She's gorgeous. It runs in the family, of course, and she's a carbon copy of Baylor with the exception of her intense green eyes. They are the color of sparkling blades of grass in the sunlight just after the rain. But Piper has an exotic beauty that the others don't have. Maybe it comes from her travels abroad. Maybe it's her unusual hair. I normally don't give a second look to women. Not ever. But right after I recognized her; when she reached up to pull the band from her hair and it fell down around her shoulders, my goddamn heart stopped. The tips of her honey-brown hair look like they've been dipped in black ink, framing her heart-shaped face that surely belongs on the cover of a magazine. Her wavy hair falls just below her collarbone and looks slightly longer in the front than in the back. Before I walked over to talk to her I had to step back. Compose myself. Take a breath. Much like I do right after the huddle and before the snap of the football.

"My ride?" Her face is pale and haunted. She looks at me like I'm the Grim Reaper. Her doe eyes assess me and I can almost see the questions racing around in her head. She pulls her shoulder-bag close against her body and looks behind me. "How do I know you're my ride and not some psycho killer?"

I surmise from her reaction that Baylor didn't tell her I was picking her up. I offer my hand in greeting. "I'm Mason, Griffin's friend. Baylor sent me to get you."

She regards my outstretched hand as if it might burn her. Her phone chirps and she glances down at it, reads the screen, then rolls her eyes. My guess is Baylor has just texted her. "Best man, huh?" she asks, looking slightly more amenable as she finally shakes my hand.

Her small hand is soft and a little damp. She's nervous. I wonder if I made her that way or if it was flying that did it. I can't help but notice how well her hand fits into mine. For a brief second, I wonder if she minds the calluses on my palms and then I remind myself that I really don't care. "And you're the maid of honor. Guess that means I'll be walking you down the aisle," I joke.

"Whatever." She pulls her hand away and I immediately mourn the loss.

There's only one other person whose touch has ever made me feel this way. I shake off the notion and reach for her suitcase. "Let me help you with that."

She stands up and her slender, graceful fingers intercept the handle before I can reach it. "I don't need your help." She walks away, pulling the large bag behind her.

I feel like a loser as I catch up to her. We must be a sight. This petite creature lugs a heavy suitcase behind her while her companion, who towers over her and outweighs her by a good hundred pounds, walks by her side. "Okaaaaaay. How about a drink?" I point to a sports bar tucked away in the corner of the arrivals area.

She stops walking and looks up at me in horror. "A drink? I don't even know you. Why would I want to do that?"

I hold my hands up in surrender. "I just figured after your long flight you might want to unwind a little. Anyway, you're about to get into a car with me. A drink seems kind of benign compared to that, don't you think?"

"I don't really have a choice about the ride, now do I? But I'm still not having a drink with you. I did enough *unwinding* on the plane." She turns her back to me and walks away as I follow the movement of her curve-hugging jeans.

"Okay, then. You're not only a bitch, but a drunk," I mumble under my breath.

She spins around. I guess she has better hearing than I anticipated. I half expect her to throw her bag at me, or at the very least, slap me. "Yes, I am," she says. "And that's why you don't want to know me. Now—Mason, was it—where are you parked?"

We walk in complete silence to my car. The entire time I complain inwardly about how I was the only one without anything better to do on a Friday afternoon than fetch Ms. Bitchy from the airport.

Not that I'm unhappy with the way I'm spending the off-season. I could be running around doing endorsements, like a lot of the other players. Even as a backup quarterback, I had several offers to choose from. But that's not me. I like my quiet life. My private life. My uncomplicated life.

I look over at Piper. Why do I get the feeling this woman is anything but uncomplicated?

When we reach my car, I pop the trunk and stand back, watching in amusement as she loads her heavy bag into it. I would offer to help, but shit, she'd probably bite my head off.

She makes no comment about the car. It's nice. Very nice. It's the only extravagant purchase I've made since going pro. And even though I bought it because I love it, not as some kind of chick-magnet, women usually fawn all over it.

I head around to the passenger side of the car in an attempt to open the door for her, but she beats me there and lets herself in. I roll my eyes at her and keep my thoughts to myself. Slipping behind the wheel, I back out of my parking space and proceed to the exit ramp. Out of the corner of my eye, I notice Piper wringing her hands and rolling her shoulders. I see the nonstop tapping of her foot on the floor mat. She must be nervous about being home after so long. I try to ease the tension.

"Your family owns three great restaurants. How come you didn't go into the business?" I raise my brow with my question as I momentarily take my eyes off the road and stare at her.

She doesn't break her gaze from whatever is so interesting outside her window. "Neither did Baylor," she says flatly.

"Okay, I'll give you that. But why backpack around the world?"

She leans against the headrest, arching her neck into it. Her hair falls behind her and my attention is drawn to a small sparkle on the left side of her nose. It's a piercing. A tiny diamond so small you can barely see it. "I don't backpack," she says. "I have a suitcase. A damn heavy one."

"I offered to carry it, Piper." I shake my head. "Are you always this stubborn?"

I think back to the conversations Griffin and Gavin have had about that very same Mitchell-sister trait. When she ignores my question, I ask another. "You didn't answer me. Why do you *travel* around the world? And why don't you ever come home? I know your sisters miss you. They talk about you all the time."

She opens her eyes and looks at me purposefully. "What are you, writing a book about me or something?"

My fingers come up to rub the bridge of my nose. This is going to be a long drive. "Okay. Well then, do you want to know anything about me?"

"Not particularly," she says, her eyes back to focusing out her window.

Maybe her sisters haven't told her about me. Maybe she's not into American football after living abroad for almost four years. Or maybe she knows who I am but simply doesn't care.

"How come your boyfriend didn't come with you?" I ask.

Her head whips around and her face contorts as if I'd asked her why the moon was green. "I don't have a boyfriend. Why would you even ask that? I'm not going to fuck you if that's what you're after."

I almost run my car off the road from the shock of her words. "Believe me, Piper, fucking you is the last thing on my mind right now. I think I'd rather throw you out the window, but then your sisters would kill me." I try to compose myself before I say anything I'll regret. "I was talking about Charlie. How come he didn't come with you?"

She looks away, but I could swear I see the hint of a smile curve her lips. It makes me wonder what she would look like if she actually smiled. I'll bet she has one of those smiles that lights up a room. One of those smiles that makes men weak in the knees and incapable of rational thought. She doesn't look like much of a smiler, though. She has a sad, vulnerable look about her. And damn it, even though she's probably the biggest bitch I've ever met, something about her draws out my protective instincts.

"Charlie isn't my boyfriend. *She's* my best friend." She plays with a small leather bracelet on her wrist, twisting it back and forth and fumbling with the charm on it. I wonder if it's from Charlie. One of those friendship bracelets that girls give each other.

"Oh." I laugh, thinking about bits and pieces of girl-talk I've overheard from her sisters. "That does make more sense now that I think about it. So, why didn't she come with you?"

Frustration spills out of her in a fiery sigh. She turns her whole body in my direction, straining the seat belt taut across her body. I try not to notice the way it tugs on the v-neck of her shirt, accentuating her ample cleavage. "You want to talk? Let's talk. So, what about you? Do *you* have a girl in your life?" Her beautifully bitchy eyes burn into me while she awaits my answer. She's obviously deflecting the conversation back to me so she doesn't have to talk about herself. Or Charlie.

"Yes. As a matter of fact, I do." I can't hold in my smile. Every time I think about Hailey, I'm positive my face lights up with pride.

I can feel Piper studying me. "Huh, you must really love her then." She says it like it's such a foreign concept, one person being madly in love with another. It makes me wonder just what happened to her—or *who* happened to her.

"I do." I nod my head. "I love her more than I ever thought one human being could love another."

She straightens herself into her seat and I wonder if I caught just a hint of disappointment cross her face. She reaches for the radio, but hesitates, looking at me first. "Do you mind?"

I shake my head and she proceeds to scan through my presets to find a station that suits her. We drive in silence, with her occasionally singing quietly to a song until she realizes what she's doing and stops. When my favorite song comes on, a song Hailey and I sing together—well she mumbles, I sing—I glance over to catch Piper doing it again and she blushes. The brief wave of embarrassment that crosses her face is just another indication that there might in fact be a decent person underneath her tough, standoffish exterior. The woman is a spicy mix of contradictions.

The music turns off as my phone rings. I push the button on my steering wheel to answer it. "What's up, G?"

"Did you get the package?" Griffin asks.

"The *package* is sitting right here," Piper says, snidely.

"You could have warned me I was on speaker, Dix," Griffin says. "And, hi, Piper, this is Griffin. I'm looking forward to meeting you."

"Yeah, me too," Piper says, obligingly.

"Sorry, G." I shrug my shoulders at Piper. "But, yeah, I'll drop her off and then meet you and Gavin at the gym, right?"

"Sounds good. I'll be there around four o'clock after my shoot. Thanks for picking her up, Dix."

"Not a problem. See you then." I click off the call and the music comes back on.

Piper turns the volume down. "Your friends call you '*Dicks*'?" she asks, wide-eyed.

"Dix," I say and then spell it out for her, "D-I-X. You know, because my name is Mason."

She draws her brows in confusion.

"Mason Dixon," I explain. "As in the line that was the northern limit of the slave-owning states before the abolition of slavery?"

She chokes on a laugh. "Your last name is Dixon?"

She really doesn't know about me, does she? "No. My last name is Lawrence. It's just what my friends call me."

"Oh, right." She rolls her eyes. "I forgot. Men always need to have stupid nicknames for each other." She turns the music back up and stares out the window again.

As we make our way into the city, she's oblivious to my frequent glances. I wonder how this girl came from the same womb as Baylor and Skylar. Aside from the obvious stubborn streak, she's nothing like them. They are kind and selfless. They would give their right arm for strangers. They love their tight-knit family and Sunday brunches.

So why in the hell, then, do I feel like this one person—this exotic bitch of a woman with her damn sparkly nose—has gotten under every single layer of my thick and callused skin?

chapter three

piper

"Sorry," Skylar says, laughing as she hugs me for the umpteenth time. "I've just missed you so much. And I know you wanted to stay with Mom and Dad, but I think their pipes bursting was fate. You get to stay with me now. It'll make wedding planning so much easier."

I look over her shoulder at Aaron, her two-week-old baby who's sleeping next to Jordan, Baylor's five-month-old daughter. I close my eyes and try not to think about my sisters' charmed lives. Okay, so maybe they've had bumps and bruises along the way, I mean what happened to each of them was awful, but right now, in this moment—I've never seen them happier. Even Skylar, who never even wanted a husband or kids, is positively glowing. And I've just been sentenced to live in the middle of it for six weeks.

I silently curse my parents, who decided at the last second to do a major remodel since half their house flooded a few days ago. But that left me with a choice. Stay with Skylar in the city, or Baylor in Maple Creek, Connecticut. Since I have no desire to stay in my childhood home with its bad memories, Skylar got me by default.

I break free from the crushing hug and go sit on the couch, watching my oldest sister pour champagne into three glasses.

"Skylar, did you get the church re-booked for the 15th?" Baylor joins us in the living room with a plate of cheese and the champagne. She hands one to each of us. "Only one drink for Skylar and me since we're nursing. But you can have the rest, Piper. I'm sure you need it after your long day."

I nod and take the glass from her. "Thanks." I don't bother telling her it's not the long day—it's the destination.

I look around Skylar's townhouse. It's amazing. Tasteful. Safe.

Then Baylor's words sink in and I snap my eyes to Skylar. "The 15th? I hope you mean the 15th of April."

She shakes her head and laughs. "Apparently you have a lot to learn about wedding planning, little sister. There is no way we could pull it off in a month. I have my doubts about being able to organize it in *two*."

"Two?" I place my glass down so forcefully, champagne sloshes out the top of it and all over the coffee table. "You said six weeks, Skylar. Six. Not eight. I have to get back. I can't be away that long."

"It's only a few more weeks, Piper." Baylor grabs a burp cloth from her bag and wipes up my mess. "It's not like you have a job to get back to or anything."

I give my oldest sister a punishing stare. "Oh, right. Like writing books is a real job, Bay."

I feel bad as soon as the words leave my mouth. I know her books have done very well. I even read one once. But I just can't get into all that mushy-love crap. Give me a good mystery or thriller. I close my eyes and blow out a deep breath.

A hand comes up to touch my shoulder. "It's okay, Pipes," Baylor says. "I'm sorry. I shouldn't have said that. I just wish you would come back home. Why do you insist on traveling all the time? What happens when your college fund runs dry? You'll need to work. Come back here, be my assistant."

"Or work in one of the restaurants," Skylar adds. "There is so much for you here."

I'm exhausted. I don't want to have this argument with them again. For the sake of peace, I say, "I'll think about it. When the money runs out."

This seems to appease them for the moment. They don't need to know the money will never run out. They don't need to know my college fund was depleted long ago and Mom and Dad send me a small stipend to live on each month. They don't need to know I'm never coming back.

They don't need to know.

"So, other than wedding planning, what should we do while you're here?" Skylar looks lovingly over at little Aaron. "I'm on maternity leave until after the wedding, so we can hang out. It'll be just like high school. Well, before you bailed on me and did a semester abroad your junior year."

High school. I cringe thinking back on it. I wonder if everyone hates it as much as Charlie and I did. She and my sisters were the only things that kept me sane my senior year. I couldn't wait to graduate and travel the world.

I need to talk to Charlie. I glance at my watch and realize it's the middle of the night in Barcelona—no wonder I'm so tired. It'll have to wait until morning.

"I'm not exactly sure what I'm going to do. I was thinking about training for the Boston Marathon. And maybe I'll help the folks out at the new place for some extra cash."

"Oh, they would love that." Skylar walks over to get her stirring baby. "You could always waitress at Mitchell's NYC, too. We're always looking for good—"

"Marathon?" Baylor interrupts. "You're kidding, right?"

"Don't you keep up with Piper's Facebook page?" Skylar asks. "It's practically the only way to get information on where she is and what she's doing."

"Oh, come on, you guys know I've never been on Facebook." Baylor raises a snarky brow.

"Right." Skylar laughs. "I almost forgot about the infamous Facebook sabotage." She unsnaps her shirt and settles Aaron against her breast for a feeding.

I roll my eyes at how my sister is simply flopping her boob around without a care in the world. "Really, Skylar?" I ask, walking away so I don't have to witness it.

"Wait, Pipes." Baylor follows me into the kitchen. "Tell me more about the marathon. I know you've been running, but a marathon? Don't you think that's a bit extreme? Anyway, don't you have to register for those things well in advance? It's next month, isn't it?"

"It is. April 20th, in fact." I pull out my phone and scroll down to find a few pictures that were taken last year. I show her the photos Charlie snapped of me in the marathons I ran in Berlin and Amsterdam. "I know it's too late to register, but they always reserve a few thousand spots for charities and contributors. I thought maybe Gavin, with his ties to the movie business and all, could pull some strings and get me in."

Baylor scrolls through the pictures of me, sweat-drenched and practically limping across the finish line. I look at them over her shoulder, proud of the one thing in my life that gives it meaning. Clarity. Purpose.

She hands me the phone and wraps me into an all-encompassing hug. "I'm so glad to see you doing something you love. I've been so worried about you, Piper. I'll ask Gavin about it."

The doorbell rings. Jordan is fussing, garnering Baylor's attention, and Skylar is still busy nursing so I walk over to answer it. I look through the sidelight to see a young man, probably my age, carrying a large bag. He's got dark-brown hair that's short and manicured—a contradiction to the sleeves of tattoos on his arms and the gauges in his ears. He's hot. European-guy hot. I wonder who the hell he is and why he's coming to my sister's house.

For a moment, I freeze. My stomach forms a large knot and my head feels light. Oh, God, they aren't trying to set me up, are they? I knew this would happen. It was one of my fears coming back home. I just can't believe they didn't even give me a single goddamn day to get over the jet lag before they started.

"That'll be Jarod from Mitchell's." Baylor fidgets with a baby chair, trying to attach it to the dining room table. "Let him in, Pipes. He's got our dinner."

A breath of relief escapes me as I open the door and let him through. And even though he's only the delivery boy and not some kind of surprise blind date, I still wonder if my sisters have an ulterior motive.

"Hi." He walks by and the smell of delicious American food permeates the room, causing me to forget about everything else in the world except the dinner this guy is carrying.

Oh, how I've missed it. I think I've missed the food here more than anything else. I can smell the barbeque sauce and I can only hope it's Mitchell's famous pulled pork. There are just some things you can't get abroad, and good barbeque is one of them.

Jarod does a double take after he walks past me. "Wow," he says, looking back and eyeing me up and down. "You could be Baylor, only a little younger and with some um . . . eccentricities."

I nod to his many tats and the gauges in his ears. "*I* have eccentricities?" I say flatly.

He laughs, putting the bag on the table and pulling out several boxes of food that, no matter how tired I am, have my mouth fully waking up and ready for a feast. "I heard you'll be in town for a while. If you need anybody to show you around, I'm your guy."

I grab a fork and dig in, not waiting for the others and not caring what a pig I must look like. "No, you're *not* my guy," I mumble through my mouthful of delicious pork. "And I basically grew up around here. I don't need the dime-store tour."

He looks slightly taken aback. I see him question my sisters with his eyes. They shrug their shoulders and then Skylar thanks him for the delivery. "You're a doll, Jarod. I really appreciate this."

"No problem." He turns away, not bothering to give me another look. "Let Griffin know I said hi, and tell him I'll see him at the gym sometime."

Skylar nods and they say their goodbyes as I scarf down the meal like a starving rat eating a prized piece of cheese.

"So, there's a gym nearby?" I ask. As long as I'm stuck living at Skylar's, I can at least spend part of every day at the gym. And if I work at the restaurant, that will afford me as little time here as possible. I look over at Skylar, who's now nursing Aaron from her other flagrantly exposed boob.

Baylor feeds Jordan a spoonful of pureed baby food. "Yes, just down the street. The best in New York." She turns to give Skylar a wink.

I swallow a bite of pork, licking the delectable sauce from my lips. "Well, do you think they'd let me join for just a couple of months while I'm here?"

"Probably," Skylar shouts over her shoulder. "Considering Griffin, Gavin and Mason own it. Well, most of it anyway. Some corporation still owns forty percent, but the guys are buying them out over the next few years."

My brows come together as I try to understand this. "They own a gym? Why would a movie producer and a photographer want to own a gym?"

"And a football player," Baylor adds.

"Football player?" I take a bite of the creamy mashed potatoes.

Skylar shakes her head. "Do you not listen in *at all* when we Skype you on girls' nights? Mason always comes up one way or another."

"Mason plays football?" I tilt my head and study her. "Oh, yeah, maybe I did hear something you said about that." I shrug my unimpressed shoulders. "I try not to listen when you and your friends get all hot and heavy over guys."

Skylar and Baylor share a look. Baylor lets out an audible sigh and goes back to feeding her daughter.

"Not only does he play football," Skylar says, buttoning up her shirt, "he plays for the Giants." She stands up and puts Aaron on her shoulder, walking towards the kitchen as she burps him. "Well, not every game. Not most games, in fact. He's their backup quarterback. Actually, he was supposed to *be* their quarterback until he got screwed over by the guy who didn't retire. Johnny something—I can't even remember his name. I don't really follow football, but I will start when Mason—"

"Skylar?" I interrupt. "Is there a point to your rambling?"

"Oh . . . uh, I just thought you might be interested in who your best man is."

"You mean *your* best man, Skylar." I get up from the table, not even finishing my dinner. There are entirely too many babies making too many disgusting little noises to keep eating. "Anyway, I don't care about who he is. And now that I know he's a famous football player, I want to know even less about him. It does explain the flashy car, however. I'm sure he has it just to impress the ladies. What a dick." I spell it out for them, "D-I-C-K, not D-I-X. So, don't you dare try to set me up with him—or anyone else for that matter."

Another look passes between my sisters. "Set you up with Mason?" Baylor laughs. "No. That wouldn't happen even if you wanted it to. That man hasn't shown interest in anyone in years."

"Of course not," I say. "He has a girlfriend."

Skylar chokes on her drink. "Girlfriend? Mason? No, he doesn't. He hasn't been interested in anyone since Cassidy. That was over two years ago and we all know how that turned out."

"But earlier in the car, he told me he was in love." I scratch my head in confusion. "I think his exact words were '*I love her more than I ever thought one human being could love another*'."

Baylor smiles. "Oh, you mean Hailey."

I shrug. "He never told me her name."

Laughing, Skylar says, "He didn't tell you Hailey is his daughter and not his girlfriend? That's classic Mason."

"His *what?*" I look between my sisters. "Isn't he a bit young to have a daughter?" I cringe as soon as the words leave my mouth.

Baylor raises her eyebrows at me. "I was younger than he was, Pipes. He's twenty-two. Plenty old enough to have kids."

"Kids?" I gasp. "As in more than one?"

"No, just Hailey." Skylar places Aaron in a bassinette. "She's about twenty months old, wouldn't you say, Baylor?"

Baylor nods. "God, that child is freaking adorable. Thank goodness she got her looks from her dad and not her bitch of a mom."

Thankfully, before I get to hear any more about the adorable little girl, the front door opens and in walks a gaggle of men. And one very cute nine-year-old boy.

"Aunt Piper!" Maddox runs across the floor and jumps into my arms.

"Mad Max!" I squeeze him tightly and spin him around. I have the best memories of Maddox. Baylor had him when she was nineteen. She moved home to work at Mitchell's and finish her degree, so she needed a lot of help from me. I was only fourteen at the time, but I became his primary babysitter. Until I left. But those few years were all it took to forge a lasting bond between the two of us. He's the only kid I really truly love to pieces. I mean, sure, I like the other ones. But I know I'll never connect with them the way I connected with Maddox.

Maddox and I catch up while the others remove their coats and head over to grab a bite to eat. No wonder they ordered so much.

Gavin pulls me into a bear hug. We've only met the one time, at his and Baylor's wedding, but he's my brother-in-law, so I let him hug me. Then Skylar introduces me to Griffin, who thanks me profusely for coming back to town to help plan their big day.

Mason raises his chin to me in greeting. No hug. No handshake from his extraordinarily large hand. Not even a word of hello. Geez, *dick* is right. It's just as well. I don't want to know him either. Not beyond the wedding duties bestowed upon us from Skylar and Griffin.

Baylor puts Jordan into a play saucer, keeping her busy with all of the toys at her eye level. "Gavin, Piper wants to run in the Boston Marathon. Do you have any strings you can pull at the studio to get her in?"

He ponders her question and then shakes his head. "I'll ask around, but I don't think so. We worked with the New York Marathon quite a bit." He turns to me. "Too bad you missed it last month, I could have for sure gotten you into that one." He points his fork at Mason. "What about you, Mason—can the Giants get her in?"

Mason gives Gavin a look of death. He spears him with his eyes as if Gavin has just asked him to cut off his throwing arm. Then Mason turns to me. He stares at my two-toned hair. His eyes hone in on my nose piercing. "*You're* an athlete?"

My jaw drops at his inconsiderate remark. "Not an athlete. A runner." I close my eyes briefly, thinking of the poetic accuracy of that statement.

Mason shakes his head. "You're not an athlete. Athletes don't have nose piercings, neon-colored fingernails, and weird hair. And your legs are too short to make good qualifying times. You know you have to have good qualifying times, right?"

I refrain from shouting expletives at the man, due to the fact that my impressionable nine-year-old nephew is sitting in the kitchen. Instead, I calmly pour myself another glass of champagne and drink it down completely.

"Plus, athletes don't drink like sailors on leave," he adds.

That's it. I walk over behind Maddox and cup my hands over his ears. "You don't know a fucking thing about me, Mason. How dare you assume that because I'm a little different, I can't possibly be someone who could have anything in common with the kind of person you are. Which at this point, I'm sure is a self-centered, fame-hungry man-whore with a tiny little penis who drives an over-the-top car to attract anything with a vagina. Well, listen up, *Dick*, and listen good. I'm registered with AIMS, which I'm sure with your pea-sized jock-brain, you don't know stands for the Association of International Marathons. And I assure you I have more than enough certified qualifying times to run in the Boston Marathon. I'm sure, in fact, that this *little* girl with her short legs and nose piercing could beat the ass off your big-boned, callus-handed, narcissistic marathon time."

I remove my hands from Maddox's ears and kiss the top of his head before walking away. It's then I notice the entire room has gone silent and all eyes are pinballing between Mason and me.

Mason walks over and ruffles Maddox's hair before proceeding to cover his ears just as I did. "In my off-season, I've been training for the marathon. And yes, I can get you in. So, Piper Mitchell—game fucking on!"

He walks to the fridge and helps himself to a beer. His faded, snug jeans show off his tapered waist and muscular thighs. He gulps half the bottle down as the rest of us watch, stunned into silence. "And I'll even let you work with my trainer at the gym," he adds. "You'll like her. She's got funky hair and odd piercings, too." He picks up an unopened box of food and tucks it under his arm. Finishing his beer, he puts the empty bottle in the trash and walks to the door. "Now if you guys will excuse me, I have to go pick up Hailey. It's my weekend." He reaches the door handle and turns back to me. "You can start Monday. After you've recovered from your jet lag. But for Christ's sake—quit drinking."

I stare at the closed door long after he walks through it. Then I look back at my sisters who are gaping at me. "Ugh! *Me* stop drinking? He just chugged a beer. How do you guys put up with that man?" I walk over and pour myself another glass of champagne just out of spite, knowing I'll have one hell of a hangover in the morning.

I lean against the counter and take a sip of the bubbly liquid. Then I notice the room is still so quiet you could hear a pin drop.

"You like him!" Skylar's smile spans ear to ear and she's practically bouncing in her chair. "Oh, my God, Piper—you like a boy. You're *not* gay!"

Champagne spurts from my mouth at her words. "Gay—you thought I was gay?" I look from Skylar to Baylor, gauging their reactions.

"Well, you've never talked about a boyfriend. You seem to have such a . . . distaste for men," Baylor says. "And then there is Charlie—"

"Who is my *best friend*," I assert. "Not my *girlfriend*. Charlie, my heterosexual friend who is currently shacking up with some random guy she shagged last year while she waits for me to return. Which is one more reason I can't stay here a minute longer than necessary. And *like* Mason? That jerk—are you kidding me? I wouldn't touch him with a ten-foot pole. I'm sure he's just like all the other stuck-up athletes who think they're God's gift to mankind. No, the only interest I have in him is that he can get me into the marathon."

My sisters share another look. When did they get so damn good at nonverbal communication with each other?

"Whatever," I pout. I fetch my heavy suitcase and head for the stairs. "I'm going to bed. I'm exhausted."

Griffin hops up and grabs my suitcase from me. "Let me show you to your room."

And only because I'm about to fall over from jet lag, alcohol and frustration, I let a man help me.

chapter four

mason

Gavin and Griffin run up behind me on the indoor track, flanking my sides. "Training for the Boston Marathon, huh?" Gavin asks. "Since when?"

"I'll bet since about two seconds after Piper said she could beat him," Griffin says.

They laugh and sprint ahead of me, not needing to pace themselves like I do. I shake my head at my stupidity for the tenth time since I opened my big mouth yesterday. I've never been the kind of person who is overly competitive. That might come as a surprise for some, considering my profession. And maybe it explains why I chose to stay with the Giants after Henley's retirement retraction instead of trying to get traded for a starting position. But for some reason, that girl—that *woman*—rubs me the wrong way and I couldn't help but accept her challenge.

I didn't sleep very well last night. I wondered if I had made false promises. I didn't know for sure if I could even get in the race myself, let alone get Piper in. But this morning, when the charity coordinator for the Giants organization returned my call saying it was all good, I breathed a sigh of relief. Or maybe it was a sigh of exasperation knowing how I let her get under my skin again. After all, I did have to pledge five figures on each of our behalves.

One day. I've known Piper Mitchell for one goddamn day and can't stop thinking about her. She's nothing like the women I used to be attracted to. Nothing like Hailey's mom. Nothing like the swarms of fans who try to drape themselves all over me when they find out I play pro ball.

"Speaking of Piper," Gavin says, as they come up behind me again, lapping me on the quarter-mile track.

I give him a hard stare. "I wasn't speaking of Piper—*you* were." I slow my pace, thinking they'll just run ahead of me.

I watch the two of them turn around and jog backwards. "You interested, Dix?" Griffin asks.

I play dumb. "Interested in what?"

"Interested in Piper, you tool."

Of course I'm interested. Who wouldn't be? Well, with the exception of guys who don't like pushy, stubborn, infuriating women. What the hell am I thinking?

"Of course not." I check my watch and head off the track to find a towel. "No offense, because you guys are with her sisters and all, but she's a grade-A bitch."

We all take a towel from the stack and wipe our faces. Gavin furrows his brow. "Then why accept her challenge? And why the marathon? I mean, that's a pretty big undertaking, Mason."

"I need to push myself. The stronger I get, the more likely I'll win that starting position."

"When do you report back for off-season conditioning?" Griffin asks.

"April 22nd," I say. Then I wait for it.

"Two days after the marathon?" Griffin shakes his head at me, laughing. "Dude, do you have a death wish?"

"It's all good," I tell them. "The first two weeks of conditioning are limited to strength training and rehabilitation. We don't get into the heavy stuff for a while."

Gavin snaps me with his towel. "Rehab—well that sounds about right, after running a marathon."

"You sure you're okay with our May 15th wedding date?" Griffin asks. "Isn't that right in the middle of off-season training?"

"I'm sure, G. I already checked with the training coordinator. We don't condition on weekends until closer to pre-season and there are really only ten mandatory days of mini-camps that I need to attend. But I plan on being there every chance I get. I'm even going to the rookie camp. I need to show everyone I've got what it takes, and sometimes that works better doing it from the ground up."

"We know you have what it takes, Dix." Griffin throws his dirty towel into the hamper. "Johnny Henley really screwed you over. But, man, you've handled it with grace and dignity—that's nothing to be taken lightly. You'll get there one day. We all have faith in you."

Faith. Every time I hear that word, I think of Griffin's first wife, Erin. She was always talking about faith, fate and family and how you should trust each to guide you. God, I miss her.

Thinking of Erin reminds me that I promised to take Skylar to get a tattoo. She wants to surprise Griffin by getting the same tattoo Erin had. Looking in from the outside, one would think their situation was really messed up. On the contrary, I think Skylar and Griffin are my fucking heroes. Not many people could have done what they did. Take a crappy situation and turn it into something great.

"You coming to brunch tomorrow?" Gavin shouts from the shower stall next to mine.

Brunch. I love Sunday brunch with the Mitchell gang, especially when I have Hailey with me. They dote on her and she loves playing with Maddox and the babies. But going would mean having another run-in with the youngest Mitchell sister. After last night, I don't think it would be wise. I don't want to ruin brunch for everyone, and I think a few days without seeing Piper will help me gain a little perspective. I don't need complications in my life that could distract me from my goal of becoming a starter. Hailey and football—that's all I can handle right now. That's all I want to handle.

After our showers, we agree to meet for drinks tomorrow and then I head to the gym daycare to grab my daughter.

I look through the large picture window to see Hailey playing next to a few other toddlers. I stare at her through the glass. She still takes my breath away every time I see her. She has this little cherub face framed by my platinum-blonde hair. I tried to tie it up into a bow, but I'm far from perfecting it and it has once again come loose, causing her long hair to mess and tangle. I know I'm in for some tears later when I brush it out. But first, I'm going to take her to the park. She loves the horses. And I will do anything to see her gorgeous little smile.

Her face lights up when she sees me coming. "Dada!" she squeals and toddles her way over to me as I melt into a pile of goo at her melodious, high-pitched voice.

I scoop her into my arms, peppering her face with kisses before I thank the staff and head out to my car. My—what did she call it—*'over-the-top car to attract anything with a vagina?'* Yes, it's sporty. Yes, it's fancy. But what she monumentally failed to notice yesterday when I drove her home, was Hailey's car seat in the back. It was my one requirement when car shopping. A great sports car with a back seat. Had I known at the time that women would drool over it, I might have reconsidered my decision and bought a mini-van. If my car is a chick-magnet, a mini-van is repellent.

Driving to the park, I momentarily think of trading in my one prized possession. But the moment passes when I rationalize it's not my problem. It's theirs—all those women who shamelessly throw themselves at any player on the roster in hopes that they'll get their fifteen minutes of fame.

I made that mistake once. I won't make it again. And although it resulted in the best thing that ever happened to me—Hailey, I'm not willing to risk it. So, ever since Cassidy showed up seven months pregnant, demanding a marriage proposal, I've been celibate. Almost two years since I've had sex. My left hand has become my best friend and my only source of relief. Funny how I even made a conscious decision to use my left hand—strengthening my non-dominant arm in the process.

After a pony ride, Hailey starts to get cranky, a sure sign that she's hungry. Mitchell's isn't far, so I make the five-block walk with my little girl on my back.

Walking through the door into the welcome blast of warm air, I practically run over the one person who shouldn't be here. I give her a disapproving stare. "Is this how you spend your maternity leave, Skylar? You know maternity leave means you don't have to show up for work, right?"

She looks sheepishly at me. "I can't help it. I don't want the place to go to shit while I'm gone. I'm only here for a few minutes to make sure it's being run properly in my absence."

I pull her with me to the hostess stand. "Table for *three*," I say, looking at Skylar instead of the hostess.

Skylar looks longingly back at the kitchen and then sighs. "Okay, fine. But only because I want to spend time with this gorgeous girl. How are you, Hailey?"

"Up, up!" She holds her hands out to Skylar who willingly sweeps her up into a hug.

Skylar has us seated close to the kitchen, presumably so she'll be able to hear if there are any crises that need her attention.

"So, where's Aaron? Too young to take out yet?"

She shakes her head. "No, we've been taking him all kinds of places, but Griffin doesn't let anyone touch him. He's kind of vigilant about it. And he carries a huge container of hand sanitizer for us to use whenever we touch things like door handles and elevator buttons. It's pretty comical, and I'm not afraid to say, annoying at times. But I put up with it because I know he's trying to keep him from getting sick. He's had enough sickness around him to last a lifetime."

I nod my head in fierce agreement. "You know, it's probably just the whole new dad thing. I was the same way with Hailey at first. Especially since I didn't get to see her very often. He'll change soon enough, don't worry." I take a drink of water that our waiter brought over. "So, is Piper babysitting?"

She coughs, choking on her own drink. "God, no. That girl hasn't babysat since high school. I think Baylor over-used her or something. She practically raised Maddox for a few years, then she hit seventeen and everything else became more important. Things like Charlie and planning for their trip after graduation."

Thankfully, the waiter comes to take our orders, averting anymore talk of Piper. *Why did I even bring her up?*

"Jarod, you remember Mason, don't you? He's going to be the best man at my wedding."

He extends his hand to me and I shake it. "Oh, yeah. Mason Lawrence, I know all about you. I'm a big Giants fan. Good luck this year, man. I hope you get to play more than you did last season."

Jarod is wearing long sleeves with markings of tattoos peeking out near his wrists. He also has gauges in his ears. He must be a damn good waiter, because Mitchell's usually only hires clean-cut servers. I notice his short, manicured hair and wonder if maybe he conceded a different hairstyle to get the job.

"You and me both. Thanks." I proceed to give him my order and then ask about getting some chicken tenders and apple slices for Hailey. "Do you want chocolate milk, sweet pea?"

She claps her hands and squeals, "Chocate!"

He finishes taking our order, but hesitates before walking away. He studies me for half a second and then turns his attention to Skylar. "So, how long is your sister in town?"

Skylar glances at me before answering. My face is stoic. "Until the wedding, so May 15th," she replies.

"Oh." He shifts his weight nervously. "So, do you think she'd want to go out with me sometime? Maybe you could put in a good word."

Skylar tries hard not to smirk. "Sure, Jarod. She doesn't date much, but I'd be happy to tell her what a nice guy you are."

"Nice?" he says, as if it's a bad word. "How about you tell her I'm your best waiter and that you're probably going to promote me to assistant manager soon. And tell her I can get VIP tickets to some sick new bands since my uncle is a promoter."

"Assistant manager, really?" she asks, her attention fully on this kid who can't be more than twenty. "I'm glad you're so ambitious, Jarod. And of course, I'll tell her all those things."

"Thanks. I'll go put your order in now. You won't forget, right?"

"No, Jarod, I won't forget. Now, hurry to table three, the patron looks annoyed."

He rushes off and I shake my head after him. "She's here only one day, and already she's got a guy after her. What is it about you Mitchell sisters?"

"Actually, two guys," she says.

"Two? Really?" My brows shoot up in question, and maybe concern.

"Oh, come on, Mason." She goes into full mom mode and pulls a bib out of the diaper bag I brought, placing it around Hailey's neck. "Don't play dumb with me. I saw the way you guys were with each other last night."

"The way we were . . . uh, you mean the fight your sister picked with me?"

"Yes." She smiles, her face lighting up and I can't help but notice she shares the same brilliant green-colored eyes with Piper. "And the challenge you put on the table. And the heat between you." She fans herself.

"Heat?" I say, incredulously, laced with a bit of denial. "You're crazy. And she's the one who threw down the gauntlet, I just picked it up. It's purely selfish, because it'll be good strength training to help me get ready for pre-season."

"Right." She helps Hailey with her straw when Jarod deposits the chocolate milk in front of her. "I just can't believe how much she's changed."

"Hailey?"

"No, Piper. I mean, she got a nose piercing and then she did that thing with her hair. She was never like that before. We were the three musketeers—her, Baylor and me; well, *four* if you count Charlie, who was always around. And even though Piper was five years younger than Baylor and three years younger than me, we still always got along so well. We did everything together. I just don't understand what happened to her."

"Europe happened to her. And Asia. And Africa," I say. "People are different there. I was overseas last summer for some exhibition games. It's a whole different world, Skylar. I think the more eccentric you are, the better you fit in." Hailey's chicken tenders are placed on the table and I cut them up into bite-sized pieces. "You just need to give her a chance to acclimate. She's been gone for so long."

"Yeah, maybe," she says, picking around at her salad. "Just don't be too hard on her, Mason. Something isn't right. Something hasn't been right with her for a long time. I know she comes off bitchy and self-centered, but she's not really like that. I think she puts up a front. So if you have even the least bit of interest in her, don't give up. I think you may be exactly what she needs."

"Me?" I gesture to the waiter boy walking by. "What about him? Doesn't he seem a little more her type?"

She shakes her head. "Don't get me wrong. I love Jarod. And he's right; he is the best waiter I have. But he's not the guy for her. She needs someone strong. Someone discerning. Someone who can look past that rough exterior and break down her walls."

"Skylar, I don't need any distractions in my life. Dealing with Cassidy, having Hailey every other weekend, and playing football—that's pretty much all I can handle right now. I don't think I could take on a project as big as your sister."

"Project?" She gives me a biting stare. "Isn't that precisely what you've done, agreeing to train with my little sister for the marathon?"

"Who said I was going to train with her? I said I would let her work with my trainer. Anyway, I think she hates me."

Skylar laughs.

"What's so funny?" I ask.

"Oh, nothing. Except that's exactly what I thought about Griffin when we first met."

chapter five

piper

There's still a winter chill in the air when I walk the ten blocks to the gym. I walk fast, trying to forget the dream I had last night. The dream I've had two nights in a row. I thought they were going away. I haven't had one in a while. Maybe it's because I'm home. It's never the same dream. Never the same faces.

I wrap my coat around myself and quicken my steps even more as I think about brunch yesterday at Mitchell's Long Island—my parents' newest restaurant. It was interesting to see how everyone has gotten along without me these past years. They've moved on. Made something of their lives. Continued living. All while I seem to be stuck like a broken record on constant repeat.

I observed the things I'd missed when I flew in for a whirlwind weekend last year for Baylor's wedding. Things like how my mom looks older and stressed out, the fine lines around her eyes and mouth more prominent than I'd ever seen them. I know she's approaching fifty, but she's always had such a youthful look about her. I guess four years make a big difference.

My dad has taken on Gavin and Griffin as his own flesh and blood. Like the sons he never had. Did he want me to be a boy? His third child—his last chance to sire a son? To have someone carry on the name of his empire? He doesn't talk to me much. Not since I left junior year. I'm a disappointment to him. A failure. I think about how different all of our lives would be if I'd just been a boy. He seemed more interested in the fact that Mason didn't show up for brunch than the fact that his youngest daughter *had*.

It made me wonder why Mason didn't show. Was it because I was going to be there? He clearly has a problem with me. I couldn't care less about him one way or the other and my only problem with him is that he possesses a penis.

My phone vibrates and I smile as I swipe to answer the call. "You have no idea how much I needed to hear your voice," I say.

"So, how's day three going?" Charlie asks. "Please tell me you are going to see that gorgeous hunk of a football player today."

"Shut up." I roll my eyes at the phone. I never should have mentioned his name to her yesterday. "No, thankfully, I'm not going to see him, but I am going to see his trainer. I'm on my way there right now."

"Is his trainer gorgeous?" she asks.

"I don't know, I haven't met *her* yet."

"Ooooooh, maybe you could have a threesome." She giggles. "I mean, you already know the guy is hot—like super-sports-hero hot. I've Googled him and Pipes, I know you don't date and all; I'm just saying, if you were ever going to—now would be a good time to start."

I blow out an exasperated breath into the phone. The only reason I don't hang up on her is that I know she's kidding. She also knows just how far she can push before I break.

"Okay, okay," she says. "Enough talk of the freakishly-hot quarterback. Tell me about all the other shit you've done since we talked yesterday."

I tell her about brunch, leaving out the details of my mom's appearance. That would make Charlie sad. My mom was like a second mother to her. Hell, she was like an *only* mother to her. Her own mother was too wrapped up in a bottle to give a rat's ass about the comings and goings of her only daughter. She was a washed-up runway model; a has-been. An over-the-hill actress who only got bit parts as someone's forty-something mother. But still, she had to keep up appearances. She would often be invited to charity functions and red-carpet premiers and because of that, she had to look impeccable.

But her daughter didn't. Her beautiful daughter that had, in her mother's words, *'stolen her looks'* from the minute she got knocked up with her.

Nobody cared what her daughter looked like. She wasn't in the spotlight. No one would notice if she had bruises on her face or burns on her arms. Charlie was good at hiding it. So good that my mother, even as close as they had become, was oblivious to it until Charlie told her senior year, weeks before we packed up and left. But by that time, she was eighteen and practically living with us. She begged my mom not to do anything about it.

Maybe that's why my mom looks so old. She's been burdened with too many secrets.

We end the call as I walk through the front doors of the massive four-story gym. *Wow*. This place is like the freaking Waldorf, except people are wearing spandex instead of tailored suits. They *own* this? Gavin, Griffin and Mason own this place? I look around the expansive space, seeing it almost completely from one end to the other through the glass walls that partition the different sections. I know immediately I will love it here. I see dozens of treadmills I can get lost on. Weight machines that beckon me, challenging me to push myself to the breaking point. Boxing rings that I know will absorb some of my aggression.

I walk up to the front desk and drop my duffle bag. "Um, I'm supposed to meet with a trainer." I fumble with my phone, pulling up the text Mason sent me. I'm sure he misspelled her name. "Uh . . . Trick?"

"I'm Trick," a soft yet masculine voice bellows behind me.

I whip around, surprised to see a woman in the place where the voice originated. She holds out her hand. "Mason sent you. Piper, right? I adore him. And your brothers-in-law. Well, I suppose Griffin isn't exactly that yet, but it won't be long. Are you excited about the wedding?"

As she rambles on about anything and everything, I take in her appearance. Just as Mason said, she's got piercings; one through her lip and one in her eyebrow. She has short, purple hair that matches her outfit—a tight-fitting sports bra that flattens her barely-there chest, and three-quarter length spandex leggings that hug her boyish figure. She's petite but very fit. Defined biceps lead down to the thick veins lining her forearms. I know instantly that I will like her.

"… and so I decided on Trick, you know, because it's gender-neutral and all."

I realize in my perusal of her wild-yet-somehow-fabulous persona, I've missed most of what she said. "Uh, sorry." I finally accept her outstretched hand hoping she doesn't think I'm a rude ditz. "Yes, I'm Piper. Mason said I can work with you while I'm here?"

She laughs, looking me up and down. "You must have really gotten to him."

"Gotten to him?" I cross my arms in front of my body, slightly uncomfortable at her perusal.

"Yes." She reaches down to pick up my bag and motions for me to follow her. "He doesn't share me with just anyone, you know. He must like you." She turns back and looks at me again, shaking her head as if she's confused about something.

"Like me? No. I think he's taking pity on me because I said I could beat him in the Boston Marathon." I still can't believe I said it. What was I thinking? He's a professionally trained athlete and all I do is run, well and box occasionally.

Trick suddenly stops walking, causing me to nearly run into her. "Wait. Hold the fucking phone," she says, doubling over in laughter. She straightens up and wipes her eyes. "You mean to tell me Mason Lawrence is running in the Boston Marathon? With you?"

I don't know why she finds this so funny. "Well, not *with* me," I say. "But he's the one who got me in. He said he's been training for a while now, as part of his football conditioning."

A huge smile sweeps across her face. It can't be comfortable. It looks like her lip ring is pulled so taut it might rip right through her flesh. "Is that so?" She starts walking again, and I follow, watching her shoulders shake up and down as if she's laughing, but without making a sound this time.

We end up in a locker room where she issues me a lock and I stash my bag for later. "I take it you've run before? What are your times?"

She seems mildly impressed when I rattle off my times to her.

"And where else have you trained?" she asks.

"Nowhere else. I just like to run."

She puts a gentle hand on me. "You mean to tell me you haven't had any formal training? You got those times by *just running?*"

I shrug my shoulders. "Well, I like to box, too."

"Box," she repeats as if I told her the sky wasn't blue. "You run and you box." She once again looks me up and down, then she walks around my body and puts her hands on my calves, then on my thighs, plying them with her fingers. She comes around and faces me. We are almost exactly eye-to-eye, with hers falling ever so slightly below mine. "If you give me five days a week, three hours a day, I'm gonna shave ten minutes off your time."

I smile. I knew I was going to like her. "Deal."

I follow her over to the weight machines, noticing how her toned calf muscles flex whenever she takes a step. I think back to what Mason said about people like me not being athletes. Trick is obviously an athlete, and she's way more outrageous than I am. Why did he even say what he did? Was it just to get a rise out of me?

I forget about anything and everything as she pushes my body to limits I didn't even know existed before. I'm certain my muscles will be excruciatingly sore tomorrow, but I've got to suck it up, I've already agreed to come back for more.

I start to question my sanity when Trick says we're done with weights for the day. She points in the direction of the treadmills lining the back wall with scores of televisions hanging just beyond them. "I've already programmed number nine for you. Just push the 'start' button when you hop on. No more than five miles today. I don't want you to push yourself too hard."

I raise my eyebrows at her and she laughs. "Don't worry, we've got a great massage staff here. The bosses said whatever you want, you get. Perks of knowing the owners, I guess." She winks at me and then nudges me off towards the treadmills.

I curse myself for leaving my iPod in my bag, but at this point, I don't feel I can walk the extra steps to retrieve it. I question my capability to do even five miles, which would be a piece of cake on any other day.

I'm glad they have televisions, but it looks like each bank of four machines shares one of them. I just hope some wanker doesn't already have it on The Weather Channel or something.

As I walk down the aisle in search of number nine, I realize almost all of the few dozen treadmills are taken. I wonder what these people do that allows them to ditch work well before noon. Most patrons are men, executives probably, or maybe salesmen, based on the fact that they're all chatting away on their Bluetooth devices. I'm relieved they all seem too busy to gawk at me.

I arrive at my designated station, a large, sleek, industrial-sized treadmill that looks more complicated than most cars. I step on and press the big green 'start' button. The belt starts whirling around, slowly working its way up to a good walking pace of 4 mph. This allows me time to take in my surroundings.

To my left is an older woman struggling to run at a mere 5 mph, sweat pouring off her brow and her middle bouncing up and down with each labored breath. I have to hand it to her for being here. I'll bet if she keeps it up, she'll lose the spare tire in no time.

In front of me is the large television that serves my pod of treadmills. I roll my eyes at the programming. Typical for a gym, I guess. It's on ESPN Sports Center. My hand wanders to the keypad on my machine that controls the television. I switch channels until I find something worth watching. It appears to be a program about medieval castles in the Scottish countryside, but I don't have my earbuds to plug in, so all I can do is admire the beauty and long to return to my gypsy lifestyle with Charlie.

"Do you mind?" a low, winded, inherently masculine voice speaks from my right, startling me. "I was watching ESPN. First come, first served, you know."

My eyes close ever-so-briefly at the voice. Then I almost trip over my own feet as the speed of my treadmill rapidly increases to a steady running pace. I don't have to look. Even as winded as he sounds, I'd know his voice anywhere.

I will myself not to turn and look at him. I can tell by looking in the mirror that he is shirtless. And sweaty. And very, very muscular.

I berate myself. *Why do I even care about that?*

I concede his point and use the keypad to return to the previous channel, hoping it will mollify him and keep his attention so that he won't feel the need to talk to me.

"Thanks, Piper." His fingers touch the controls of his treadmill, slowing his breakneck pace to match mine.

I nod and try to feign interest in his show, willing time to go faster so I can hit the showers and run hot water over my screaming muscles.

Minutes go by in silence. He's no longer watching ESPN. He's watching me. I can feel his stare burning into my flesh until I can't stand it anymore. "What?" I bite, giving him a brief glance.

"Nothing . . . geez." He holds his hands out, palms up and gives me a shrug with his broad shoulders, one of which his earbuds are now draped over. "I guess I thought you might be a little grateful, that's all. I mean, Trick is kind of awesome, right?"

"What, you think I *owe* you something now, is that it?" I contemplate stopping the treadmill and ending this whole stupid shenanigan. "Because if that's the case, I'll leave right now. I don't owe anyone anything. Ever."

He looks taken aback. "No, Piper. You don't owe me anything. Except maybe a 'thank-you.' You know, some people do things out of kindness and not selfishness."

"Not in my experience," I tell him.

His eyes narrow and soften. "Well, you've obviously had the wrong experiences then."

If he only knew.

"Obviously." I yearn for my earbuds to drown out his voice. To drown out the world so I can do what I do best.

Mason's treadmill beeps and then slows, ending his program. The sense of relief that overtakes my body is palpable. It's short-lived, however, because he doesn't disembark from it right away. Instead, he stares at me, his curious eyes being drawn to the small tattoo behind my ear. I don't feel comfortable with the way he's studying it. I reach up and pull my hair from the band, releasing it so it falls around my shoulders to conceal that private part of me.

He looks dejected. "See you later, Piper." He grabs his towel from the handlebars, throwing it over a shoulder.

In the mirror behind the televisions, I watch him walk away. His blue running shorts are wet with sweat, causing them to mold and stick to the globes of his ass. His broad back takes up more real estate than two normal-sized men put together. His muscles ripple as he stretches his neck from side to side, his frame tapering off to a slim and fit waist. My eyes then travel down to his calves. They are chiseled muscle, toned and tight, even when he stops walking to speak with someone.

"Nice, huh?"

I startle at the feminine voice and then realize I've been caught staring by the woman on the treadmill next to me who has slowed to a walk.

I shake myself out of whatever world I was in and answer her. "I guess. If you're into that sort of thing."

"Honey, who isn't into that sort of thing?" She pins me with her thoughtful stare in the mirror. "Oh, unless you're gay. I know that's the 'in' thing these days with you young kids. Doesn't bother me at all. In fact, my niece is gay." She smiles. "Hey, she's about your age—"

"No, ma'am, I'm not gay," I cut her off. *Why do people keep saying that?* "I'm just not interested, that's all."

"Oh, that's too bad," she says. "He's a nice boy, young Mr. Lawrence. And a mighty fine football player, too." She wipes her brow with a towel. "He sure is focused, that one. In all the times I've seen him run on the treadmill, I've never once seen him remove his earbuds." She winks at me. "Until today."

"He's a friend of the family," I tell her.

She nods with a smile. "Oh. I guess that explains it then. Well, enjoy your run."

"Thanks." In the mirror, I watch her walk away until she passes Mason, who is now talking to Trick. His eyes catch mine and he smiles. I immediately shift my gaze back to the television while I finger the keypad until I find the medieval castles once more.

After my five miles, I head back to the locker room only to find Mason still talking with Trick. I try to sneak by, but they're blocking my path. Mason shoves his bottle of water at me. "It looks like you need this."

I eye it with disdain. "I have my own. Thanks."

"Whatever." He proceeds to down the rest of it and then tosses it into a nearby trash bin. "So, you really think you can beat my time in the marathon?"

I glance over at Trick, who is watching our exchange. Her eyes widen and she nods at me, giving me a healthy dose of self-confidence.

"Yeah. I think I can beat your time."

"Care to make a friendly wager on it?" he asks.

I think of my meager bank account compared to what must be his monumental one. I shake my head. "I don't think so."

"Oh, come on." He nudges me with his sweaty elbow and something strange happens to my insides. "If you're so sure you'll win, what does it even matter?"

"Aren't you rich enough already, Mason? I don't know why you would want to win fifty bucks from me—which, by the way, is probably more than I can afford."

"I'm not talking about money, Piper. *That* I take very seriously. I'm talking about a date." He looks over at Trick and gives her a wink before returning his attention to me. "If I win, you go on a date with me."

My confidence fades, along with all the color in my face. I try to recover quickly. "I thought you didn't date."

"I don't. All the more incentive for you to beat me."

I do my best to remain composed. "Dating you is no prize, Mason." There is no way I would go on a date with him. Or anyone, for that matter. "But for the sake of argument, what would I get if I win?"

He laughs at my stab. "What do you want?" A prodigious smile cracks his face as he awaits my reply.

I can't believe I'm even contemplating this. I shouldn't be. I know better than to take a bet from any man. But damn it, I want to beat him. I want to wipe that testosterone-laden, egotistical, self-serving grin off his face. I look at Trick. She's smiling and holding up all her fingers as she mouths *'ten minutes'* at me.

Feeling bold, and taking my strength from Trick, I blow out a breath and concede. "Fine. But can I get back to you on what I want?"

"I'll tell you what, Princess. You don't even have to pick your prize now. It won't matter anyway, because you have no chance of winning, but if you do—you can have whatever you want. The sky's the limit."

I roll my eyes at his narcissistic ass. Like he could give me what I really want. It's just like a man to think he can swoop in and save the day.

On tired legs, I walk past him into the locker room and turn around one last time. "For one, I want you to never call me Princess."

chapter six

mason

What was I thinking making that bet with Piper Mitchell? *A date?* I haven't been on a date in two years. I don't want to go on a date with *anyone*, let alone the one woman who seems to infuriate me at every turn.

In the shower, I contemplate how I avoided her at the gym for the rest of the week, switching my workouts to afternoons instead of mornings. I needed to be able to concentrate on the task at hand: getting stronger, fitter, more deserving of the job I'm after.

Watching her run on the treadmill was too much of a distraction. I had to slow my speed when she was next to me. I swear to God I could smell her, and her scent was doing things to my body that I had to ignore, or risk being mortified in front of the gym I work out in—the gym I own for Christ's sake. I felt like I would fall over my own feet if I kept up the pace I needed to.

When I finished my run and spotted that sexy little tattoo of a black rose behind her right ear, it was all I could do to keep from losing my shit. By the time I left her to the rest of her workout, I couldn't keep my eyes from drifting back over to her. I tried like hell not to look, but it was like her body was a tractor beam and I had absolutely no control over my own vision. I had to look. I had to watch her tight ass bounce up and down with every stride she took. I couldn't tear my gaze away from her alluring breasts in the sports bra that was as green as her eyes.

Shit!

Before I fully comprehend what's happening, I realize my dick is standing at full mast. I'm beyond the point of stopping this freight train, so I let my mind continue to fantasize and let my left hand go to work. I can see those emerald eyes staring into mine as she licks her lips in anticipation of taking me fully into her mouth. I imagine the faint and fleeting sparkle of the small diamond in her nose as I look down on her pleasing me. I can almost feel her soft, pouty lips encompassing my shaft, her tongue swirling around the tip.

My hand moves faster and my heart races. With my other hand, I steady myself against the wall of the shower, warm water running over my shoulders. My guttural shout echoes through the bathroom as my orgasm overtakes me and my release slowly swirls down the drain of the grey-tiled travertine shower.

Breathless, I let the water run over my head as I recover from the powerful climax. Then I vow to figure out a way to get the princess out of my head.

~ ~ ~

Skylar opens the door to her townhouse, greeting me with a hug. When I see her eyes, I could swear I blush like a freaking girl thinking of how, not an hour ago, I came all over my shower wall to those same brilliant-colored eyes she shares with her little sister. I quickly look behind her to see if anyone else is home. My heart rate decreases slightly when I see the lights out with no activity. "You're not bringing Aaron?"

She swats my arm playfully. "To a tattoo parlor? I don't think so." She pulls her purse onto her shoulder. "No. Aaron is with my folks for the day."

And Piper? I have to keep myself from asking, rationalizing how I don't care where she is or who she's with.

"Okay, then. Let's get going." I take her arm and escort her down the front steps. We make a left turn and head for the subway. I didn't bring my car today. I wasn't sure how safe it would be at the tattoo parlor. I've met the owner before, Spike. He's the one who came to the townhouse and did Erin's tattoo. The same tattoo he's about to ink into Skylar's lower back, in the very same spot he inked it into Erin. "You ready for this, Skylar?"

She has a bounce in her step when she turns to smile at me. Her dark-blonde hair is pulled back into an effortless wavy ponytail. "Oh my God, Mason, yes! I'm so excited. Do you think Griffin will be okay with it?"

I know he will be. He's got two tattoos of his own. One in memory of his mother. The other for Erin. I think he'll be over the moon when he sees it. Tattoos can be sexy if done tastefully. I don't have any myself, but not because I'm opposed. I just haven't come across anything I want to permanently etch into my skin. "He's gonna love it. It's a great wedding gift to him. And a perfect way to honor Erin." I have to catch myself before tears burn the backs of my eyes. "I'm really proud of you, Skylar. Have I ever told you that? I think you are one of the best people I've ever come across, and I'm damn proud to be a part of your wedding."

She stops walking, pools of tears welling in her eyes as she nods her head at me. She grabs my arm and we walk down the steps to the subway station.

Twenty minutes later, Spike is pulling out the stencil for her tattoo. "I knew you'd be back," he says to Skylar, referring to her and Griffin's visit earlier this year in an effort to track down Erin's surprise tattoo. "Have a seat right here. I'll go get the equipment." He directs her to a chair that is similar to something you'd find in a medical exam room, only it looks like it can be changed into almost any position. "Grab some coffee if you want," he says, nodding to the corner of the room which houses one of those single-cup brewers with an array of flavor selections off to the side.

While I'm perusing the coffee choices, the bell on the front door chimes and we all instinctively turn our heads in that direction. My heart beats powerfully in my chest as I watch Piper walk through the door. Before she notices me, she shares a smile with her sister. "I'm stoked to watch this," she says to Skylar. "You inflicted a lot of pain on me when we were little, so I'm going to enjoy every second of this."

Skylar scoffs, "I did no such thing."

"You did, too," Piper quips like a petulant child. "You and Baylor always pulled my pigtails. It got to the point that I begged Mom to just cut my hair off."

"Oh my God, I had totally forgotten about that." Skylar brings a hand up to hide her surreptitious smirk. "I remember now. We used to chase you out in the field behind our house. I'm so sorry, Piper. Can you ever forgive me?"

"Maybe," she says, raising her voice so Spike can hear, "it depends on how loudly he can make you squeal."

Spike chuckles and they laugh. I watch them interact, falling into a comfortable banter between two sisters who were obviously close growing up. It makes me wonder why Piper chooses to stay away. She has a great, close-knit family here. She could get a job at the drop of a hat. Why has she chosen the life she has? Did the apple really fall that far from the tree?

It's like she has two personalities. One I'm seeing now, as she talks with her sister. The charming, carefree, confident gypsy, with easy laughter filling her gleaming eyes. But there is the other side of her; when her 'Mr. Hyde' comes out, turning her into a skittish raccoon, fighting for her life and tearing through everything in her path.

I shake my head, ridding it of the thoughts infiltrating my brain. Thoughts of taming the beast within. Being her protector. Her confidant. The reason she stays in New York, even.

I turn my attention back to the coffee machine when I hear an unforgiving, "What's *he* doing here?"

And, Mr. Hyde has made his appearance once again. I pick up my freshly-brewed cup and head over to where the sisters are sitting. In an equally malevolent voice, I say, "Actually, *he* is just leaving." I turn my attention to Skylar. "Now that Piper's here to keep you company, I'll just take off."

I hold my coffee out, offering it to Piper. "Here, want this?" She eyes it as if I've offered her a goblet of poison. Then she pulls a bottle of water from her bag.

Skylar protests with a whiny shrill. "What? No. You promised you'd be here, Mason. You said you'd hold my hand. I need both of you or I'll chicken out, I know I will."

She starts to rise from the chair. I take a deep breath and blow it out audibly through my pursed lips. Then I gently push her back down. "Fine. I'll stay." I look over at Spike to see him bringing the supplies over. "How long did you say this will take?"

Spike sets up a tray next to Skylar's chair. "Well, there's no color and it's a pretty basic design. I'd say two hours."

"Two hours?" Piper says, incredulously. She gives me a brief glance and rolls her eyes.

I feel the same way, sister. I don't want to be in the presence of Piper Mitchell any more than she wants to be around me. She's trouble on a freaking stick. A loose cannon. A woman on the edge. I do not need that kind of complication right now. No matter how many times she may appear in my fantasies.

An hour later, I'm busying myself answering emails and texts one-handedly while Skylar keeps a death-grip on my other hand. The sisters chat away, interrupted only by occasional squeals of pain from the elder one. My eyes start to bug out from looking at the small screen for so long. I put my phone in my pocket and stand up to stretch, being careful not to drop Skylar's hand.

It's then that I notice the bracelet on Piper's wrist. I saw it before, in the car on the way back from the airport, and it occurs to me that I don't think I've ever seen her go without it. While her attention is otherwise occupied, I take a closer look. It appears to be a made of intertwining leather bands around a charm depicting a rose. The rose is so dark it's hard to make out. The entire bracelet is black—almost goth looking, a contradiction to the multi-colored, non-descript, Bohemian-style clothing she seems to prefer.

Suddenly, Piper's left hand breaks free from Skylar's. I look up to see she's caught me staring at it. She tucks it behind the table, replacing it with her other one. I question her with my drawn brows, but she ignores me, going back to their conversation about what hours she's going to work at Mitchell's NYC this weekend.

Oh, this is news. She's waitressing at NYC? That means she's working side-by-side with that waiter boy who wants her. What was his name, Jacob? The one with all the tats.

"It's Jarod," Skylar says, now staring at me over her shoulder. She winks at me, and if the ground could swallow up a two-hundred-and-twenty-pound quarterback, it'd be a welcome burial. *Did I really fucking say that out loud?*

I try saving a little face. "Uh, right, Jarod. He seems like a good kid." I pry my hand away from Skylar, flexing and fisting it to get the blood flowing again. "I have to hit the restroom. Spike?"

He points the way as I try to walk unceremoniously out of the room while everyone quietly laughs.

When I'm fully immersed in the bathroom, I lock the door and walk over to the sink, putting my hands on either side of it while my head slumps between my shoulders. I raise my head and look at the unfamiliar guy in the mirror. The love-sick puppy lost in a grown man's body. I blink my eyes once, twice—then I concede the facts. I want her. I want Piper Mitchell.

I just wonder how far I'm willing to go to get her.

chapter seven

piper

I wake with a start. Sweat is pooling between my breasts, soaking the shirt I sleep in. I try to shake off the nightmare when it occurs to me—this is no nightmare. It's Aaron wailing at the top of his four-week-old lungs in his bedroom down the hall. I shut my eyes tightly waiting for the incessant crying to cease. It doesn't. I roll over and pull the pillow over my head, shoving it into my ears to muffle the noise.

It's no use. I won't get back to sleep. I sit up and throw my legs over the side of the bed, cursing Trick and my sore muscles. It's been two weeks of training and even my hair seems to hurt. I rise and look in the mirror, detecting a hint of defined muscle in my upper arms. Why do my arms need to be so strong for a foot race?

I quickly throw on my workout gear and grab my gym bag. I head down the stairs, snagging a banana from the fruit bowl on my way out the door. "Later!" I shout as I walk through it. I'm sure I wasn't heard. Aaron is still screaming.

My thoughts take a bad turn on my way to the gym and I find myself scanning the nameless faces on my walk. I watch expressions of men my age as they catch my eyes. *Do they know me?* I scan my memories, my dreams, much like how the FBI runs facial recognition on criminals. Have I seen them before?

My feet quicken, feeling the panic rising up through my tense body. I can't wait to get on the treadmill and lose myself in a run.

~ ~ ~

Hours later, my mind calm and my legs like jelly, I pick up my bag and leave the locker room, fresh from a shower. Trick gives me a thumbs-up as I exit the front door of the gym. She must have known what I needed today. We sparred in the ring and I was on fire. She worked me hard, but I'd say I gave her a run for her money. I find myself smiling despite the beating my body took today.

The smile quickly dissolves, along with most of the blood in my face, when I absentmindedly run into a man outside the gym doors.

"Oh, sorry, young lady," he says, not recognizing me as I do him, because he's busy picking up the book he dropped when we collided.

I try to step away, but my feet won't move. My blood boils as I stare down at him. Despite the fact that my fists have already had a workout today, I ball them tightly and contemplate pummeling the old bastard. The only thing keeping me from jumping him is the thought of where I'm standing—right in front of the gym my brothers-in-law own. Bad press could hurt their business. Bad press could also bring attention to me, something I can't afford.

Before I fully come to my senses and walk away, the man stands. The blood drains from *his* face as well, but we both know it's not for the same reason. I feel rage while all he feels is shame. "Piper?"

I turn my back on him and will my legs to move.

"Piper Mitchell, is that you?"

My legs propel me slowly away from him.

"Piper, I know it's you. Please, stop and talk to me."

I don't stop walking, but I turn my head so he will hear me loud and clear. "I don't have anything to say to you, Mr. Tate."

He grabs my arm and I stiffen, being pulled into one of my nightmares. "Piper, I just want to know if she's okay. Please, if you won't tell me where she is, at least let me know if she's alive and well."

Boldly, and nothing like what I do in the majority of my dreams, I rip my arm away from him. "Are you kidding me? You really have the balls to ask me if she's okay? Maybe if you would have cared enough to find that out ten years ago, she *would* be okay."

He gasps, tears welling up in his eyes. Tears that have no right falling onto his bastardly cheeks. I shake my head at him and try to walk away again. He forcefully grabs my shoulders, restraining me. "Is she dead? Oh, my God, what did I do?"

Large hands rip Mr. Tate's arms off me, shoving him back against the brick wall of a building which I'm sure will result in a bruise down the bastard's back. "Is there a problem here?" Mason asks me, his raging eyes burning into Tate's.

I blow out a relieved breath. "No, no problem. He was just leaving." I walk in the opposite direction, back towards the gym where I feel safe. Then I stop, letting Tate's words of regret get to me. I curse myself for what I'm about to do. I'm about to put his mind at ease. Something he's not entitled to, but I do it anyway. I turn briefly. "The answer is no, she's not dead."

I slip into the gym before I can hear another word of his pleading. I'm quite sure Mason won't let him follow me in here. Even Tate isn't stupid enough to take on a professional football player. Plus, he's twice his age. He looks old. Very old. As if the burden of what he did has aged him beyond his years. Good, he deserves that. He deserves that and more.

My bag slides off my shoulder as I hunch over, my hands meeting my knees as if I'd just been kicked in the gut. "What is it about men that make them think they can either abandon you or hurt you?" I ask no one.

"Did that asshole hurt you? Who was he?"

I close my eyes at Mason's voice. In my panic, I didn't realize he was standing next to me.

My silence fuels his anger. "He did. Fuck, I'm going to kill him," he says, walking back towards the door.

"No!" I shout, stopping him. "It's not like that, leave him be."

He walks back over and his massive hand cups my chin, gently raising my head until our eyes meet. "Piper, are you okay?"

I bob my head in an awkward nod and take some deep, calming breaths. Then I pick up my bag with trembling hands and sling it over my shoulder. "I need to go."

He takes my bag from me with little effort. "You're not in any condition to go anywhere, Princess." He takes my elbow and leads me towards the café in the gym. "And I'm not convinced you'll be okay if you do. What you need is to sit down and get a cup of coffee and a bite to eat."

"Would you quit calling me Princess? Why the hell do you even do that anyway? And what makes you think you know what I need?" I pout at him, stopping our progress.

"I know exactly what you need because I'm well aware that you just had a grueling workout and you're weak and exhausted because of it. I'm aware that you followed said workout with what looked like a very stressful encounter with that asshole. I'm aware that you're stubborn as hell and won't listen to a goddamn word anyone says to you despite the truthfulness of it. And I call you Princess because that's exactly what you are, traveling around the world on Daddy's dime without a fucking care of how it affects others."

I realize that while he was talking, he guided me into the café and we are standing next to a booth in the back. He shoves me down into it. "Now what the hell can I get to feed you, *Piper?*"

"Ugh!" I try to leave but he has me cornered in the booth. I'm acutely aware, however, that I'm not panicking. On the contrary, I'm confused by just how safe I feel with him towering over me. "I do not travel around the world on Daddy's dime," I lie. "I have a college fund and this is the way I choose to spend it."

"Toe-may-toe, toe-mah-toe," he says, while simultaneously texting on his phone. "It all comes from the same place. I hear about where you've been traveling. I know what things cost. Your college fund ran out long ago, Princess. Unless, of course, your parents were expecting you to go to Harvard Med."

My jaw drops at his temerity. I'm in no mood to fight with him, especially since he's right. So I cross my arms and rest my head back against the booth. It does feel good to sit down. But I'm not about to tell him that.

Two minutes later, someone arrives with coffees and a couple sandwiches. I smirk at them sitting on the table when I realize he must have texted the order. "You holding me captive?" I wince at the words after they come out of my mouth.

"No." He slides in next to me, leaving a respectable distance between our thighs. "I'm simply insisting you eat to get your strength back so you can fight off predators on the street."

I concede, reaching out for what looks like a turkey sub. "He's not a predator."

"Then who is he? I can't let you leave if I think you're in danger." He sips his coffee and reaches for his sandwich. He looks at me hesitantly, warring with himself. Then his eyes change and a warm comforting wave washes over his face. I've seen this look before in my parents and my sisters. Concern. "I know something has happened to you. This man, does he have anything to do with it?"

I freeze upon hearing his words. *He knows?* How could he possibly? I contemplate my choices here. I just met Mason and I feel no obligation to tell him anything. I stare at him. He has this welcoming look about him. He's a huge guy, but he seems like a gentle giant. His icy-blue eyes beg me for answers.

"You're not leaving until you tell me, Piper."

Well, at least he didn't call me *Princess*. He holds my untouched coffee out to me. As I reach for it, my hand forcefully collides with his, sending the cup toppling over to the other side of the booth, the hot liquid narrowly missing both our hands.

"Damn. Sorry about that," he says, thinking it's his fault. "You didn't get burned, did you?" He runs his hand up and down my arm looking for damage. My instinct is to pull away. Every fiber in my body is screaming at me to retract my arm. Yet I let him check me out, my heart thundering in my chest while he does. I let him turn my arm over, inspecting it from fingertip to elbow, because something about his touch is different. Different than anything I've ever felt.

He finishes his examination and motions for someone to come clean the spill. "I'll get you another."

"No, it's okay," I say, with a shaky voice I pray he doesn't discern. I pull a bottle of water from my bag. "I have a drink."

I'm not sure what persuades me, but in a split second, I decide to confide in him. Maybe it was his gentle touch. Maybe it's the way he makes me feel protected. Maybe it'll appease him and get him off my back. But am I throwing Charlie under the bus by telling him?

"Nobody knows about this," I say, silently apologizing to Charlie. She'll understand. I know she will. "Nobody except me, my best friend, and my mother."

He tentatively picks at his sandwich as if what I'm about to tell him will hurt him. "Okay. Tell me."

I look around the café to make sure we're alone. "That man was Charlie's father."

"Charlie's dad?" His brow furrows in anger. "Did he do anything to you? To her?"

"Yes and no. I mean to her, not to me," I say, fumbling over my words. "Well, he didn't do anything *to* her. It's more like what he didn't do."

Mason's confused eyes question me.

"It's a long story," I say.

He drops his sandwich and leans back into the booth. "I'm not going anywhere. I have all the time in the world."

I can't believe I'm about to divulge such information to a virtual stranger. What do I really know about Mason Lawrence? Other than what my sisters have told me and the stuff I've Googled about him in the last few weeks—I roll my eyes at myself—I barely know him at all. But all the articles, all the stories I've heard from friends and family, they all say the same thing. He can be trusted. He's an honorable and genuine guy, if one can truly exist. And deep down in my gut, I know I agree.

"He left Charlie and her mom when Charlie was twelve years old." I dare to look up at him. He doesn't comment. His eyes encourage me to continue. "Her mom was famous. A runway model and actress. But after Charlie was born, she lost her modeling contract and the roles stopped coming in. She turned to drugs and alcohol. And she, uh . . . blamed Charlie for her lack of work."

"What do you mean *blamed?*" he asks.

"Exactly what it sounds like. She hit her. She hit Charlie." My heart races as I reveal her secret, hoping I'm not damned to hell for doing it.

Mason contemplates my words as he looks at me over the rim of his coffee cup. "And he knew about it?"

I nod my head. "Yeah, we're pretty sure. Charlie heard them arguing about it once. Her mom threatened him. Told him if he ever breathed a word of it, she'd end his career. He was a fairly new screenwriter trying to sell his screenplays, and she had enough clout to keep that from happening."

"So he chose his career over his daughter?" Mason balls his hand into a fist and hits the table, causing everything on it to jump. "Fucker."

I realize in this moment what I had forgotten. Mason has a daughter. I've never seen him with her, so it never occurred to me until this minute that he's a dad. He's probably envisioning someone hurting his daughter. I push the thought out of my head, not wanting to even contemplate it.

"And that's why she wanted to leave the country after high school?" He shakes his head, confused. "But she's a grown woman now. Her mother can't hurt her anymore." He slams his coffee on the table, causing it to spill out the top. "Wait . . . your *mom* knew about this?"

Unmindfully, I put my hand on his arm to calm him. I instantly pull it back when I feel the spark that ignites between his flesh and mine. I ignore the unfamiliar feeling in my belly and proceed to explain. "Only after it had ended and we were getting ready to leave the country. Anyway, there wasn't anything my mom could do about it. Charlie asked her to keep quiet, saying she'd deny all of it if my mom went to the authorities. It would be Charlie's word against hers."

"But why stay away all this time? Why not just move out of the house when she turned eighteen?"

"Because that's not the end of the story," I say flatly, clamping down my emotions.

"Shit," he says, shifting in his seat, putting his large arm on the bench behind my head, but not quite touching me. He doesn't even know Charlie. Doesn't barely even know me, yet his eyes are filled with concern and trepidation. He nods at my water bottle. "Do you want something a little stronger than that?"

A quiet laugh escapes my nose and I shake my head. "I'm in training, remember? No alcohol."

"Right. You're saving it for our date," he deadpans.

I tense. He must realize he's hit a nerve. He quickly adds, "I was joking, Piper. So, you were saying there's more to the story?"

I blow out a breath and rub the tension from my neck. I can sense his hand behind me, moving towards me then dubiously pulling away, as if he's having to keep himself from touching me. My pulse quickens and another sigh escapes me, leaving me wondering if it's because he almost touched me. Or because he didn't.

I push my sandwich away, feeling sick over what I'm going to tell him. "Charlie's mom was a drunk. She hung out with other drunks. Sometimes the guys she had over to the house would . . . do inappropriate things to Charlie."

"Fuck," he mumbles under his breath. "I'm so sorry."

I nod. "Yeah, me, too. But it happened more than a few times. It's why she won't come back. Some of the guys were famous. She didn't ever want to risk seeing them or her mom, even on television. It's easy enough to avoid American T.V. over there."

"So you went with Charlie and have been traveling with her ever since?" he asks.

"She's my best friend," I respond, twisting my bracelet as my fingers often do when I'm nervous. "It's what we do for each other."

"You're one hell of a friend, Piper." He relaxes a bit, seemingly mollified that I'm not in any danger. His eyes shift to the anxious activity of my hands. "Is that who gave you the bracelet?"

"Mmm hmm." I move my left hand, putting it down on the booth next to me and away from his prying eyes. "Hey, if you're done with the interrogation, can I go now? I have a shift at the restaurant."

He stands up, but doesn't move out of the way. "Which restaurant?" he asks, waiting for me to answer before letting me out of the booth.

"Skylar's. It's where they need the most help."

Mason purses his lips. He looks pissed. Then he lets me by. I start to walk away, but his voice pulls me back. "Speaking of Skylar. She was supposed to accompany me to a Giants charity function next weekend, but she bailed on me. Griffin has some epic photo shoot he wants her to tag along on. Can you help a guy out and go with me?"

I look at him like he's grown another head. "I don't date, Mason. And last I heard, neither do you."

"That's exactly why I need someone with me, you know, to keep the airheads away. Come on, Princess, it'll be very low key."

I sneer at him. "I thought we agreed you weren't going to call me that anymore."

He laughs. "I remember no such agreement. But I tell you what, if you go with me, I promise to use only your proper given name."

I can't believe I'm actually considering this. A date with Mason.

No, not a date. If Skylar was going with him first, it's definitely not a date.

Because he doesn't date.

And I don't date.

Ever.

"What's the charity?" I ask, trying to prolong my need to answer.

"I believe the proceeds will help fund adoptions for couples who can't afford it."

My heart pounds in my chest. I close my eyes and expand my lungs with a needed breath.

"Fine," I say, walking out through the front doors of the gym, wondering what I've just gotten myself into.

samantha christy

chapter eight

mason

I pull up to the curb, double parking for a minute while I exit the car to go get her. When I close my door I have to hold onto the car for balance. There she is, waiting at the top of the porch stairs at Griffin's townhouse. I stare at her while she fumbles with something in her purse. It's not warm outside on this April evening, yet my palms instantly become sweaty and my breathing ragged.

On my two hands, I can count the times I've seen her. She's always been pretty in her workout gear or bold shirts with belled sleeves paired with jeans. But this Piper—she takes my fucking breath away.

Her dress is pale blue, not a color I'd ever predict she'd wear. If I had to guess, I'd say the dress was borrowed—picked by one of her sisters, perhaps specifically to match the color of my eyes. It doesn't cling to her every curve. No, this dress is much worse than that. This dress keeps you guessing at what's underneath. The hem falls slightly above her knees, showing off her shapely calves, and the bust is just snug enough to reveal her modest cleavage. It's enticing without being solicitous. It's not her at all and I try to stifle a laugh as I watch the way she shifts around uncomfortably in the high heels she's wearing.

I know for a fact she'll be talked about at the benefit. She'll stand out like a sore thumb. Not for the obvious reasons one might think, but because she's so unlike most of the narcissistic women who will be there. It's like she has a timeless beauty, young yet sophisticated and worldly at the same time, much as I might classify someone like Audrey Hepburn or Jackie Onassis.

I hope my attempt at getting to spend time with her doesn't backfire on me. For a moment, I consider not attending; begging her to let me sweep her away to a secluded restaurant where I can get to know her better. Someplace where I know she might be more comfortable than a place fans or paparazzi might prey on our every move. If I know anything about Piper Mitchell, I know this—she doesn't like attention. I'm not sure what I was thinking inviting her to this. I told her it was no big deal. But the truth is, it's a Giants benefit and even as low-profile as this one is, it'll still garner some press and unwanted attention.

She spots me as I walk across the sidewalk. Then she grabs the rail to help her navigate the stairs. I take two at a time in an attempt to reach her before those heels have her tumbling down to the unforgiving pavement below. I reach out for her, but am stopped by her biting words.

"I can manage a few steps, Mason. This isn't a date, remember?"

I pull my hand away, but stand ready to catch her if she falters. "Right. Not a date. Of course not." I hope my pants don't catch on fire, because according to the pounding of my heart and the tightness of my trousers, this is totally a date, and I'm a big fat liar.

She may not let me help her down the stairs, but I'm sure as hell not going to let her open her own car door. I beat her to it, shaking my head when I see the disagreeable look on her face. "Humor me, okay? I've got on a monkey suit and you look . . . well, you look incredible. So, I don't care if we're on a date or not, I'm holding the goddamn door for you. Here and all night. Get used it to it, Princ . . . uh, Piper."

The hint of a smirk crosses her face and she nods at the car door, allowing me to open it for her. She awkwardly situates herself in the low-riding seat, making sure her dress doesn't creep up in the process. When she seems satisfied, and perfectly in position, I grab the seat belt and lean across her to secure it.

She puts her hand in the way, halting my progress as she takes the belt from me. "I'm not a child, Mason. I can do it myself."

"Sorry, old habits, I guess." I close the door and let her belt herself in, having told my second lie of the evening. It's not an old habit, it was an excuse to touch her, smell her. And in that second when my head was in the car, inches from her body, it was like fireworks were shooting through my veins. The pure feminine fragrance of her scent still surrounds me, the subtle whisper of fresh flowers lingering in my nostrils.

It's hard to keep my eyes on the road as I drive to the museum that's hosting the benefit. Her hair is down, the dark, wavy tips of it brushing against her collarbone. It looks soft and for a brief second, I imagine it cascading on my chest as she straddles me. I shift around in my pants, hoping she doesn't notice. She doesn't. She's looking out her window, making me wonder if she ever does anything else while riding in a car.

I turn on the music to ease the piercing silence and we make it almost the whole way without conversation. Until I see her messing with her bracelet. I think she does it when she's anxious. I try to alleviate her fears.

"I really appreciate you doing this, Piper. You're helping me out a lot. As a player, I'm required to attend a certain number of functions, but I almost always pick the smaller ones. You don't have to worry, we'll be in and out in a few hours. All you need to do is stand next to me and pretend to enjoy yourself."

"I'm not just doing it for you," she says, momentarily taking her eyes of the road to fiddle with a strap on her dress. "Skylar said she'd disown me if I cancelled. She said it was really important to her that I come and not let you down."

"You wanted to cancel?" I say, trying not to sound defeated as I pull up to the valet stand in the parking garage.

She nods. "I'm not very good with crowds."

"And yet you want to run in the Boston Marathon, next to . . . oh, about thirty thousand other people?"

She laughs silently, spurts of air blowing out her nose as she exits the car when the attendant opens the door for her. "That's different," she says, as if it's a real explanation.

I get my valet ticket and offer Piper my elbow before making our way through the garage. She stares at it, rolling her neck that I can only assume is tight with tension. If I could just reach out and work my fingers around her exposed shoulders, kneading the anxiety from her body. I long to pull her close to me; to put my arm around her waist and escort her properly. My body is twitching with the need to touch her. But I know I have to take it slow. She's skittish. Wary. Lost. And if I want any real shot with her, I have to be patient. The shit that happened to Charlie must have really messed with her head. I suppose it's why she has a hard time trusting men. Trusting *me*.

I drop my hand to my side, walking next to her through the garage and up to the front doors of the museum, feeling empty and alone for the first time in several years. I'm not sure what is driving my incessant want of this woman. She's never shown interest in me. She hasn't acknowledged our electrified touches. Has she not felt them? Is this simply about the chase for me—wanting someone I can't have? Or maybe I just need to feed the beast.

No. It's more than that. I could go out and get laid any day of the week. Hell, I can guarantee there will be at least a dozen women here tonight willing to strip down right there in the parking garage if I'd let them.

"There you are, baby." I cringe at the high-pitched nasally voice as we walk through the large double-doors into the massive entry hall. Case in point.

I give Piper my best apologetic look. I should have prepared her for this possibility, but I really didn't think she'd show. I turn to my ex-girlfriend. "I told you not to call me that."

She waves a conceited hand at my remark, dismissing it as she turns her attention to Piper. Like most of the women here, Cassidy is wearing a short, skin-tight dress accentuating her store-bought cleavage. Her wrist, neck and ears display a gaudy amount of expensive jewelry. And the price tag that resulted in her hair being straightened to within an inch of its life probably cost a week's worth of child support.

Cassidy's eyes rake over Piper from head to toe in a long, silent, sizing-up moment, as if Piper were a stray mutt brought to a dog show. I take a second to notice the differences between the two women. Cassidy is the complete opposite of Piper. Her too-long hair, extending all the way down to her waist, is blonde with strawberry highlights brought out by the loud color of her fire-engine-red dress. Her face is heavily painted with makeup, eyeliner so thick and black it makes her eyes look cat-like. Her lipstick matches her dress and is slick and wet; looking like a single touch from her lips would send one's clothes straight to the dry cleaner.

In contrast, Piper looks young. Innocent. Natural. She has makeup on, but in a tasteful way that makes it look like she doesn't. Even with her inky-black hair tips and miniscule nose piercing, she looks tame and demure compared to the predator assessing her as prey.

"Who's Snow White with the bad dye job?" Cassidy raises her drawn-on eyebrows at me.

I scowl at her furiously. I've never felt the need to hit a woman as much as I do this very second. My heart sinks and I close my eyes, shaming myself for subjecting Piper to this feeding frenzy. Am I so selfish that I'm willing to bring her to this mosh pit just to spend a few short hours with her?

I'm ready to grab Piper's hand and march her right back out the front doors when she turns to me and fires back, "Who's Barbie with the collagen lips and fake tits?"

If I had a drink, it'd be spewed all over the ladies in front of me. I can't hold in my laughter, much to Cassidy's displeasure. I give Piper an approving nod, happy to see it's not just me she can stand up to. "This is Cassidy Whitmeyer, Hailey's mother."

"Oh, right, the ex-wife." Piper holds out her hand in greeting.

Cassidy sneers at it then ignores her hand completely.

"Girlfriend," I say, correcting Piper.

"What?" she asks.

"Cassidy is my ex-girlfriend, not my ex-wife. We were never married." I lean close and whisper into her ear. "Thank God."

I could swear I see Piper shiver as my hot words flow over her bare neck. "Oh," she whispers back. "When my sisters referred to your ex, I just assumed..."

"No way. Not her." I pull back reluctantly, wanting to spend every breath nuzzled close to Piper's flowery-scented skin.

Cassidy lunges forward, putting herself between Piper and me. "And this is?"

Piper answers before I can. "Nobody. I'm nobody. Just a friend." Her eyes plead with mine as she gives a small shake of her head. I take it to mean she doesn't want me to say her name, but for the life of me, I can't figure out why.

"And does *nobody* have a name? She looks familiar." Cassidy asks me with no regard for Piper.

Piper taps her on the arm, to which Cassidy stares at the offending gesture and then questions Piper with her catty eyes.

"Just call me Snow," Piper deadpans.

Cassidy gives her a bitchy smirk. "Cute," she says.

I feel I'd better end this standoff before Cassidy makes her even more uncomfortable than she already is. I try to sound friendly when I ask my ex-girlfriend, "So, who's watching Hailey?"

"My mother," she says, still staring down Piper.

"And who are you here with?" I ask.

She turns back to me with a big smile. "Jealous, are you?"

"Not even a little bit, Cass." I take a meaningful step towards Piper. "No, I'm just hoping whoever it is will come looking for you so you can quit monopolizing our time."

She purses her surgically-enhanced lips and narrows her scornful eyes at me. "Would it surprise you to find out I'm here with Johnny Henley?"

My stomach churns and I feel sick. I know he's my competition and all, but that's a low blow even for a veteran player.

"Ha!" she says. "I'm only kidding. I'm here with Anthony Moore. He's a journalist." She points across the room to a man who is scribbling away on a notepad while standing among some of my teammates. "Should I invite him to join us?"

Piper shifts uncomfortably and whispers to me that she's off to find the ladies room. I watch her walk away, my eyes following her every careful step in those ridiculously high heels until she turns the corner. Finally, I give my attention back to Cassidy. I should have known she'd weasel her way into to this function. She's done it many times before. It's like she's keeping tabs on me. I'm not sure why; she's sleeping with half of New York City, probably including the judge who refused to give me more time with my kid. I made it clear to her long ago, when she showed up pregnant, that my only interest in her was that she keep our daughter happy and safe. As long as she continues to fulfill her end of the deal, I'm happy to keep paying the astronomical amount of child support she managed to get out of me.

Knowing she's here with someone from the press makes me even more relieved that Piper didn't let me reveal her name. I'm not sure what Cassidy would have done with the information, but I'm sure it wouldn't have been anything good. I get the distinct feeling she's not overjoyed that I may have started dating after all this time.

"No, Cass, you shouldn't invite him over, because there is no *us*. Please just leave me alone and go back to your little lap dog."

She turns her nose up at me. "I don't know why you hate me so much, Mason. Don't you think we should get along—for Hailey's sake?"

"As far as our daughter knows, we *do* get along. And that's exactly how I intend to keep it. I'll do anything for her, including pretending to like her mother." I step away from her, grabbing two champagne flutes from a waiter's tray. "Now if you'll excuse me, I have to go find uh . . . Snow."

She puts a hand on my arm, causing a bit of champagne to slosh out of a glass. "What's up with the fake name? And that hair, it's so last decade. Couldn't you have found someone a little less hideous, baby?"

I burn her hand with my punishing stare. "Get your hand off me, Cassidy. And watch yourself. You have no idea the legal teams I have access to, do you? You just remember—as soon as I decide to fight you, you'll be sorry."

"Are you threatening me, Mason? Do you really think a judge is going to give you Hailey?" She laughs. "You—a wanna-be football player who isn't even home half the year?"

She hits a nerve. It's exactly why I haven't fought for custody. Hailey needs structure and stability. A full-time parent who isn't traveling every other week from August through January. And even though Cassidy is a certified slut, I have to admit she's been a decent mom.

I see Piper round the corner and tear myself away from Cassidy. "Goodbye, Cass."

I meet Piper halfway across the expansive room. I hand her the glass of champagne. She accepts it while regarding it woefully. "I thought we weren't drinking," she says.

"We're not. But one toast won't hurt, will it?" I hold my glass out to her.

Her shaky arm extends to clink my glass, but she uses too much force, sending both our drinks shattering onto the shiny marble floor. She blows out a deep, regretful breath and apologizes. "I'm sorry, I'm so clumsy sometimes."

I push the broken glass to the side with my shoe as I see two waiters race over with a mop and broom to clean up the mess.

From behind, someone speaks softly in my ear. "See—hideous. Is she even house-trained, Mason?"

I turn to give Cassidy a biting stare as she shrugs her shoulders and keeps walking.

"It's okay, Piper. No harm, no foul." I show her my injury-free arms, happy the shards of glass didn't slice through my throwing hand. "Let me see your hands, did you get cut?"

She holds up her hands and I reach out to inspect them, bowled over once again by the warm sparks that ignite between us when we touch. I look up to catch her watching my perusal of her arms. Her breathing stops. She's just as affected by this as I am. But for some reason, she's trying her best to hide it.

"Maybe I need that drink after all," she says, pulling her hands away.

chapter nine

piper

Mason tries to flag down a waiter, but I start to walk away. "It's okay, I'll go get them from the bar. Be right back." Before he can follow me, he gets cornered by somebody who looks important. Somebody who looks like old money. Somebody who is dragging a fashion model behind him.

I turn my attention towards the bar, passing by all the waiters who are offering glasses of champagne. I curse myself for letting Mason and Skylar talk me into this. And meeting his ex? That was a tortuous ordeal. I once again forgot he even had a kid. What am I doing letting myself get involved with someone like that? *No—not involved with, just doing a favor for*, I reason.

I'm so out of my comfort zone right now I fear anything could set me off. I contemplate bolting out the side entrance. Then I could ditch the five-inch heels and slip into my more agreeable running shoes; falling into that zone where nothing exists but me and my breathing. But morality claims my conscience and I vow to stick it out for Skylar. And maybe a little bit for me.

He said it'll just take a few hours. I check the large clock on the wall and see that only leaves ninety minutes. Mason Lawrence might be an incorrigible quarterback, but he does seem genuine. He stands up to every good thing I've heard about him. And the fact that he enjoyed watching me diss his ex—that was simply an added bonus.

I wait at the bar behind two very large men who seem to be socializing more than ordering. Men who must have had tailor-made tuxedos to fit their burgeoning bodies. One of the men is African-American, sporting long brown dreadlocks that fall far beyond his broad shoulders. The other is all but bald, a tattooed '88' on the back of his neck with the New York Giants logo transposed over the top of it. Don't these guys sometimes get traded to other teams? And what if his number changes? I remember the pain from getting my tattoo and I wonder just how hard it would be to remove one.

"She likes your ink, Saunders," a low, burly, Darth-Vader-like voice pronounces.

The man with the tattoo turns around and gives me a face-splitting smile. "Well, what do we have here?" He regards my dress with carnal appreciation. "I don't think I've seen you around before. Who do you belong to?"

My jaw drops. "I don't belong to anyone." I try making myself taller. It's a futile attempt considering these guys probably tower over me by a full foot, even with my five-inch heels. "Instead of just standing there, how about letting me by for a drink?"

"What are you ordering?" the guy with dreads asks. "Whatever it is, I'm buying."

I clutch my purse tightly, thinking of the vast emptiness in my wallet. I thought the drinks at these benefit things would be free. All of a sudden sweat dots my upper lip and I feel claustrophobic with these giants hovering over me. I feel the anxiety rising like a slow wave gaining momentum right before it turns into a tsunami. I pivot away from them and notice how crowded the atrium has become in just a few minutes. People are teeming around, making introductions and pointless small talk. I scan their faces, hoping I don't recognize anyone and praying none of them recognize me.

I find myself frantically looking around the room for Mason. When my eyes spot him, he's staring directly at me. He looks aghast when he studies me, and he quickly extracts himself from the fashion model trying to drape herself on him. He races across the gleaming marble floors towards me, his long legs churning up the distance between us in just a few strides.

"Relax, honey," I hear the tattooed man's voice behind me as a heavy hand grips my waist. "He was just kidding. It's an open bar." He runs his hand up my rib cage.

My body stiffens at his suggestive touch. Bile rises in my throat as my knees threaten to buckle. But before the panic outright consumes me, Mason reaches my side, threading his arm around my back while brushing off number 88 at the same time—a guy who's arguably a hundred pounds heavier than he is. "Piss off, Saunders," he says. "Go find someone else to reject your ugly face."

Much needed oxygen fills my lungs as a wave of relief courses through my body. I feel Mason's strong arm around me, keeping me from collapsing. But what's utterly confusing is, instead of sending me spiraling further into a full-on meltdown, his touch feels therapeutic. Safe. Pleasant even.

The two burly men walk away, muttering their apologies to me as I beg the floor to swallow me whole. I pray the entire venue didn't just witness my silent hysteria.

Mason gently escorts me to a quiet corner of the room. Worry darkens his expression. "Jesus, Piper, are you okay? What did they say to you?"

"Nothing." I shake my head. "It was nothing. They were just being friendly. I'm sorry. I hope I didn't ruin this for you." I move my weight back and forth between my feet that are now aching in these pretentious shoes.

"Ruin it for *me*?" he asks. "Not possible. Besides, I'm the one who dragged you here. I shouldn't have let you wander off. *I'm* the one who's sorry. I swear I won't leave your side again. You'll be safe with me."

"Safe? You think I need you to keep me safe?" I bite, cringing at the tone I've taken with him after he's shown me nothing but kindness tonight.

A look of dismay flashes across his face, making me feel even worse over my harsh words. Then he laughs it off. "I've seen you box, Piper. I'm pretty sure you can handle yourself."

"You've seen me box?" I don't remember ever seeing him at the gym except for that very first day.

He looks slightly embarrassed, which I find amusing on such a big guy. "I've watched you a couple of times, yes."

My body heats up at the declaration. My first instinct is to tell him not to ever watch me. To *'piss off'* as he told those other men. But the way I feel right now—knowing he took the time to notice how proficient I've become; knowing he thinks I can take care of myself when nothing can be further from the truth—it's a strange, yet comforting connection that I've only felt with one other person on earth. The one person I abandoned in Barcelona.

Before I can filter my words, I open the can of worms that shouldn't be opened. "Why did you watch me?"

"Why do you think, Piper?" He cocks his head to the side and raises an eyebrow.

I asked for it. I ran right into it head-fucking-first. I have no excuse for baiting him like that. I've seen the signs from him. I've felt it in his touches. But what he doesn't understand is that it can never happen. "Uh . . . I can't . . . um, I think I'll take that drink after all."

He gives me a poignant look and then grabs two glasses of champagne from a passing waiter.

He tries to hand me one but I wave it off. "I was thinking of something a little stronger."

"You know where the bar is," he says, depositing the untouched drinks on a nearby table. "Lead the way."

We walk up to the crowded bar and work our way up to the front where we watch the bartender prepare us a couple of Jack and Cokes. I savor the burn of the first alcohol I've had in three weeks. Then I look across the room and see the fashion model he was talking with earlier. The one who seemed to have no problem trying to get cozy with him. "Who's that woman?" I nod my head at her.

"Her name is Janice Greyson. She's the owner's daughter." He points to the well-appointed older gentleman on her right. "That's her father standing next to her. He's the big boss."

"I thought you said this was a small charity function." I shift around again, my feet really starting to hurt now. "Why is the owner of the Giants here?"

"Janice is the one who organized the benefit. Not to mention she's very close to the cause being that she's adopted. It makes sense her father would come to support it." He nudges me gently with his elbow and adds, "Plus, I think he's trying to set me up with her."

My stomach churns, a slight sick feeling building from within, reminding me how empty it is since I was too nervous to eat earlier. I throw back the remainder of my drink. "I'm going to get another."

"Are you sure about that, Piper? The marathon is only a few days away."

I balk at him, "What are you, my dad?"

He holds his hands up in surrender. "Fine, fine. I'll take you to get another. But if you lose the race on Monday, don't come crying to me." He winks and something inside me melts.

His stare is intoxicating and I question my choice to have that second drink. The liquor is making me brave and stupid at the same time, reminding me exactly why I shouldn't have it.

I'm mesmerized by the bartender as he expertly mixes scores of drinks seemingly all at once. It almost becomes a ball and cup trick to figure out which ones are ours. I stare intently until he places mine on a napkin in front of me.

"Dix! It's good to see you, brother."

I watch as Mason and the tall stranger enjoy one of those guy handshake-turn-hugs, patting each other affectionately on the back as they share a few words.

The man turns his attention to me, but unlike some of the others, he doesn't try to undress me with his eyes. "And just who did you find to escort your pathetic second-string ass to this thing?"

Mason hits him with a reserved, playful punch and looks at me. I shake my head at him, eyes wide with trepidation. "This is . . . uh, a friend of the family. Garrett, meet Snow." He winks at me. "Garrett and I went to Clemson together. He's the pathetic second-string running back for the Giants."

"Friend of the family? What family—you mean to tell me you have a life outside of football?" Garrett says to him before turning to me. "Snow, huh?" He laughs and I'm sure he's going to make fun of my 'name.' "It's a shame my wife isn't here, you'd get along great. Her name is Autumn."

"Where *is* your better half?" Mason asks, scanning the room.

"At home probably puking her guts out. I don't know who decided to call it *morning* sickness, because she's got it all goddamn day long. I just came to make an appearance and write a check." A waiter hands him a glass of champagne. He tips it at us. "And drink. The woman won't let me drink at home anymore since she can't."

Garrett excuses himself to talk to some of the other players. Then Mason introduces me to a few other people, smirking at me every time he uses my new name. While some of the others in our group hold conversations about their children or their pregnant wives, he pushes my hair to the side and whispers into my ear. "I knew I'd find some way to call you a princess tonight."

When his hot breath flows over my ear, tiny hairs on the back of my neck stand at attention and I notice an involuntary hitch in my breathing. When I turn to question him, I see he noticed, too. His gaze is fixed on my neck and his hand is still holding back my hair. His eyes dilate and he blows out a deep breath.

I conjure up every ounce of willpower and pull away, my hair falling back down around my shoulders as he stares at the dark tips when they meet my flesh. "What do you mean?" I ask.

"You know, Snow White. She's one of those Disney princesses, right?"

I break into a huge smile as laughter bubbles from within me. "Oh my God, you're hopeless, you know that?"

He studies my face as if he's in awe. "Piper Mitchell, I do believe this is the first time I've ever heard you laugh. I think I'll make it my mission to produce that sound from you more often." He leans in close and my eyes flutter in anticipation of the feel of his breath on me again. "And I'm not hopeless—" he puts a strong arm around me and pulls me ever so slightly closer to him "—I'm hopeful."

Squelching the lava running through my veins, I tell him I need to use the bathroom again. It's a lie I hope he doesn't detect. I need to get away. Distance myself from him for a minute to gain a little perspective.

Sadly, perspective is hardly what I get in the well-appointed restroom that's nothing more than a flurry of women applying makeup and spreading gossip. But mostly what I notice are the three pregnant women sitting on the bench, comparing stories while working the circulation back into their feet. I make quick time of my business and exit the ornate ladies room. "Is *every* woman here pregnant?" I mutter to myself.

"*You're* not," Mason says, surprising me as he leans against the wall outside the bathroom. "And count your lucky stars. From what I've seen and heard, it's no walk in the park. Morning sickness, stretch marks, and weird-ass cravings. Not to mention all the moodiness." He points to the men's room. "I'll just be a second. Wait here, okay?"

I nod, watching him disappear behind the bathroom door. "Yeah, lucky me," I say under my breath, ignoring his command when I head back in the direction of the bar.

A few minutes later, Mason finds me downing a third drink, standing shoeless by the service entrance in an attempt to avoid the cameras now making their way around the congested atrium. He shakes his head in mock disgust. I shake mine back at him and realize that it doesn't stop when I do. My head is spinning. He smiles sympathetically, taking my empty glass and placing it on the ground, picking up my shoes in the process. "Winning that bet is getting more likely all the time. Let's get out of here."

He opens the service door behind me, pulling me through into the brisk nighttime air. With whiskey coursing through my veins, I don't notice the chill. But that doesn't stop him from removing his jacket to place it over my shoulders.

Before now, I didn't realize how truly large he is. His tuxedo jacket is longer than my dress and envelopes me like a black hole. As he puts my arms in the sleeves, rolling them up as if he's dressing a little girl, I study him. I never noticed how unique his hair is. He has this platinum-blonde hair normally reserved for west coast beach bums. It falls into an effortless part, courtesy of the cowlick above his left eye. It's not very long, but it has an edgy look that is slightly this side of rebellion.

His icy-blue eyes are bright, even in the relative darkness of the evening. I've never seen this exact shade of blue before. I glance down at my dress and it dawns on me why Skylar insisted I wear this one in particular. I can't stop the roll of my green eyes before I look back at his dress-matching blue ones. I can't remember ever admiring a man's eyes the way I am right now. The alcohol has made me brave. Bold. Careless.

When he's finished dressing me in his jacket, he turns his attention to my feet. He lowers himself to the pavement and lifts one of my legs to put on my heels. My foggy head swims with a little-girl fantasy, and then I almost fall over when he seems to read my mind. "See, and now you're Cinderella," he says, slipping on one of my shoes. "That's two."

Two princesses. *Ha!* My life is anything but a fairy tale. Those are reserved for people who aren't stupid, like me. For people who pay attention to details. For people who never go looking for trouble. I frown, watching this prince of a man put on my shoes, knowing not he nor anyone else could ever fill that role for me. But for just a split second, deep inside the far reaches of my spinning head, a voice tries to be heard. A voice that tells me how, just maybe, someone like me can have a happy ending.

"Ouch," I say, attempting to walk alongside Mason back to the car. I halt our progress and lean against a wall, sinking down and looking very unladylike as I once again remove my shoes. "Feet hurt."

Before I can stop it from happening, I'm picked up and cradled in the arms of my sizeable escort, being carried helplessly through the parking garage. My body and my mind are at war with each other. My mind screams for him to let me go, but my body relishes the feel of his arms around my back and thighs, holding me tightly against his chiseled chest. My body shudders as my face falls against his neck. I inhale, dragging his clean, athletic scent deep into my lungs.

My eyes close at his intoxicating aroma when, suddenly, I'm falling into a dream. There are hands everywhere on me, grabbing at my clothes and jockeying for position on my body. Only this time, I fight. I lash out, screaming bloody murder while my fists swing at anything and everything. I hear my name being called over and over as my self-defense training kicks in, refusing to let me be claimed as a victim.

"Jesus Christ, Mister, what's wrong with her?" a strange voice bellows.

Strong hands shake my shoulders, causing my eyes to open as I'm pulled from the nightmare. "Piper. Piper, wake up," Mason implores. My drunken eyes try to focus on the young guy on the ground holding a hand to his face.

"What happened?" I ask, eyeing the kid on the floor of the parking garage.

Lines of worry collect near the corner of Mason's mouth. "He was just trying to help me get you in the car when you starting fighting us. You punched him, sweetheart."

My chin falls to my chest as reality sets in. "I'm so sorry." I watch the kid stand up, rubbing his reddened jaw. "I didn't mean to do that," I tell him. I turn to Mason. "I'm sorry." I duck into the car and close the door, wanting it to swallow me up and spit me out in another dimension.

I see Mason exchange a few words with the attendant; shaking his hand and forking over what I think are several very large bills much to the kid's pleasure. I blow out a deep sigh. He's paying him off so he won't press charges. Or maybe so he won't go telling the story to one of the many journalists inside the building.

When Mason gets in the car, I'm barely awake, alcohol pulling me under as my head rests against the window. I sit wallowing in regret over how badly this could have turned out for him. For me. I don't even put up a fight when he reaches across me to secure my seat belt. But I do everything I can to ignore the intensity of his touch as his fingers brush up against me when he gently grabs my neck and turns my head towards him. "Piper, what's going on? What happened back there? Tell me. I can't understand unless you talk to me."

I pull my head away from his hand. "I told you when we first met, Mason. You don't want to know me. Maybe you'll believe that now. Just take me home."

We drive home without talking, neither of us bothering to turn on the radio. He scrubs a hand over his jaw. The debate going on in his head is apparent. The tension between us is palpable. The silence in the car is deafening.

He finds a parking spot in front of Skylar's place and sprints around the car to help me as I quickly exit and stumble my way up the porch stairs. "That's where you're wrong, Piper," he says, stopping me short of the front door. "I *do* want to know you." He cups my chin with his hand, raising my fallen head so our eyes meet. "Believe it or not, you're worth knowing."

Without bothering to acknowledge his words, I slip through the front door and shut off the porch light, watching his defeated body shuffle back to his car. Under the dim light of the streetlamp, I see him pound the steering wheel in frustration before he drives away.

I take a bottle of water and some aspirin upstairs with me and lock myself in my room, not even bothering to undress before I fall onto the bed.

Suddenly, it occurs to me that he called me sweetheart back at the parking garage. My heart pounds at the recollection. And my head aches when my mind grasps the notion that of all the events that took place at the benefit—this is the one I choose to focus on. Not the humiliation I imposed upon him tonight. Not the damage I inflicted on the poor kid's jaw. Not the complete ass I made of myself all evening. No, my stupid, under-the-influence-of-too-much-whiskey brain keeps playing his endearment over and over, like a looping movie reel.

Mason didn't even seem to care about how I embarrassed him. In fact, I recall him saying he wanted to help me. Protect me. Keep me safe. I try to imagine for a second the possibility of being with him. But then my stomach wretches and I dart into the bathroom just in time to empty its contents into the toilet.

I clean myself up and look in the mirror, shocked to see I'm still engulfed in his jacket. The heady smell of his cologne travels across my every nerve ending. I pad back to my bed, mindlessly

black roses

wondering what happened to my heels. Then I drift asleep, surrounded by the intoxicating scent of the only man my body has ever craved.

chapter ten

mason

It's Marathon Monday. Thousands await the gun to sound and start the third wave of runners. As I stand among the herd, I scan the crowd looking for the only reason I'm here. I know I won't find her. She's much further up in this wave than I am. She has actual qualifying times from other marathons, so even though I got her in under the charity waiver, she gets to start with other people who have similar qualifying times.

I've never run a full marathon before, just a couple of half ones last year for various benefits. But the only qualification I really needed, other than the available slot, was a decent pledge amount and a promise to be able to finish in under six hours. I've been training hard with Trick, so I figure I can do it in a little more than half that time. In fact, my one mission today is to catch up to the mercurial princess, watch her fabulous behind for a mile or so, and then beat the black spandex running pants right off her gorgeous body.

I saw her before the race, but she didn't speak to me. I could tell she was mortified over what happened the other night. She all but ignored me. I told myself it wasn't me; that it was the crowd. And maybe the nerves she was feeling over the possibility of losing and having to hold up her end of the deal.

For a minute, I even contemplate losing on purpose just to see what she would ask for. But despite my curiosity, and the very tiny part of me that wants to see her cross the finish line ahead of me, I still know that, being a guy, I'd rather have her see me as this strong alpha-male type, not the pussy who got beat by a five-foot-nothing girl who is half his weight soaking wet.

And I really want a date.

The gun sounds, but there isn't much movement in the herd. I suppose it takes a while for almost ten thousand runners to get started. There are officials trying to keep eager participants from trampling others in their quest to fulfill their dream of running in this momentous race. Finally, we creep forward; a pack of sardines vying for position in a too-tight space. It makes me wonder how Piper is handling the crowd. I've never felt so claustrophobic. I noticed she had her earbuds and iPod with her this morning. Although it's discouraged by the race organizers, and forbidden among those going for prize money, it may be the one thing that allows her to get through marathons despite her distaste for crowds.

I, on the other hand, am not listening to music today. I'll admit, it's therapeutic, and it does get me through grueling runs on the treadmill. But I know I will thrive on the incessant crowd noise. Just like when I'm playing in a game, the noise is encouraging. Motivating. It's what will get me across that finish line. Well, that and the impending date with the woman who manages to both infuriate me and get me hard in the same goddamn breath.

black roses

It doesn't take me long to advance my position, weaving in and out, passing the slower runners and leaving them in my wake. Occasionally, I'll hear a pointed shout from someone in the crowd who recognizes me. I'll tip my chin or wave at them, but after a few miles, I find my stride and get consumed with thoughts of the past weekend.

I lost a lot of sleep Friday night, worrying about Piper. I know she was drunk, and she does seem to have her issues with men, but what could have driven her to hit the poor valet who was just trying to help me with her? It's like she was lost in a dream—or living a nightmare.

When I called Skylar the next day to check on her, I was invited to dinner at the townhouse. A dinner Piper would not be attending because she was scheduled to work. Griffin and Skylar often have me over, taking pity on the bachelor who can't even boil pasta correctly. I lose myself in my punishing pace and the memory of that night.

"I can't believe she hit him!" Skylar said. "She said nothing to me about it this morning. She left early for a run and then went to her shift at the restaurant."

"I don't know what happened. One minute I was carrying a drunken Piper with sore feet, limp in my arms, and the next she was flailing around, batting blindly at us when he helped me with her." I put my fork down and stared meaningfully at Skylar. I wasn't sure if she knew about Charlie and I didn't intend to betray Piper's trust, but I wanted to figure out what was going on with her. "Has anything happened to Piper? You know, to make her the way she is around men?"

"*As in, has anyone hurt her?*" Skylar studied me, pondering her own question. "Um . . . I don't think so. She's just never been much into guys before. In fact, Baylor and I thought she was gay until we saw the way she was with you."

"*The way she was with me?*" I asked, innocently.

Griffin laughed, joining the conversation as he put a juicy hamburger on my plate. "Oh, come on, Dix, the girl is smitten. Even if she won't admit it to herself, it's pretty obvious to the rest of us."

I smiled at the affirmation. I'd suspected as much, but hearing it from them, it made me want to pound my chest like a goddamn gorilla.

"Still, not being into men doesn't exactly explain what happened the other night," I said.

"I don't know." Skylar got up to refill my water glass. "She changed a lot when she did that semester abroad her junior year. I suppose something could've happened then, but you think she'd have told us. We were really close. She came back a different person, but we just thought it was the experience that changed her."

"Different how?" I asked.

"When she came back, all she wanted to do was work in the restaurant to make money for traveling. She stopped helping with Maddox and spent all her time with Charlie or at Mitchell's. She even quit studying theater. She was all about acting before that, wanting to earn a scholarship to a school of the arts. But after she came back, she didn't audition for a single production. She was obsessed with her plans to travel after graduation."

black roses

"She used to act?" I recalled Piper saying Charlie's mom used to be an actress. Did that have anything to do with her turning her back on it?

Skylar's face lit up with pride. "Yes. She was good, too. Even from the time we were little, she was always dressing up and performing monologues for us. I remember she got the lead role as Anne Frank when she was only a sophomore. She was really talented. Baylor and I kept telling her she was wasting all that talent following a pipe-dream to travel the world. We knew she would go incredible places, but we always figured acting would be what would take her there. I mean, she was only making slightly more than minimum wage at the restaurant, so how could she afford to go? We were shocked when Mom and Dad said they were going to let her use her college fund for traveling. They had always been adamant about their kids getting a college education, yet they gave her carte blanche with the money they'd saved for years."

"Skylar, having a passion for travel is one thing," I said. "But doesn't it strike you as odd that she came back a completely different person than she was before she went away?"

"You said it yourself, Mason. When we talked about her before, you said life is different overseas. People are different. I think she just found the place where she thought she fit in more than she did here. She was always a wanderer, a gypsy, but we assumed it was all part of her creative process." Skylar took a drink from the beer I rejected, being only two days before the race. She blew out a frustrated breath. "I don't know. Maybe it was partly my fault. By that time, I was in college myself, commuting into *the city to get my degree in restaurant management. It consumed me, and when I wasn't studying, I was partying. I suppose I kind of hung her out to dry."*

Griffin grabbed her hand. "It wasn't your fault, Sky. People grow up and change, and there isn't a darn thing you can do about it."

As the miles go by, I think about Griffin's words. People do change. *I* changed. In college, I used to be that cocky football player Piper thinks I still am, sleeping with any woman who would lift her skirt for me. It took something huge, something monumental, something completely unthinkable and life-altering to get me to change my ways. It took Hailey. And although I agree with Skylar that Piper's semester abroad could have changed her, I feel there's more to it than that. I wonder if there is more to the Charlie story than what she's telling me. What if Piper was abused by the mother's drunken friends, too?

My stomach turns over thinking about another man's hands violating her. I run faster, trying to catch up to her. With every step, I vow to protect her. With every labored breath, I promise to keep her safe. With every drip of sweat, I swear to become the reason she remains in New York.

Around the three hour mark, I spot her. Even among the many clusters of runners and the endless sea of competitors, I find her. I should know what she looks like from behind, I've watched her enough at the gym this past month, much more than I've led her to believe. I would know her backside anywhere.

In a very Piper-like manner, she's running alone, away from the pack and off to one side. I slow my pace so I don't catch up, watching her from behind as I admire the fluid grace she exhibits with every pounding stride. Her tight running pants hug every demure curve of her hips and ass. Her light-green tank top reveals a line of sweat between her shoulder blades that have gotten more defined thanks to Trick's punishing workouts. Her bi-colored ponytail bobs up and down, the stray wisps of hair being held back by a headband that matches her shirt. She's gorgeous. Statues should be made from her alluring mold. If my body wasn't almost at its breaking point, I'm sure I would be tenting my running shorts by the mere sight of her.

It's now when I realize the race is almost finished. Barely more than a mile to go, according to my running watch that I've completely ignored. While competitors have been falling behind, dropping out and cramping up, time has flown by for me, thoughts of Piper fueling my every step. If I can run a marathon at the simple thought of her, I can only imagine what I could do with her by my side.

I come up next to her and pace her for a second, eyeing her in my periphery. Finally, she seems to notice I'm here. A devious smile curves her sweat-laden face. She pulls an earbud from her ear. "It's about time," she says.

I laugh as much as one can after running almost twenty-six miles. "About time? I'm gonna win the bet, you know." My lungs burn trying to keep up with my words and still take in the oxygen I require.

"Game on, *Dix*." She breaks away, pulling ahead of me.

"Oh, I don't think so, *Princess*." I muster all of my energy and sprint past her, putting a sizeable gap between us before I settle back into my marathon pace, hoping I don't pass out from the exertion of trying to impress her.

Every fifty or so strides, I peek over my shoulder to make sure she's not gaining on me. So far, she's not closing the gap too much. But I wonder if I've just cut off my own legs, deploying my last energy reserves too soon which would allow her to make a fool of me, sprinting ahead of me at the finish line.

I concentrate on my breathing, reminding myself there is just one more mile to go. One mile to get my name in the history books for something other than football. One mile to secure a date with the only woman I'd ever run a marathon for.

One. More. Mile.

I turn again to exact Piper's position, but she's not there. I look over my other shoulder to see if she's passing on that side, but she's not there either. I slow my pace so I can turn my body around more efficiently. That's when I see her. And after more than twenty-five grueling miles, I stop running. One mile from victory, I concede the race to thousands of others who will cross the line before me.

I stop, because a hundred yards back, Piper is sitting on the ground, blood staining her lower legs as race officials hurry to her side. I sprint towards her, ignoring my screaming muscles and oxygen-deprived lungs. My instinct to protect this girl overtakes my physiological need to breathe. When I stop in front of her, I eye the cuts on her knees and the gravel-scraped abrasions on her hands. I gasp at the blood trickling down to discolor her white running shoes.

But when I find her eyes, I'm surprised to see she's not worried about her injuries. Her eyes are darting around at the crowd, scanning it frantically as her body begins to shake. I've seen this look before. She's having a panic attack. It's the same look she had the other night. I search my brain to find a way to help her.

"Are you okay, Miss?" I hear from paramedics and bystanders hoarding around her to help.

She panics even more at the onslaught of people surrounding her.

I hold my hands out to my side, attempting to clear people away from her. "Please, back away. She's claustrophobic." I grab a bottle of water someone is holding out and retrieve a roll of gauze from the paramedics I pushed aside. They attempt to reach her, but I block them. "I said back off if you want to help."

"Piper." I get down on my knees, gravel grinding into them as I talk softly to her. "Piper, it's okay. I'll help you." I assess her injuries while pouring water over her cuts to clean them. It doesn't look that bad, a couple of scrapes that have all but stopped bleeding. She continues her distraught survey of the crowd and I follow her gaze to try and figure out what she's so afraid of. Is he out there? Charlie's dad? Or worse—some asshole who hurt her?

I need to get her out of here. Away from these people. And I quickly realize what I need to do to snap her out of it is get her back up and running. If I've learned anything about Piper this past month, it's that she runs to shut things out. To clear her mind. To escape from her demons.

I have to work hard to keep the bystanders at a distance, warning the paramedics with my eyes and even lying to them about having EMT training. They finally believe me and retreat even further. Apparently they don't watch much football, a circumstance I wouldn't have been grateful for until this very second.

Something on the pavement next to her reflects the sun's harsh rays, catching my eye. I reach out and pick up Piper's leather bracelet, running my finger over the intricate curves of the black rose. I quickly shove it into the tiny zippered pocket of my running shorts, grateful I even saw it. I don't know what it means, but I know it's important to her. It may even be her most prized possession, something that occurred to me the other night when she wore it to the benefit. I momentarily wonder if it has ever been removed from her wrist before this very second. Visions of Piper naked, wearing only the leather bracelet, hinder my quest to help her through this. I berate my wayward thoughts, trying to focus solely on the task at hand—fixing this beautiful, broken girl.

"Piper, look at me." I cup her face with my hands and force her to make eye contact. "It's me. It's just you and me, sweetheart. We can do this. We only have one mile to go and we'll go down in the books. You've worked so hard for this. Come on. You can do this."

I get to my feet, making sure her eyes stay on mine, putting myself between her and the crowd. I hold out my hands to her, offering them to help her up. "Look at me," I tell her. "Only me."

She blows out a long, deep breath and then puts her hands in mine, allowing me to help her up. She winces, but I know it's not necessarily from her scrapes. I'm in pain, too. Our muscles have begun to stiffen and I wonder if we are even capable of finishing the race after stopping for a few minutes.

"One more mile, Piper. Piece of cake." She lets me take her elbow so I can make sure she's steady on her feet. "We'll go as slow as you need."

She studies me, warring with herself over the decision she's about to make. She nods her head. "Okay." It's the first word I've heard her say since she fell. And I know right now, that no matter how long it takes for us to finish, it will be a victory.

I let her set the pace. She walks faster than I expected and I hear the cheers from the crowd, applauding her for continuing the race. Not two minutes later, she's increased our speed to a steady jog. When we come around a corner and spy the finish line off in the distance, I hear Piper gasp. I look over worried that she's panicking again, but instead, I have the pleasure of witnessing a slow, triumphant smile creep up her face. It's not something I thought I'd see today—if ever again.

"What is it?" I ask.

She points to the race clock that shows the time for the third wave. "Trick was right," she says, her smile not faltering. "She did it. She shaved ten minutes off my time, even with my fall."

Then she turns to face me, still keeping our pace while saying something truly amazing. "Thank you, Mason."

I almost trip over my exhausted feet, absorbing the words of gratitude I never thought would cross her lips. I shake my head. "You're welcome, Princess. And you're wrong, it wasn't Trick, it's you. *You* did it."

I see tears well up in her eyes. Tears of joy. Tears of gratitude. Tears of happiness. But she never lets them fall. She holds her chin high, nodding at me before she turns back to watch our approach of the finish line. I make a split second decision.

She doesn't even notice when I fall back and let her cross first.

chapter eleven

piper

I've never before felt such exhilaration crossing a finish line. Was it Mason? Was it not letting my fears consume me?

When I saw that face in the crowd, every horrible nightmare I've ever had came flooding back to me. Until that moment I could almost pretend the faces in my dreams weren't real. That they were figments of my imagination. But now I know for sure—those faces belong to actual people. Those monsters do exist. And every fear I've had over returning home has just been validated. Even in Boston, camouflaged by thousands of runners, I can't hide from them.

But as panic pulled me under, to depths I'd never experienced before, Mason appeared before me, possibly giving up his one shot at finishing the Boston Marathon, doing the one thing he's proven to be good at time and time again. He protected me.

He protected me from one of the guys in my nightmares. Protected me from the unwanted attention from the paramedics. Protected me from certain self-destruction. Only one other person has ever been able to comfort me the way he does and she is thousands of miles away. It's one of the reasons I don't like leaving her side.

It's one of the reasons I'm starting to like being by his.

I'm reeling when Mason comes up next to me, walking alongside me as we cool down from the grueling race. "Nicely done," he says, a smile cracking his sweaty, captivating face.

Still bathing in excitement and adrenaline, I jump at him, wrapping my arms around his neck in an uncharacteristic hug. "We did, it!" I squeal, breathlessly.

"You bet your ass we did."

We're both dripping with sweat, breathing heavily and we really should be walking around to keep loose. But this embrace is like no other, knocking whatever wind I had left right out of me, rendering me incapable of voluntary movement. His large hands grip me, one spanning my lower back, the other between my shoulder blades. I don't know if it's the excitement of the race or the unadulterated fear from seeing the face of one of my assailants in the crowd, but in this moment, I don't ever want him to let me go.

I've never felt so safe before. An absurd realization considering we're standing among thousands of strangers. The way his arms envelop me, gluing me to his much taller, broader body, makes me feel both protected and wanted at the same time. No, not wanted—*needed*. Because the way he's holding me right now, it's like he needs me as much as I need him, making me wonder what he could possibly need that he doesn't already have, or couldn't get at the drop of a hat.

As I peek around him and watch more people cross the finish line, it dawns on me that he came up from behind me after the race. I pull away and draw my brows at him. "You didn't have to let me win, you know. You helped me enough. I don't need your pity, too."

He laughs, mumbling something about 'Mr. Hyde.' Then, shaking his head at me, he says, "I didn't let you win, Princess, I got a cramp. It still hurts like a bitch." He leans over to massage his calf. Then he grabs my elbow, pulling me along. "Come on, let's keep walking or we'll wind up stiff as a board."

We walk around, being herded off of Copley Square with the other finishers, off to massive tents with EMTs, massage stations, ice baths and endless tables of electrolyte drinks and carbohydrate snacks. We follow a path around the square, adding almost another mile to the distance we've already covered, but I know if we don't do it, we'll pay dearly later.

As my breathing regulates and I start to come down from the high, I find it hard not to look around at the hordes of runners, officials and bystanders without feeling anxiety creep back up. Instinctively, my right hand grasps my left wrist in search of the one thing that calms me.

Panic strikes. My hand fumbles around my arm, searching frantically for the little straps of leather—my fingers needing to mindlessly trace the outline of the flower that has come to define me. But it's not there. Instantly, my pulse shoots up when I realize it must have broken free from my wrist when I fell.

I look down at the abrasions lining the arm that broke my fall. "Oh my God. No no no no no." I couldn't have lost it. Not that. Tears sting the backs of my eyes and threaten to fall at the thought of it. I don't know if it's the exhaustion from the race, or the face in the crowd, but for the first time in a long time, my throat tightens and I feel I may do something I haven't done since April 25th—exactly five years ago this Saturday—cry.

I turn around ready to sprint back to the spot of my fall when Mason grabs my arm, softly restraining me.

"I have to go!" I yell, trying to break free of him.

"Piper." His grip is firm, yet gentle, as he keeps me from leaving. "It's okay—look." With his other hand, he unzips the small pocket of his shorts; the one meant for carrying identification or a car key. He pulls out my bracelet and holds it out to me.

How did he even know that's what I was looking for? "What? How?"

"It must have come loose when you fell." He examines it. "It doesn't look any worse for wear. Here, let me tie it back on for you."

I hold out my arm, studying him as he carefully places it around my wrist. Sweat has darkened his hair, lengthening it so it touches his eyebrows. His blue irises become darker, reflecting the midday sky, focusing on the task as he struggles to tie the small bands of leather with his large fingers. The intoxicating pulses that result from his touch rouse something deep inside me. I stand here, exhausted from running, terrified of the monster I saw among the crowd, arms and legs scraped up and stinging from my sweaty skin, yet all I can think about is the man who is touching me.

He smiles. I wonder if he's feeling exactly the same thing. The way he glances up and holds my stare confirms my suspicions.

When he finishes securing my bracelet, he examines my scraped up arm and knees. "Come on, let's finish our cool down and get you to medical. Then we'll find Griffin and your mom."

I almost forgot about them. Since the race is on a Monday, not everyone could spare an entire day to come see us run. I didn't want my sisters lugging their tiny babies hours away just for a brief glimpse at me when I jogged by. But my mother insisted on coming, once again confirming her support in every choice I make.

Hours later, after replenishing our food and water stores, we say goodbye to Mom and Griffin as they head back to New York.

Most of the runners who aren't local, choose to stay overnight to stave off the stiffness that would result in a long car ride home. Mason was generous enough to get me my own room and last night he even had room service prepare me a huge plate of pasta so I could carb-load before the race. He didn't offer to join me. In fact, he didn't contact me at all before the race. We even came separately; me on the train and he in his car.

I thought for sure I'd scared him away after my behavior at the benefit. Not to mention the parting words I left him with. But his touch today told me a different story. And for the life of me, I'm not sure why he wants to waste his time on someone like me.

I told Mason I wanted to turn in early. But I can't relax and my muscles ache and burn, so I go for a walk to keep loose. The sun is just starting to set over the tall downtown buildings when I emerge from the hotel. Metropolitan Boston is much like New York except everyone doesn't seem to be in as much of a hurry. People stroll leisurely down the sidewalks that seem quiet and not overcrowded with buskers.

I stop and purchase a hot dog from a street vendor. As I eat, I pass by the Charles Playhouse, a place my mom used to bring me once a year to see smaller off-Broadway productions. Seeing the posters of upcoming shows causes me to lose my appetite. I throw the remains of my dinner into a trash bin and try not to feel sorry for myself. I reason that it's better this way. If my name was up in lights or plastered in playbills on graffiti walls, it could make me a target. A victim. And that's one thing I don't intend on being ever again.

Back in my room, a few Tylenol and an ice bath have me relaxing enough to fall asleep, hoping exhaustion will stave off the nightmares.

∼ ∼ ∼

Too many hands are touching me, each taking a piece of clothing off my languid body. I don't fight them. I don't want to fight them. What they are doing feels good. I recline on the massive bed and invite more. My body feels alive, like I'm floating on air. I look around the room at the drunken faces. Boys of different shapes and sizes, shouting and cheering me on. I randomly grab a hand and put it to my naked breast, relishing the razor sharp bolts going straight to my groin when fingers pinch my nipples. Rock hard penises are thrust at my face and onto my body, each one wanting a piece of my flesh. I reach out and rub the velvety steel length of one of them, unsure of the face it belongs to. I'm mesmerized by the silky softness of the erection as a small bulb of moisture exits the head.

Fingers move within me, the initial burn turning into something else that causes my insides to ignite with need and desire. Every so often, I feel spurts of warm wetness on my stomach along with blissful-yet-agonizing shouts of release. Pleasure builds within me. Fingers pinch my nipples and rub my clitoris. Hands take turns kneading the tender flesh of my behind. My hips are elevated and my legs held wide open. I scream out in painful pleasure as I watch the face of one of the boys as he fills my tight walls with his shaft. I move someone's hand aside and take over the punishing assault on my clit until I'm screaming out exaltations into the cheering crowd. Then the boy's face becomes another. And then another. The faces all blur together and I start to feel faint, exhausted from the pain. From the pleasure.

I don't want to do this anymore. I try to push one of the boys away, needing to give my body a break from the punishing paces I'm putting it through.

He doesn't budge.

Pain sears through me as he enters my raw channel. I try to throw him off me, but hands are restraining me. "No!" I scream. "Get off me!" I yell and lash out and kick my legs.

A loud cracking noise fills the room and another person jumps onto the bed. "Piper! Piper, wake up!" a voice commands, much deeper than the other voices in the room. Someone grips my shoulders, shaking them. "Wake up, sweetheart."

I snap out of the nightmare, my blurry eyes frantically searching the room for the boys who were just here. But all I find is a half-naked Mason, holding me down in an attempt to keep me from kicking him.

"Piper. It's me, Mason. You're okay. Look at me. It's just me. Only me. You're okay now."

As I wake further, he lightens his hold on me. He reassures me over and over and over, until I stop lashing out at him and collapse down onto the bed. I have no fight left in me as he turns me away from him, cradling me from behind, enveloping me with his comforting protection. "Shhhhhh," his whisper sooths me as his breath rolls over my ear. The gentle rhythmic motion of his hand up and down my arm causes my eyelids to get heavy, sleep once again pulling me under as I hear him say, "I'm never going to let anyone hurt you again."

Eat up, Princess. And call me when you're ready to collect your winnings.

I rub the sleep from my eyes, staring at the note Mason left by the bed, right next to a large, domed tray reeking of heavenly breakfast food. Through the broken, splintered door to his connecting room, I can see that he'd packed up and vacated sometime after my nightmare.

My heart races when it comes rushing back to me. The nightmare. Mason breaking down the door and holding me until I went back to sleep. I can only imagine what he must think of me now. But then I recall the words he said as I fell asleep.

Momentarily forgetting what I did yesterday, I attempt to hop out of bed when my screaming muscles vehemently protest. I rub and knead the knots in my legs until I can finally move myself from the bed to the floor, where I stretch until I can no longer ignore the alluring smell of breakfast. I salivate knowing what must be under the silver dome. American breakfast. I missed it almost as much as good barbeque.

Two hours later, after the bellman insisted he accompany me to the train station, I'm riding the train back to New York, the soft side-to-side motion lulling my tired body until I drift off to sleep, still holding his note.

I startle awake, looking around to gauge if anyone heard me call out in my dream. And then I realize something momentous happened. I had a dream. A *dream*—not a nightmare. I was with Mason and he was walking me down the aisle at Skylar's wedding. Everyone was there, my sisters, my family, friends and neighbors.

Even Charlie was there. But when we got to the altar, we didn't part ways to stand in our respective places to the sides of the bride and groom—we *were* the bride and groom. I was wearing a virginal white dress, the train extending back to the first row of pews. Mason was in the tuxedo he wore to the benefit. We recited our vows and then everyone cheered as we ran out of the church and right into our reception that was teeming with activity. The gorgeous three-tiered cake was cut, the pale-blue garter belt was slung, and the beautiful bouquet of black and white roses was thrown into the air to be caught by Charlie. It's then when I shrieked in excitement, waking myself up.

I shake off the dream, writing it off as a product of all the wedding planning Skylar and I have been doing lately. But in the back of my mind, I wonder if deep down in my subconscious, it's something I want. Over five years I've gone without having anything but nightmares. Five years! And the star of my first regular dream is none other than the author of the note I'm still clutching.

I stare at it. Who is this man? I've done nothing but push him away, despite his innumerable selfless deeds. And then after everything else he's done for me, he finds my bracelet. I swear to God, if knights in shining armor do exist, I guess that would make him mine. I mean, he broke down a damn door for me.

I'm tired of letting the past define me. I'm tired of living in fear every single day. I look around at the men on the train. Surely not *all* of them are bad. I think of Gavin and Griffin and the happiness they've brought to my sisters' lives. I think of the Playhouse and the show posters in illuminated cases. I realize for the first time, that if I don't let myself have a life, I'm letting *them* take it away from me. They've already taken so much. They made me a victim long ago. But maybe *I'm* the only person who is forcing me to continue to be one.

I make a split-second decision and take out my phone to compose a text.

Me: I know what I want.

Mason: Anything, Princess. You name it.

Me: I want you to stop calling me Princess.

Mason: You beat me in the Boston Marathon and that's all you can come up with?

Me: Actually, there was one more thing.

I hesitate so long, he texts me three more times asking what it is. I've already typed the words into my phone. I just haven't had the courage to hit 'send.'

Mason: Are you still there?

I think back to the dream I had earlier. I can't ever remember having an honest-to-God dream that was all hearts and flowers and not some twisted version of *that* night. I grasp onto this one sliver of hope and take the leap.

Me: I want to go on that date with you.

chapter twelve

mason

I occasionally throw a football in front of seventy-eight thousand people. I've given a dozen speeches at middle schools and high schools in the Tri-State area. I sometimes get to mingle with the rich and famous. But, this—walking up Griffin's porch steps to fetch Piper for a date—*this* has my nerves so far on edge that I feel sick to my stomach.

I'm not sure I'll get another chance. I've got one shot at this. She's fragile. Broken by some horrible event that haunts her in her sleep. Fractured to the point of sheer panic at both the benefit and the marathon.

I haven't seen her since her nightmare after the race. That night was both incredible and awful at the same time. When I heard her blood-curdling screams come from the room next to mine, I thought she was being attacked. I didn't even think twice about breaking down the door. And when I got to her, I was relieved yet gutted watching her relive something from her past.

I was able to calm her down, and to my surprise, she even let me hold her until she fell asleep. I lay there watching her for hours. My body was begging for sleep, my muscles exhausted and my energy stores depleted, but I couldn't rip my eyes from her beautiful face. I'll admit, I took liberties she may not have given me if she were conscious. I brushed her hair aside and touched the small tattoo behind her right ear. I nuzzled my head into her hair, inhaling the flowery scent of her shampoo. I put her small hand in mine and held it for dear life—I'm just not certain for whose, hers or mine.

But then I left. I know how embarrassed she gets after her panic attacks. And no matter how much I wanted to stay and have breakfast with her—no matter how much I wanted her to trust me and open up to me about what happened to her—I knew it wasn't the right time. I needed to give her some space. So I packed my things and tipped the bellman to keep her safe.

The hair on my arms prickles when I recall getting the text from her. Of all the things she could've asked for, she asked for a date. Maybe she felt bad because I let her win.

She had second thoughts when I told her Saturday was my only free night. She tried to convince me to go any other night. But this is the first week of conditioning, and that comes with a lot of meetings and engagements. And even though I want this woman more than I've ever wanted anyone, I'm not about to give up a part of myself to get her. Everything I do at work is for one specific purpose, to show my value as a team player, potential leader and top-notch quarterback who is deserving of the starting position.

She cancelled twice on me already, and I suspect her sisters have put the pressure on. I don't really care why she's doing this or how we got here because I've only got twenty days. Twenty days before the wedding. Twenty days before she packs her bags and heads back to her nomadic life.

Twenty days to convince her to stay.

I ring the bell and look through the sidelight in anticipation. I see the indecision when Piper comes from the kitchen. She hesitates. She exchanges words with someone I can't see. She even shakes her head and starts towards the stairs to her room. Then something causes her to turn around. It's then she catches me watching her through the small window.

Her eyes close. Her chest expands before I see her blow out a long breath.

One chance, my head screams. *Don't fuck this up.*

Skylar comes into view, handing Piper her phone and giving her a nudge in my direction. My eyes are trained on her as she slowly walks across the hardwood floor. She may be nervous. She may not even want to do this. But that doesn't keep her from looking heart-stoppingly gorgeous. As in, my heart genuinely skipped a beat. In twenty-two years, that's never happened to me. Not even when I was drafted by the Giants.

It must have actually skipped a hell of a lot more than that, because I feel weak. And completely out of my mind at the thought of this petite, remarkable creature being capable of bringing me to my knees easier than a three-hundred-pound linebacker.

She opens the door and I drink her in. Her hair is soft and wavy, like she just came from a day at the beach, looking casual as if she hadn't taken any time on it whatsoever, yet it's perfect. Her emerald eyes reflect the rich color of her blouse, making them an even deeper shade of green than usual. Tasteful makeup accentuates her eyes and I break out in a smile, knowing she took the time to get ready for our date after all.

"What's that?" She nods her head at what I completely forgot I was holding.

I put my proverbial tongue back in my mouth and extend my arm, offering her the 'bouquet' of candy bars I had the chocolate shop down the street put together. "I heard you say you missed American candy while you were away."

"You brought me a bouquet. Of candy?" she says in amusement, her mouth easing into a grin she can't control.

"Well, I wanted to be original and not bring flowers like your other dates."

"I don't date," she says with the lift of her eyebrow.

"Except tonight," I remind her.

"Don't get cocky. I'm just honoring our bet." She tries to sound bitchy, but I can see right through it. She's as transparent to me as if we'd been twins separated at birth. I can see through the façade she puts up to make her appear stronger than she thinks she is.

I don't know what happened to her to make her this way. What I do know is that I work day in and day out with some of the biggest, beefiest, most muscular guys in the country. And I own a gym that gets used by a few of the world's elite athletes. But this girl—this broken, flawed, extraordinary woman—I think she just might be the strongest person I know.

∼ ∼ ∼

"What can I get you to drink, Miss?" the waiter asks.

Piper hides behind the menu, putting it between us and the prying eyes of our attendant. She whispers, "Is this one of those places that will bring a bottle of wine and open it right here at the table?"

I chuckle and whisper back, "This is one of those places that will follow you into the bathroom and wipe your ass if you want them to."

The menu drops onto the table and Piper bursts out laughing. Her laughter is poetic. Exhilarating. Contagious. I start up as well. We try to stop but then one of us looks at the other and we crack up into a fit of giggles. I've never seen her look more beautiful. It's as if all the stress that goes along with . . . being *her*, is momentarily lifted. Her eyes water and she dabs at the corner of them with her linen napkin.

Our waiter clears his throat, reminding us that he's still anticipating our order.

I pick up the wine menu and ask Piper, "Does a Chardonnay sound good?"

She nods and I proceed to place the order.

Another server brings us a hot loaf of bread and fills our water glasses from a crystal pitcher. I break the bread, putting half of it on Piper's plate. "How do you feel now, five days after?"

"Pretty good. Just this morning, I went for my first run since the marathon. You?"

"I started offseason conditioning on Wednesday." I instinctively rub my sore thighs. "They've taken it easy on me because of the race, but I probably pushed myself a little too hard trying to impress the powers that be."

"What exactly is offseason conditioning?" She tears off a piece of her bread and pops it into her mouth.

"It's a nine week program that keeps us from squandering away the muscle and agility we gained during the previous season. The first few weeks are limited to strength, conditioning and rehab—which decidedly I was in great need of." I continue to explain the details of our workout program when she starts choking on a piece of bread.

She drags in ragged breaths between coughs, looking embarrassed to be drawing any attention. "Are you okay?" I hold her water out to her. "Here, try and take a drink."

She pushes the glass away, instead reaching into her bag to pull out a water bottle. I notice she always carries one with her and I wonder if it's a habit she got into while traveling. You can never be too sure about the quality of water in strange places.

She stops coughing and I nod at the bottle. "Are you a water snob or a germaphobe?" I joke.

She shrugs and caps the bottle, placing it back into her bag. "I just like this particular brand, that's all." She shifts uncomfortably in her chair. "So, you want to be the starting quarterback?"

"Doesn't everyone?" I ask.

"No. Everyone doesn't," she says, her unease abundantly clear. "Why would you want all that attention?"

The sommelier brings us our bottle of wine. Piper watches with great interest as he opens the bottle and pours a taste into my glass. "Yes, this is fine. Thank you," I tell him as he fills our glasses and places the bottle on the table.

"I don't play football for the attention, Piper. I play football because I love the game."

She takes a drink of her wine, eyeing me over the top of the glass. "Why is it so important to you?"

"Have you ever had anything you were really passionate about? Something that defines you to your very core? Something you felt you would die if you didn't do?"

Piper shrugs and her eyes fall despondently to the table when it dawns on me she did have something like that. Skylar told me acting was her life when she was growing up. And yet she gave up her dream to travel the world aimlessly.

Or something forced her to give it up.

"Maybe you just haven't found that one thing yet, Piper. You're young. You still have a lot of years to figure it out. I was lucky. My dad signed me up for peewee football when I was five. He was my coach until I went to high school. It was something we always did together. We bonded over football. I guess that's part of why I want this so badly. I think he would've been proud of me."

Her eyes snap to mine. "Would've been?"

I nod. It's been almost seven years, but my voice still hitches when I tell her, "My parents died in a car accident when I was sixteen."

Piper gasps, covering her mouth in horror. "Oh, my God. That's awful. I'm so sorry, Mason."

"You can't imagine how losing someone that close to you can change your life. I wanted to die along with them. I was their only child and didn't have any relatives I could stay with. It was my football coach who helped me out of my depression. He took me in, letting me live with him until I went away to college. All of my anger, all of my aggression, all of my self-loathing—he got me to put it back into football."

"Why did you hate yourself?" she asks, sympathetically, or maybe empathetically. "It wasn't your fault."

"It *was* my fault. I was driving." I relive the moment in my head for the millionth time. I'll never forget how time stood still and seconds became a lifetime. "I'm not sure I'll ever understand what I was thinking when I swerved off the road to try and miss hitting a squirrel. A fucking squirrel. It wasn't even someone's pet. When I crashed sideways into the tree, I traded my parent's lives for a goddamn rodent."

She looks sick, her pale face displaying a look of horrified disbelief. "Did you really want to die?"

I swear the way she asks me the question, it's the most introspective thing I've ever heard come out of her pink, pouty lips. I don't look away from her. Her question burns a hole into my brain. Into my soul. She's been there, too. She wanted to die. I'm sure of it. And it completely guts me.

I nod, holding my hand out and turning up my wrist so she can see the evidence. "Yes, I did." I take a deep breath and go out on a limb. "I killed my own parents, Piper. I've been to hell and back. So you see, there is nothing you could tell me that would make me think any differently about you."

"Are you ready to order, sir?"

Of all the times for a waiter to interrupt a conversation.

Piper stands suddenly. "Excuse me for a minute. Can you please order for me?" She scurries away in the direction of the bathroom and I'm more than a little relieved that she didn't take her things with her. I watch her walk away, wondering what the hell happened to her that made her want to die, and wanting to do everything in my power to make it better.

After placing our order, I hear her phone ping and vibrate on the table. I realize she forgot to silence it. I look towards the bathroom to see if she's on her way back when it chimes again. When I don't see her, I decide I'd better silence it for her. After all, this is a pretty upscale place. I reach out to it when I see the text that pops up on her screen.

Charlie: I know you don't want to hear it, but I couldn't let this day go by without wishing you a happy 22nd. I love you, Pipes.

Her phone goes dark again and it takes all my willpower not to pick it up and make sure I read it correctly. Today is Piper's birthday?

No wonder she wanted to cancel. She probably wanted to do something special with her family. Either that or she didn't want me to feel the pressure of having our first date on such a momentous occasion. But why would she not want to hear it from Charlie? Are they fighting?

I don't let another second go by without calling the waiter over to make some last-minute arrangements.

Then my phone rings. *Cassidy.* I have no choice but to answer it. She's got me by the balls when it comes to that. I would never forgive myself if something ever happened to Hailey and I didn't know because I was too stubborn to answer the phone.

"What is it, Cass?" I ask, brusquely.

"Well, good evening to you, too, baby."

I roll my eyes. "Cassidy, is there a point to this call, or are you just trying to ruin my evening?"

"Of course there's a point to the call. I wanted to let you know that Hailey climbed the stairs all on her own today without any help from me."

"That's great, Cass, but I'm sure this could have waited until tomorrow. And you will remember to keep the safety gate locked, right? Just because she can climb the stairs, doesn't mean she won't fall."

She huffs into the phone. "God, Mason, I'm not stupid."

The waiter comes by to ask a question about our meal.

"Are you out with the guys?" she asks, after hearing my brief conversation with him.

"It's really none of your business who I'm out with."

She's silent for a beat. "Oh, so you're on a date? I thought you didn't date, Mason. Who is she?" More silence. "It's the girl from last week, isn't it? Snow White? Oh, God, baby. I mean, seriously, if you want to date, I can think of about a thousand girls who would be better suited for you than little Miss Awkward."

During her tirade, Piper has rejoined me. She sits down and picks up her phone, I guess trying to mind her own business while I'm on a call. I don't much like her reaction when she reads Charlie's text. She shifts in her chair as if it suddenly became uncomfortable. A wave of sadness overcomes her and it makes me unhappy that she's not getting along with her best friend on her birthday.

"I'm not interested in your recommendations, Cass. And what I do is no concern of yours."

Piper snaps her eyes to mine when she hears me say Cassidy's name. "*Sorry*," I mouth to her, shrugging my shoulders and hoping I'm not completely ruining this date by talking with my ex.

"It absolutely is my concern," Cassidy barks into the phone. "I can't have you trolling around with God only knows who. How did you meet her? Is she one of your ridiculous little fangirls? Do you even know anything about her?"

I try to lower my voice, but anger boils up inside me. My boisterous whisper betrays the calm and cool exterior I'm trying to exude to Piper. "You're one to talk. You have a goddamn revolving door in your apartment. God knows what Hailey is witnessing. So don't you dare presume to tell me when and whom I can or can't date."

"But—" she tries to get a word in.

"I'm hanging up now." I bring my voice up to a normal decibel. "There is a beautiful woman sitting across from me and I refuse to ignore her for any longer than necessary." I end the call and put my phone down, noticing the blush sweeping across Piper's cheeks.

"You are, you know," I tell her. "You're beautiful, Piper. If I didn't tell you that already, I should have. And I'm sorry for taking that call, but I never know when it might be about Hailey."

"It's fine." She waves it off, and then starts picking at the tablecloth as if she's never received a compliment before. "I understand you'd do anything for your daughter."

"Do you like kids, Piper? I know you have a special connection with Maddox, but I never see you with Aaron or Jordan. You don't have a problem with me having a child, do you?"

I watch intently as she picks at the white linen, knowing she's thinking deep thoughts, and I wonder if my being a dad is going to be an issue for her. She's only twenty-one, well twenty-two, but still she may be too young to take on the responsibility of being with a guy who has a kid. Because she's right—I'd do anything for Hailey. And no matter how much I want Piper Mitchell, if she can't accept my daughter, that's a certified deal breaker.

chapter thirteen

piper

My heart pounds so hard against my chest wall, I'm sure Mason can hear it. Thankfully, our waiter interrupts what I'm sure would have been a very awkward conversation, depositing meals in front of us that I imagine should come from a diner with red-and-white-checkered tablecloths, not a high-class restaurant with expensive linen ones.

An unexpected smile cracks my face. "You bring me to this fancy restaurant; one that actually *does* have attendants in the bathroom that would probably wipe my ass; and you order me barbeque?" I laugh, looking at the slop of Carolina pulled pork on top of a thick Kaiser roll.

"I'll never forget that first night we met," he says. "When we had the argument about you being an athlete. I'm sure you remember the one?" He winks at me and I roll my eyes. "You had barbeque sauce in the corner of your mouth and I can't even begin to tell you what I would have done to be able to wipe it off." I try unsuccessfully not to grin at the visual in my head. "I knew you probably would have kicked the shit out of me. And now, after seeing you box the way you do, I know it for a fact. But I thought, since we're on a date and all, that if it happened again, you'd be kind enough to let me wipe it."

For the second time tonight, I feel heat creep across my face and I'm sure my cheeks are pinking up to match the shade of my borrowed lipstick. I fidget nervously with my bracelet and then pick up my wine, absentmindedly putting it to my mouth, allowing the liquid to touch my lips before I realize what I've done. My eyes go wide and I quickly put down the glass and wipe the wetness from my frown.

"Something wrong with the wine?" He sniffs his before taking a drink.

I shake my head. "No. I guess I'm just not a big fan of Chardonnay," I lie. *It's my favorite*. "Sorry."

"I'll get you something else. What would you like?"

"Nothing, thanks. I think I'd like to dig into this great-smelling sandwich."

He pushes the tiny serving bowl of barbeque sauce towards my plate. "Don't forget to really load up," he says, smiling.

I laugh. "I was right," I say, trying to get a grip on the pile of meat, dripping sauce from a bun that's larger than my hands. "You're incorrigible."

"Who said I was incorrigible?"

"Nobody." I get some sauce on my finger and lick it off. I look over at Mason who is watching the action intently, his dilating eyes trained on my lips as I see him shift around in his chair. I didn't mean anything sexual by it. I really was just licking my finger. But the way he's looking at me right now, it's like he wants to eat me alive. And every part of my body, right down to the cells that make up my beating heart, is afraid that's exactly what he wants to do.

But the same parts of me are also terrified that it's not.

I stare at him, wondering how the simple act of me licking a finger could make him lose his shit. "All football players are alike. You think you can get whatever you want, whenever you want without regard to anyone. And you never change. I know what goes on. I've heard about plenty of famous players in their forties who are on their third wives, girlfriends on the side, and a felony assault charge that was conveniently dropped to boot. What is it about being famous that makes you think you can disregard all the rules of basic humanity?"

I immediately regret my words. I know I said them out of fear. Fear of the unknown. Fear of what this date could lead to. Maybe I'm sabotaging the night on purpose. He's never given me any reason to doubt his intentions or his humanity.

He puts down his fork and looks me directly in the eye. "That's not me, Piper. I'm not like Charlie's mom, if that's what you think. I don't believe the world is at my disposal. I don't expect things to get handed to me on a silver platter. I fight for what I want. And right now I want two things—football and you."

My breath catches, his words taking me completely off guard. He doesn't give me time to respond. "I know football players get a bad rap for being . . . well, for being *players*, but I'm not like that. I'll admit I wasn't careful when I was younger. I made a mistake. I got careless. But I'm not a bad person. Have I done anything to make you think I am?"

"What about at the airport?" I ask.

"Airport?"

"When you gave that woman your phone number."

"Huh?" He tilts his head and studies my face. "What woman?"

"The one with the kid. I think he was lost and you helped him find his mother. Then you gave her your phone number. Are you telling me that's not being a player?"

The strong muscles of his jaw try to suppress a smile before the features of his face soften with boyish charm. "It was an autograph, Piper. Not a phone number. I talked about football to try and calm him down. Turns out his dad was a big fan, so he asked his mom if it was okay for me to give him an autograph."

"An autograph?"

He shrugs; a slow graceful movement of one muscular shoulder.

I close my eyes and shake my head. "I'm sorry. You've actually been pretty nice to me considering some of the things I've said to you. But how do you know you won't become those people? I mean, you're just at the beginning of being famous. What happens if you get that starting position? What happens when women throw themselves at you whenever you leave your apartment? What happens if you want one of them, but they decide they don't want you? Are you going to just take what you want, Mason?"

He pushes away his half-eaten plate of food, seemingly losing his appetite. He pours the remaining wine into his glass and drinks it in one long swallow. "No, Piper. I'm not going to *take* what I want. But I am willing to fight for it. That's where I'm different from them—the men in your past."

"You don't know anything about me," I growl at him, giving him a biting stare.

His face falls into a frown and I can tell he regrets his comment just as much as I regret mine. "You're right, I don't. But

I would like to. I hope you'll give me the chance to get to know you better. Now, eat your sandwich or you'll waste away. I'm willing to bet you ran more than you should have today. Am I right? What did you do, five, six?"

I shrug. "Seven."

He laughs. "See, I know a lot about you already. I knew you would never stick to the marathon recovery guidelines."

We talk about running for the remainder of the meal. It's a safe subject. I tell him about the marathons I ran in Amsterdam and Berlin last year. I tell him how Charlie got me into running back in high school. I even show him some pictures on my phone.

"This must be Charlie," he says.

"That was taken in Austria the day after she broke her leg. We were supposed to go mountain climbing the next week, but obviously, we couldn't."

"There aren't any men in these pictures," he says, taking the liberty of paging through more of my photos. "Does that mean I don't have any competition from guys with really cool accents?"

I shake my head. "I don't date, remember?"

He laughs. "Me neither. Until tonight. In fact, this is the first date I've been on since Hailey was born."

My jaw slackens with disbelief. "You haven't been on a date in almost two years?"

His eyes scrunch together like he's working something out in his head. "Technically, a little over two years. Not since Cassidy showed up pregnant."

"How is that even possible? I don't know any guy who can go that long without . . . um . . . *dating*." I feel a wave of heat cross my face and wonder if there's ever been another time in my life when I've blushed so many times over the course of one evening. I know there's not.

I take a drink of water from my bottle to cool me down.

"I told you, Piper, I'm not like most guys. I'm one-hundred-percent dedicated to my daughter." He raises his hand and examines it. "And apparently, my left hand."

In a very unladylike manner, water spews from my mouth in a fit of laughter. Mason chuckles as he wipes droplets off my phone. He looks at the picture again before handing it back to me. "Charlie is the spitting image of her mother," he says, eyeing the picture of Charlie with her blue cast and me supporting her on her crutches as we pose in front of the ski slope she broke her leg on. Charlie is a redhead. Her long, wavy hair a carbon-copy of the once-famous actress I grew to despise.

"I used to see her mom in movies when I was a child," he says. "Stole her mother's looks is right. She's stunning."

I've never once before been jealous of Charlie. Yes, she's always been the beautiful one. The one men fawn over. The tall, mysterious redhead they take home while her awkward roommate sleeps alone. But right now, despite how I've always been relieved that she gets all the attention, my eyes fall to the table as a foreign feeling courses through me. It feels a little like defeat. "Yeah. She is, isn't she?"

"Yes, of course she is." He leans over the table, reaching his hand up to my mouth. I tense when his fingers meet my lips. My pulse races and my breathing stops at the feel of his gentle touch. He swipes his thumb across my bottom lip, retracting his hand to reveal the barbeque sauce he'd wiped off. He puts his thumb into his mouth and sucks the sauce off. I almost fall out of my chair. I think that must be the single most sexy thing I've ever seen a man do. Then again, I've never regarded men as sexy. Until now. Until Mason. "But she doesn't hold a candle to you, Piper. You're gorgeous, don't you know that?"

Before I can disagree with him, or even have the time to blush, the Maître D comes over with a bottle of champagne and a plate of Tiramisu with a lit candle in it. He wishes me a boisterous happy birthday and several tables around us applaud as he pops the cork, pouring us each a glass of what looks to be an expensive Brut.

I feel I might be sick right here in front of Mason at this fancy restaurant that serves barbeque on request. I pull my water bottle out of my bag and take a long drink. "I uh . . ." I fumble with the bottle and look around nervously to make sure people are no longer watching. I push the fancy confection away from me. "I don't celebrate my birthday, Mason. How did you even know?"

"Who doesn't celebrate their birthday? At least until they hit fifty and want to live in denial." He laughs.

"*I* don't," I say, with the conviction of a serial killer.

I watch the crinkle form between his eyebrows. "How come?"

There's a pregnant pause and I feel he can sense me scrambling for an answer. The wheels turn in my head so I can quickly give him one. I blow out a long breath to bide some time. "I just don't think we need to celebrate the fact that we're dying. You do know that from the minute we're born, we start dying, right? We are literally born to die. There is no other certainty in life. And every birthday we celebrate is just one more reminder of how much closer we are to death."

He studies me while I speak and I wonder if he can perceive how my words tell a much different story than my eyes do. Does he believe all that crap I just spewed out? "So you're a glass-half-empty kind of girl?"

"No, I'm a realist," I quip. "So tell me, which one of my sisters do I have to kill?"

"Neither. It's my fault." He nods his head at my phone. "While you were in the bathroom, you got a text. I know it was wrong for me to look, but when I glanced down and saw Charlie wishing you a happy birthday, I couldn't let the night go by without recognizing it. I didn't go through your phone, Piper. I swear I just saw the text flash across the screen. I'm really sorry."

His eyes fill with regret and beg me to forgive him. I try to see it from his point of view. I get that most people celebrate their birthdays and he probably just thought I didn't want to put the pressure on him for our date. Mark it down as one more noble thing he's tried to do for me.

He has no idea. No idea that for the last four years, I've gotten so drunk I almost ended up in the hospital. Not because I was celebrating, but because I was trying to forget. Forget the worst day of my life. Forget the unimaginable pain of losing that part of me I could never get back. Forget the day I stopped living.

His eyes fill with compassion. "Okay, so no birthday." He leans over and blows out the candle, removing it from the dessert. He picks up my champagne glass and hands it to me. "To us, then. To completing the Boston Marathon—a distinguishable accomplishment only a select few can claim."

How he can manage to pull me from the depths of self-abhorrence, I'm not quite clear on, but at his remark, I crack a tiny smile and take my glass from him. "To you, for making it possible for me to finish."

We clink glasses and drink. I down the whole thing in three swift gulps. Mason laughs. "Ahhh, so I've found your drink. Unreasonably overpriced champagne it is." He pours me another. As I watch the bubbly liquid effervesce in my glass, I remind myself what happened the last time I drank too much around Mason. I ended up panicking and punching out the valet. I vow to limit myself to two glasses—enough to loosen me up and allow me to enjoy the evening Mason is trying so hard to orchestrate.

"Come on." He gets a forkful of Tiramisu and offers it to me. "It'd be a shame to waste this dessert that in no way, shape or form even begins to resemble a birthday cake. I'm not even sure why they brought this, I mean what idiot serves Tiramisu for someone's birthday? This is obviously an '*I finished the marathon*' cake."

I laugh and take the bite, holding his inviting stare. I'm not sure what it is that makes it so intimate when one person feeds another. Mothers feed their kids all the time. So why then, when he pulls the fork slowly from my mouth, do I feel a shockwave traveling all the way from my mouth to the very core of my being?

I take a sip of my champagne and try to form a coherent sentence. "Actually, it means 'lift me up'."

"Uh, what?" He loosens the top button of his blue dress shirt and I realize he's just as flustered by my bite of cake as I am.

"I lived in Italy for six months," I explain. "Tiramisu means 'pick me up' or 'lift me up.' So, you see, it *is* appropriate. You literally lifted me up in the race and forced me to continue. I don't know if I'll ever be able to truly thank you for that." I fiddle with my bracelet, twisting the charm around it on my wrist. "As a matter of fact, I have a lot more to thank you for than just the race. I'm sorry it's taken me so long to say it, but I really appreciate everything you've done for me."

His face lights up as he digs in and offers me another bite. "Believe me, Piper. It's been my pleasure."

Someone clinks a spoon on a glass and our attention turns to the table beside us. We watch a man make a toast to his son who is graduating from law school. My eyes fall on Mason as he longingly witnesses the exchange between father and son. We cheer along with the other patrons and raise our glasses in toast.

When the applause dies down, I reach across the table and place a sympathetic hand on Mason's arm, relishing the electrified heat that I've come to expect with our touches. "I'm so sorry about your parents. I can only imagine how horrible that must have been for you. I'm sure they would be proud that you've accomplished so much."

He nods, not taking his eyes off my hand that still rests on him. He covers my hand with his other one, holding it in place on his arm. "Thank you. I've learned to live with it. It's a part of who I am. But I won't let it define me." His eyes capture mine, burning into the far reaches of my mind as if he knows my deepest, darkest secrets. His thumb caresses my knuckles, sending a comforting warmth through me. "Bad things happen to good people, Piper. We just can't let our past dictate our future."

I pull my hand back and he instantly releases it, smiling over at me, almost like he senses my fear of being held down. He picks up his drink and touches the rim of it to mine. "So, where am I taking you next Saturday, Piper?"

chapter fourteen

mason

Jarod delivers our orders, interrupting the conversations at the table, and it reminds me of last night. The waiter had shitty timing. I never did get an answer from Piper about a second date. Then when I took her home and walked her up the stairs, this two-hundred-twenty-pound quarterback was afraid to repeat the question for fear of rejection.

I didn't try to kiss her. I wasn't going to push my luck. I was grateful she didn't run out on me after all the mistakes I made seemingly putting my foot in my mouth more than once. She wasn't ready. But she was conflicted, I could tell. As we stood on the porch, she kept staring at my lips, a sure sign she was thinking about kissing me. There was nothing more I wanted to do in that moment. The pull was so strong I had to physically restrain myself by grabbing the railing behind me. Her lips were so soft and vaguely pouty. Simply perfect. And since I'd touched them earlier when I wiped the barbeque sauce from them, I knew exactly what I was missing.

I only hope I have another chance.

But as I watch Jarod serving the food, I notice his eyes never stray far from Piper. He wants her. What if I've opened up the door to her dating and now he's going to take the opportunity I've afforded him? Why the hell did we have to have brunch *here* today? Why not Maple Creek or Long Island?

"Hey, Piper," Jarod says, putting her omelet in front of her. "Are you working later?"

She shakes her head. "No. Not until tomorrow."

His faces falls in disappointment. "Oh, well, me too. I guess I'll see you then."

"Yeah, I guess so," she says, smiling up at him.

Smiling. It's a rarity for Piper Mitchell. Why is she smiling at him? As I ponder it, she looks over at me to catch me staring. Her smile gets bigger. And just like the fucking Grinch, my heart expands and almost bursts through my chest. I think for a brief second that maybe I'm the one who put the smile on her face. Perhaps she's simply in a good mood after our date? She seems relaxed today. Carefree. Dare I say . . . happy.

I glance over at Jarod, who is still paying close attention to our table. Probably because the owners and his manager are all in attendance. I'll give her the day to think about it. Then I'll catch her at the gym tomorrow. Before she comes to work. Before the tatted-up boy has a chance to ask her out and butt in on my girl. Because that's exactly how I see her. *Mine.* I can't bear the thought of anyone else being with her. Touching her. But deep down, I know that's exactly what happened in her past. And not in a good way.

I start to lose my appetite.

"So, how'd it go last night?" Griffin elbows me from his seat next to mine, whispering so nobody else can hear. "If I had to guess, pretty damn good. I've never seen Piper wake up in a good mood. That woman is not a morning person."

"Really?" My previous thoughts fall away as a smile threatens to split my face open.

"Yeah, I'm telling you the girl was walking on cloud nine. She even made coffee for us. That's a first. Whatever you're doing, just keep on doing it."

"Did she say anything?" I ask, hesitantly.

"What are we, in high school?" He laughs.

"What's so funny," Skylar asks from across the table.

"Nothing," Griffin replies. "I was just noticing what a good mood my friend here was in."

All eyes turn to me. Then one by one they go across the table to Piper, who instantly blushes and looks slightly forlorn by the attention.

"Must be this fantastic weather," her dad says.

"Must be," Skylar adds, winking at me.

Piper gives her a dirty look. I think she must have kicked her under the table, because Skylar whispers loudly, "What?"

I look around the table and see exactly what I want for my future. For my daughter's future. The Mitchells are one big happy family. Bruce and Jan have taken me in as one of their own. If they only knew how much I wished that were true. They did an impressive job raising three incredible daughters.

Bruce is a big guy like me. Intimidating as hell sometimes, but once you get to know him, you realize his bark is far worse than his bite. Still, I'm not sure I'd want to be on the wrong side of a conversation with him. I've heard enough about how that can go from Gavin and Griffin. They both had to earn his trust the hard way, after abandoning his daughters.

Jan shared the gorgeous color of her eyes with both Skylar and Piper, and she dotes on Hailey as much as she does her own grandchildren. It makes me sad that I can't have my daughter with me every day. The more I'm around the Mitchells, the more I realize what true family is. Perhaps it's time to think about hiring the lawyer I always threaten Cassidy with.

As if my thoughts conjured her up out of thin air, Cassidy walks through the front doors of the restaurant, carrying Hailey in her arms. This must be a coincidence. No way would she have been invited here. She fits in with the group about as much as square peg fits into a round hole.

When she sees me, Hailey squeals, "Dada!"

My eyes instinctively go to Piper's to see her reaction. For a split second, her eyes light up and her face brightens. Then as quickly as it happened, her eyes fall to the table in a sad stare. In my mind I convince myself she was delighted to see my daughter but not so happy about the woman holding her.

I get up from the table and walk over to greet my little girl, pulling her into my arms for a big hug.

Everyone at the table greets Hailey, fawning over her pretty dress and stylish hair. Almost everyone.

Finally, someone acknowledges her mother. "Oh, hey, Cassidy," Skylar says, trying to be polite.

"Hi," she says, her eyes perusing the table, stopping dead when she sees Piper. If looks could kill, Piper would fall forward into her half-eaten cheese omelet. Cassidy raises her hand, pointing a ridiculously long and manicured fingernail at Piper. "You. You're that girl from the benefit." She looks around the table at Baylor and Skylar. "I knew you looked familiar. You're one of *them*, aren't you?" she says, her expression filled with bitterness. "You're a Mitchell sister."

Baylor says, "I guess you haven't been formally introduced. Cassidy, this is Piper, our younger sister."

Cassidy snorts, mumbling, "Piper, Skylar, Baylor . . . how very cute," without any regard to the parents that named them who are sitting right here with us. "You're the one in the picture."

Piper looks confused. "Cassidy showed me a picture once," Baylor explains. "She thought it was a picture of me but I told her it was my little sister."

"Interesting." Cassidy's eyes dart between Piper and Baylor. "You could almost pass for twins." She gives a pointed stare at Piper. "That is if Snow White would have stayed away from the dime-store hairdresser."

Piper rolls her eyes and pretends not to be affected by her words as she rises from the table. "If you'll excuse me," she says, irritation pinching her brow. "I have to take my dime-store hair along with my God-given boobs to the bathroom."

I watch her walk away, wanting to yell at my ex but not in front of our daughter. "Cass, that's enough. We're trying to enjoy brunch. Is there a point to you being here?" I ask.

"I promised Hailey take-out today. Apparently you've gotten her addicted to the chicken nuggets here."

I smile at my daughter. "You like Mitchell's, sweet pea? You're a smart little girl."

Hailey claps her hands. "Mit-tels. Yummy Mit-tels."

All those at the table laugh with delight. I put her down so she can be showered with kisses from everyone present. Everyone but the one person I want to see my daughter warm up to.

Mindy, a waitress and good friend to Skylar, comes out with Cassidy's packaged order. She hands it to her along with the bill and crouches down to greet Hailey. "Hello, Miss Hailey. How are you today? I like your pretty dress."

"Go poopy," Hailey says without a care, now straining into her diaper.

Mindy laughs. "I'd love to help you out with that, sweetie, but I'm serving food today and I don't think my bosses would appreciate it very much."

Cassidy shoves the takeout bag at me. "I'll clean her up." She whisks Hailey away to the bathroom leaving me with her food and, conveniently, the bill.

I open up my wallet and pay Mindy, who asks, "How does Cassidy do that? I swear she manages to get out of paying the bill every single time."

I laugh. "Are you suggesting she has my daughter trained to poop whenever the bill comes?"

"I wouldn't put it past her," she says. "But I'm not sure anyone is *that* good at manipulation."

"Oh, I don't know. She's pretty damn good."

When I get to thinking about all the manipulating she's done with me, my entire body stiffens when I realize she's in the bathroom. With Piper. That can't be good. I quickly excuse myself from the table and head down the hall. Before I round the corner to the bathrooms, I hear Cassidy's voice and stop to listen. She must have cornered her in the hallway.

"What is it with you Mitchell sisters?" she asks.

"Exactly what is that supposed to mean?" Piper replies.

"You all go after the rich and famous ones. What makes you think you're any better than the rest of us?"

"First of all, I'm not *going after* anyone," Piper says. "And you don't know anything about my sisters, so why don't you shut the fu—, uh, just shut up about it."

I'm amused, and slightly impressed, that Piper is censoring herself in front of Hailey.

"Mama, poopy," Hailey reminds her.

"Just a minute, baby." I hear movement and then I have to concentrate to hear her growling whisper. "It was you he was with last night, wasn't it? Do you really think you're good enough for him? You dress like a pauper. You have that thing on your nose. It's so last decade. You're just so . . . normal. You realize Mason Lawrence can have anyone he wants, right? Why do you think he would choose someone as plain as you? Unless of course you're fucking him. Are you fucking him? It won't last, you know. He'll use you up and throw you away just like all the others. He'll go through all of his little fan girls until he realizes who he needs to be with. The mother of his child. He will do anything to make Hailey happy. And Hailey wants her Mommy *and* her Daddy. And as soon as she's old enough to ask for it, he'll give it to her. He does every time. So go have your fun, but know who he'll end up with in the end."

"He'll obviously want to be with you because you're such a great mom," Piper deadpans. "Cussing and talking the way you do in front of your daughter; you should win the Mother of the Year Award. How proud you must be. You don't even realize what you have, do you? You don't realize it because instead of seeing her as a gift, you see her as a tool to getting what you want. I feel sorry for you, Cassidy. For you and your pathetic life. Now run along and pretend you're a mother who actually cares that her daughter messed her pants."

I'm stunned by their exchange. I'm enlightened by Cassidy's admission. I'm encouraged by Piper's declaration. She thinks children are a gift? Perhaps it won't be so hard to forge a bond between them after all. But before I can process all of this information and get out of the way, Piper rounds the corner smacking right into me.

"Ooof." I put my hands on her arms to keep her from falling.

She looks up at me bashfully. "Uh, did you hear any of that?" she asks.

I give her a confirming nod. "Pretty much all of it. I was coming back to rescue you from Hurricane Cassidy. But apparently you didn't need my help."

Her eyes fill with regret. "I'm sorry I said those awful things about your kid's mom. I shouldn't let her get to me like that."

"Are you kidding? Everything you said is true." I look her straight in the eye. "And everything *she* said is not. I hope you know that. I told you last night, you were the first date I've had in years. There hasn't been anyone else, even in passing. Those things she said, she said them to scare you away. I had no idea that she's been waiting for me to get back together with her. I promise you that will never happen. You were the first woman I've wanted to be with since Hailey was born. You're the *only* woman I want to be with."

I both see and hear her sigh of relief. Her eyes soften. She believes me.

I realize my hands are still on her arms and she has goosebumps; the fine hairs prickling my fingertips. It's not cold in the hallway. It must be me. She's reacting to my touch. Better yet, she's making no attempt to pull away from it. Now may be the right time to ask her out again. While we have this connection. This fire that's coming from her and going straight to my groin—right through every bone in my body—and directly to my goddamn heart.

"Piper—"

"Is everything okay back here?" I'm cut off by Jarod, who is eyeing my hands on her arms with disdain.

She backs away, putting too much distance between us and my hands fall down to my sides, heavy with emptiness.

"Everything's fine, Jarod. We were just heading out to the table." Piper walks away, glancing back at me over her shoulder with sympathy, as if she knew what I was about to ask and Jarod ruined the moment. That look—does it mean she would have said yes?

Jarod glares at me before going back to his duties.

Fucking waiters and their bad timing.

chapter fifteen

piper

He was going to ask me out again at brunch yesterday. I know it. I could sense it; feel it in his touch. Lying here in bed, I can still feel his fingers on my arm. First, holding me up so I didn't fall when we collided, then brushing lightly against my skin as we spoke. It was hard to concentrate on what he was saying when all my focus was on those inches of my flesh that were touching his.

However, I'm glad he didn't ask. I would have said no. I'm only here for a few more weeks. And once I leave I'm not coming back. What would be the point in going out with him again?

I had another dream about him last night. I find it strange that ever since I saw the face in the crowd, the face that should have me fighting demons every night in my sleep, I've had more good nights than bad. More dreams than nightmares. More hope than despair. But I know my dreams are just that—dreams of what could never happen. I could never have a real relationship with a man. I could never be with someone without the ugliness of my past destroying any shred of a bright future. My fate has been sealed. My destiny shrouded in a darkness I can never overcome.

I reach my hand out and place it on the vacant pillow next to me, for the first time in my life, mourning every what-if and could-have-been. I reach down into the very depths of my soul, looking inwardly around every nook and cranny to see if there is any small part of me—just one little piece I think I can give to him.

I touch my lips. I remember the fire he set in my body and the shivers he sent down my spine when he touched them the other night. The memory of it has my fingers wandering into my panties, something I've done sparingly over the years and only to release tension. Never before have I touched myself while thinking of a man. Never have I let my fingers circle my clit while envisioning another person. Never have my fantasies gone so wild that I find myself moaning at the very thought of him.

My hips begin to move involuntarily as I spread the wetness around, making my fingers glide soft and easy over my hard nub. My mind goes back to the night he protected me; spooned me until I fell asleep. I imagine him brushing my hair aside and tracing my tattoo before placing his lips on it. I imagine his lips and hands traveling down my body, softly, slowly and gently like no others have ever done. I slip a finger inside of me, pretending it's his. I think his name might even escape my mouth in a breathy moan when my thighs tighten, my belly clenches and I spiral down into a shuttering orgasm unlike anything I've ever experienced.

Then without thinking too much about it, I pick up my phone.

Me: Was there something you wanted to ask me yesterday?

He texts me back immediately and I break into an enormous smile, so sudden and unexpected it hurts my face.

Mason: Yes. I just wasn't sure you were ready to be asked.

Me: Today is a new day.

Mason: Okay, then. Will you go out with me on Saturday?

Me: Yes.

I throw my phone down and head into the bathroom.

When I emerge from my shower, I hear commotion downstairs. I throw on a t-shirt and yoga pants and head down to see what's up. I'm just off the bottom step when squeals of laughter fill the air. I look over to see Griffin giving Hailey a piggy-back ride around the living room.

My heart thunders. Where there's Hailey, there's Mason.

In two seconds flat, I take inventory of my appearance. Hair—wet. Clothes—frumpy. Makeup—none. I spin on my bare feet and attempt to make a mad dash upstairs before I even have a chance to think about the fact that he's seen me at my worst before. He's seen me at the gym. He's watched me shatter in front of thousands of people, sweaty and broken. He's witnessed me drunk and disheveled. So why, in this moment do I care if he sees me like this?

"Hey, Princess."

I hate that name. I want to walk over to him and shove it right back down his throat. But somehow, he's made it seem more of an endearment than a putdown. The way he says it, I realize it's the same tone he uses when addressing his daughter.

I protest anyway, on principle. "I thought we agreed you weren't going to call me that anymore."

"Okay, then. Hey, sweetheart." He winks at me.

I roll my eyes. I roll them despite the fact I love the way the word rolls off his tongue. My mind flashes back to the first time he used it. When I was drunk and having a nightmare in his arms. Then again at the hotel when he was comforting me. I can remember every single time with indisputable clarity. When he says it, it's not condescending like the way some men, and a few women, say it. He's sincere. Assured. Confident.

I feel the heatwave across my face and chest as I recall the fantasy I had just a short time ago. Oh, my God. Was he here? Was he in the same house, just down the stairs even, when I was coming to the thought of him?

Skylar appears from the kitchen, carrying a happy Aaron in her arms. I look at her with him. I look hard, as if seeing them together for the first time. I realize I've pretty much ignored the baby while I've been here. I've made excuse after excuse not to be around him. Skylar has stopped asking if I want to hold him. I stare at her with him, watching as Griffin swoops in to kiss her cheek on his way by, swinging Hailey as she makes excited noises. It's a freaking Norman Rockwell painting. I want this. I want this so much my heart hurts.

But deep down, I know I can never have those things. The happiness. The sense of well-being. The joy.

They all died with my spirit five years ago. I can't get them back. Charlie can't get them back—Lord knows she's tried. What makes me think Mason can help me feel them again? In only two short weeks, no less. I re-think my text earlier. I shouldn't have sent it. I was in some weird state. Some alternate post-orgasmic reality where I thought I could be normal.

"Good," Skylar says, placing Aaron in his bassinet, turning on the mobile of dancing bears hanging over his head. "You're both here." She goes to stand by Griffin's side. "We need to talk to you."

Oh, hell. She's going to try and set us up. My eyes glance at Mason, who, by the look on his face, has no idea why he's here. Skylar's never been one to interfere. Baylor—she's the meddler. She wants everyone's lives to play out like one of her sappy romance novels. But Skylar, she's always pretty much left me alone. I can feel it coming, though, percolating up out of her as if it's been festering inside her and must come bursting out.

I sigh and wait for my sister to embarrass me.

What comes out of her mouth, however, doesn't make me blush after all.

"We're postponing the wedding," she says.

I look between them. They have nothing but love for one another. Their wedding is all they can talk about lately. It's nauseating, to tell the truth. So what on earth could keep them from going through with it? "What? Why?" I ask.

"I'm not ready. It's too rushed. I'm only doing this one time and I want it to be perfect." She leans in close to Griffin and gives him a squeeze. I catch a fleeting look from him that tells me he's not completely on board with the postponement. "The dress designer called yesterday. Piper, you know we've had issues with the dress for weeks now. Well, it's not going to be finished in time. I love that dress. And the church, well, when we moved the date a few months ago, we picked the only date available." She sighs. "I don't want to get married on a Thursday."

She twists a lock of her hair. She's nervous and it makes me wonder why.

"When will the dress be ready?" I ask. "Surely Griffin or Gavin can pull some strings and get you a weekend wedding. Who says you even have to get married in a church. Why not here?"

Skylar and Griffin share another look before she turns her attention back to me. "Don't freak out. I've already contacted Charlie to make sure she's okay with it. She is, so you should be too."

"You contacted Charlie? Why would you do that? What is she okay with? Just how long are you postponing the wedding?" My hand goes to my wrist and I start to fiddle with the thin leather straps of the bracelet. Whenever I think of Charlie, I touch it. Whenever I think of *anything* I touch it. Deep down, I know it's just a silly symbol. But it has come to mean so much more. It represents the piece of me I no longer have. Once again, I'm grateful Mason found it on the ground next to me. I've only known him for seven weeks, but he seems to be taking care of me at every turn. I find myself reconsidering my reconsideration of our next date.

Skylar twists her hair again. "Two months."

"Two?" I ask incredulously, looking between the three of them to see none of them are as bothered by this as I seem to be. "Two?" I ask again. I'm sure I heard her incorrectly. "But the dress is almost done. All she has to do is add the lace. How can that take two months? If it's the church, you can just get married here like I said."

She shakes her head. "It's already done, Piper. We rescheduled it for July 7th. We had to call in a lot of favors, so there's no way we are changing it again."

I search my mind for reasons they may not have thought of. Reasons they have to marry sooner. I look over at Mason when I find one. "You have football. You'll be too busy. Don't you have to start practice by then?"

"Nope. We pretty much have the month of July off. I don't have to report to training camp until the 30th."

My eyes dart between all of them and then focus on Mason as my blood starts to boil. "You *knew* about this? You knew and didn't say anything?"

"He didn't know," Griffin says. "He's my best friend, Piper. I know his schedule almost as well as he does. This was all Skylar and me. I'm really sorry if it puts a crimp in your plans to return overseas. But I have to live with this woman for the rest of my life, and I'm damn well not going to start off by refusing to give her the wedding of her dreams."

I calculate it in my head. Four months. That is how long I'll be away from Charlie when all is said and done. Charlie. My rock. My touchstone. My very sanity. I start to panic. "I have to text Charlie." I take the stairs two at a time, ignoring my sister calling out to say she's made breakfast for everyone.

~ ~ ~

We've been texting for thirty minutes. Texting about random movie trivia. Then random music trivia. And now we've moved on to random book trivia. It occurs to me we obviously have way too much time on our hands.

Charlie and I work occasional jobs to supplement the money my parents send, but it's a few days here and a few days there. We do all sorts of odd jobs, but mostly waitressing—something we both despise, and usually end up getting fired for punching out some asshole who grabbed us. It's never in a classy place like Mitchell's. It's usually some dive bar that has a hard time keeping their help due to the unruly clientele. So we've learned to budget our money and make the most of what we have. It's meant giving up a lot of things, like private bathrooms and a good wardrobe. But it lets us do what we want, when we want, and that's all that matters.

Mason calls me Princess. His vision of what my life is like and the reality of it are two very different things. I'm sure he thinks we're living in posh hotels, being waited on hand and foot by concierge service.

Charlie and I continue texting mindless drivel. We're avoiding the conversation we both know we need to have.

Charlie: Sooooooo...

My fingers pause. Here it goes.

Me: Yeah

Charlie: 2 more months, huh?

Me: I'm so sorry.

I feel terrible leaving her alone for so long. Then it occurs to me there is no reason I need to be here. The wedding is practically all planned. I could hop on a plane and be back with Charlie tomorrow. I could return to New York in July. Excitement courses through me, right before my chest becomes heavy when I think of Mason.

I have to put down the phone with this realization. I can leave my sisters. My mom and dad. Maddox even. But the thought of leaving Mason, who I barely know, has my stomach clenching with hollow grief. I close my eyes and mentally trace the hard angles of his face.

No. Charlie is my priority. She is where my allegiance lies. We made a promise, a vow even. It was always supposed to be the two of us against the world. No matter what.

I ignore the ache that settles just behind my heart.

Me: I'll come back. There's no need for me to stay here. I'll leave tomorrow and just fly back for the wedding in July.

I stare at my phone awaiting a reply. I startle when it rings and Charlie's face pops up on the screen. I swipe my finger across the screen to answer it.

Before I can even say hello, she's screaming at me. "You will do no such thing, Pipes. Your sisters need you there. Besides, I already have a ticket to Sydney. I leave tonight."

Two emotions are battling in my head. Relief and sadness.

And then there's the guilt. Guilt over the relief I feel that she's not begging me to come back. Guilt over the small part of me that wants to be somewhere other than with her. And guilt over the fact that it's because of a man. We swore we'd never let a man come between us. Never let a man weasel their way into our lives and then rip the rug out from under us like all men do. Eventually, they all do it. All relationships end. Death, divorce, boredom, violence. They all end badly.

I selfishly wonder if she's moving on without me. We've never been apart for this long. "You're going to Australia without me? What about, uh, what's his name, Donovan? Is he going with you?"

"Donovan is last month's news. You didn't really think it would last, did you? You of all people know better than that. He was good for a few weeks of food and shelter. It's all good."

It's not good. It's never good when she says that. I know her better than the birthmark on my left thigh. "What happened?"

"Nothing really. Pretty much the usual."

She doesn't have to elaborate. The usual means he slept with someone else. Sometimes the usual means coming home to find our shit packed and left on the doorstep. But it always means they've had their fill of her. I'll never understand why. Charlie is beautiful and sexy and, based on the stories I've heard, a goddess in bed. I'll never fully understand why men go through her like a dirty dishrag. She's bitter, yes. But who wouldn't be, having been through what she's endured. Maybe it's me. When guys find out I'm not good for a threesome, they don't usually want a third wheel hanging around and sleeping on the couch.

"Men suck," I say. Then I try once more. "Why don't I meet you in Sydney? It'd be fun. We can do a walkabout again."

"I said Donovan was history. I didn't say I was going alone." I can almost hear the smirk through the phone. "How else do you think I could afford the ticket? They are like two thousand apiece. We're running out of money, Pipes, in case you haven't noticed. I mean, your parents have been great. Real life savers. But at some point, we are going to have to talk about—"

"Not now. We don't have to talk about this now. Can I please just get through this wedding?"

I hear her heavy sigh. "Sure, Piper."

"How long will you be down under?"

"I'll be back by July. Then who knows? I'll just have to see which way the wind blows." She laughs. "Or who *I* can blow to set us up for a few more months."

I laugh with her, but it's not genuine. I hate the fact she sleeps with men to put a roof over our heads. She claims she enjoys it. I don't buy it. It's going to break her more than she's already been broken. Of course, that's why we're perfect for each other.

"Promise me something, Pipes."

"Anything." I'd do anything for her.

"Promise me you won't close yourself off while you are there. You have this incredible opportunity to get to know your family again. This one chance to maybe have something you never thought possible. Promise me you won't close the doors that may be opening to you."

"What did Skylar tell you?" I snap, my eyes burning through the floor to where I know my sister is eating breakfast.

"Nothing much. But from what she did say, I can tell that being back there is good for you. Maybe you can finally heal. Maybe you can slay those demons once and for all."

"She obviously talks too much. Being back here is *not* good for me. It brought back the nightmares, Charlie. I belong with you. Cradle to grave—it's what we've always said."

"I know. If that's how it turns out, I'm all good. Just promise me you won't give up something special simply because you feel you owe it to me. You owe me nothing. And no matter what, we will be best friends forever. Never doubt that."

She doesn't sound like herself. It makes me wonder if this new guy has her thinking about something more permanent. I don't push though. I never push. Just as she never pushes me. Nudge maybe, never push.

"Fine," I promise. "But just make sure I know where you are, because on July 8th, I will hunt you down."

"Sure thing, sister," she says, before moving on to describe her new man and their sex life in nauseating detail.

samantha christy

chapter sixteen

mason

Her inky black tips whip around in the breeze, lashing across my face when I come up behind her. I put my arms on either side of her, caging her in as she looks out upon the city.

A swift updraft catches her hair and I get a glimpse of her tattoo. My eyes quickly trace the delicate shape of the lone rose, and I long to touch it with my fingers as I did the night of the marathon. There is a story behind every tattoo, any tattoo worth having anyway, and I'd bet my right arm that Piper's story is a game changer.

My arms tighten around her and I lightly press my front to her back. "You have absolutely no idea how much I want to kiss you right now."

Her body tenses. I rest my chin on the top of her head and close my eyes, inhaling the intoxicating scent of her hair.

"But I'm not going to," I say. "Not today."

I feel her relax under me, taking in ragged air as if it's the first breath she's had all day.

I brush her hair aside and move my mouth behind her ear, right above her tattoo. "I know it may be expected, being our second date and all. And we are in arguably a very romantic place." I look around the observation deck, recalling a movie I once saw. "In fact, isn't this the same spot where Warren Beatty met Meg Ryan on New Year's Eve?"

She shakes her head. "You're confusing movies. It was Warren Beatty and Annette Benning. But they never met here. She didn't show."

"That's awful," I say. "And not romantic at all."

"Actually, it is. He tracked her down months later and found out the reason she never showed up was that she was hit by a car and paralyzed—on her way to meet him that day. She never wanted him to know what happened to her."

I'm not even sure she's aware of how she's leaning into me as she explains. I play along. I know the movie, of course. But what surprises me is that *she* does. I wasn't sure Piper Mitchell had a romantic bone in her body. But it's there. With my fingers on her wrist, I can feel the racing of her pulse as she describes the way they got together. I can hear the longing in her voice. She may put up the façade of not needing a man, not wanting that one great love, but I can see through the bullshit she lays out for the rest of the world.

"So he accepted her, flaws and all?" I ask. "Even though she thought she was damaged goods?"

My question drives a thick layer of silence between us. I've made her think. That's good. Because I know with one-hundred-percent certainty that whatever happened to her doesn't matter to me. Not in the least.

She strains her neck, peeking back at me before looking at the ground and shaking her head. "Why are you going through so much trouble, Mason? You know I leave in a few months. If you're ready to date again, there are so many other girls. I mean, don't get me wrong, I had a great time tonight, and I really appreciate your efforts, but what do you expect to get out of all this?"

"What do I expect?" I try to reign in my anger, wondering what another man must have expected from her to cause her to become so bitter. "I don't expect anything, Piper. I like being around you. This feeling I get when you're near me—I like it. I want it for as long as I can get it. No strings. No expectations."

"But why here?" she asks. "Why did you bring me to the top of the Empire State Building?"

"I wanted you to see something." I turn her body and tilt her chin up towards the horizon. "I know you grew up not far from here, and I'm sure you've been up here before. But my bet is you've never taken the time to see this."

Silence drapes us once again as we watch the sun while it sets, turning the sky from blue to purple to orange, with streaks of light dancing through the clouds, making their silver linings glow. We quietly observe the yellow ball being swallowed up by the building to the west.

At some point, however, I stopped watching the sky and started watching her. Shivers visibly move down her body when she becomes aware of my stare.

I slowly turn her around to face me and I rub my hands up and down her arms, feeling every hair stand on end at the pass of my fingertips. "Every day is a new beginning, Piper. When the sun sets, it takes all the bad shit with it, wiping the slate clean. It took me a long time to learn that." I put my wrist in front of her, revealing the scar that spans across it—a reminder of what I've lost—a reminder of what I didn't.

She traces the raised bump with a finger, sending shivers down my spine. I lift my other hand and finger the bracelet on her wrist, wondering if it represents *her* loss. And for the first time, she doesn't pull it away.

When I look down into her eyes, she's looking at my lips. She's thinking about me kissing her. My pants tighten as I imagine tasting her pink pouty mouth and devouring her sweet scent as our tongues mingle.

Her gaze shifts to someone walking up behind me. I'm almost relieved her eyes went astray, because with the way she was just looking at me, I'm not sure I could have stopped myself from crashing my lips onto hers. But she's still fragile. She's not ready. Hell, maybe she'll always be fragile, but she's learned to relax around me. Her anxiety, however, is lurking just under the surface, and I fear if I do anything to rush things, I'll lose her.

"A rose for pretty lady?" I hear in a heavy Eastern European accent. I turn to see a stout man carrying a basket full of roses of various colors.

"Do you happen to have a black one?" I ask, pulling my wallet from my pocket.

The man's eyes widen with his audible gasp. "Black? No no. You no want black." He shakes his head. "Black mean death. Black mean no love." He looks back and forth between us. "You no love her?"

In my periphery, I see Piper shifting uncomfortably from one foot to another. How does one answer that question on a second date? No matter what I say, I'm screwed. I'm not stupid. I keep my mouth shut.

The small man shakes a finger at me. "I see you. From across the way, I watch you. You no need black rose, you need maybe pink. Red even, no?"

black roses

I eye all the different colors in his basket. "Okay Mr.—"

"Trudowski"

"Okay, Mr. T, Tell me about the meaning of these roses."

His eyes light up as if I'd asked him to talk about his grandchildren. "Roses have many meaning. I tell you what mean to me." He pulls a white rose from the bunch. "White represent purity, innocence, young love. But also loyalty. It say 'I'm worthy of you'." He places it back in the basket and retrieves another one. "Yellow rose mean friendship, caring, affection." He exchanges yellow for orange. "Ahhh, this one good for young lovers. It meaning desire and attraction. Passion." His eyes bounce between Piper and me as he explains.

Picking up a pink one, he says, "Pink have many meaning. Elegance, grace, happiness even." He puts it down to find the final color among the bunch. "Red rose need no explain. Everyone know red. Now you decide. I have customer over there." He points to a young couple kissing and showing a little more PDA than would be deemed socially appropriate. "They red no doubt. Yes, red and orange."

I pluck four flowers from the bunch. Every color but red. Then I hand over a rather large tip as he thanks me profusely.

"Red," he says, before walking away. "Next time we meet, you choose red. You see. Trudowski know things."

We watch the man walk away, meandering over to his next potential sale.

Our eyes then meet over the top of the roses I'm holding. I hand them to her one at a time.

I give her the white one first. "You are worthy of this rose. You are worthy of everything and anything this life has to offer. I give this to you because I will be here for you, whether it be seven weeks or seven years. I'm here. I'm not going anywhere."

She takes the rose and her eyes flutter closed as she inhales its scent. "But—"

"I'm not done," I interrupt. "I have three more to go." I hold out the yellow one. "For our friendship. You push me to be a better friend, a better person, a better man. And I'll value that long after the petals fall from this flower."

She takes it, opening her mouth again to say something. I raise my finger to her lips. "Can you keep those pouty lips quiet for two minutes and let me finish?"

Her mouth closes, sealing it shut before she bites the edge of her bottom lip. The small movement causes me to have to rotate my hips and situate myself so she can't see what her mindless gesture is doing to me.

I hand her the pink rose. "Mr. T says this one represents elegance and grace—both of which you possess. But I believe it also has other meanings. Promise. Possibility. Admiration. Gratitude. You give my life promise, Piper. For years, I've lived for one person and only one person, my daughter. Being with you, I'll be damned if I'm not seeing the possibility of another future and for that I'm grateful." I shrug my shoulders. "Well, that and I remember in junior high on Valentine's Day, people would give pink roses to those they secretly admired. I've never done it until now."

She sighs. I can't tell if it's a happy one or a sad one. I'm praying for the former. "Mason—"

"Ah ah ah." I hold up my hand. "I have one more."

I hold out the orange rose. "Passion," I say, punctuating the word with prolonged silence. I point my finger between us. "You can't deny it exists here. And I'm pretty sure you can't even deny feeling it all the way back in the airport the first day we met. Am I wrong?"

She raises a brow at me. "Oh, am I allowed to talk now?"

Her sassy, sarcastic voice sends tingles through me. I laugh. "Please."

"Thank you for the flowers." She bundles them together and takes the time to appreciate each individual scent.

"I'm sorry he didn't have black. I know it's your favorite."

Her hand absentmindedly comes up to finger the tattoo behind her ear. "Why would you think that?" A crevice forms between her eyes as she questions me.

"It's kind of written all over you." I nod to her neck and then I pick up her wrist and fondle the bracelet as she watches.

After a moment, she pulls away. "No, they aren't my favorite."

"Then why have them all over your body?"

I know I'm pushing her for information. Information she may not be ready to give yet—or ever, for that matter.

"As a reminder I guess." She twists the rose charm around the leather straps of her bracelet.

"A reminder of what?" I ask.

She's standing right in front of me, but her eyes are about as distant as I've ever seen them. She looks pained. When she answers me, her voice is brusque, alerting me I may have crossed a line. "As a reminder that I don't like them—what is this, the Spanish Inquisition?"

I laugh to try and lighten the mood. "You are a complicated woman, Ms. Mitchell. You know that, right?"

She shrugs and turns around to view the night sky along with the twinkling lights illuminating the neighboring buildings.

I cage her in my arms again. "You know, Mr. T seems to be an expert on roses. He said that all roses have many meanings. Maybe you just need to find another meaning for yours."

I brush her hair aside and gently rub my thumb across her tattoo. "Maybe one day you'll feel comfortable enough to tell me about it."

"There is no one day, Mason. I'm only here for two more months."

"I'd better work quickly then," I say.

She cranes her head around, revealing the question in her eyes.

"If I only have two months to convince you to move back here, I'd better work quickly."

Her eyes fill with several emotions all at once. Hesitation. Sadness . . . Regret? "I won't be staying in New York."

"What if you fall in love with me, will you move to New York then?"

She shakes her head. "No way would that happen."

"Why not? Do you not like the way I look? You think I'm hideous, admit it," I joke.

Small bursts of air leave her nose, cueing me in on her lifting mood.

I raise an arm and smell my pit. "Do I smell bad?"

She snickers quietly. "Only at the gym."

"I know it's not my kissing," I say. "I realize you haven't experienced one of my kisses yet, but I'm one hell of a kisser."

"Who told you that, your left hand?" She's now audibly laughing at her own joke. Her melodious laugh is so contagious, I can't help but join her.

I turn her around to face me again and her eyes seem to mimic my own, not being able to decide if I want to gaze deeply into hers or stare at her inviting lips. My mind is at war, knowing this may be the perfect moment for a kiss, but at the same time, fearing it may drive her away.

After only a moment, her mood becomes somber. "I don't fall in love, Mason."

"Do you really believe you can control that, Piper? Falling in love or who you fall in love with?"

"Love is a farce," she says, looking down at the roses. "People make money off it." She holds her hand up, putting the flowers between us. "Case in point. Florists, greeting-card companies, chocolate vendors, jewelers—they all bank on the concept that there is actually some all-encompassing emotion that will conquer everything. It's crap. It's a business. And if you buy into it, you're full of shit, too, Mason."

I want to argue with her, tell her billions of people aren't all under some kind of spell cast upon us by commercialism. But I don't. Whatever happened to her broke her so completely that I'm not sure she can ever be put back together. Especially not in two short months. You can't tell someone like Piper about love, you can only show them. I'm just terrified I don't have the time.

"Okay then, I'll happily concede and agree I'm full of shit." I take her hand that's free of the roses. "So, Piper Mitchell, will you hang out and *not* fall in love with me until you have to leave in July?"

She stares at our joined hands. I wonder if the same energetic heat is flowing out of them across her body, just like the crescendo of waves are cresting across mine.

She smiles, looking slightly relieved. "Yes, Mason. I'd be happy to hang out and not fall in love with you."

"Care to make a little wager on that?"

Her eyes widen. "A wager? On if I'll fall in love with you or not?"

I smile from ear to ear. I may have just figured out how to keep her here after all—that is if her gargantuan-sized stubborn streak doesn't interfere. "Yes. If you fall in love with me, you move to New York. If you don't, you go back to Charlie and your life as a wanderer without a single argument from me."

She scrunches her eyes. Well at least it's not an outright 'no.' She's actually thinking about it.

"But what's in it for me? Let's say . . . hypothetically, because it will never happen, that I fall for you. You win the bet and I move to New York. But if I win the bet, I go back to my life which I already plan on doing anyway. So you see, I don't stand to gain anything by winning."

She has a point. I think on it a beat. "Okay. I win—you move to New York. You win—you get whatever you want. Just like the marathon. You don't even have to tell me now. The sky's the limit."

She contemplates my offer. "What if I want to keep traveling the world? *In style*."

I laugh. "Anything means anything, Princess."

She rolls her eyes, knowing full well she walked right into that one. "Fine. But your bank account may be about to take a huge nose dive. If you think child support is bad, wait until you see the damage I can do at a spa in Dubai."

"It's a deal." I go to extend my hand, but realize we never let go. I lean close, bringing my lips down to just above her ear. I've every intention of winning this bet. It may just be the most important wager of my life. I draw out my words and let my hot breath flow over her ear. "Game fucking on."

chapter seventeen

piper

I would never do it. Take money from Mason. But it'll be fun to see him squirm about it.

It's not going to happen—me falling in love with him. With anyone. I've only ever been in love one time. For one day. With one person. One moment even, before everything was taken away.

My dreams have changed lately. They give me a glimpse of what my life might be like if that fateful day never would have happened. If the choices I made were different. If I could be like every other twenty-two-year-old woman.

The nightmares, although becoming fewer, still plague me. They alternate between the versions where I fight my predators, and the ones where I don't. Years ago when I first started having the dreams, I never fought. Not one time. My mind simply played that fateful night over and over again with frightening clarity.

Maybe I'll never know which version of my nightmare was real. Maybe I'll never know what really happened that night—being sentenced to a life of what-ifs and could-have-beens.

And even though Mason will never win the bet, I'll always be grateful that he allowed me to dream again. Dreams like when I was a little girl. Fairy tales that are so far out of my reach, it's laughable. But dreams nonetheless.

One might say I was stupid to take the bet, especially given my history with them. But bets have kind of become our thing. Small or big, they always seem to work their way into our conversations. Last week, he bet he would beat me in bowling. I think the man is determined to find all my weaknesses; all the things I miss when I'm overseas. He won, of course—I mean, come on, I hadn't bowled in over five years—earning him tonight's romantic dinner at a fine French restaurant.

The sommelier brings two glasses of champagne, placing them between us on the elegantly-appointed table. I eye my glass, willing myself to pick it up and take a drink. It's a simple task really, one that billions and billions of people do every day.

Pick it up, Piper.

Pick. It. Up.

I reach over with a shaky hand, imploring my fingers to wrap around the stem and bring the glass to meet Mason's as he so patiently waits for me to do.

I awkwardly grasp the glass while I bring my eyes to meet his—to watch his expression as I pretend to catch the base of the glass on my bread plate, tipping and spilling the entire contents all over the beautiful tablecloth. "Oh, shit," I say, feigning the accident.

For a moment, he studies me. He studies me as if he suspects my action was deliberate. But I'm well practiced. A master of clumsiness so to speak. There is no way he could know. He studies me, but he doesn't judge me. His eyes are soft, not accusing. Sympathetic, not embarrassed.

He finally turns his attention to the spill, using his napkin to soak up the mess before it cascades from the table onto the floor. The waiter hurries over to finish the job and Mason asks if we can have our own bottle of it brought to the table, "just in case." He winks at me.

"Piper, I'm not sure if you've ever made this observation about yourself, but you are quite clumsy when it comes to drinking."

I smile and shrug. Most men—most *people*—just get annoyed with me and my accidents. Mason is different. He treats it as one of those quirky things that endears you to another. "It's too bad we can't all be as skilled and adept with our hands as you are."

The sommelier, a petite female delivering our bottle, blushes horribly, looking very uncomfortable to have been privy to that part of our conversation. I quickly run the words through my head again and realize the reason.

"Football," I spit out at the flustered woman. "He plays football. You know, with his hands? Ugh . . ." I cover my embarrassed face with my hands as Mason laughs right through the pop of the cork.

He picks up my glass, holding it out to me carefully and with meticulous caution.

I smirk at him as I take it from him, our fingers lightly brushing each other's as the glass exchanges hands. My breath hitches at the touch and it's not lost on me that he notices.

Mason ever-so-gently clinks his glass to mine, but before he drinks, he asks, "Are you moving to New York yet?"

I shake my head as my eyes intentionally roll to the ceiling. "No, Mason, I'm not in love with you."

"Yet." He smiles, taking his drink.

"Ever," I rebuff.

He checks his watch. "I still have six weeks, Piper. Never say never."

"I didn't say never. I said *ever*. But whatever—it won't happen." I take a bite of the scrumptious canape placed before me. "But I'll sure as hell enjoy being fed like a queen while you try."

He laughs and I try to ignore his crystal-blue gaze warming into a heated stare as he watches me eat.

After our Chateaubriand gets served, I ask him, "So how's training camp going?"

"It's not called training camp this time of year. We're still in off-season conditioning. Full blown training camp doesn't start until late July. That's when we turn our lives over to the league for six or seven months. To end conditioning, we have a mini-camp in mid-June and then we have free time until we report to training camp."

"So you get the month of July off?" I ask.

"Technically, yes. But we still work with our trainers and sometimes we attend pre-season functions. Mostly it's just six weeks of stress and anticipation of the upcoming season."

"When do you find out if you get the starting position? Do you have a tryout or something?"

He chuckles, confirming just how little I know of American football. "No. I won't get the starting position as long as Henley is around. He's a Heisman-winning player. He's popular with the fans and managers. But mainly, he's just one hell of a quarterback."

His words make me wonder, causing my brow to furrow. "Then why stay here in New York if you know you won't get the job?"

"He'll have to leave sometime. The guy is forty-one years old which is practically elderly in this sport. He was supposed to retire this year but changed his mind after the playoffs. I suspect it won't be long. One more season, maybe two." He looks out the windows, out onto the many lit-up buildings that tower over the busy streets. "I love it here. I love New York. And while I wait, I'm getting stronger. Better. So that when I do get the job, I'll secure a future for me and Hailey right here where I want to be."

"Won't it be surreal for Hailey, growing up with a famous father?"

"I don't know. I mean, I did a lot of my growing up without a father at all. Whatever happens and wherever my career takes me, I swore the day Hailey was born not to let it affect her or our relationship. Sometimes that can be hard with Cassidy holding the reigns most of the time."

"Speaking of Cassidy," I say, finding the perfect opportunity to extract information without seeming too interested.

"Can we not speak of her while we're on a date, Piper? Thinking of her will completely get my mind off that incredible dress you're wearing. You look beautiful tonight. You look beautiful all the time, but wow . . . that dress."

I find it hard to hold in my smile watching him attempt to not look at my breasts. It's another borrowed dress, and it shows off a bit more cleavage than I'm used to advertising. But it's fancy and appropriate for the venue. Mason is nothing but chivalrous as he keeps his attention on my face, my arms, my hands. Anything but my boobs. I wonder if he made a bet with himself to not look directly at my chest this evening. I try to imagine what he will reward himself with if he wins.

Tingles pulse through my nerves thinking about what that could entail. Anxiety follows the thoughts as I take another drink from my champagne flute.

"Let's talk about Hailey instead," he says. "I have her this weekend and I was wondering if you'd like to join us for a picnic tomorrow afternoon."

"You have Hailey this weekend?" I ask. "Who's with her now?"

"She's at my neighbor's apartment. I trade babysitting for football tickets."

I raise my eyebrows. "Sitter too expensive for you? I thought you professional athletes were rolling in money."

"I can afford a lot of things, Piper. That doesn't mean I have to spend money on them. Plus, it's a lot more fun figuring out how to barter for what I need."

Amazement, or maybe amusement, flashes across my face. His words make me think of Charlie and my life abroad. "I spend a lot of time bartering."

His face falls, his smiling gaze going dead sober. "Uh, not to sound like I don't think you have many talents, because I'm sure you do, but what exactly do you barter with?"

I know what he's thinking. And he'd be right if Charlie were sitting across the table from him instead of me. She has gotten us plenty of meal tickets and free stays by letting men use her. "I barter with my time. I run errands for people, sometimes work in their shops or bars for a free stay in the flat above. Once we lived with an old guy in Wales for a few months, just because he wanted company. His wife had recently passed away and he lived in this huge castle-like home. He gave us a place to stay and three hot meals a day, just so someone was there. We played Monopoly with him every Sunday night."

He looks slightly shocked. "And that's all he wanted, companions?"

"Yes. That's all." Then I tease, "Well, what he and Charlie did behind closed doors, I couldn't tell you. But for a ninety-year-old man, I'd say he's got stamina."

His mouth drops open and his eyes fill with rage as if I'd said *I* was whoring myself out.

I laugh. "I'm only kidding, Mason. God, if you could see your face right now. Mr. Longfellow was quite the gentleman. And more than a little feeble. I assure you, it was all very proper."

"Longfellow, huh?" he chuckles, lightening his mood. He reaches across the table and runs his fingertip along the bridge of my nose, down to my tiny piercing. "And what did you have to do to get this?"

I feel his touch throughout my entire body and I pray he doesn't sense the way my pulse shoots up as if I'd just started a race. I try to control my breathing, but with the way he's looking at me right now, my entire autonomic nervous system just went into overdrive.

He drops his hand back to the table, close to where mine rests, and I find myself willing him to inch it over and put it on me. Right now, in this moment, my body is winning the war over my mind. And my body craves his touch.

I must have been staring at our hands too long. Or Mason is a mind reader. Because he moves his hand towards mine and threads two of his fingers around two of mine. It's almost the way childhood friends might hold hands, light and casual, but . . . *holy crap* . . . it's anything but. Every feeling I had on top of the Empire State Building last week comes rushing back. The words he spoke ring in my ears. *What if you fall in love with me, will you move to New York then?*

This foreign feeling rushing through my body like a tidal wave—it's not love. That I'm sure of. But what is it . . . Lust? . . .

Desire? I'm positive I'm the only living twenty-two-year-old on earth who can't discern these emotions.

"Piper?"

Oh, hell. He must think I'm an imbecile. "Right, my piercing. Uh, remember how I said I would work for shop owners? Mrs. Kranstein owned a boutique and spa in Berlin. I worked for her for about a month."

"A month?" he questions. "Just how many piercings do you have? And, um . . . where are they?"

I can't help my face-splitting smile. I'm just not sure it's the result of his joke, or the way his thumb is now lightly caressing the back of my hand. "Just the nose. Well, and these." I lift my free hand and point to my ears.

"Well, I like it—the nose piercing. Not too over the top and pretentious. It's subtle. Intriguing. Sexy."

More of those indescribable emotions course through me. I've never wanted a man to call me such things. I've never before strived to *be* such things.

I'm also one-hundred-percent sure I'm in for disappointment. I'll disappoint him when he touches me. I'll disappoint my sisters when they find out what a failure I am. I'll disappoint my parents if I never make something of my life.

But more importantly, I'll disappoint *me* if I don't even try. So when he asks me once again to spend tomorrow afternoon with Hailey and him, I agree.

∼ ∼ ∼

When we return to Skylar's, I see through the sidelight that the townhouse is dark. Only the lights over the stove illuminate the kitchen in a soft glow. Skylar and Griffin must have turned in early. Little Aaron has been wearing them out.

Mason comes up behind me. His fingertips trail down my arms, sending quivers of anticipation charging through me. He takes my hand in his. "I'll walk you in. Just to get you settled."

The three glasses of champagne I had tonight unite and decide that allowing him inside after our date is not an abhorrent idea after all.

As I walk to the kitchen to deposit my purse on the counter, every hair on my neck is acutely aware of how he follows me, step for step. I steady myself against the cold granite, wondering if I can handle what comes next.

Kissing—that's what comes next.

I slowly turn around keeping my eyes glued to the ground. I've kissed a few men over the past few years. Kissing is safe. Kissing doesn't scare me. Probably because it's the one thing that doesn't plague my dreams. My lips belong to *me*, not them. It's the stuff *after* the kissing that terrifies me.

Still, those I've kissed in the past didn't stick around for an encore. And I could hardly blame them. Each benign encounter felt like a kiss from my father. No excitement. No fireworks. They were plain. Unexciting. Ordinary.

Part of me hates the thought of ruining what Mason and I have. Once we kiss, everything will change. It will be awkward and forced. I will stiffen like a board. He will pull away, feigning some kind of forgotten appointment or family emergency. It happens. Every time. Just because kissing is safe doesn't mean I'm any good at it.

When I was little, before my life went to shit, I used to practice kissing my handheld mirror. I imagine the men who have endured my kisses have a similar experience—feeling as if they are kissing something inanimate. Empty.

"Don't think about it, Piper. Just do it."

Mason's voice startles me, reminding me I'm not alone. It's now I realize I've been staring at his lips. This whole time, I've been mindlessly staring at his full, firm, inviting lips, probably looking like a feline in heat.

"Mason, I'm not sure—"

Before I can tell him all the reasons for not wanting to ruin what has become a beautiful friendship, his lips meet mine.

And I don't stiffen.

I melt.

I melt into his firm yet soft lips, the heat from them searing through my body, a tornado destroying everything in its path, leaving me utterly destroyed in its wake. Ruined for any other lips that may try to claim mine in the future.

Every atom in my small universe is focused on the movement of his mouth against mine. Every particle of my being is hoping he won't ever stop. Every thought that infiltrates my head gives me reasons to pull away.

But I don't.

I don't.

Realization consumes me. I want this. I want him. I want normal.

Instead of my mind flashing forward to what usually happens next, causing me to freak out and send them running, my thoughts wander aimlessly, recalling small moments in time from the past few months. Moments like when I first saw Mason in the airport and my knees went weak. Moments like when he protected me in the parking garage and at the marathon. Moments I watched him at the gym when he was unaware of my admiration.

Before I fully comprehend what's happening, our tongues mingle together in a perfectly choreographed dance that has me feeling it all the way down to my toes. He's tasting me, feasting on my mouth, devouring my lips. He breaks the kiss and our lungs simultaneously fill with the oxygen we've deprived them. His lips go on to find my neck, and I'm absolutely sure he can feel my racing heartbeat under his prodding mouth.

A sigh, that sounds more like a mewl, unwittingly escapes my throat as my head falls back to give him more room to work. His hand comes around behind me, pressing him tightly against me, his strong chest flattening my breasts. His hard groin against my belly.

I feel the panic climbing my spine like rungs of a ladder. It's fighting with the warm tingling sensations shooting through each arm, leg, finger and toe.

Mason pulls away, just enough to spare me his erection. It's almost as if he heard my silent plea. He stares into my eyes, forcing the anxiety back down into the pit of my belly where it always lurks, waiting to rear its ugly head.

His arms gently caress mine and he smiles. Not a full-blown face-cracking smile. A soft, alluring, intoxicating smile that curves up one side of his mouth more than the other. I find myself staring at his lips once again as they part when he asks, "Are you moving to New York yet?"

I let out a sigh of relief. A laugh of comfortable friendship. A smile of . . . happiness? "Not hardly," I reply.

He kisses me on the top of my head and turns to leave. Just as he reaches the door, he spins around. "Just so you know, I'm not moving to New York either. But it's not out of the realm of possibility. I really, really like New York."

My eyes narrow as I allow his words to sink in.

He winks at me and then disappears through the front door.

chapter eighteen

mason

I sit on a blanket and watch Piper with Hailey as they kick a soccer ball between them in the park. Well, as much as a twenty-two-month-old can kick a ball. But I think she's getting the hang of it. 'Uncle' Gavin has made sure of that, being he was a soccer star during his years at UNC.

Piper seems to be getting more relaxed around her as the afternoon wears on. At first, when we were eating lunch—a fabulous spread courtesy of Skylar and Mitchell's—Piper didn't even make eye contact with Hailey. I was worried. No, terrified was more like it. These two girls are the most important people in my life and if they don't get along there isn't even a choice in the matter.

But now, after I intentionally stepped away, pretending to get a call from my agent, I dare to hope that maybe there is a chance at this after all. Piper's demeanor is guarded and a bit forced, but at least I see potential there. And I won't give up. I won't give up until the fat lady sings and does the damn hula in her thatched skirt and coconut bra.

I haven't taken the easy road in love, that's for sure. Figuring out Piper Mitchell is like trying to do one of those Chinese puzzles. Just when I think I'm getting somewhere, I wind up back at square one.

I lost a lot of sleep last night thinking about her. We have a connection. A deep undeniable bond I've never felt with another woman. I hesitate to even use the word soul mate because it makes me sound like a pussy-whipped lap dog, but damn it if that's not exactly how I feel.

I've analyzed every look and every conversation, much like how I study and scrutinize game film at practice. I've tried to dissect every anxiety attack. She came close to having one last night. That kiss, it was—shit, it was better than all the sex I've had rolled together in one big package. That kiss was epic. If I wasn't already falling for her, that kiss was reason alone to.

She kissed me back which was somewhat unexpected. When our eyes met, there was a clear hesitation. I could almost hear the wheels in her head spinning—deciding to choose door number one or door number two. In the end, she not only chose the right door, she fucking decimated it, burning it to the ground with the heat that exploded between us. And the sound that came from her when I kissed her neck, that fantasy-provoking mewling sound will stay with me far beyond the six weeks I have left with her.

That heat, however, was almost instantly squelched like a flame deprived of oxygen the instant I pressed into her and she felt my hard-on. I knew immediately. I could feel the panic rising in her as much as if it was my own. I knew I had to stop or I could push her past her breaking point. And breaking Piper would wreck me.

But then something happened when she was on the brink of anxiety pulling her under. She looked at me. Hell, she looked *into* me. And I swear I could see the wave of calm wash over her beautiful face. It wasn't unlike what happened before in the parking garage and at the marathon. Somehow, when our eyes connect, her panic wanes. I'm not conceited enough to think I can fix her and remove all the demons in her life, but maybe I'm the one who can make her realize life is worth living after whatever happened to her.

Hailey runs over and jumps on my back, knocking me forward onto the grass. I pull her around to my front, pinning her on the ground so I can tickle her pint-sized ribs. Her sweet, childish laughter seems to echo through the park.

This is living.

I look down at my scar and give thanks to Coach Braden for saving me. I look up at the clear-blue sky and hope my parents can see their spectacular granddaughter. I look over at Piper to see her studying my interaction with Hailey. I could swear her eyes get misty, but as soon as she catches me watching her, she clears her throat and starts kicking around at the ball abandoned by her feet.

What was that look? I can normally read her easily. Like an old favorite book. When it comes to how she reacts to me, she's completely transparent. I know she has feelings for me. Feelings that run far deeper than she wants to admit. But when it comes to Hailey . . . well, it's like that Chinese puzzle.

My daughter rubs her eyes, my clue that the day has taken its toll. I pick stray pieces of grass from her platinum-blonde curls and then look at my watch. My heart sinks. It's almost time for Cassidy to pick her up. The days I'm with her fly by in an instant, the hours are like minutes and the seconds tick away painfully fast.

I gather up our things. "Time to go, sweet pea."

I swing the backpack on one shoulder and Hailey up on another. "Ready?" I ask Piper.

She nods, picking up the soccer ball before we make our way through the park and out to the subway.

The whole way, Hailey points out and counts every bird she sees, making meaningful adult conversation almost impossible. Then she starts humming her favorite Disney song. "Sing, Dada," she begs. I can't deny her request, so I pull out my phone and tap on the screen, finding the song to accompany me.

Few things embarrass me. Singing a girly princess song in front of the woman I'm trying to impress is definitely one of them.

When we make it to the platform, I take a moment to admire Piper. Her hair is windblown and her skin slightly pink from the strong afternoon sun. I realize I don't want the day to end. And I'd really like some alone time with her. "Come back to my place," I say, hopefully.

Her eyes flicker between Hailey and me. "Won't Hailey's mom be there soon?"

"Don't worry about Cassidy. I'd really like you to come with us. There's something I'd like to show you."

The number five train to Skylar's place pulls up alongside us and the doors open. She looks at me. We stare silently at each other until the train pulls away, leaving her standing beside me. She smiles. "I suppose I could come over for a few minutes."

Hailey smacks my face with her little hands. I guess I've been giving too much attention to Piper for the last thirty seconds. Piper laughs as Hailey plies and prods my cheeks as if my face were made of clay. It's the first laughter I've heard from her since last night. And for what feels like the first time today—I breathe.

"What's *she* doing here?"

Cassidy's stinging words slice through the thick, tense air of the hallway outside my apartment.

"You're early, Cass." I give Piper an apologetic glance.

"Mama!" Hailey squeals at the sight of her mother, squirming out of my arms so she can run over to her.

Cassidy all but ignores our daughter's embrace as she fires daggers from her eyes at Piper while I unlock the door.

"I'll just get Hailey's things." I move aside to let them all in. I drop my keys on the entry table before turning to Piper. "You can freshen up in the bathroom if you want." I point to the door next to my bedroom. "It's right through there."

Relief is apparent on her every feature as she scurries away without a word. But it only lasts a moment.

"Pie-pie," Hailey wails, running after her, giving her legs a hug from behind.

I glance at Cassidy. I can practically see the smoke coming from her ears. Her hands ball into fists before she marches over to Hailey, ripping her away from the endearing grip she has on Piper's leg.

It's hard to hold in my smile. Hailey has just given Piper her seal of approval. Something she doesn't dole out to just anyone. More must have been going on at the park than I realized. Or maybe Hailey senses the same enchanting qualities in Piper that I do.

A fleeting look of terror crosses Piper's face. *Damn.* What was I thinking bringing her here and forcing a confrontation like this? I obviously wasn't thinking with my head. Another part of my anatomy maybe, but definitely not my head.

Piper smiles compassionately at Hailey as she's dragged across the room by her mother. "It was very nice seeing you again, Hailey. Thanks for playing soccer with me."

She turns to Cass. "Cassidy, always a pleasure." She spins around and walks through the bathroom door, shutting it and leaving buckets of sarcasm in her wake.

Cassidy gathers up her things. Hailey knows the drill by now. The older she gets, the harder it is for her to leave without tears. I won't deny that I've shed a few of my own the times she reaches for me, begging to stay.

As if adding fuel to the fire that is my heightened emotional state, Hailey runs over to me and holds up her hands, big balls of tears balancing on her lower lids for a second before spilling over and trailing down her little round cheeks. "Dada!"

Cassidy watches us as we hug, neither of us wanting to part. "You know, if we just lived together, you'd see her all the time and she would never have to be this sad when we leave. She'll cry herself to sleep tonight. She always does the days she leaves you."

A piece of my heart breaks off. Just like each time my daughter leaves. I'm not sure if what Cassidy says is true, but the thought of it tears me up.

"Time to go, sweetie," Cassidy says, pulling her from my arms.

From behind me, I hear the door to the bathroom creak as Piper is either opening it to see if the coast is clear, or to listen.

Right on cue, Cassidy leans towards me, placing an unwelcome kiss on my lips faster than I can stop her.

chapter nineteen

piper

The front door slams shut behind Hailey and her mom, leaving the air rich with tension and discomfort. I walk over to it and grip the handle, turning it quickly, pulling the heavy steel door towards me.

Mason races over and puts his palms by either side of my head on the door, forcing it closed. "Where are you going?"

"Is *that* what you wanted to show me?" I hit the door with my open palm. "That you're getting back together with your ex-wife?"

He sighs so long and hard I can feel the back of my hair part under his heavy breath. "She's *not* my ex-wife."

"Girlfriend. Whatever." I stare at the blue steel door just inches from my face. "You could have just told me."

"I'm not getting back together with her, Piper. I told you that already. I'll never get back with her. She's a manipulative shrew."

"But you kissed her. Is that you *not* getting back together?"

"You're wrong." His hands lower, caging me in place. "I didn't kiss her. She kissed me. Just another one of her spiteful tactics. She's threatened by you. I haven't had a woman in my life in a long, long time."

"Hmph," I pout through my closed mouth. "It sure looked like you were kissing her."

"I was *not* kissing her. God, you are so stubborn, woman." He puts a hand on my arm and I tense. He immediately removes it, placing it back in its previous spot. "She surprised me. I was saying goodbye to Hailey, and before I knew what was happening, she swooped in like the predator she is."

I shake my head, not knowing what to believe. Cassidy is everything I'm not. She's extraordinarily beautiful, walking-the-catwalk-in-Milan beautiful. And although her breasts aren't real, even *I* think they're spectacular. She oozes sexiness from every pore. I'll bet she doesn't cringe when men touch her. I'll bet she doesn't feel her skin crawl just thinking about being with a man.

It would be so much easier for him—for any man—to be with her over me.

He takes my silence as incredulity. "Piper." He gently puts his hands on my shoulders and spins me around to face him.

I can't look directly at him. I stare blindly into his chest as my thoughts stray to what it might look like under his tight-fitting polo. I have a pretty good idea. After all, I've seen him shirtless at the gym.

He puts a finger under my chin, raising my head until our eyes are forced to meet. "I wasn't kissing her. Believe me, if I was kissing her, that's not what it would have looked like." He grabs my face, his hands on either side, his thumbs meeting in front to rub across my bottom lip as he stares at the slow gesture. "*This* is what it would have looked like."

He leans down and his lips crash into mine so forcefully, it propels my body against the door behind me.

"Ugh." When the hard steel meets my back, my mouth opens and my breath escapes me, right into his welcoming kiss. He takes the opportunity to push his tongue into my mouth. His silky, firm, demanding tongue. His tongue that has infiltrated my every thought since he kissed me last night.

After his tongue relentlessly takes everything it can from me, his mouth parts from mine, never once leaving my skin as he trails feathery kisses from the edge of my lips over to my ear.

My head tilts as he devours the space between my earlobe and my shoulder. He slowly works over every centimeter of my skin, studying it with his lips. Each flick of his tongue sends electric shocks spiraling through me. Each light sucking movement causing tremors across my body.

Never in my life have I felt this way. I'm standing on air. No, I'm floating. I get it now—what people mean when they say they are on 'cloud nine.'

All too quickly, he pulls away, and for the first time, I'm left wanting more. Needing more.

Craving more.

And if his triumphant smile is any indication, it's written all over me like a cheap romance novel.

He places a chaste kiss on my lips and laughs. "Was that just our first fight?" His hand lingers on me, tracing the curve of my neck.

Smiling, I say, "No, that would have been the airport. You know, when you called me a bitch and a drunk."

"Oh, right." He has the decency to look shameful.

"It wasn't even our second fight," I say. "That was at Skylar's when you said I wasn't an athlete and my legs were too short to run a marathon."

His eyes fill with regret. "I was a dick, Piper. I'm really sorry. I think I was just trying to fight my attraction for you from the very beginning. Anyway, you proved me wrong. Those little legs beat my ass and now you have bragging rights."

"Whatever." I roll my eyes, knowing he let me win. "So, you find me attractive, huh?"

"You have no idea, do you?" his eyes snap down to his tented pants.

My pulse races. And not in a good I'm-standing-on-a-cloud kind of way. It races in a turn-and-open-the-door-and-run-for-dear-life kind of way.

In typical Mason fashion, he senses my anxiety and pulls away. He grabs my hand. "Come and sit down. Can I get you a drink? Maybe an adult beverage?"

I want this. I want him. Maybe if I get a few drinks in me, I'll relax.

What the fuck are you doing, Piper? My conscience screams at me, knowing good and well the position that could put me in. I try to push my pangs of conscience aside. I try to push my fears aside. Mason is a good man.

Mason is a good man, I repeat over and over inside my head.

"What, no more juice boxes?" I joke. Then instead of sitting on the couch, I follow him to the kitchen. "I can help."

He pulls out a bottle of Jack. It's unopened and I wonder if he got it specifically for me, after seeing it was my drink of choice at the benefit. I watch him expertly mix it with just the right amount of Coke, splitting a can between us and not going too heavy on the liquor.

I take my glass from him and we walk back in the living room to sit on the couch.

"What was it you wanted me to see?" I ask.

He narrows his eyes in question while taking a drink.

"At the train. You said you wanted to show me something at your apartment."

"Oh, that. Yeah . . . well, you're looking at it."

"What?" I look around.

"My apartment. I wanted to show you my apartment."

I shake my head in mock disgust.

"What?" he says. "It worked, didn't it? I got you to come back here. I just never planned anything out beyond that. I have no idea what to do with you. I mean, I haven't been on an actual adult-like date where a girl comes back to my place before, so I'm not sure exactly how this works."

I have to hold in my giggle. Mason Lawrence—hot, sexy, almost-famous football player—doesn't know what to do on a date. But then I realize, neither do I. Hell, I don't even read my sister's romance novels. Do we watch television? Play a board game? Get out our phones and text our friends?

I take a drink. "Um . . . do you have any movies?"

He lets out a relieved breath. "Movies, yes! I have lots of movies." He hops off the couch and opens his entertainment center to reveal an impressive stockpile of titles that probably cost more than my first car.

I follow him over and peruse his collection. He has all the great sports movies, of course. He has some documentaries, sci-fi, and even some romantic comedies. I survey the hundreds of films surrounding his massive T.V. But I gasp and my fingers stop browsing when I spot one in particular.

Mason recognizes the way my eyes hesitate when they come across this specific title. He reaches out and pulls it from the case. "Okay. *Roxanne* it is. Are you a big Steve Martin fan or something?"

"Something like that," I say, my gaze fixed on the floor as I make my way back to the couch.

I was always in love with Cyrano de Bergerac. It was my favorite play of all time when I was little. I wanted to play Roxane. Maybe not from the original play that was written entirely in verse, but some of the later adaptations. And although I love the Steve Martin/Daryl Hannah movie version, it has always bothered me that they spelled her name wrong, adding an 'n' to it.

My heart is heavy as we watch it. I haven't seen it in years. I didn't realize I still craved acting so much. What I wouldn't give to change things.

"I think you would make a wonderful Roxanne," Mason says.

Completely ignoring the movie, I turn to him. My eyebrows scrunch and my nose crinkles. Why would he say such a thing?

Duh—of course. Realization hits me.

"Skylar told you. Or was it Baylor?"

He puts his arm on the back of the couch behind me and hooks an ankle over his knee, giving me his undivided attention. "It was Skylar. But I wish I would have heard it from you. I wish I would hear a lot of things from you."

I shake my head. "I don't like to talk about myself."

"You were an actress. A damn good one based on what I've heard. Was it Charlie's mom that made you quit? Did you think you would grow up to become like her?"

"I told you, Mason. I don't like to talk about myself. Can we just watch the movie please?"

He turns back towards the television. "Sure. We can watch the movie. But maybe one day . . ."

I close my eyes and sigh. "I told you, there won't—"

"I know, I know." He holds his hands up in surrender. "There won't *be* a one day. But that doesn't mean I won't try like hell to change your mind about it."

Halfway through the movie, it occurs to me that my head has fallen and rested against Mason's shoulder and that we are holding hands. And now that I'm aware of it, I can't concentrate on anything else. His thumb rubs slow circles across my palm, putting me in a trance. The heat surging between our bodies is increasing by the minute.

He can't see that I'm not even watching the movie anymore. My eyes are closed. They are closed as I try to imagine a 'one day.' I try to imagine Hailey playing next to us on the floor. I try to imagine family birthdays and holidays, Sunday brunches and vacations. I dream of the what-ifs and the possibilities.

Then I remember dreams aren't always good. Sometimes they are just twisted versions of the truth that your mind tries to accept. And no matter how much I want to accept that I could have a normal future, my dreams remind me of how that could never be possible.

"Piper," I hear him whisper. "Are you tired? Would you like to turn off the movie?"

I look up at him and I can tell by the look of worry on his face that he now realizes I wasn't asleep, but rather in another world. Suddenly, his hands cup my face. "You look sad. What's wrong?" he asks, his thumb slowly tracing my bottom lip. It's a gesture I've come to crave.

My eyes shift focus between his lips and his mesmerizing blue irises. When our eyes meet, the intensity of his dark gaze takes my breath away. I try to answer him, but I'm speechless.

"God, Piper. I . . . " His words fade away as his mouth starts to move towards mine.

My body responds to his movement immediately, my pulse racing and my breathing becoming ragged. His lips haven't even touched mine yet, but I already feel the air under my feet, raising me back up to the cloud.

Cloud nine—that is where I want to live. It's my happy place. The place where nothing bad can happen and nobody evil can hurt me. Pain doesn't exist. Hearts don't get ripped to shreds. Girls don't get raped.

His lips crash into mine. Soft kisses quickly turn hard and demanding as my tongue meets his, stroke for stroke. He tastes like rum and Coke, with a hint of spearmint. He tastes amazing. He tastes of everything I want my life to be. He tastes of heaven.

Once again, he trails soft kisses over my neck and jaw. He takes extra time when his lips meet the skin behind my ear that is branded with ink. Part of me feels the urge to pull away. That piece of me is private. But he sucks on it lightly and I find I can't move. I'm putty under his lips, his mouth, his skillful tongue. Almost as if my tattoo is a direct portal to my pain, he draws some of it out of me, extracting pieces of it with every gentle touch.

My fall from the cloud is instantaneous when I feel his hand trail up my ribs and gingerly cup my breast. I can't breathe. Fear grips my spine like a vise, squeezing the air from my lungs as my body stiffens and trembles. Panic builds quickly, not wasting time giving me much warning. I cry out as anguish consumes me.

His hand retreats abruptly. "Piper, sweetheart. Look at me."

I'm shaking, the tremors in my hands clearly visible.

Mason holds my hands tightly in his. "Look at me," he implores. "Look into my eyes."

I take a deep breath and raise my eyes to meet his.

"It's me, sweetheart. It's Mason. Don't take your eyes off me." He smiles. He smiles my favorite smile. The one that raises only half of his mouth. The smile that tells me he's a good man.

Mason is a good man, I repeat over and over in my head.

"Listen to me, Piper. And listen good. When I touch you, it's not to use you or hurt you. When I touch you, it's so I can worship you. And every time you allow me to see you—feel you, is a gift I intend to treasure."

He squeezes my hands and then releases them, moving one of his hands up my rib cage again. My eyes try to close in fear.

"Eyes on me, sweetheart. It's only me. We both have shit in our past. But this—this here is so much different than anything I've ever felt. I'm not going to hurt you. I'm going to cherish you with every touch. Let yourself feel me. Let go of everything else."

Our eyes lock together as his hand meets my breast. He cups it gently, letting his hand take the weight of it slowly. His eyes beg me to relax under his touch. My heart begs me to comply.

I breathe through my emotions. Slowly inhaling through my nose and out through my mouth. If my eyes start to stray, he urges them back.

Slowly, methodically, he traces the fleshiness of my breast over my top. When his knuckles lightly brush over my nipple, I struggle to keep my eyes open because the sensation flowing between us is overwhelming.

Our eyes burn into each other. Mine telling stories that shouldn't be told. "Are you okay, sweetheart?"

I nod.

I'm okay.

I'm okay!

"Can I put my hand under your shirt?" he asks.

I inhale another cleansing breath and then I nod once more.

He untucks my shirt and places a hand on the bare flesh of my stomach, causing ripples of pleasure and nervousness to tumble my insides. His eyes never leave mine as he works his hands up my rib cage all the way to my bra. He caresses me through the thin cotton before pulling the cup down to free my breast.

The sensations build as he continues his manipulation. My nipples are stiff and he pinches them lightly. A pleasurable sound escapes me, surprising even myself. This is what passion feels like. This is the exact feeling I dreamed of as a girl. No—it's better. This feeling is beyond any of my dreams.

I dare to let my hand fall onto his thigh, giving his leg a reassuring squeeze. I smile hearing his quiet gasp, knowing what my hands on him can do. It's the first time I've purposefully touched him, other than maybe that hug I gave him at the marathon. Even when he's kissed me, my hands have lain at my side. But looking into his eyes right now, I have nothing but desire to put my hands on him.

I start to move my fingers, inching them further up towards his lap. I look down to see what I'm doing as I reach for the bulge in his pants.

In a split second my confidence turns to panic. *No, please, no.* I silently plea to my mind and body. But despite my attempt to gain control, waves of anxiety crash over me, pulling me under so I can't breathe. Tears sting my eyes, but I refuse to let them fall even as frustration overcomes me.

"Piper." He peels his hand from my breast and then removes my hand from his erection. He cradles his fingers under my chin, forcing me to look up at him. Gently, he touches my face, his fingertips sliding over my cheekbones to caress my lips. "You lost eye contact, sweetheart." He leans down to kiss me, placing both hands on either side of my face. He kisses me until I go limp in his arms. He kisses me until I can't think of anything but how much I want this feeling to last.

Emotionally exhausted, we lie back against the couch and hold each other. Eventually, Mason speaks in barely more than a whisper. "Thank you for tonight," he says, pulling away, making sure my shirt is situated. "And thank you for trusting me." He hugs me, molding me into his arms as a feeling of calm washes over me. Then he gently kisses my forehead and says with a mischievous smile, "Just so you know, I'm dangerously close to moving to New York."

My heart falls into the pit of my stomach as my distant eyes fall to my lap. I sigh. "You don't want to move to New York, Mason."

"Why not?"

"New York is a dark and scary place," I explain. "Demons lurk in the shadows. Filth lines the streets. People are homeless and broken."

"It doesn't have to be scary, Piper. Not if you go with someone you care about. New York can be great. Magical even."

I shake my head. "Not for me."

"Can we stop talking in code now and have a real conversation?" he asks. "I'm serious about you. I want you to give us a real chance. Don't you think we deserve that? Don't *you* deserve that?"

I spring up off the couch and walk across the room. "Thank you for the wonderful day, Mason. I had a great time."

He shakes his head and rakes his hands through his hair. "Are you really going to ignore what we have here? You can't possibly tell me we don't have this incredible connection. I've never felt this way about anyone, Piper. Can you honestly say you don't feel the same?"

I reach for the door. "I'm not capable of having feelings for anyone, Mason. Please, don't follow me. I'd like to be alone."

As I walk through the doorway, his words chase after me. "You may be living here temporarily, but you might as well be back over there—in Egypt maybe. Because you are living in fucking denial."

The door slams shut, silencing any words that dared to come after.

chapter twenty

mason

I'm trying hard to participate in conversation. After all, Piper's sisters did go through the trouble of securing a sitter so we could all go out tonight. It's a momentous occasion. 'Couples Night.' Even Piper used the term when we discussed it earlier this week. I dare to hope she's beginning to think of us as a couple; even after her disappointing exodus last weekend.

It's been almost a week. Six whole days since I've seen her and she's all I think about. I can't stop imagining her lips and how they molded to mine as if we were made to flawlessly complement each other. It was amazing to be able to caress and comfort her and have her trust me, if even for a short time. And damn it if I can't stop thinking about her breasts and how perfectly they fit into my hands. Hell, I can't even manage to get her out of my head on the football field. Two things I live to hold—a football and Piper.

Actually, a football, Hailey and Piper.

But can they all go together? Is there any way I can work some miracle and convince her to stay?

I have five more weeks.

I shift myself in my pants and look away from her, concentrating instead on the conversation Gavin and Griffin are having in an attempt to lose my erection. We're at a bar now, but they are busy arguing over what they ate for dinner earlier.

"I'm telling you, they weren't scallops," Griffin says. "It was shark meat."

"Well, what the hell is the difference?" Gavin asks. "And who the hell really cares?"

Griffin shakes his head. "Oh Lord, don't let my future wife hear you say that. It must be nice to be married to a romance author instead of a restaurant manager. I never hear the end of it. I don't even like to go out to dinner with her unless we go to a five-star restaurant. It's like being engaged to a goddamn food critic. I haven't been with Skylar all that long, but believe me when I say I know the difference between a scallop and shark meat. I know it nauseatingly well."

I laugh at his comment and they both turn to me. Griffin leans in so only Gavin and I can hear. "Hey, Dix, glad you could tear your eyes away from my fiancée's sister's chest long enough to give us the time of day."

"What?" I feign ignorance and they simultaneously raise their eyebrows at me. "Shit. Was I that obvious?"

"Does this mean you're a thing?" Griffin asks. "I mean, it'd be nice to know I didn't put off marrying the mother of my child for nothing."

My mouth drops open. "You *what?*" I glance over at the girls to make sure they aren't listening. "You mean to tell me you postponed your wedding to get us together?"

Griffin gives me a pointed stare and nods his head.

"Holy crap," I say. "So the dress excuse, and the church—"

"All a sham," he says. "The dress was delivered the day before we postponed." He nods to Skylar. "It was all her idea. I want to marry her yesterday. But when Piper came home from your first date, it was like meeting an entirely new person. I'm telling you, the girl was walking on air. It took Skylar all of five seconds to pick up the phone and start moving the date."

"That's fucking huge, man," I say, reaching over to shake his hand. "And it's probably one of the nicest things anyone's ever done for me."

He shrugs. "Hey, it was the least I could do after you set me straight and dragged my ass back from Miami."

"So we're even now." I smile, giving him an appreciative pat on the back. "But seriously, thanks, man."

"You two pussies gonna hug, or can we order some more drinks?" Gavin teases.

Griffin waves a hand to get the attention of the women sitting opposite us at the table. "You ladies ready for another?"

Piper quickly stands up. "I'll get them."

Baylor tries to pull her back down. "Isn't that what waitresses are for? Sit down, little sister."

"I just don't want to wait," she says. "Everyone good with the same?"

The others all nod and then I get up to help her. It's the third time she's gone up to the bar to order. I wonder if it's because she doesn't want me to pay. I've paid for our dinners without her putting up much of a fight, so I'm a little confused by this behavior. Maybe she's changed her mind after what transpired last week. I thought it turned out okay. I mean, yeah, she started to have a panic attack, but it never escalated. We connected. She felt something. I'd bet my life on it. She couldn't have faked that kiss. Those noises.

Shit! My pants are getting tight again.

Back at the table, we are distributing drinks when someone comes up behind me, cupping their hands over my eyes. "Guess who?" the sultry voice asks.

I know the voice. It's the same one that pops up on my voicemail almost weekly, asking when I'm going to take her out. "If I guess wrong, will you have me fired?" I joke, reaching up to remove her hands from my eyes so I can see Piper's reaction.

Her eyes flash to the floor and I see a wave of sadness cross her face. But she recovers quickly when she notices me staring. She plants on a smile then sips her drink. A nod of her chin, along with a raised brow, tells me I should acknowledge the person standing behind me.

I turn around and Janice Greyson pulls me into a breast-crushing hug. "Thank God someone interesting showed up. My dad has me entertaining a group of *the* most boring executives. I think I might slit my wrists before the night is out."

In my periphery, I see Piper's jaw drop. I look Janice in the eyes. "You're not very observant are you?" I ask.

How many times have Janice and I been at the same functions? How many times does she come out to the field and stare at me during drills? And all that time, she never noticed my scar. *Everyone* notices my scar eventually. Unbelievable.

"What?" she asks, feeling around her mouth. "Do I have something on my face?" She gets a small compact out of her clutch.

"No. It's nothing. Forget it."

"Oh, well, in that case, how about you take the boss's daughter for a dance and save me from the geriatric brigade." She sneaks a peek at herself in the tiny mirror, smoothing the hair on the side of her head, before placing it back into her purse.

"Sorry, Janice. My dance card is full tonight."

Her eyes finally take in everyone else at my table, landing on Piper, who's more than a little drunk. She points at her. "You were at the benefit." She holds out her hand in greeting. "Janice Greyson, daughter of Neil Greyson."

When Piper gives her a questioning look, it's hard not to laugh.

Janice continues, "You know, Neil Greyson. As in the guy who owns the Giants."

"Oooooooh," Piper draws out, as if she's just now learning this. She shakes Janice's hand. "Piper Mitchell, daughter of Bruce Mitchell. As in the guy who likes to fuck my mom."

Shocked and speechless, Janice mumbles, "I guess I'll see you around then, Mason."

"I guess so."

Everyone at the table watches Janice walk away and then all at once, we burst into laughter. But my jovial spirit dies the instant I hear it. My eyes snap to Piper and my stomach turns as I listen to her drunken, maniacal laugh. This laugh—it's not like her usual melodious school-girl giggle. This laugh; this hollow, cackle of a sound, it's eerily familiar. I don't like it. I don't like it one goddamn bit.

I have to sober her up. I walk around to her chair. "So how about you dance with me so I'm not a big fat liar?"

She feverishly shakes her head. "I don't dance."

I laugh and lean in closer. "You don't date either, yet here we are on our sixth date."

She turns her head to face me, our noses mere inches from each other. "Fifth," she says. "The benefit doesn't count."

I smile. I smile big. She's counting, too. "Okay, fifth." I take her hand in mine, giving her a tug. "Come on, one dance. Everyone else will come." I raise my voice and say, "You guys are up for a dance, right?"

Before Griffin and Gavin even process my question, Skylar and Baylor are dragging them onto the dance floor with ear-to-ear grins. I get the feeling they would do anything to get Piper and me together. To get their little sister to stay in New York. I can't say I blame them. I feel the exact same way.

We all dance in a group, but my eyes never stray far from her. The way her body maneuvers on the dance floor mesmerizes me. Much as it does when I watch her run. She has that same fluid grace in her dance moves.

The liquor flowing through her seems to loosen her up, making her relax and be present in the moment. Something I've observed is quite hard for her to do. My plan, however, is to sober her up before bringing her home with me. The last thing I want is to take advantage of a drunk Piper—something I'm sure would kill our relationship faster than a hot knife slicing through butter.

After a few songs, sweat starts to dot her brow and she removes her light cardigan, tying it around her waist to reveal a tank top that hugs every curve of her beautiful figure. She raises her hands above her head, dancing with her sisters in a carefree manner I've never witnessed before. I think this is the real Piper. The happy, easy-going, untroubled Piper from before she was broken by whatever secrets she hides from the world.

A new song starts and the entire population of the dance floor simultaneously breaks into the choreographed arm movements made popular by a stupid YouTube video. We smile and laugh and sweat and dance. It's the best time I can remember having since before my parents died.

Piper and I stare at each other without a care of how ridiculous we must look as we mindlessly do the silly dance. I mouth one line of the lyrics to her. Something about missing her before she came into my life.

Words I wish I could tell her without scaring her away. Words that I know would.

As if I had orchestrated it perfectly, the next song that plays is a slow one. I waste no time pulling her into my arms, our sweat-drenched bodies mashing together.

It could be the alcohol. It could be the endorphins. It could be the way our bodies fit together like the seam of a flawlessly-made football. But watching her now—seeing her look at me like this, our eyes burning into each other with this intensity, I know one thing for sure. I'm moving to New York.

In fact, I'm so fucking deep in New York, I can't see past my knees.

"Come home with me tonight," I breathe into her ear.

～ ～ ～

I can barely keep my hands off her. It was exponentially hard to sit at our table in the bar knowing she was coming home with me. But the longer we sat there, the more she sobered up. She was so out of it, she knocked over a few glasses of water. I ended up just buying her a few bottles of it—less likely to spill.

"Have a seat." I point to my sofa. "Get comfortable. Pick a movie if you'd like. I'll be back in a minute."

In the kitchen, I prepare her favorite drink. I know she has sobered up, but I think she might need a bit of liquid courage for whatever might come next. For what I hope comes next. My dick twitches when I think about kissing her again. I know we need to take it slow. I'm willing to do that. Hell, I *want* to do that. But I don't think I can go another day without kissing her again.

I return to the living room, placing our Jack and Cokes on the coffee table behind her. When she turns around, I'm more than a little aware of how she's removed her cardigan again as my eyes hone in on her already pebbled nipples straining the material of her tank top. I'm also aware of how longingly she's looking at the movie in her hand.

"You really like that one, huh?" I ask, lifting my chin at the same title we watched last week.

"Yeah." She nods. "I always wanted to play Roxane. She's my favorite heroine."

I recall the original story in my head. Cyrano never thought he was good enough for Roxane. He saw himself as ugly, unworthy of the love of a beautiful woman. I wonder if Piper likes the story so much because she relates to *him*, not *her*.

She sits down on the couch, dropping the movie before she pushes her drink to the far side of the coffee table. Her tongue darts out to stroke her lips with a soft, sensual lick. "I didn't come here to drink, Mason." The smile that follows her words is slow, naughty, and completely breathtaking.

Fuck.

That may be the sexiest thing I've ever heard her say.

Instantly, blood rushes to my dick. But I know better. "You're still drunk, aren't you?"

She shakes her head. "Haven't had a drink in hours. I'm fine." She looks up at me all doe-eyed and libidinous. "And I'd like you to kiss me."

She doesn't have to ask me twice, but I make her anyway. The edges of my mouth curve into a grin. "Can you say that again? I'm not sure I heard you correctly."

She giggles. It's the light, airy laughter I love. Not the disturbing, demented laugh of earlier. And right now, I can't recall a sweeter sound in the world.

Her blush confirms her claim of sobriety. "I'd like you to kiss me," she says, with even more authority.

I drop to my knees in front of her. "There is nothing I'd like more." I lean in, cupping her face in my hands. As my body draws closer to hers, I notice the hue of her irises turning an even deeper shade of green. Her eyes reveal far more than she wants me to know. They tell me how much she wants this. Wants *me*.

"You're stunning," I mumble, right before staking my claim on her lips.

The moist heat and the forceful demand of her mouth has me reeling, igniting a bone-melting fire that burns deep within me. I tip her head back, cradling it in my palm as my hungry tongue savors her intoxicating taste.

My hands explore her neck, her back, her thighs, as my mouth takes everything from her that she's willing to give. Every kiss with her is better than the last. Every feeling more intense. Every touch more explosive.

Her legs part, inviting my body closer to hers. My fingers lightly brush across her ribs, just below the curve of her breasts. I wrestle our swollen lips apart, needing her to look at me. "Is this okay?"

She nods, never breaking eye contact with me as my thumbs trace the underside of her heaving breasts. When my hands cup her fully, her jaw goes slack and her mouth partially opens, a breath of air escaping along with a whimper that has my dick painfully straining against the fly of my jeans.

I lean close to her ear and let my breath flow over her. "Can I see you, sweetheart?"

She trembles. "Only if I can see you," she says, her voice dropping a purposeful octave.

I take it back—*that* was the sexiest thing I've ever heard her say.

My mouth twists into a tight-lipped grin. I don't even hesitate. I reach behind my neck to grab my shirt, pulling it over my head and discarding it into a careless pile on the floor.

I can't say my ego doesn't get a little inflated when her eyes go wide as they rake across my chest. I'm not naïve, I know what I look like. And I work damn hard for this body. But I've never wanted to be worshiped for it outside of what it allows me to accomplish on the field. Not until this very second.

The way her eyes trace every ridge and ripple of my abs makes the thousands of hours I've spent on them worth it. Women always look at me with wanton stares. As if I'm a slab of prime meat for them to order up. A hard body. A conquest. But Piper looks at me the way no one else ever has. With reverence. Wonder. Respect.

I pick her hand up and place it on my chest. Sensations assault me as she follows the same pattern I'd traced over her tank top. And damn if her hands don't feel like pure heaven on me. A few more minutes of this and I'll go out of my mind.

I put my hands over hers and direct them to the hem of her top. She hesitates for a beat; her breathing visibly quickening. Then she slowly lifts the material until the elastic gets caught up on the curve of her breasts.

I run my hands up her stomach, grabbing the thin layer of cotton to complete the movement of pulling it over her head.

Then I stare.

I stare like a fool. Like an adolescent seeing his first pair of tits. But, *holy shit*, I've never seen anything this spectacular. Her teardrop-shaped breasts are creamy white, clearly never having been touched by the sun's punishing rays. Her rose-bud nipples pucker even tighter under my heated gaze.

"My God, you're beautiful." The instant my hands meet her silky flesh, I rip my admiring gaze from her body and look into her eyes to find them smoldering with unspoken desire.

I knead and ply and pinch and tug. I worship her breasts with my hands and fingers until the urge is so strong, I can't control it. "Eyes on me," I command, before my mouth falls upon her chest, my tongue rolling over and flicking a stiff nipple.

Surprisingly—thankfully—she doesn't pull away. Instead, she arches her chest into my mouth, further fueling my siege. Her hands meet my back, her fingernails lightly scraping up my spine, sending more heat into my already thickened blood.

I glance up to see her heeding my order to keep watching me. I smile against her breast and she blushes, a warm, lazy grin tugging at her swollen lips.

Her hips grind and gyrate in a punishing rhythm that causes sweet, hot friction to build between us. I can't get enough of her flesh. My hands, my lips, my mouth, my tongue—they chronicle every inch of her, all the while sending up prayers that this not be the last time I ever feel her like this.

I want her to feel how I do every time I look at her. I want her to feel the desperation. The passion. The all-consuming need.

I want her to *feel*.

I don't think she has in a long, long time.

My fingers dip beneath the waistband of her jeans, running along her supple stomach from hip to hip. I slowly unbutton them, carefully watching her face for signs of panic, being ready to retreat in an instant.

She doesn't stop me. In fact, every movement her body makes urges me on; her hushed, needy noises fanning the flames and fueling my desire. My eager fingers find their way through her soft curls and under her panties to find them soaked through.

But then her legs stiffen and clench shut, and a distressed sound of pain echoes off my walls, completely gutting me. My eyes snap up to see that her head has fallen back onto the couch and her eyes are tightly closed.

"Piper, look at me."

I still my hand, but leave it on her sex. "It's me. Only me." I maneuver my other hand behind her neck, angling her head forward. "Open your eyes, sweetheart. Watch me worship you. It's just me," I repeat. "I want it to be only me. Always."

Her eyes meet mine and I'm floored by the emotion. Slow waves of realization cross her face. I look deep into her, far into the reaches of her being. I recognize that look. I can almost see her fighting her demons. I can almost see her slaying them.

In an unhurried, but purposeful movement, her legs relax and fall open once again. I glue my eyes to hers, holding her with my stare; imploring her to take what I want so desperately to give her. I've never looked at a woman as I've pleasured her. And, my God, the intensity of it is so overwhelming I have to pause before I move again. Before I can even breathe.

My fingers begin to explore as I drag them through her wetness, moving them up to coat her pulsating clit. Her breath hitches when I hit the engorged bundle of nerves, circling my finger around and around. I grind my hips into her thigh, applying much needed pressure to my throbbing erection.

"Only me, sweetheart," I remind her over and over again. I don't want her mind wandering away to anyone else—any*thing* else. My voice becomes a chant, a chorus telling her how beautiful she is and what she does to me. I tell her to let go.

Her legs tense again, but her eyes tell me it's in a good way this time. Her breathing becomes ragged, her throaty noises more audible until she stiffens completely, crying out muddled exaltations of pleasure.

Watching her orgasm is like witnessing a flawless pass to completion. The sweet spiral of pigskin as it leaves my hands, flying a pristine arc through the air and falling effortlessly into the hands of my receiver. *Fucking perfect.*

Her sexy screams, her smoldering gaze, the sweet friction of rubbing myself against her—they all culminate and throw me over the edge right along with her. And for the first time since middle school, I come in my own goddamn pants.

I remove my hand from her pants and cup her face before crushing my mouth on hers, thanking her with my kisses for the gift she's given me. Her hands come up to cover mine, accepting my bid of gratitude. Her fingers slide over my hands and grasp my wrists, her thumb absentmindedly tracing my scar over and over.

When I pull away, she takes a moment to catch her breath. Then, keeping my hand in hers, she turns it over and touches the red raised flesh once again. "How did it happen?"

My eyes briefly close, savoring the significance of this moment. She's going to win the battle against her past. And it starts now, by letting her into mine.

I stand and pull her up with me. "Let's get cleaned up. Then I'll tell you."

chapter twenty-one

piper

We lie on his couch, my head resting on his thigh; Mason methodically fingering locks of my hair. I'm more relaxed than I can ever remember.

Maybe it's the powerful orgasm I just experienced. Maybe it's the strong blue eyes looking down on me. Maybe I've turned a corner.

Maybe.

"So." He breathes out a long, tumultuous sigh. I suspect what he is about to say is something very personal and private. "You pretty much know the gist of it. They died in a crash. I was driving." He pauses, and although I'm not looking at him, I can feel his head shake from side to side. "I was sent to a temporary home until they could find a permanent place for me to live."

"It must have been horrible. I'm so sorry." I strain my neck to make eye contact so he understands that when I say *'I'm sorry,'* I mean it. It's not just a platitude. It's not just a thing I say when I hear something unpleasant. I hope my eyes convey it's deeper than that. That I understand the meaning of pain. Heartache. Utter destruction.

He nods. "It was. Losing my parents was unimaginable. But what came after was almost worse." He grabs my hand and holds it against my chest, rubbing his thumb across each of my brightly-painted fingernails.

His face is etched with sorrow and my heart hurts for him. I know how hard it must be to talk about a traumatic experience. Maybe I should have kept my big mouth shut. Why did I even ask him? It's not fair of me. Not when I know I can't share my own past. "Mason, you don't have to. It's okay."

"No, it's fine," he says, squeezing my hand. "It actually helps to talk about it sometimes."

"Okay." I squeeze his hand back in reassurance.

"The coroner's report shows they died at the scene. But they weren't sure if they died instantly." He clears his throat, struggling to keep the desperation from his voice. "I like to think they did. That they didn't know what was happening. That they didn't have time to think about dying and how that meant they'd never see their only child again. Never see each other again—the loves of their lives."

He draws in a ragged breath. His hand grips me a little tighter and I notice it has become damp.

"The dreams started the night after the funeral. My mind went wild, each night delivering me a different version of the accident I had little memory of. I'd blocked out everything that happened after hitting the tree. After hearing the bark split and splinter while the hard steel crunched and buckled around it.

"Night after night, the unforgiving dreams came relentlessly. It got to the point where I didn't sleep much. My grades plummeted. My social life ceased to exist. I stopped participating in spring workouts. My will to live was slowly being sucked out of me every time I relived that day in my dreams."

I run my fingers along his scar. I have no words. I don't pretend to know what he went through. But I know loss. I know excruciating heartbreak. I know nightmares. Hearing the raspy hitch in his voice, the way he tries to look strong for me when he's obviously a wreck on the inside—it makes me want to cry for him.

But I don't. I haven't cried for anything or anyone. Not since that day.

He sighs, pulling himself together. "Some nights are better than others. Some nights my parents tell me there was no pain, no suffering, no blame. Those nights I watch them peacefully pass away. But then there are the ones where I watch them die horribly. Bloody and mangled, one or both of them screaming out in pain. I'm held captive in a seat belt that won't release. I can't reach them. I try to comfort them with my words. I say I'm sorry. That I fucked up. But they become still and stare blankly, their faces pale as the life leaves their bodies.

"Other times I do reach them and hold their hands as they slowly slip away. Then there are the dreams where they die instantly, not giving me the chance to say goodbye. To apologize for killing them." He pulls his hand from mine, wiping the sweat on his jeans before bringing it back to grasp my fingers again. "For months and months, every version of that night played out differently in my dreams. It made me crazy. I couldn't eat. I couldn't sleep. I didn't know what really happened. I still don't."

Oh my God.

My heart races. My throat stings. My eyes hurt from suppressing tears that beg to fall. Does Mason even know how much we are alike?

Maybe he would understand.

I want to comfort him, but the huge lump blocking my airway keeps me from speaking, so all I can do is caress his hand to let him know I'm here. That I'm listening.

"The lack of sleep wreaked havoc on me and one day I just snapped. I couldn't live with the guilt anymore. The doctors said I actually went temporarily insane from my chronic insomnia. That's why they didn't commit me—well after my mandatory seventy-two hour stay. They gave me anti-anxiety meds that caused me to sleep for two days straight.

"My coach, Coach Braden, petitioned the state to become my legal guardian when I was released from the hospital. The therapists they had me see didn't do much good. It was Coach who helped me. He pushed me to play again. He took me on the field every day after school and worked me until I nearly passed out from exhaustion. Most nights I was too tired to dream. But it was his words that got to me. Just a few simple words—but I'll never forget them. He said, *'if you die—they die along with you. If you live—they live through you. You are their legacy.'*

"Those words are what I see now when the bad dreams come. I want to make my parents proud. I can't change the past. I can't not swerve to miss the squirrel and crash into that tree. But now I know it was a mistake. A momentary lapse in judgment. I may be the reason my parents died, but I didn't die with them. I was given a second chance—a third even. And I plan on living. Living for them. Living for me."

He takes some calming breaths. His revelation clearly done.

I try to swallow the lump that has taken residence in my throat. I clear my voice. "I spill drinks on purpose."

I can't look up at him. I can, however, feel a wave of tension leave his body. His hand relaxes in mine. His breathing becomes more regular. The tense muscles of his thigh slacken under my head.

"I had begun to suspect as much," he says. "Do you want to talk about it?"

My eyes close. "Yes." My heart beats wildly and panic builds in my belly as my memories overpower me. "No."

"When you're ready." He runs a soothing hand through my hair.

"I'll never be ready, Mason. Because once I tell you, you won't want me. I know I can never be the person you need me to be."

"You're wrong, sweetheart." He brings my hand up to his lips and places a gentle kiss on the back of it. "You are exactly the person I need you to be. You aren't perfect. God knows, I'm not perfect. But I think we just might be perfect together."

My heart opens and lets him etch a piece of himself inside.

"We all see ourselves differently from others," he says. "We see the worst. In my eyes, I'm a murderer. I don't yet know what you think is the worst version of yourself. But this I'm sure of—nobody else sees you that way. Least of all me."

∼ ∼ ∼

"Oh my God, Pipes," Charlie wails through the phone. "You have to tell him."

"Why? So he can think about all those other hands on my body when he's touching me?" I blow out a frustrated sigh.

"No. So he can begin to understand you. He bared himself to you, Piper. Not many men can do that. It's obvious to me he has major feelings for you."

I shake my head in disagreement even though I know she can't see me. "It's different. What happened to me—*to us*—is different."

"Yeah. It's a lot different," her accusing voice berates me. "What happened to you, to me, was awful. Unimaginable even. But Jesus, Pipes, he watched his parents die right in front of him because of something he did. That's some monumentally fucked up shit."

"What happened to him is terrible," I say. "Of course it is. But it doesn't make my skin crawl when I touch him. I don't think I could take it if he looked at me that way. You know after . . ."

"You can say it, sister. After the best orgasm you've ever had." She laughs, lightening the mood.

I can feel my face redden in my dark room. "Okay, yes. And the only orgasm I'm one-hundred-percent sure I've had at the hands of a man. I don't want to ruin that. If I leave, I wouldn't be able to stand the memory of him being repulsed by me."

Silence.

I look at my phone to see if we're still connected.

"Charlie?"

"*If?*" Her loud word startles me. "You said '*if,*' Pipes. Are you thinking of moving to New York?"

I choke on my saliva as I guffaw into the phone.

"What is it?" she asks.

"Nothing," I say. "Inside joke, I guess."

She laughs. "Now you have inside jokes with him? Girl, you've got it bad."

"I do not," I insist, albeit not whole-heartedly. "And I'm not moving to New York. Even if I wanted to move to New York, I wouldn't. I'm not in the least bit equipped to move to New York. Plus, you're over there. Cradle to grave, remember?"

"First of all, I'm not even going to pretend I just understood what you said. Second, cradle to grave doesn't mean we have to be attached at the hip. Cradle to grave can mean talking on the phone every day, showing up for momentous occasions, and taking kick-ass vacations together. You're my best friend, Piper. You'll always be my best friend. No matter where we end up."

"I'm not moving to New York, Charlie."

"Whatever." I can almost feel the eye-roll in her words. "Let's get back to the juicy stuff. What happened right after you had the greatest orgasm of all time? Did he hold you? Did he want to fuck? Did you say thank you? You should always thank a guy for a good come, Piper."

I laugh. "I'll remember that for next time. We didn't do anything," I say. "That's when I asked him about the scar and he said we could talk after we cleaned up."

"Cleaned up? What—as in you spilled a shit-ton of drinks in your usual endearing fashion?"

"Bitch," I tease. "I don't know, cleaned up. You know . . . I used the bathroom and he changed clothes."

"Why did he change clothes? Was he expecting a sleepover?"

"Of course not. He just threw on a new pair of jeans."

"Really? And just what was he wearing before that?" she asks.

"I don't know, another pair of jeans, I guess. God, why the third degree?"

"So he changed from one pair of jeans into another?" Shrieks echo through the phone, piercing my ear. "Oh my God, Pipes—the man jizzed in his pants!"

My jaw drops. "He did not," I say, unbelievably.

"Are you sure? I mean, you were kind of busy coming yourself. Maybe you just didn't notice." She giggles.

"Oh, God. Do you really think . . . uh, I thought . . . I mean, I didn't even touch him there."

Laughter dances through the phone. "You have much to learn my young apprentice. Yes, I really think so. And I really think this is a good thing. A great thing. Maybe the best thing. Tell him, Piper. If you want any chance at a meaningful relationship with Mason, you have to tell him."

Long after our conversation ends, her words resonate through me.

His words resonate through me. *I want it to only be me. Always.*

A foreign feeling grips the edges of my heart. I think it might be called hope.

chapter twenty-two

mason

Her hand is warm and inviting in mine. We haven't parted skin for the entire span of the two-hour movie. And thank goodness it's dark in the theater, because the way her pinky rhythmically moves against the outer seam of my pants has had me sporting painful wood for the duration.

Even when she takes drinks of the bottle of water I bought her, she manages to maneuver it with one hand, holding the bottle between her legs to cap and uncap it. I've never been so jealous of a piece of damn plastic.

Shit.

I remember the reason I bought her the water bottle in the first place. *I spill drinks on purpose.*

My hard-on quickly deflates as I ponder the reality behind that statement. I'm pretty sure I have an idea of what must have happened. And the thought turns my stomach. It makes me ashamed to be a part of the entire half-population that could even contemplate doing such a thing.

"What a great film," she says, her voice startling me, but in a kind of fantastic way that pulls me from ugly thoughts.

"It was," I agree. "They had me fooled. I thought for sure the guy's brother was the killer."

"Me, too. I love it when things don't turn out the way I expect."

I smile and give her hand a squeeze. "I'm glad to hear you say that."

People excuse themselves to walk past us, so we stand up and join the herd exiting the theater. We continue discussing the film in the lobby when a commotion grabs our attention.

Security guards drag a belligerent man past us. "I paid for a fucking ticket. Same as everyone else," he yells, kicking at them while they attempt to usher him to the front door. He makes eye contact with me. "You!" he says.

I'm used to getting recognized in public, it's hardly anything new. But the way he looks at me, it's not with the normal fan adoration. It's with disdain. And his pin-point pupils in the dim light alert me to his apparent state of drug-induced inebriation.

"Wait!" a familiar voice calls out.

I, along with the security guards and the rest of the lobby, turn to see who's yelling.

Cassidy.

She runs up to the two men who have the unruly guy in choke hold. "He's with me," she says.

"Then we're going to ask you to leave as well, Miss," one of the guards replies.

"Ugh!" She stomps her foot like a tantruming three-year-old. Then she sees me. Her eyes are hazy and unfocused, her tiny pupils mirroring those of the man she's trying to defend. She's higher than a kite in trade winds.

"Cassidy," I say. "Are you fucking kidding me?"

"Mason!" she says excitedly, shouting too loud for our close proximity. "Tell these rent-a-cops to let Nick go."

One of the security guards turns to me—recognition becoming apparent as he looks at me. "Are these two with you, sir?"

Funny how throwing around a football, even part-time, earns me that title.

Ignoring him, I ask Cassidy, "Where is Hailey?"

"At my mom's for a sleepover. Why?"

I turn to the guard. "No. They're not with me." I grab Piper's hand and walk out of the theater.

~ ~ ~

"Tell me about her," Piper says, settling into my couch. "Why is it that you and my sisters hate her so much? I mean, other than the fact that she seems like a complete bitch."

I draw my brows together. "Nobody's told you yet?"

She shakes her head. "All my sisters tell me is how great you are. When I ask about details, they say the same thing every time—ask you. I've never known them to be so opposed to gossip. I figured you told them not to tell me."

A welcome pang grips my chest. *She asks about me.* "Why would I tell them that?"

"I don't know. Everyone has secrets," she says sadly.

I ignore her inward reference. "Cassidy is no secret. And she was different back then. Back when we, um . . . dated." I shrug innocently.

"I get it," she says. "You slept around. It's a pretty normal thing for college guys to do, Mason."

"Yeah, well that was then. Not anymore. She made sure of that."

"How?" Her eyebrows furrow, causing an adorable crinkle to form on the bridge of her nose. "Why haven't you been with anyone since?"

"Because she trapped me."

"Trapped?"

"Got pregnant on purpose."

Her jaw drops and she looks slightly green. "Oh, my God. Who would do that?"

"You got me," I say. "But I was naïve and she had me snowed. She played the part of the demure sorority girl. She played it very well. We hooked up a few times." I look over to gauge her reaction, putting my arm around her shoulder to pull her close. "Are you sure you want to hear this?"

She nods confidently.

"When I told her I didn't want a relationship, that football was my sole focus, she asked me for one last goodbye, um, you know . . . "

"Goodbye fuck," she says bluntly. "Okay, what happened next?"

My two-hundred-twenty-pound body tries to shrink into the couch on her harsh, but true, words.

"Well, I gave her what she wanted." I shake my head at the memory. "She left right after. And when I went to remove the condom, I discovered it wasn't there. I knew I put one on so I searched the bed and found it . . . completely dry and totally empty."

I cringe. "Cassidy could be kind of rough with me so I guess I didn't feel it come off. I didn't think much of it until she showed up seven months pregnant demanding a marriage proposal."

Still mortified every time I think about that night, I stare mindlessly at our entwined hands, entranced by her deep blue nail polish. It has not escaped my attention that the longer I've known her, the more she tends to favor the color. I'll bet if we stood before a mirror and she put her fingertips on my face, they would get lost in my eyes. That's how dead-on she is with the shade of blue she's chosen. I can only hope it's intentional. A sign of her deepening feelings for me.

"Do you—" she clears her throat, "Do you think you would have had kids if that didn't happen?"

"Of course," I say without hesitation.

I think of Hailey. Her round cherub face, her disobedient platinum curls, and my fierce love of everything about her. "Maybe not right away. Mostly because during the season my schedule is so hectic. But sure, I guess I've always wanted kids. How about you? Do you see kids in your future?"

It's a question I've wanted to ask her before, but didn't have the balls to for fear of her answer. Her eyes go distant and she shrugs. I remind myself how young she still is—we are. *Don't push her.*

"I've never seen Cassidy like that before," I say, changing the subject. "I'm pretty sure she was stoned out of her mind."

"That could be bad," she says.

"That could be very bad." I don't even want to think about the possibilities. I promise myself I'll contact my lawyer first thing Monday to find out what my options are.

"Hey, can we stop talking about my ex and start talking about something a lot more fun?"

"Fun?" she asks. "Like what?"

"Like your lips . . ."

A smile tugs at the edges of her closed lips, right before her tongue comes out to wet them. Her eyes fall to my mouth.

" . . . and how you're thinking about kissing me right now."

"Am not," she lies through her pearly whites.

My cheeks hurt from suppressing a huge smile. "It's okay to want me, Piper. I want you, too. I want you so much that I think about you every minute of every goddamn day."

Her hand trembles in mine. "I'm scared," she confesses.

"And you think I'm not?" I turn to face her, taking both her hands in mine. "Everything about this"—I pull a hand away to wave a finger between us— "terrifies me. But I have feelings for you. Huge feelings. Feelings that override any apprehension, concern, or doubts I have about us."

She nods and I can see her try to swallow her emotions. "Me, too."

Jesus. Did we do what I think we did? *Did we just fucking move to New York?*

I stand up and offer her my hand. "Come with me." I nod to my bedroom. "I promise you we'll only go as far as you are comfortable with. I have to see you again." My gaze shifts to the breasts still concealed beneath her blouse.

Her eyes flit nervously back and forth between me and the bedroom.

"Look at me, sweetheart," I beg. "Keep your eyes on me. It will be okay. It will be perfect."

"If by perfect, you mean a train wreck with multiple casualties, then you're about right."

My heart sinks before I see her eyes brighten with the beginnings of a smile. "A joke? You made a joke about having sex with me, Mitchell? You know that's not very good for my ego, right?"

"I have a feeling your ego can take it, *Dix*."

Laughing, I reach down and scoop her up into my arms, carrying her back to my bedroom, making her the one and only woman who has ever crossed the threshold.

After kissing her senseless on my bed, I remove her clothes, watching her cheeks pink up in the soft light I intentionally left on in the room.

When I peel her jeans off, I spy a birthmark on her left thigh. About the size of a silver dollar, it looks like the state of Texas. It's the sexiest thing I've ever seen. I trace the beauty mark with my tongue, never breaking eye contact with her. She makes soft mewling sounds, causing my already hard dick to pulsate in time with my heartbeat.

I push a finger inside her. Then two. Her head falls back against the pillow. My mouth breaks the seal on her skin. "Eyes, sweetheart," I remind her. "I'm the only one who's going to touch you here."

Her body trembles as my fingers work inside her, crooking forward to try and find that one spot—that Holy Grail that will drive her wild.

I add my tongue to the campaign, cupping her behind and tilting up her hips to match my slow, circling rhythm. Every cell of my body erupts with need as I taste her muskiness and watch her squirm and writhe beneath me. When I lightly rake my teeth across her clit, her hips buck against my mouth and her nails dig into the meaty flesh of my shoulders.

She is pure energy beneath me, her legs wrapping around my back before she stiffens and pushes them into me in time with her throbbing clit.

Hands, fingers, lips, tongue—it's a challenge to do everything I want to do to her while keeping eye contact. But damn it if it doesn't make every touch, every caress, every moment more intense.

Her tight walls squeeze my fingers and her groan of sweet release just about finishes me. Her eyes glaze over, the deep green irises burning into mine as she tumbles over the last edge of pleasure.

I climb up her languid body, my painfully hard erection straining against her shin, her knee, her thigh. I balance on my elbows above her, resting myself at her entrance. I reach over and retrieve a condom from my nightstand drawer. I show it to her.

Her eyes close and open on a ragged sigh. Then she nods slowly.

"Are you sure, sweetheart? I don't want to hurt you."

Her mouth trembles as she reaches up to touch my face with tentative fingers, brushing them back and forth across the soft hair on my jaw. "Yes. I'm sure."

A longing like nothing I've ever experienced washes over me, my need to protect her is fierce. I trace my thumb over her quivering lips. "You'll always be safe with me."

I sit back on my haunches and tear open the small square package. I watch her study me as I roll it on and then hover over her. She's so fucking nervous. Her hands are shaking. Her breathing accelerates, causing short successions of hot breath to roll over my face. I watch her swallow.

I can't do this. I'm afraid I will break her. I reach deep inside for my willpower and gently pull away, but she grabs my shoulders, bringing me closer.

"Mason, please. I'm sure." Her tender, conceding eyes contradict her apprehensive movements.

I've never wanted anything so much in all my life.

"Sweetheart . . ." I lean in to kiss her, the head of my throbbing dick begging for entry, riding the edge between too much and not nearly enough. I start to push in slowly, torn between savoring the surreal sensation of sliding up her tight walls and needing to keep her grounded. Sheltered. Safe.

I won't last long. I'm not even an inch inside her and I can feel my balls tighten. I close my eyes and try to think of something, anything, to hold off my own release so I can see her enjoy this.

But then she lashes out, her arms flailing blindly. A guttural, painful scream tears through the air, making my heart tumble uncontrollably into the trenches of my clenching stomach. My eyes fly open to see her staring blankly at the ceiling, her eyes hollow as if nothing is behind them but an endless pit of fear.

"No, no, no, no . . ." her quiet plea shreds me, pummeling my body like blows to the gut.

I was barely seated within her so I pull out instantly and roll to her side. "Piper. Sweetheart, it's me."

"No, no, no, no . . ." she chants with every quick breath, lost in a nightmare that I provoked.

Guilt flows through me like hot lava, my mind wildly grasping at anything that could fix this. I take a deep breath against my rising panic and clench my teeth against the wave of helplessness. I shake her lightly. "Piper, look at me," I command. "It's Mason. Only me. You're okay, sweetheart." I repeat the mantra over and over, until she hears me.

She looks around the room surprisingly, as if expecting to see something or someone else. Then she snaps out of it, recognition rolling in waves across her face as it contorts with a mixture of misery and embarrassment.

She sighs, closing her eyes and pulling the covers over her naked body. She throws an arm across her face, shielding her eyes from me. "I thought I could," she says. "I'm sorry."

I lay on top of the covers that surround her, pulling her close to me, spooning her without letting any part of my skin except my hands touch her. "God, no. *I'm* the one who's sorry. I never should have pushed." I run my hand gently down her arm, my fingers coming across her bracelet. I slowly trace the charm. "You weren't ready. I should have known."

"You didn't push me Mason. I wanted it. I *want* it. I'm just not sure I can." I feel her chest rise and fall in a deep sigh.

"Shhhh." I hold her tightly and she lets me. We lie like this for long minutes, just listening to each other breathe. I need her to know I'm here for her. I need her to feel it. I'm all in.

Shivers run down my spine as she takes in and lets out an insurmountable quantity of air. She's about to talk. Secrets are about to spill from her lips. Horrifying, gut-wrenching secrets.

"You know how when you wake up from a dream and you could swear it was real?" she asks. "How you can't understand how something with such clarity and detail didn't really happen?"

I nod my head into her neck. "Yes," I breathe my answer into her hair. I absolutely fucking know.

"I'm not a virgin," she quietly reveals, emotion breaking her voice. "But I don't remember losing my virginity."

I stiffen, taking her hand as I brace myself to hear everything she has to say.

"And I don't know who I lost it to because there were so many boys. So many . . . " Her words fall apart, trailing off as sick fear coils my insides.

My brain takes a second to get from '*I don't remember losing my virginity*' to '*so many boys.*' And then all of a sudden, my mind starts to put pieces of the puzzle together.

She spills drinks on purpose.

She can't remember.

So many boys.

Fuck. My stomach rolls. Bile burns my throat and a rage I can barely control pounds at my temples. I try to push down my emotions. Because this—what's happening right now—is huge. She trusts me enough to open up to me. Maybe she even *loves* me enough to do it.

"Piper." It's all I can get past the colossal knot in my airway. I have to remind myself to breathe as I caress her arm gently. She needs to know I'm not repulsed by her revelation. And even though all words are lost to me, I try to reassure her with my touch.

"I didn't even know it happened. Not for a long time after," she says in a troubled whisper that I strain to hear. "I was sore the next day. Really sore. I thought it was because I had started running with Charlie the day before." She pauses and clears her throat, clearly uncomfortable as she continues, "There was some blood. But I was always a little irregular where that was concerned."

I get lost in the haunted sorrow of her voice as I brush her hair behind her neck and let my fingers attempt to rub some tension from her. My eyes fall onto her tattoo, making me wonder what it has to do with her assault.

"I started having dreams. Flashbacks," she says. "Each one revealing a clue to what happened to me that night. But at the time, I didn't know the nightmares were real. They're never the same. Sometimes I fight. Sometimes I run away. Most times though, I participate willingly."

Her breath comes in short spurts of air, tension rolling off her in palpable waves. "They say I was most likely drugged with sleeping pills since I never felt sick after. They told me it was unlikely I even put up a fight—that those drugs are meant to relax you and almost put you in some sort of alternate reality."

The aching throb in my chest turns into unrelenting fury in my gut. Anger clouds my brain and rage bubbles deep in my blood. I want to ball my fists and hit something; hurt something as deeply and as punishingly as she's been hurt. It takes everything I have to lid my own emotions and offer her a comforting word. "God, Piper. I'm so sorry. I can't even imagine—"

Her neck strains as she looks back at me, cutting off the first words I could muster. "But you *can* imagine," she says. "You might be the only one who can, Mason. I have no idea what happened to me that night. Every dream I have is a different version. I may never know what happened. Just like you."

Shit. More of the puzzle pieces fall into place. "The marathon. Did you see someone? One of your attackers?"

She nods. "I think so. But I'll never know for sure. He could have been anybody; or nobody. Or he could have been one of the guys who assaulted me. Or"— I feel the bunching and quivering of muscles in her neck—"he could have simply been a drunk kid at the party having a good time, clueless to the fact that he was raping a girl."

Oh my God. Her murky waters run far deeper than I can fathom. Flashes of my own dreams—dozens of them—shuffle through my mind. I know all too well what not knowing the truth did to me. It almost killed me. But with help, I got myself to a place where I could manage it. I wonder if Piper will ever be able to get there.

black roses

I damn well plan on being around to do everything in my power to make sure she does.

chapter twenty-three

piper

In a break between customers, I stare out the window, daydreaming about waking up in Mason's arms this morning. I didn't dream at all last night. The nightmares never came, and the reality of waking up with him after my revelation is better than any dream I could have conjured up anyway. Except maybe a dream where I get to live a normal life. Like a normal girl. A girl whose world didn't come crashing down around her on her seventeenth birthday.

I thought it would ruin me—ruin us—once he found out the worst parts of me. And although I feel lighter than air today, deep down, I still have reservations. After all, can anyone really know all the secrets of another? What if he can never accept what I've been through? What I've done.

What if I'm not capable of being the kind of woman he needs? Sex is supposed to be good. It isn't supposed to be this dreaded experience that takes you to the depths of your own fiery hell. Even Charlie seems to like it despite everything that happened to her.

Still, he was right. It did help to talk about it. All those hours I sat on a couch with therapist after therapist, refusing to talk. Maybe if I'd just opened up to them.

You have to tell him, Piper. Charlie's words echo in my head. Would she approve—or would she scold me for leaving out pertinent details?

The way he held me all night was surreal. As if he accepted all my faults. The ones he knows about anyway. He stayed on top of the covers, keeping the warm fleece sheet between us, strategically bunched up in the space between his groin and my backside, presumably so I wouldn't freak out over his erection.

My breath hitches just thinking about his penis. He thinks I'm scared of it. I guess in a way, I am. I'm scared of all penises and what they could do to me. What they have already done to me. But, his in particular seems to make my mouth water instead of making my stomach turn. Last night, before my total and complete meltdown, I would steal glances at it. When he wasn't commanding that my eyes connect with his, and when his stare would inadvertently fall to my breasts—I would look at him.

I wanted to take him in my hand so badly. So badly I thought I could do it. I really thought I could—

"Hey, Piper."

Jarod startles me, pulling my gaze from the window.

"What's so interesting out there?"

"Hi, Jarod." I turn around and tighten the strings of my apron. "Nothing. Just taking a mental break, I guess."

"Oh. Well, what time do you get off today?" he asks.

"I'm only scheduled to work lunch, so I'm off at two."

He smiles and I realize what I hadn't before. He's attractive. Handsome, even. His dark brown hair, his chocolate eyes and his olive skin all hint at a Latino heritage that gives him a slightly exotic look. The gauges in his ears add an edge to the overall picture, along with his full sleeves of tattoos which are presently covered up by his long-sleeved dress shirt. I've never looked at him this way before. I've never looked at any man this way. Not until Mason.

"I'm off after lunch, too." He shifts his feet nervously. "Do you maybe want to catch a movie or something after work?"

Men have asked me out before. Lots of times, even though I try to remain anonymous and unapproachable. And I usually have no problem blowing them off and telling them where to stick it. But this is Jarod.

I look around the restaurant and take in all the men here. Some sit with children; some with a group of men. Most are with what appears to be their significant others. But instead of emphatically assuming that each of them is a rapist—a conclusion my unyielding mind settled on years ago—I try to look past that pre-conceived notion and figure out their story. I realize I've changed. Mason has changed me. And not all men are monsters.

Jarod and I are friends, so I feel kind of bad when I have to suppress the smile that's threatening to curve my lips as I say the words I never thought would pass through them. "I'm sorry, Jarod. Thank you, but I can't. I'm seeing someone."

His eyes meet the floor. Then he nods. "It's Mason Lawrence, isn't it?"

I nod. I half expect him to rant about how, of course, any girl would choose a famous athlete over a waiter. I'm fully prepared to defend myself and set him straight. But he doesn't utter a word about it. Instead, he says, "He's a lucky guy."

"Thanks, Jarod," I say as he walks away, swinging a towel over his shoulder in defeat. *But, I'm the lucky one.*

I look back out the window and watch the busy world rush by, wondering if maybe I could fit in and be a part of it. Maybe I'm ready. Maybe I'm ready to move to New York.

Maybe I already have.

~ ~ ~

I float through the rest of my shift, the usual customer annoyances having little effect on me.

Throwing my dirty apron in the laundry pile, I gather my things and head out the front door, dropping my phone when I collide with someone in my buoyant exit.

Crap. I look down at my phone. *I think I broke it.*

But before I can lean down to retrieve it, biting words lash out at me, dampening my mood much more than the broken phone. "Well if it isn't Piper Mitchell, the very same one I saw leaving Mason's building early this morning."

My eyes snap to Cassidy's and an unwelcome pang of dread splinters through me like a warning beacon. "What were you doing there at seven o'clock this morning?" I ask, acutely aware of my silent gratitude to the many pedestrians bustling about us. "Are you stalking him?"

Hatred clouds her hazel eyes. "I have every right to be there. He's the father of my child." Her lips draw back in a silent snarl. "And whether or not he realizes it, I'm the most important woman in his life and I always will be. Especially if he knows what's good for him."

My mouth gapes open. "Is that a threat, Cassidy?" My body stiffens in automatic defense. "Are you telling me you'll try to take Hailey? Because you'd be in for one hell of a fight."

Her deranged laugh causes the hairs on my neck to rise. "You don't even know him," she says. "You've been around for ten fucking minutes." Her nostrils flare and her face reddens in anger. "*I've* been in his life for years. And I'm willing to bet he doesn't know the slightest thing about you, does he?"

Unease washes over me. "What's that supposed to mean?"

"I told you I thought you looked familiar when we first met, but it took me a while to put it all together. This morning, when I snapped a picture of you coming out of his building, it all started to make sense. It's then when I remembered the picture I showed Baylor last year," she says. "I thought it was her, but she set me straight."

Her apparent lunacy is starting to scare me, even beyond the whole she's-taking-stalkery-photos-of-me feelings. But she has my full attention as she digs through her purse, pulling out what looks to be a weathered photo.

She grips the photo in her hand, not allowing my eyes to fall on it. "When I was in high school," she says, "I would go into the city for parties. Wild parties. I first saw Mason at one of them. He may not have known me at the time, and we didn't hookup until college—" she pauses to release a sigh that drips with school-girl infatuation, "—but, he's the reason I went to Clemson."

Oh, my God. Stalker is right. My unease is quickly turning into pure undiluted fear.

"I only knew it was a matter of time before he fell for me. I was very, um . . . persuading."

Thoughts of her *persuading* him sicken my insides.

"Anyway, back to the point." She shakes her head as if pulling herself back from fantasy. "I know what went on at those parties." She gives me a hard stare. A knowing stare.

My gut clenches as jagged pieces of my nightmares slice through my mind. My lungs burn, begging for the un-replenished air that's left them. My foreboding body falls back against the building for support.

"Mason thinks you are some sort of prudish princess." She rolls her eyes. "Snow White, was it? Well, *Princess*, I wonder what he would say if he knew you frequented those kinds of parties. If he knew you were the kind of girl who gets off when more than one boy touches you. If I told him that you like to suck some nameless guy's dick while another one fucks you at the same time. Do you think he'd ever look at you the same way? Do you think he wouldn't be repulsed by the very sight of you . . . "

Gooseflesh ripples up my back as I try to keep the nightmares, the slivers of memories, at bay. Mason knows. I told him. So I shouldn't let this get to me. But she pushes on, punishing my resolve by describing in detail what did or could have happened that night. Her repeated graphic verbal illustrations cause waves of nausea to roll through me. I feel the blood drain from my face. I fear I might faint, so I put my hands on my knees right before I horrifyingly lose my lunch on the sidewalk beneath me.

Still unable to stand straight, I can feel her eyes burn into me as I glance up at her. The sheer desperation in my naïve eyes must betray me and I can clearly see the moment her mind erupts with comprehension.

Evil distorts her face as she assesses me from head to toe. "Oh, my God," she says, studying me, her eyes hard and cold like a freezing wind. "So Snow White isn't a slut. She's a victim."

If the contents of my stomach weren't already spectacularly displayed in front of me, they would be now. My body begins to shake uncontrollably. But as I watch the scheming wheels spin behind her bitter eyes, the terror of her knowing my secret pales in comparison to what she says next.

She shoves the tattered picture in front of me. My hesitant eyes take it in. It's a picture of me. On *that* night.

"So, Princess," she says, malevolence dripping from her words. "Boys had sex with you without your consent? How can you be so sure *he* wasn't one of them?"

Tension closes like a fist around my heart as I look closely at the picture. There in the background, with his arm around the shoulders of another boy, is Mason.

He's so young. His soft, light beard hasn't yet made its way to his face, but it's unmistakably him. But what makes me wretch up more nothingness from my empty stomach is that the boy he's with—he's one of the nameless faces in my dreams.

I clench the picture with shaky hands, crumpling it in my fist as I try to muster the energy to run. After all, running is what I do best. I take a deep breath. Then another. And as soon as my lungs fill with enough oxygen to give my body the will to move, I walk away. I walk away leaving my broken, shattered phone on the sidewalk in a pool of my vomit.

"Okay then," I hear her call out after me. "I guess you can go ahead and keep the picture." I attempt to block out her laughter as it bounces off the building behind me. My feet can't get me where I need to be quickly enough.

～ ～ ～

The plane's engines scream in my ear as we taxi down the runway. Announcements come over the speakers following the pre-recorded safety video. Flight crew walk down the aisle checking seat belts and closing overhead compartments. I've seen it all a hundred times before. It all becomes drivel in the background as my thoughts overcome me.

His face isn't one of those in my nightmares. But there are so many. And he was there at the party. The proof is sitting back on my parents' kitchen counter along with a letter to Skylar, explaining how I can't stay for her wedding. Lame excuses of an emergency with Charlie. I hope she won't hate me for missing her special day.

I can't stay. I can't walk up the aisle with him. I can't stand across the altar from him knowing he could be one of them. It would explain how he was so quick to accept what happened to me. How he kept telling me nothing in my past could change the way he felt. How he was always protecting me. How he held me tightly last night, silently sobbing behind me. Maybe guilt was consuming him.

Could I really have fallen in love with a boy who raped me?

Denial shoots through me. I try to convince myself it wasn't him. But there's no denying the truth in the picture. I turn up my music, mindlessly staring down upon the shrinking city. And as the water below slowly overtakes the land in the window, I bid a final goodbye to New York.

chapter twenty-four

mason

Pre-season is over. I don't report to training camp for almost six weeks. It couldn't have worked out better. I plan on spending every minute I can with Piper and Hailey. The latter may involve kissing a little ass where Cassidy is concerned.

My lawyer said it shouldn't be too hard to get joint custody. It's pretty common these days, even when people have demanding jobs like mine. But it will take time.

I can't begin to think of how Cassidy's behavior could affect my daughter. I would go for full custody, but without proof—without hard evidence of her somehow endangering Hailey, I don't have a case. I can only hope it was a one-time thing. I've seen her drunk plenty of times, but in the city, where driving isn't involved, it didn't seem like that big of a deal. But Saturday night was different. She was completely out of it. And that asshole she was with. I shudder to think Hailey could be exposed to someone like him. I've always known Cassidy was a slut, but if she's into drugs. *Shit*. I don't even want to think about it.

I'd rather think of Piper. We passed a major milestone over the weekend. What happened to her is unbelievable. Worse than I imagined—which was maybe some old boyfriend forcing himself on her, or at the very worst, a random stranger assault. But, God, multiple boys raping her while she was obliviously whacked out on sleeping pills? That sickens me. And I know all too well what it's like to not know the difference between nightmares and reality.

She trusted me. She opened up to me and then she let me hold her all night. I know she believes she'll never be ready to give herself over to me completely, but I think she's wrong. In a few short months, she has conquered so many fears. She's let me kiss her. Touch her. Put my tongue on her. And the orgasms she's had—if I tried to choreograph the perfect orgasm, I still wouldn't have come close to even being in the same damn ball park as the reality of watching her lose control and enjoy the ones I've given her.

As I put myself through the paces on a treadmill, my mind goes wild just thinking of the sexy birthmark on her thigh. The alluring tattoo that sits just below her ear. Her perfect creamy breasts that I swear were made specifically to fit my hands. The sweet, musky scent between her legs.

Stop it.

I increase the speed of my treadmill and the volume of my music so it's hard to think about anything but keeping up my punishing pace.

When my run is finished, I look around the gym. I came early, hoping to run into Piper. With my days free for the next month, I thought we could work out together.

We haven't talked since she left my place yesterday morning. We both skipped Sunday brunch out on Long Island. I think she needed time to process everything. If what she said is true, other than Charlie and her parents, I'm the only other soul who knows. Hell, I'm still processing it myself. I'm still reeling over the fact that her admission connected us on some surreal level I never thought I'd experience with a woman.

I'm in love with her. I'm sure of it. And as soon as I can, I'm going to tell her. I'll spell it out with Mr. T's roses if I have to. Anything to make her understand that I'm all in. I'm in this for the long haul. No matter how long it takes. I'm talking marriage, kids, side-by-side burial plots. The whole nine yards.

I stare at my water bottle after taking a drink—a little piece of plastic that has so much more meaning than I ever thought it could. I vow to have a dozen cases delivered to my apartment as soon as I leave here.

I look at the banks of treadmills. I look at the weight stations. I walk past the boxing rings, hoping I'll catch a glimpse of her.

"How's my favorite underrated, underutilized football player?"

I turn around, smiling at my favorite gender-neutral friend. Okay, my only gender-neutral friend. "Hey, Trick. How's business?"

"Good. Busy," she says. "So busy I'm thinking the bosses need to give me a raise." She winks.

I laugh. "Glad to hear it." I look over my shoulder, visually sweeping the premises once again. "Did I miss Piper?"

She looks up at the large clock on the wall. "Huh." She tilts her head, studying it. "No, you didn't miss her. She hasn't been in yet," she says, turning back to me. "Kind of unusual for a Monday since the restaurants are closed. In fact, I don't think she's missed a Monday morning workout since I met her, not counting the day of the marathon."

My good mood dampens and my heart suddenly finds itself in the pit of my stomach.

Something's wrong. And I'll bet it has everything to do with Saturday night. Has she changed her mind about me now that I know her secret? Maybe she thinks I'll see her differently; that I won't want to touch her after knowing what happened. Nothing could be further from the truth. I just have to make sure she understands that.

I pull my phone out to text her.

Me: Hey, sweetheart. I missed you at the gym. Can I see you today?

I make some small talk with Trick and a few of the gym patrons, but my attention is largely focused on my phone—waiting, willing it to vibrate with a reply.

Clean from my shower, I throw my gym bag over my shoulder and head in the direction of Griffin's townhouse. She hasn't texted me and if she's having second thoughts, she needs to see in person that *I'm* not.

Skylar smiles when she sees me, holding a sleepy Aaron in her arms. She opens the door and then cranes her neck to look behind me. "You're alone?" she asks. "Where's Piper?"

I try to ignore the twist in my gut. "I was hoping you could tell me. I haven't seen her since yesterday morning."

Worry etches lines beside her eyes. "She didn't stay with you again last night?"

"No." I look past Skylar to the stairs, hoping Piper will come bounding down at any second. "She didn't. Last I knew she was going into work."

She waves me in, depositing Aaron in a nearby cradle. "She did. She worked the lunch shift yesterday." Her questioning eyes sweep over me. "I'm confused. Because obviously you spent the night together on Saturday, and then you both begged out of brunch. We all assumed the two of you had finally gotten together and wanted some, um . . . alone time." She winks. "But then I found out she took a shift at NYC. Did you guys have a fight or something?"

I shake my head with a sharp jerk. "Not at all. Quite the opposite. That night was one of the best of my life. Maybe *the* best. She finally—"

I stop my words mid-sentence. Skylar doesn't know.

"She finally what?" she asks.

"Um . . . I think she finally realized that maybe we could be a couple."

A triumphant smile sweeps across her face. "I knew it!" She claps her hands and then winces when she remembers the sleeping baby just yards away. "Wait. Then why is my little sister M.I.A?"

I shrug and run both hands through my hair in frustration.

"What, you think she's having second thoughts?" she asks.

We share a look of defeat and then simultaneously pull out our phones to start texting and calling anyone who might have a clue.

I'm getting nowhere on the phone with Baylor when I see it in Skylar's eyes. I don't know who she's talking to, but the way she's looking at me right now—it's the same damn way the doctor looked at me in the hospital seven years ago when he told me my parents were dead. Her eyes are full of unspoken words. They are heavy with sorrow. Her sympathetic gaze never falters from my prying eyes as she listens, nodding along with whatever she's hearing.

She peels the phone slowly from her ear, closing her eyes as she sets in on the table in front of her. "What did you do to her?" she asks, her voice hollow, as if not knowing to accuse or support me.

My head tilts to the side as I ponder her question. "Do to her?"

A heavy weight settles in my chest. *Oh, God.* I pushed her too far Saturday night. She's having some kind of delayed panic attack. "Nothing," I say blindly, before flashbacks of her desperate chants send a burning wave of grief raging inside me. "I thought it was okay. I thought she was okay." I tip my head back and blow out an agonizing breath. "Fuck, Skylar. What did I do?"

"I don't know, Mason." She walks over to me and grabs my shoulders, her petite frame forcefully turning my large one. She guides me towards the door. "But you'd better damn well figure it out. I've just been informed by my mother that she's gone. She left New York and she's not coming back. Not even for my wedding." She opens the front door and pushes me through. "I love you. But I love my sister more. I hope whatever happened is just a misunderstanding. Fix this, Mason."

The door slams shut behind me and I stand here, empty. As empty as I was the day my parents died.

I look down at my wrist, a constant reminder of what I lost. It makes me think of Piper's bracelet. She touches it when she's nervous, same as I do my scar. And I wonder—does it give her strength, or does it slowly suck the life from her?

I tap her name on my phone, but before I even hear it ring, it goes to voicemail. I plead with her to call me. To let me know where she is. To come back.

I text her repeatedly as I rush back to my apartment, heading straight for the parking garage so I can go the only place I think may hold the answers.

Long Island.

~ ~ ~

Four angry eyes meet mine at the front door of her parents' house after her father rips the door open. "You've got balls coming here," he says. "I should call the police."

Piper's mom puts a hand on him, holding him back when he looks like he's going to lunge at me. "Bruce, wait," she begs, warring emotions evident in her teary eyes. "Look at him. He seems utterly wrecked. This is Mason. He's practically part of the family. Maybe she's mistaken."

"Mistaken?" he spits at her as if she were a stranger. "You think our daughter is mistaken about this psychopath raping her?"

Jan cringes. Bruce hits the door with his fist.

I die inside.

She thinks I raped her? Oh, God. I did push her too far.

I double over, my hands meeting my thighs as I fight for breath. I'll never be able to forgive myself. My body crumples, my back hitting the porch wall as my head finds its way between my knees. "No, no, no," my broken voice stutters. "I'm so sorry. It's all my fault. She said she was ready. I thought she was ready."

I can hear Bruce cussing over his hurt hand. Jan is crying—disappointment flowing with her tears. Her hand comes up to cover a heart-wrenching sob. "What kind of monster thinks a drugged-up sixteen-year-old can consent to sex?"

"Sixteen?"

It takes a minute to sink in. "What? Sixteen? No." I look at their broken, angry faces. "Bruce, Jan, I'm confused and you are scaring the hell out of me. She told me what happened to her. She finally opened up to me Saturday night after I, after we . . ." I try to clear the desperation from my voice. "We tried being together but she panicked. That's when she told me. She told me about the night she was raped and the boys who raped her. She slept in my arms after that. I thought she was okay." I look at them, my expression pained and puzzled. "When she left my place yesterday she was okay."

Bruce cradles his right hand gingerly as hatred clouds his eyes. "Told you about it? What's to tell, you were there. You were one of them."

"One of them?" I look up at him, my heart pounding painfully hard. "As in one of the sick bastards who raped her? What are you talking about? I just met her a few months ago."

"Are you calling our daughter a liar?" He looks like he wants to hit me instead of the door.

"No, sir." I stand up and steady myself on the wall. "I just think she's confused because we had, well, we tried to have . . . " I shake the uneasiness from my voice. I need them to believe me. "I know about her nightmares, about the faces she sees, maybe after our encounter, she thought I was one of them."

"Or maybe *you're* the one who's confused," he barks. "My daughter is no liar, and neither is the picture."

"Picture?" I look between them, frustration and worry bleeding from my eyes. "What picture?"

"Wait here," Jan says. Then she turns to Piper's dad. "Don't hit the boy, Bruce. You'll go and break your other hand."

Bruce nods, heeding her request. He stares me down, pinning me to the wall with his wrathful eyes.

After what seems an eternity, Jan returns, handing me a photo. It's a picture of Piper—young and confidant. Her long honey-brown hair is all one color, falling far longer than it does today. Beautiful.

Then I'm sure my eyes betray me when I see myself in the background. "I don't understand," I tell them, hoping they can read the despair in my eyes. "I never met Piper until March of this year. I'd never seen her before. Where was this taken?"

Jan's eyes betray her, revealing sympathy I'm not sure she wants me to see. She grabs my elbow, escorting me into their home. She gives her husband a look of warning as she guides me into the kitchen. I put the photo on the table and accept the water she offers me, eager to quench the intense thirst spawned by oppressive anxiety.

"What do you know about that night?" she asks.

"Only what she told me, Jan. Please, tell me what's going on here." The bitter agony welling inside me is crippling. "Where is she?"

Bruce picks up a chair, turning it around backwards before he puts it down next to me, offensively straddling it and leaning his arms on the top rail. "Let me tell you a story," he says, his voice deep and rough, edged with a deadly calm. "Once upon a time there was a sixteen-year-old girl. A beautiful, talented, outgoing sixteen-year-old girl who never knew a stranger. She doted on her nephew, helping her sister raise him when she was young and alone. She was a great daughter, a loyal friend and a gifted actress."

His eyes go dark and distant. "Then one night, a few weeks before junior year, she went to a party with some drama friends. They weren't her usual crowd, but she was determined to fit in with everyone—jocks, geeks, bookworms; she didn't want to be labeled or belong to only one group. There were football players at the party and some of her friends were trying to impress them. On a bet, she took some shots of alcohol with the football players." He pauses to push the photo closer to me. "Shots you and your friends gave her. Shots that were full of drugs so you could have your way with her."

His uninjured fist pounds the table next to the picture.

I stare at it. And like a movie playing in slow motion, a night from high school floods my memories and my world is pulled out from under me like a cheap fucking rug.

That laugh. Her maniacal, eerily familiar laugh that sent chills down my spine a few weeks ago. It was from *that* night. I remember it now as clearly as the terror on Jan's ashen face. I was seventeen and I was drunk. Not wasted drunk, but I had a good buzz going. Coach Braden would have kicked my ass if he knew I was drinking so close to the start of the season. By then, almost a year and a half after my parents died, he was more than my coach. He was my father figure. My guardian. My savior.

My friends had talked me into going to what was touted to be an epic party. The best summer blowout ever. It was at some rich kid's house in the city. The place was gigantic and I remember wandering long hallways searching for an unoccupied bathroom. I passed by a slightly open door, a bedroom based on the noises coming from inside it. Clapping, cheering, and groans of pleasure were seeping through the crack in the door. Sex oozed from the dimly-lit room. I was seventeen. Of course I looked. There were several guys surrounding a bed, none of whom I knew more than to thank them for pouring me a beer from the keg. A girl was squirming around on the bed, arching her hips and making all kinds of sexual noises that had my young mind fantasizing for days.

"Everything good in here?" I asked. All heads turned to me. A few guys looked annoyed as if I were going to join in and take a piece of

their pleasure. The girl on the bed, whose face was obscured by some guy's bare ass, crooked a finger at me, inviting me over with the gesture. *"No thanks,"* I said, as I shut the door and went to find a bathroom. That's when I heard it. Her crazy libidinous laugh.

It was Piper. She was the girl on that bed.

For the second time today, my head falls between my knees to keep the bile lining my throat from further rising. "It's all my fault," I choke out. I try to tell Bruce and Jan what happened that night. I barely get through it without getting sick on their kitchen floor. "I could have saved her. I didn't know. Oh, God, I didn't know. I was right there. Right there . . . "

When I go silent, finding no more words to defend my actions, Jan stands up and wraps comforting arms around me. "Mason, thank God," she cries, her tears falling in time with my own. "I knew it couldn't have been you. Piper was confused. She said she never saw your face in her nightmares. But that picture. The boy next to you—he was one of them. So she assumed. We assumed."

In a very motherly fashion, she rubs my back in slow easy circles with the palm of her hand. "I'm sorry I ever thought—" she clears the frog from her throat, "—I mean, you're like family, Mason."

"I should have known better," I scold myself, still trying to comprehend how close I was to her. I could have easily barged in and stopped what was going on.

"You were just a boy yourself," Bruce says. "It's not your fault. You didn't know she was being raped." He looks pained. "And from the way she's explained it to us, neither did she."

My heart clenches in my chest once more. My throat burns and my eyes sting. I look up at them to see their anger has turned to nothing but sympathy. I'm sure my face is a wreck; red and swollen from rubbing my hands over it; wet from all the tears that have fallen. "I love her," I tell them. "Please tell me where she is."

"We don't exactly know, son," Bruce says. "I'm not even sure she knew where she was going when she left yesterday. And her phone got . . . left behind."

I shake my head, unwilling to accept it. "I have to find her," I beg. "Please, you must have some idea."

They share a look. And goddamn if it's not another look that twists my insides. "Mason, this may have been a big misunderstanding, but you have to know, she may still never be capable of having a relationship with a man who has a child."

My questioning eyes flit between them. "What does that have to do with anything? Hailey's no bother. She's a wonderful little girl."

Jan nods. "She absolutely is. And we love her. But there is more to this story than you know." She puts a hand on my cheek. "But it's not our story to tell."

She pulls out her phone and taps the screen. "We may not know where she is, but we know someone who probably does."

I take the phone from her to see the name on the screen.

Charlie Tate.

chapter twenty-five

piper

"No, I don't need a bellman," I say. "I don't have any bags. No hay bolsas."

The desk clerk runs my card, giving me a sympathetic look. I can see he's wondering what my story is. Running from an abusive husband? Kicked out by a cheating boyfriend? I'm sure he's seen it all.

I sign my receipt and ask him if I can use the hotel phone, not having yet replaced my cell. "¿Puedo usar el teléfono por favor?"

"Sí." He pushes the phone towards me.

"Long distance." I hold my arms wide open, hoping he understands my gesture as I don't recall how to say the words in Spanish. I flash him my best damsel-in-distress look, even adding a lip quiver for good measure.

He looks behind him, beyond a glass door into the office, presumably at his boss. She looks busy at the moment. He types a code into the phone and hands me the receiver. "Is fine," he says in broken English. "You look like nice girl. Hurry, use telephone fastly."

Thanking him profusely, I dial Charlie's number. I know she won't answer, she's a bonafide call screener. Plus, it's like three o'clock in the morning in Sydney. Just as well. I don't want to have to explain everything now. I'm exhausted. I just want her to know I'm back in Barcelona. It's part of the sisters' code—always tell each other where we are. Sometimes we're the only ones who ever know.

The sisters' code.

It's something we came up with when we were twelve, after her dad left and she started living her own personal hell. She didn't want to be her mother's daughter anymore, so she asked me if she could pretend she had mine. My mom treated her like a daughter anyway. And Baylor and Skylar learned that where there was one of us, the other wasn't far behind. For all intents and purposes, she *was* a Mitchell sister.

"Hey, hermana, it's me. I'm just following the code. I'm back in Barcelona and I can't wait to see you when you return from down under. My phone broke, so if you need to get me, just call this number. Love you. Hope you're having a blast with, wait . . . what's his name? Anyway, just thought you should know. Bye."

I push the phone back in place and thank the desk clerk again before dragging myself up the stairs to my room to get much needed sleep.

～ ～ ～

Loud knocking wakes me and I curse the noise when the numbers on the bedside clock tell me I've only been asleep for twenty minutes.

I cover my head with a pillow, hoping the intruder will just go away. "Por favor limpie después," I beg the supposed housekeeper to come back another time.

The incessant pounding doesn't stop. I angrily slide my tired body from the bed and pad over to the door, ripping it open as I yell, "I'm sleep—, oh, my God . . . Charlie!"

Her all-encompassing hug propels me backwards into the room. "I missed you so much," my muffled words tread through her thick red hair. Then I push her away. "Wait. Why are you here? What happened to Syndey and what's-his-name?"

She steps back outside the room to pull her heavy suitcase over the threshold. I can't suppress my smile. It feels like old times. Safe. Comfortable. Familiar.

"Oh, that." She avoids my pointed stare, placing her bag on the ottoman before she unzips it. "Pfft, it never would have worked out."

My jaw slackens. My eyes narrow. I point an accusing finger at her. "You lied."

She starts to unpack her suitcase, dumping the contents into random drawers.

I put my hand on hers, stopping her from grabbing another handful of clothes. "You broke the code, Charlie. Why did you lie? You know I know you too well, so don't feed me any shit."

She rolls her eyes. "Technically, it wasn't a lie, Pipes. I had every intention of going with him. I just changed my mind at the airport" —my punishing stare prods her on— "when his wife showed up and threw her phone at me." She rubs a spot on her shoulder, wincing.

I pull her in for a hug. "Oh, sweetie, I'm so sorry. Not again. Men fucking suck."

She laughs half-heartedly. "Well at least this one didn't actually suck dick like the last guy."

I close my eyes and shake my head, appalled at the situations she ends up in sometimes.

She looks around my hotel room and then at her semi-unpacked bag before squinting her eyes at me. "Speaking of how men suck, why are *you* here? And where's your stuff?"

My throat stings and my heart hurts. It actually hurts—as if it's not all completely there—like I left some of it back in New York.

She sees the expression of defeat on my face. "Oh, Piper. What happened?" She leads me over to the bed, patting the spot next to her when she sits down.

Her mouth gapes open as I tell her the incredulous story. Then she cradles me until I fall asleep.

When I wake, I'm pissed off at the light for coming through the curtains and touching my face. But at second look, I realize it's morning light, not evening. I check the clock. I slept for almost eighteen hours.

On the bedside table there's a note from Charlie telling me she's gone to work, stocking shelves at a small tourist boutique by the cruise port. I smile, thinking she's got an actual job instead of relying on a man to put a roof over her head. At least for now. Until she does something stupid again like sleep with the boss and get fired by his wife.

After a long, soothing shower that washes the travel filth from my body, I sift through some drawers to borrow a t-shirt and jeans. Jeans I need to roll up at the cuff due to the differences in our height. I draw the line, however, at wearing Charlie's underwear and since I've been sporting the same pair for two days, I decide to go commando.

I sling my purse over my shoulder and head out on a shopping spree. I never went back to Skylar's to collect my things and I'm going to need some stuff to get me by until my dad can ship my clothes over. Out of habit, I've always kept my passport in my purse, and that along with a credit card was all I needed to get a plane ticket. Everything else was expendable.

Including Mason Lawrence.

My heart sinks. I'd gone a whole thirty minutes without thinking of him. I try to convince myself it wasn't him in the picture; that maybe his bitch of an ex-girlfriend had Photoshopped him in or something. But how would she have known I was there and that the picture was of *that* night? I'll never forget the clothes I was wearing. Months later, when I finally realized what had happened, I burned the pink low-cut sweater and hip-hugging capris.

Even if Mason was one of them, maybe it was just like I told him and he was simply a drunk, horny kid joining the orgy. Could he even be to blame if that were the case? Even so—I can never forgive him for knowing about it and not telling me the truth once I told him what happened to me. Did he think he could be with me knowing what he did? How could we build a relationship on that? On the heels of the second worst night of my life.

The nagging voice in my head says it isn't so. That I jumped to conclusions. That maybe it wasn't even him in the picture. It could have been his, what do they call it . . . doppleganger?

Mason is a good man.

I remember chanting the mantra over and over in my head while he kissed me. Touched me. Put his tongue on me. *No! Stop it, Piper.*

He was different all those years ago. He's admitted to it. He would sleep with anyone in a skirt until he screwed up and knocked one of them up. It was him in the picture. My head knows it. My gut feels it.

My broken fucking heart hates it.

Out of habit, I reach for my phone to check the time before realizing I don't have it anymore. I look at the new watch on my right wrist that tells me it's almost time for my daily coffee. It's the one indulgence I allow myself even when I get down to my last pennies.

Who needs a phone anyway? Especially when I'm sure it's jam packed with texts and voicemails from *him*.

Approaching my favorite café, I wonder if maybe they'll let me work there again. For coffee, food, and perhaps a few weeks' stay in the flat overhead like we did for a stint last year. I don't know, though, I kind of left without notice when Charlie got some dude to fly us to London.

But the hotel I chose in haste is far too expensive for more than just a day or two. We have to start looking for another place. Maybe go back to where Charlie was crashing before yesterday; probably some youth hostel with disgusting shared bathrooms and little to no privacy.

I stand in the busy line, not recognizing any of the employees. Pay is low and turnover is high. But I don't need much, so when I make my way to the counter to place my order, I pull an application from the box attached to the wall and shove it into my purse. Then, as usual, I walk on my tiptoes from the order line to the pickup line—my eyes trained on the barista preparing my latte. It's not hard to follow it here since they write everyone's name on their cups.

"I guess you won then," a deep, pained, familiar voice says behind me.

My heart thunders. It's a resounding noise that reverberates throughout my entire body. It can't be.

I spin around and stare at him for seconds. Minutes. An eternity.

It's him. The only man I've ever loved. Even against my own will, my body responds to his voice. His face. His mere presence.

My very next thought, however, is that I'm going to eviscerate my so-called best friend and hang her from her pink fucking toenails until they rip from her body, letting her fall and drown in a pool of her own blood.

"Piper?" the guy at the counter calls out.

I turn around and stare at the offending cup on the counter that displays my name. *Shit.*

Mason comes up next to me, plucking my latte from the tiled surface, depositing it into the trashcan next to him. He reaches into his pocket and throws money on the counter—Euros even. "Make her another," he commands. "Just like that one." He nods to the trashcan. "And keep the change. Comprende?"

The barista's eyes go wide when he sees the denomination of the bill lying on the counter. He's clearly confused by the situation, but he pockets the money anyway and seems to understand enough English to follow Mason's order. "Sí. You got it, amigo," he says, happily.

Mason and I stand side-by-side in silence as my new drink is made while we watch. He doesn't talk. He doesn't try to get me to look at him. He doesn't do anything but stare at every move the kid makes, from writing my name on the cup, to mixing cappuccino with the perfect amount of milk before he places it in front of me again.

Mason nods his head at the kid in thanks. I get the impression he doesn't speak much Spanish.

I pick up the drink but I can't make eye contact with him again. I'm afraid if I do, I'll remember him in a flashback of one of my dreams. They come back to me like that sometimes. When I see a smile that might have belonged to one of them, or hear a vaguely familiar voice, or hear the drunken cheers of partying men.

If I remembered him there—doing those things to me—I don't think I'd survive it. Not after what we shared. And knowing he could potentially be the—

"Piper, sweetheart." He puts a hesitant hand on my elbow. "Please sit down and let me explain."

All of my defenses click in as I rip my arm from his gentle grip and shove him hard in the ribs. "Don't ever fucking call me that again." I walk away, begging my legs not to collapse out from under me.

chapter twenty-six

mason

"Wait!" I ignore the tender, stinging flesh over my ribs and run out the door behind her. I say to her backside, "Don't you at least owe it to me to listen? I mean I did come all this way."

She stops and turns around; conflicting emotions flowing from her eyes instead of tears. I try to read her like I've been able to do so well in the past. What is it I see behind those incredible green irises—anger? Regret? Indecision?

It's the last one I grip onto despite the way her words jump out to bite me.

"I told you a long time ago, I don't owe anything to anyone. Ever."

She's right. She doesn't owe me anything. Especially after what she thinks I did to her. Hell, she should be throwing her scalding-hot coffee at me, not giving me a second chance.

"Right," I say, grasping for words that might get her to stay and hear me out. "Then how about you do it out of the kindness of your heart." I gesture to a table in front of the café. It's in the corner of the courtyard, out of the way but still in view of the many other patrons. I want her to feel safe. That will always be my top priority whether she ends up with me or not. "Please. Sit down. You don't have to talk. Just give me the time it takes for you to finish your coffee."

She looks around at the other tables, taking inventory of the fact they are pretty much bustling with activity at this popular mid-morning hour. A sigh escapes her and my heart lurches forward in my chest. She's going to let me explain.

She walks over to the table, pulling out one of the two chairs and placing it as far away from the other as she can get it. She sits down, removing the lid from her steaming latte. "I'd say you have about ten minutes. Talk fast, because when this is done, I'm gone."

I explain every nauseating detail to her, same as I did with her parents. And when I check my watch to see how many minutes have passed, I see it's been more than twenty. And her coffee sits on the table. Untouched.

A sliver of hope lines my words. "I was there, Piper. But I swear to you I wasn't a part of what happened. I had no knowledge of anyone spiking drinks. If I had, you have to believe I would have stopped it. You'll never know how guilty I feel for being so close to you and not doing anything. I had been drinking myself that night. Not a lot, but enough to cloud my judgment. I had been to some pretty wild parties back then. And full disclosure, I'd been with more than one girl at a time myself. Consenting girls," I quickly add. "I'd pretty much seen it all. Nothing shocked me.

"I asked," I say, closing my eyes and shaking my head because I still can't believe it was her. "I asked, just like I told you a minute ago. Even though I couldn't see you, I asked if everything was okay. You gave me a thumbs-up. God, if I could only turn back time." I run desperate fingers through my hair, gripping the back of it with pent-up anger and frustration. "A fucking thumbs-up, Piper. I thought it was consensual. I thought the girl—I thought *you*—were okay. All I saw was a girl having a good time."

Finally, she makes a movement other than twisting her bracelet. Her shaky hand reaches for her drink and she takes a sip of what I'm sure is now lukewarm coffee. She doesn't make eye contact. She simply stares at her drink, mindlessly tracing the black ink of her name written across the side.

When she speaks, her words slay me. "A girl having a good time, huh?"

I nod shamefully and my voice thickens with regret. "I'm sorry."

She clears her throat and tries to compose herself, sitting up straighter in her chair and smoothing a wrinkle on her jeans. She's fighting it bad. Even though I've never seen her shed a single tear, she's clearly destroyed by this. "Well, at least now I know which dream is accurate." Her voice is distant and emotionless.

"We don't know that for sure, Piper," I explain. "I was only there for a minute. Seconds even. I left the party shortly after. I don't know what happened after that, but I like to think the drugs wore off and you fought back—kicking them in the balls, making those bastards incapable of procreation."

Her face pales. Then she quickly gulps down the remainder of her coffee and I know I'm running out of time. "Where did you get the picture?" I ask. It's a question I pondered all the way here. I'd never seen it before. Surely if I had, I would have remembered her unmistakable, stunning face.

What she says makes my stomach turn.

"Cassidy."

"Cassidy?" I ask, confident I heard her correctly, but not quite believing how that would have come about.

"Yeah. As in the mother of your child?" Emotion once again finds her words as they drip with anguish and maybe bitterness.

"How in the hell did Cassidy have a picture of the two of us from a party that was six years ago?"

As she tells me the incredulous story, I have visions of my ex lurking outside my building, following me, following *Piper*. Waves of unease and dread climb my spine. This is the same person who has been entrusted with my daughter eighty percent of the time.

I knew Cassidy was territorial, but I had no clue she had been stalking me since high school. As far as I can remember, I didn't meet her until college. It makes sense now. Of course it was her. She's trying to break us up. Stake her claim on me.

"Why do you think she gave you the picture, Piper?" I ask, needing her to come to the same conclusion.

She nods her head as if she knows where I'm going with this. "She threatened me with it. I think she was trying to end us," she says. "She implied that she was going to tell you I was a slut who likes to sleep around. She said you wouldn't want someone like that."

I guffaw loudly. "Nothing like the pot calling the kettle black."

I immediately regret my words and try to backpedal. "I didn't mean you're the kettle. I mean, you're not a . . . Shit, Piper. What more can I say? I'm sorry."

"I know what you meant." A sad smile darkens her eyes. "She told me she knew what went on at those parties. She was very . . . specific. And my nightmares all started flashing before me as brutally as if she were hitting me with her fists. She saw my reaction. I couldn't hide it. It was awful. And then I knew it. I knew the second she realized what really happened that night."

Her whole body visibly tenses and her tongue rakes over her dry teeth before she continues. "She laughed, Mason. She actually laughed about it. What person—what *woman*—could even do that?"

My hands come up to rub my face, the heavy stubble on my neck reminding me I've not showered in days. In all of my twenty-two years, I've never wanted to physically harm a woman more than I do this very second. "A goddamn monster, that's who."

How could I have been such a terrible judge of character? Even back when my dick was making all of the decisions, how did I not see through her bullshit then? "Don't you see? When she knew she wouldn't be able to use the picture against you, she found a way to use it against *me*. She's been jealous of you since day one, Piper. She'd do anything to break us up. Apparently that includes humiliating you and accusing me of rape."

Piper drains her cup and places it ceremoniously on the table. "It doesn't matter. I mean, I'm glad you weren't one of them. But you'll never look at me the same way again. You were there. You were just outside the door. You saw me like that. You can't un-see it, Mason."

She stands up and I stand with her, moving closer to her. "It doesn't matter to me, Piper. None of it. The way I feel about you—"

"It matters to me," she interrupts. She raises her outstretched hand, meeting my chest to halt my progress towards her. The harsh movement causes me to wince at the unwelcome pain on the tender flesh over my ribs. "I'm sorry you came all the way here, Mason. But for more reasons than you know, I can't be with you. It's better we found out now."

Desperation courses through my body, inexplicable sorrow flowing into my heart. "Better for whom? For you—so you can live in denial, knowing you could have had a chance at happiness?

Better for me, knowing I let the love of my fucking life walk away?"

Her breath catches and her hand comes up to press against her chest.

"That's right, Piper. I love you. I love everything about you. Even the parts you think are ugly and broken."

She looks physically pained. Her expression is tight with anguish and she steadies herself on the chair beside her. Her head shakes slowly and her eyes fall to the ground. I can feel her take an emotional step back. "No. I can't. I'm sorry. Please let me go."

Her words are daggers, sending stinging blows straight to my jugular.

As she walks away from me, I call after her one last time. "You won the bet then, sweetheart. What do you want?"

Her steps falter. She turns her head but doesn't make eye contact. "Nobody's a winner here, Mason."

I drop into my seat, the wind being knocked out of me as much as if I'd taken a tackle to the gut. I watch her get smaller and smaller as she walks further away, every step she takes tearing another piece of my heart out.

This woman was tailor-made for me. I'm certain of it. We were cut from the same fucking cloth. There is no way in hell I'm leaving Spain without her. But how in the world am I going to convince her when she's as stubborn as her older sisters?

As I sit, my thoughts are spinning. I'm trying to develop a plan to make her hear me when a couple walks by, catching my eye. A woman is talking to her male companion in Spanish words I don't understand. She stops suddenly and puts the man's hand to her pregnant belly. Their smiles stretch from ear to ear as they exchange what appear to be words of love and excitement.

Then it dawns on me.

No, it hits me like a ton of goddamn bricks.

She said there were more reasons she couldn't be with me. Her dad said she may never be able to be with a man who has a child. She's standoffish with kids.

Fucking hell.

The horrific possibilities rush through me. Did she get pregnant that night and have an abortion? Or worse, did the assault render her incapable of having children? *Oh, God*—the comment I made to her about kicking the guys in the balls so they couldn't have kids.

My chair tips over in my quick exit to run after her. She has to know none of that matters. If she doesn't want kids—we won't have them. If she does—we'll adopt.

But as I run through the busy streets, frantic to find her, one thought slows me down.

Even if she can get past this and allow herself to love me, could she ever accept Hailey? Because my daughter and I—we're a package deal.

There has to be some way to have them both.

Not able to locate Piper, I get out my phone and tap the screen. "Just one more favor. Please, Charlie?"

~ ~ ~

I spot her immediately. Well, me and all the other red-blooded males at the café. Her picture doesn't do her justice. She's stunning. Taller than average, her long dark-red hair bounces in carefree waves around her shoulders. She tucks it behind her ears, scanning the crowd until she spots me.

Her hazel eyes don't give much away as she studies me. We spoke on Monday of course, when I called her from Bruce and Jan's house. But I can tell she might be skeptical. My ears still hurt from the verbal lashing she gave me over the phone. Apparently, she had already seen Piper and had to step out of their hotel room to wring my neck, cussing me out not only in English, but in several foreign languages. Impressive.

I couldn't get a word in edgewise, not until Jan took the phone from me, explaining the gist of the situation to Charlie. Then upon my arrival, mere hours ago, she told me where I could most likely find Piper. She was dead on. I only had to wait for thirty minutes before she showed up seeking her daily vice. Charlie refused to give me the name of the hotel. I think she was afraid it wouldn't go well. Unfortunately, she was right.

She makes her way to my table, men parting like the Red Sea to let her pass as their tongues go wagging. She really is the spitting image of her once-famous mother. I wonder if she gets recognized for it over here. For me anyway, the anonymity here is refreshing, even for a lowly backup quarterback.

I stand and greet her. "Charlie. Thank you for meeting me." I hold out a welcoming hand, torn between offering her a drink out of politeness and getting right down to business.

I err on the side of chivalry. She does have a lot of clout with Piper, after all. "What can I get you?"

She shakes my hand, a strong confident handshake delivered with eye contact. Such a difference from the shrinking flower I'm in love with. It makes me happy to think maybe Piper has a protector in Charlie.

She takes the seat next to mine. "Nothing, thanks."

As I return to my seat, she assesses me. Not in a sexual way. Not in a confrontational way. Almost in the way you'd look at a stray dog from the pound when deciding whether to take him home or not.

"So, *you're* the one." She leans back in her chair, folding her arms under her breasts.

My frustrated hand runs through my hair. "I didn't do it, Charlie. I swear I wasn't one of them—"

She holds a curt hand up to stop my words. She's tall, but she's not a large woman, her petite, swan-like frame commanding far more respect than I gave her credit for. "That's not what I meant," she says. "I meant you're *the one*. Her chance at happiness. Normalcy. The one who is going to finally take her from me."

"What? No." I'm appalled she would think I'm trying to do that. But before I can defend my actions, I realize that's exactly what I'm trying to do. "Well, shit. Yeah, I guess that is pretty much what I want. But I only want to take her back to New York. I don't want to take her from her best friend."

She laughs. It's a throaty, sultry noise that causes heads to turn. "It's okay, Mason. It's great, in fact. I've been waiting for this day."

I look around. I've obviously missed something. "I'm confused."

"She thinks she's here for me. She's always thought that and I've let her. But it couldn't be further from the truth."

I draw my eyebrows at her, begging for clarification.

"I know Piper told you about me. Knowing her, it was probably to deflect questions you had about her behavior. Am I wrong?"

"No, you're not wrong. She really freaked out when she saw your—" My mouth clamps shut into a thin, regretful line. I'm not sure she knows about their confrontation.

"My father," she says. "It's okay. Piper and I tell each other everything."

I look at her out of the top of my lashes.

She nods. "Everything."

I roll my eyes at the insinuation. But I'm glad to know she has a friend like that.

Griffin. He's my Charlie. We've gotten each other through some tough times.

"If you know everything there is to know about her then maybe you can help me understand why she's running away from me. From this. Is it really because I was there that night, or is it because of my daughter, Hailey?"

Charlie's face breaks into a warm smile. "God, she's gorgeous, Mason. You better keep a short leash on that one when she hits puberty."

"You've seen her?"

"Of course. Piper showed me some pictures she had taken in the park." Compassion floods her eyes. "She doesn't dislike children, you know. It's just hard for her to be around them."

My heart sinks. "So something did happen after her attack."

She shrugs. "Not my story to tell," she says. "But I will tell you this—she's my kindred spirit, that girl. We've been through some shit, she and I. Things nobody should have to go through. But her staying here is wrong. She healed more in the few months back there with you than in the four years she spent over here."

My mouth opens and then closes. I stare wide-eyed for a full five seconds. "Really? I got the feeling the only thing I ever did was bring back her nightmares and stir up all the crap she was trying to forget."

"Don't you see, Mason? She needed that. She needed to confront her demons before she could move on from them. I've come to terms with what happened to me. Well, sort of. Okay, maybe not." She rolls her eyes. "I may be sleeping around Europe, and I'll always hate my so-called parents, but my past doesn't control me like it does Piper."

I take a drink of my tepid coffee, eyeing her speculatively over the rim of my cup.

"Whatever," she says, defensively. "Don't shrink me."

I hold my hands up in mock surrender. "Wouldn't dare to try."

"Smart man." She snatches my drink from me, removing the lid and taking a smell before gulping it down. I get the idea she doesn't much care where her next meal comes from. It pains me to think Piper could be the same way.

"I've made some calls," she says, putting the empty cup in front of me. "And I've decided I like you, Mason. So I'm going to help you. In this case our girl might not know what's best for her. It's clear to me she wants to love you. I'm just not sure she thinks she's capable of it."

"What can I do? Where is she?" Just hearing her say those words gives me hope.

"Not so fast. Let me talk to her first. She's going to resist, you know that, right? But you are good for her and I'm afraid she may never find another guy like you. You're a rare breed, Mason Lawrence, and I won't let her miss out on this opportunity because of me."

"What are you saying?"

She lets out a sigh. "I'm leaving. If I'm gone, she has no reason to stay."

"No, Charlie." I shake my head. "I can't let you do that. It's not the answer. Maybe you could go back to New York."

Her head swings violently from side to side. "I'll never do that. I don't belong there. But Piper does—with you. She's your responsibility now. Don't fuck this up or I will hunt you down and kill you with my bare hands. I don't care how impressively big you are."

She stands and I stand with her. "Give me an hour," she says, pulling a hotel key card out of her pocket and placing it on the table before me.

I offer her my hand but she pulls me in for a tight hug instead. I moan when her arms squeeze my angry, tender ribs. "Football taking a toll on you, big guy?" She laughs.

"Something is, but it sure as hell isn't football."

She gives me a questioning look and then she untucks my shirt, raising it to reveal the small area of red flesh on the right side of my ribs, just below my throwing arm. Her head tilts to the side as she studies what's there. "I'm not even going to pretend I know what that means, but it sure as hell better have something to do with our girl."

I smile down at her, tucking my shirt back in.

"You'd better wash it," she says. "It looks like pieces of your shirt fabric got stuck to it. Did you take the bandage off too early? They say four to six hours, you know. Just run warm soapy water over it and put a little ointment on it, then let it air out."

"You seem to know an awful lot about the subject." I raise an eyebrow at her.

"I'd show you, but then I'd have to kill you," she jokes.

"Listen, Charlie, if there's anything I can ever do for you . . ."

"Just take care of her, Mason." She smiles a brilliant smile and walks away.

"Count on it," I call after her.

black roses

I look at the key card and then at my watch. This is gonna be the longest fucking hour of my life.

chapter twenty-seven

piper

I stare at the sweaty girl in the mirror, watching her keep a punishing pace on the treadmill in a futile attempt to run from her past. Run from him.

It's ironic really, how fittingly accurate this is. I'm running on a treadmill—a device that by its very nature keeps you from moving forward.

It's better this way. He's a rising star. I'm a train wreck. He has a daughter to raise. He doesn't need a girlfriend who clearly needs parenting herself.

He has a daughter to raise. The words bounce around in my head as I struggle to keep that fateful day from overtaking my thoughts. I don't think about it. Ever. Except on one day every year. And today isn't that day.

I turn up the pace, making it impossible for me to think of anything but breathing.

Then I see her in the mirror, approaching me from behind. I don't miss Charlie's disapproving look when she spots my distance on the digital display. Our reflections have a stare down, then her lips start moving quickly, undoubtedly scolding me in her sister-like manner. But I can't hear her over the loud music so I point to my earbuds and shrug.

In slow motion, she dramatically raises her arm, pressing her finger on the button controlling my speed. She glares at me with a raised brow while repeatedly pressing the down arrow until the belt below me stops moving completely. Then she steps up on it, getting right in my face before ripping the earbuds from my ears. "Fifteen miles, Piper? Are you fucking crazy?"

"I do run marathons, Charlie. This should come as no surprise to you." I step off the machine, finding a towel to wipe my face.

She huffs and grabs me by the elbow, pulling me out of the hotel gym, all the way back up to our room. She doesn't say a word. Not until we are standing in front of the door. She holds her palm out. "Key," she demands.

"Where's yours?" I ask.

"Lost it."

I roll my eyes and take my key card out of my back pocket, handing it over to her like an obedient child. She looks pissed. Nobody wants to be on the bad side of pissed-off Charlie.

She opens the door, pushing me through and guiding me over to the bed. "Sit."

I look down at my brand new sweat-drenched workout clothes and ask, "Can I at least shower first, Mom?"

"No. You can't. Sit your stupid, skinny, stubborn ass on the bed and listen to me."

"You forgot steaming, as in mad," I say.

"Mad?"

"Yes, Charlie. You sold me out. You're the only one who could have known where I would be. You told him where to find me. Why did you do that?"

"Because you needed to hear the truth, Piper. When you were sleeping, he called me and explained the whole thing. The man jumped on a plane and flew across an ocean for you. And he did this knowing the worst parts of you."

"Not the worst," I say, my eyes meeting the ground.

"The worst," she repeats. "Everything else was just circumstantial."

"How could he ever see me the same way, Charlie? After he knows it was me on that bed. Having an orgy with multiple boys."

"God, you are so fucking dense!" she yells. "Can you not see that man loves you? He loves you despite all that shit. Hell, maybe he even loves you because of it. You're a survivor, Pipes. But until now, you've been surviving by running. Running from New York. Running from men. Running from yourself. It's time to stop."

My fingers lightly trace the outline of my bracelet. "I don't know if I can, Charlie."

"Yes. You can. And I'm going to give you the push you need to do it."

I eye her inquisitively. "What have you done?"

"It's not what I've done. It's what I'm going to do. I'm leaving, Piper."

"Leaving?" I tilt my head back to better study her face. "What, are you going to Australia with that douchebag after all?"

"Leaving as it I'm taking off by myself for a while. I'm going on a journey to find my inner peace."

"What? Why are you going all Buddhist on me?"

She smiles, pushing herself off the bed. "We've leaned on each other for so long, Piper. Even when you were in New York the past few months, I was still tethered to you. I'm not sure I know how to be me without you. You're my inspiration. If you can figure it out, maybe I can too."

"Figure it out?" I laugh. "Are you kidding? What makes you think I've figured anything out? Have you not even *seen* me these last few days?"

"You can lie to yourself all you want, my friend, but we both know you were like five seconds away from staying in New York until that bitch showed you that picture."

I sigh. She's right. I thought about it a lot on Sunday after waking up in his arms. Hell, if I'm being honest with myself, I thought about it long before that. But there are a hundred things that could go wrong.

She pulls her suitcase out of the closet. I spring off the bed to stop her. "Stop, Charlie. If you need to leave for yourself, fine. But you leaving doesn't change anything. I still can't be with him. I told you what happened when I tried. I can't be with *anyone*."

She rips her suitcase away from me, quickly dumping the contents of the drawers into it. "That's a choice you'll have to make, Piper. But you'll never know unless you try. You are twenty-two years old. You're never going to get this time back. When you are old and grey and on your deathbed, tell me this, will you regret not going after this once-in-a-lifetime love? If not, you're not as strong as I gave you credit for." She stops packing to look me straight in the eyes. "Remember—nobody can hurt you without your permission."

I blink, soaking in her words. "Now you're quoting Gandhi?"

The door to the hotel room swings open and my heart stops beating as Mason crosses the threshold.

"I'm sorry," he says to Charlie. "I couldn't wait an hour. I couldn't risk letting her run."

Charlie smiles at him and then turns to me. "He's a smart man. You'd be crazy to let him get away, Pipes." She pulls me in for a hug. A soul-crushing, heart-wrenching hug that reeks of finality. I've never felt this vibe from her before.

She really is leaving.

I hug her back with everything inside of me. Because no matter what happens after she walks out that door, I know our lives are changing forever.

She drags her suitcase into the hallway before the door slams shut behind her. The sound echoes dramatically off the walls as it leaves me alone with Mason in this room that's shrinking with every silent second we stare at each other.

"I'm sorry," he finally says. "I know what she means to you."

"It's okay." I shrug back my feelings. "I've been through worse."

His breath catches and his face looks pained as if my words physically hurt him.

"You look like you've had quite a workout."

I'm wondering if he's talking physically or mentally, but I don't bother asking. "Why are you here?" I say instead. "I already told you it wasn't going to work between us."

"I know you did. But I'm here to change your mind." He conspicuously stands between me and the door, his penetrating eyes begging me to listen.

"You can't." I retreat, going back to the bed while pulling the tight elastic band from my hair that's starting to give me a headache. I toss it on the bedside table.

"Piper, I'm in love with you." His hand comes to his chest, right over his heart as if to punctuate his declaration. "And it's a goddamn miracle. It's something I never thought would happen. I was happy with my life—well I thought I was anyway. As happy as

I could be . . . considering." He absentmindedly runs a finger along his scar. "Football and Hailey. That's all I needed. But the day I met you, all that changed. I knew I needed more. I don't care about your past. What happened, happened *to* you, Piper. It wasn't a choice. But this—today—this is a choice. You can't deny you have feelings for me. You may even love me. But you have to decide to allow yourself to."

Reluctantly, I shake my head. "Even if you could get past seeing me like that. On that bed with those boys. Even if all that didn't matter to you, I still don't think I could be with you."

"Why not, Piper? Do you think you're damaged goods? Because I can assure you, it's quite the opposite. It would be a privilege to be with you."

I'm exhausted. Emotionally. Physically. I'm tired of holding back with him. Maybe if I tell him, he'll realize once and for all that I'm right. I close my eyes because I can't stand to look at him as I bear my soul. "Because your daughter may always remind me of the one I lost."

The air is audibly sucked from the room and into his lungs. I hear him step across the floor before I feel the bed sink down next to me.

"You had a daughter? Oh, Piper." He runs a soothing hand down my back, landing it on the bed below, but still keeping his arm so close I can feel the heat from it through my thin running shorts. "Will you tell me about it?"

With my eyes still closed, I say, "You'll hate me if I do."

"I could never hate you, sweetheart. You were young. It's understandable, expected even that you'd have an abortion after what happened to you. And if you can't have kids now, we'll deal with it."

"No. You don't understand."

"Then make me."

"Mason . . . it's too hard."

He rubs my back again while I try to control my breathing that threatens to be out of control. "It's okay," he says. "I'm here. I'm not going anywhere."

I inhale. And exhale. And inhale. It takes me ten whole breaths before I can speak. And then—maybe it's his soothing hand on my back. Maybe the weight of my secrets has gotten to be too much. Maybe I'm just ready. Whatever it is, I start talking and words spill out of me faster than water from a broken dam.

"You know how hours, sometimes days later, you'll remember a dream? Well, that started happening more and more after the night of the party. I thought it was some normal part of puberty, dreaming about boys and sex. Then months later, I got the flu. Well, I thought it was the flu, but it didn't go away. My mom finally took me to the doctor in November, almost four months after the party. It's then when I found out I was pregnant. I didn't even know I'd lost my virginity."

"Oh, God, Piper."

He tries to comfort me, but right now, I don't want his hands on me. I scoot away from him and lean on the headboard, hugging my knees to my chest.

"My parents didn't even believe me at first. After all, they'd been through it with Baylor already. But it didn't take long to piece it together based on the estimated date of conception they gave me after the ultrasound. I didn't remember much about the night of the party. I just thought the few shots I took got me drunk. The friends I went with joked around about making out with random strangers and losing track of me for a while. I just thought maybe I'd done the same.

"My parents took me to the police, of course. But they basically told us there was nothing they could do because I didn't report it immediately. They said they'd go through the motions, fill out the paperwork and check out the residence. However, they said it would be a futile effort. After that, I started having different dreams. Dreams of fighting back. Maybe it was wishful thinking. Maybe it was more memories coming to the surface. But the thing is, I would never know who the father of my child was."

A sick feeling washes through me. "You'll never know what I felt the moment I saw that picture and Cassidy accused you of—"

"Shit." He blanches. He actually loses all color in his face that always seems to be tanned from the sun. "You thought I could have been the father. And then you thought I would hate you for aborting my child. Maybe even as much as you hated me for raping you."

My hand comes up to my mouth, covering the sob I feel welling up from deep inside me. "I didn't have an abortion, Mason."

Tears that have been building for over five years finally fall down my cheeks in an endless stream. Fire chokes my throat as I try to explain. "My seventeenth birthday was the day my daughter was born." I heave and hiccup my way through the words. I look up with tear-blurred vision to see what his reaction is.

I'm met with a broken face that mirrors mine. I haven't seen a man cry since the day my dad found out I was raped. I'm pretty sure Mason quietly sobbed into my back the night I told him about my assault, but watching him cry—seeing the sympathy and sorrow flow down his face and drop onto his jeans, that is entirely different. And it wrecks me. All at once, as if I'd been beaten over the head with it, I realize I don't want to do anything to make this man sad.

Our eyes lock and emotions swell between us. Suddenly and simultaneously we reach for each other, planting our knees on the bed beneath us as we embrace. And we cry. I cry five years' worth of tears. He cries for me. He cries with me. And oddly, it becomes one of the best moments of my life.

Minutes later, maybe hours, I've lost track of time, he lowers us to the bed and I settle into the crook of his neck. My arm swings over his chest.

He sucks in a sharp breath of air that has me wondering if I've hurt him. "Are you okay?" I stutter, my voice still thick with tears.

"I've never been better. And not even my defensive line could drag me away, sweetheart." He kisses my hair. "Can you tell me more?"

I nod into his shoulder. "I know I could have kept her. I'd seen Baylor do it. I'd *helped* Baylor do it. But she had loved her baby's dad. I didn't even know who my daughter's father was. He was just some nameless face in my dreams. I knew I couldn't stay in Connecticut or anywhere near it. I couldn't stay knowing I could run into any one of them and not even know it. Would they remember me? Ridicule me? Proposition me?

"I wasn't equipped to raise the baby by myself, or even with Charlie, and don't think she didn't offer. But I was afraid the baby would be a constant reminder of what happened. I didn't want to look at her like that—like she was the product of something horrible. I wanted her to grow up with two loving parents, not a single teenage mom with an ugly past."

The way Mason's chest rises and falls with each breath calms me. "So now you know why I don't celebrate my birthday," I say. "I didn't die that terrible night of my assault in August. My seventeenth birthday was the day I died. It's the day I gave up my daughter."

He struggles to steady his breathing, exhaling deep sighs into my hair. My smelly, sweaty hair that still reeks from my workout. He runs his thumb methodically over my knuckles, giving me the courage to say what I've felt for a long time.

"Ironically, on my twenty-second birthday, the day my daughter turned five, you brought the life back into me."

"Piper." He breathes my name like a prayer. He lifts my chin so my puffy, red eyes meet his. "Why did you think I would hate you?"

I shrug into his shoulder. "Because you have a daughter. Because you could have turned your back on her. You could have given her away, but you didn't. So how can you love someone who did?"

Air spurts from his nose in a quiet huff. "Is that what you think? Because you are sorely mistaken. What you did was the greatest and most selfless act of love, sweetheart. You gave up a piece of yourself so she would have the chance at a wonderful, happy life. It was the ultimate gift. Hate you? I'm not sure I could ever love you more than I do this very moment."

At a loss for spoken words, I squeeze his chest. He sucks in another painful breath and I shoot a questioning look at him. "Are you injured?"

"Not particularly," he says.

"What do you mean, not particularly? You keep wincing when I touch you here." I purposefully press my hand hard to his chest, by the ribs of his right arm.

Pain lines his face, causing me more than a little concern. I sit up and grab the hem of his shirt. I look at him for permission and he nods, rising up to sit on his haunches. I slowly peel it up his body, expecting to see him battered and bruised from football.

Instead, what I see brings more tears to my eyes. Now that the dam has burst, I question ever being able to stop it. And right now, I'm helpless to stop the raging flow.

There, etched on his angry, red, tender skin, is one word in script.

Roxane.

samantha christy

chapter twenty-eight

mason

"What? How?" she asks, a finger carefully tracing the red edges of the tattoo.

I give her a casual shrug. "I had a lot of time to kill while I waited for a flight over. I would have gotten your real name, but I know you like to remain anonymous."

Her tear-rimmed eyes shoot up to mine. "You spelled it right."

"Of course I did." I smile. "How could I not after hearing you go on and on about the travesty of the misspelling from the play to the movie." I wink at her and her face softens into an easy grin. It's the first sign of hope she's given me. Aside from trusting me with her story.

She's come this far, I wonder what will happen if I push her a little more. I sweep her hair back, revealing her rose tattoo. "Will you tell me about yours?" I ask. "And this?" I touch her bracelet.

She looks down at the dark rosebud entwined in leather on her wrist and I can almost see the memories flashing behind her eyes. "Charlie gave it to me the day my daughter was born. She was the only one, other than my parents, who knew where I was. Everyone else, including my sisters, thought I'd taken the spring semester of my junior year abroad. But in reality, I went to a place my parents found in upstate New York. A farm where an older couple took in people like me—pregnant teens who wanted to hide from the world. I helped them with farm chores and cooking and they let me stay for the duration. There were two other girls there when I arrived. One left within a few weeks, the other shortly before I did. We didn't exchange addresses or phone numbers." She stretches her head to one side, her hand coming up to grab the back of her neck as tension visibly rolls off her body in waves. "Nobody wanted to remember."

I push a lock of stray hair behind her ear and ease my fingers around her neck to replace hers, hoping I can help knead the stress away as she tells her painful tale.

"I got to hold her for an hour before they took her away."

I can tell another sob burns deep in her throat, but she's trying hard not to let it out. She closes her eyes, suffocating grief settling in and grabbing hold of her. "That was the best and worst hour of my entire life." She swallows hard, wiping balls of tears away with the pads of her thumbs. "She was beautiful. She had a full head of dark-blonde hair and beautiful blue eyes. I know all babies have blue eyes, so I don't know what color she ended up with. But it didn't matter to me. She was perfect in every way."

Heartache stings me as thoughts of losing my parents blur my vision. "You never saw her after that?"

She shakes her head. "It was a closed adoption. I knew it would be better that way. Especially after seeing her. I couldn't imagine getting updates and pictures but not being a part of her life. What if something terrible happened to her? I don't think I would survive knowing that. So I spent the whole hour studying her flawless face, explaining why I couldn't be her mom. I cried a river that day, after they took her from me. When the nurse came in and picked her up out of my arms, she took my entire life with her. But I knew it was for the best. I knew she deserved more than a teenage mom who could barely get out of bed most mornings.

"I don't know a lot about what happened to her. But what I do know is that she went to a heart surgeon whose wife was a nurse who planned on staying at home with the baby. They were in their thirties and had tried for ten years to have a child before adopting." She nods her head. "It was a good place for her."

I finger her bracelet. "And this?"

"Right," she says, watching me twist the charm as if she'd forgotten it. "Charlie drove up with my parents that day. I cried in her arms for hours, giving myself that one day to grieve. And then I promised never to cry over it again. That's when she gave me the bracelet. She knew there would be no pictures. No reminders of my daughter. I was confused as to why she got me the charm of a black rose. To me, it represented death—*my* death. But she told me it wasn't a black rose at all, it was simply a pewter rosebud—a perfectly formed rosebud that had yet to bloom. She said every time I looked at it, I would think of the baby and how she will flourish and grow and blossom into a brilliant young woman with a life full of endless possibilities because of the sacrifice I made."

I thread our fingers together and squeeze her hand in mine. "I knew I liked Charlie. She's bright, that one."

Piper quietly laughs. "So she's always telling me."

She looks down at our entwined hands like she just realized we were touching. "That was the day we decided to go to Europe. We planned to go the next year after graduation. It was the perfect solution. I didn't want to risk running into my daughter. Because I swear, Mason, her face is etched into my brain for all of eternity and I think I would recognize her anywhere. Also, I didn't want to have a run-in with any of the boys who attacked me. And Charlie—well you know *her* reasons for leaving."

I can feel her relax, tension leaving her body with every word she speaks. This is therapeutic for her. And with each part of her story that she reveals, I see pieces coming back together to make her a whole person.

I brush her hair aside, exposing her neck. "What about your tattoo, sweetheart?"

Her hand comes up to rub it like I've seen her do so many times before. "I got it on my eighteenth birthday. A budding rose, a reminder of what I hope would become of her; but a black rose for the death of the relationship we would never have."

She becomes quiet. After talking and crying for almost an hour straight, the room becomes strangely silent. Strange but wonderful. And I realize for the first time, that *she's* holding *my* hand instead of me holding hers. Her small fingers rub over my knuckles, sending erotic, and totally-inappropriate-for-the-situation, sensations straight to my groin.

"So that's it. You know everything about me. Except maybe that I had a dog named *Mutt* when I was little. He ran away when I was seven."

"*Mutt*, huh?"

She nods, still rubbing her fingers over mine.

"Are you okay?" I ask, searching her eyes for answers. After all, she just tore open all her wounds and bared her soul to me.

Her eyes narrow as she ponders the question. "I think I am. Is that crazy?" Her burgeoning smile warms not only my heart, but other parts of my anatomy.

"No. It's not crazy at all. Talking helps. Believe me. And I'm here anytime you want to talk about it. In case you haven't noticed, I've got some pretty big shoulders you can use for crying on whenever you need them."

Her smile falls and my budding erection threatens to abate. "Do you think you'll ever be able to see me as a woman, like you did last weekend, and not the girl on that bed?"

Suddenly, I have visions of Saturday night. Of her writhing under my tongue, pawing at my sheets as she watched me bring her to orgasm. I drop her hand and stand up at the side of the bed, pulling down my pants and boxer briefs in one fell swoop, my hardened dick springing proudly when it's released from its confines. "I don't think that will ever be a problem, sweetheart."

Her eyes go wide at the sight of me. Not in fear. Not in panic. But in appreciation; passion. And it's damn sexy.

Her hand twitches as if she wants to reach out and touch me. My dick jumps at the very thought of her hand gripping me. But then as quickly as my hopes were raised, they are dashed.

"I can't," she says.

I nod. Of course she isn't ready for this. She needs time. I berate myself, reaching down to pull my pants up, but her words stop me dead.

"I just ran fifteen miles. I need a shower." Her heated gaze skates over my chest, then lower.

Holy shit.

The way she said it. It wasn't a blow-off or an excuse. It was an invitation.

"I could use one myself," I say, stepping out of my shoes and pulling off my pants. "I haven't showered since Monday. What day is it?"

She laughs. "Wednesday."

I look to the bathroom and then I raise my eyebrows at her. Her teeth grasp the edge of her bottom lip, causing even more of my blood to run south. A slow smile tugs her lips upward. "I've never had any bad dreams about showers," she says. "Just like I never had them about kissing."

I smile and it feels as if my face could crack open. "And look how good you are at kissing." I take two steps over to her and hold out my hand.

She looks at it with dark and lidded eyes, her lips twitching into a shy yet sensual grin.

My heart all but leaps from my chest.

I pull her into the bathroom and turn on the shower. It's nice. It's got several nozzles including one of those rain showerheads on the ceiling. As it warms, I slowly remove her running shorts and tank top, peeling them off her body to reveal inch after beautiful inch.

It's bright in here. Daylight is shining through the window and strong fluorescents are overhead. I notice very faint white lines on both sides of her stomach. I fall to my knees and place my lips on them, tasting her salty flesh. I show her I love every part of her, even those parts she thinks are damaged.

I have damaged parts, too. Maybe together, if we add up all of our good parts, we can make one whole unblemished person.

She runs her hands through my hair as my mouth devours the intoxicating scent that clings to her skin. Out of the corner of my eye, I see steam coming from the shower, so I stand and walk her backwards into it until her back hits the wall.

Water pours over her, wetting her hair and running down to stream off her breasts. I've never seen anything more beautiful.

My lips claim hers in a wet, demanding kiss that spawns provocative noises from her. We kiss long and hard, exploring each other with our tongues and mouths until we can no longer breathe, our lungs burning from the lack of air.

While my hands probe her breasts, hers grip the back of my hair, tilting my head back so her lips can assault my neck. She stops wandering when she finds my pulse, sucking the fleshy skin of my neck into her mouth. My dick throbs against her and I worry it will cause her to panic. Instead, she surprises me, reaching between us, gripping me with her small hand, running her fingers along the sensitive head, driving me absolutely fucking insane.

Everywhere she touches me, electrical currents pulse beneath my skin. Her hand slowly moves from root to tip and my body aches with the need for release.

My fingers trail down her water-slicked stomach, down through her soft curls to find the hot wet heat of her center before slipping inside her. Her breath catches somewhere between a sigh and a moan.

I don't have to remind her to look at me. Our eyes meet with a force that sends shockwaves through our bodies, her hunger and passion matching my own. The base of my spine tingles as my body is battered by sensation after sensation. I bite down on my lip, tasting the blood that results from an endeavor to hold off my inevitable finish. This isn't about me. This is about giving her a memory that can overshadow the nightmares. I pull back, my steely erection falling from her soft, wet hands as I try to even out my breathing.

"Do you have a condom?" she asks, her eyes raking my body with a heat so intense it practically melts me.

Shit. Those five words almost make me come on the spot. *Hell yes, I do.*

"Wait here," I say, a desperate edge of command lining my voice. I step out of the shower, soaking the tiles of the bathroom and the carpet of the bedroom with the water rolling off me. I all but slip and fall on the bathroom floor in my haste to get back to her, catching myself on the counter in what I'm sure is a comedic, naked splaying of my enthusiasm.

Her laughter echoes off the walls of the stone shower, making my heart expand with the notion that she wants this.

Before I'm even back in the shower, I've ripped the condom from the wrapper and rolled it on my rock-hard penis. As soon as I step back in, she catapults herself into my arms and I lift her up, cupping my hands beneath the soft globes of her ass as she clasps her legs around my waist.

My hardness touches her between the legs, squished between our slickened bodies. She looks down to see how close we are to being joined. "Yes," she says, water spilling over her shoulders, adding warmth to the heat surging between us.

She looks back up at my face, a crackle of energy passing between us. Raw. Hot. Carnal. I've never seen her eyes make such urgent demands. And as she works her fingers through the back of my hair, she whispers, "Yes, Mason."

Fuck. I never knew my own name could sound so sexy.

"Sweetheart," I breathe into her, my lips closing in to savor her mouth once more, reminding her it's only ever going to be me. "God, I love you, Piper. Only me. Always."

As we kiss, her hands probe my shoulders, my neck, my back, sliding effortlessly over my wet skin, building me to a point of no return. I break the kiss and tilt her hips up as I enter her, the snug grip of her tight walls stroking me to the brink of ecstasy.

I can't help but groan when I hit the end of her. The feeling of skin on naked skin, me fully seated inside her—I've never felt such deep satisfaction. Such unadulterated joy.

I watch her with every roll of my hips, gauging her response as I start a slow and steady rhythm in and out of her. I can feel the impending climax begin to tighten my balls and tense my gut. I push her hard against the wall, keeping one hand under her bottom while I move the other one between us.

Her eyes never leave mine. Not even when they glaze over as her passion crests and she convulses in pleasure around me. Ragged murmurs of gratification leave her lips as her pulsating body milks a vigorous orgasm from me.

I brace us against the wall, my legs barely able to keep me standing. Then I bathe in the potent feeling of warmth and contentment that is stronger than I can ever remember. Her head falls to my shoulder, our bodies still connected as I cherish the steady beat of her heart against mine.

Shivers course through her when the water turns tepid. Without breaking our seal, I carry her delicately over the puddled floor of the bathroom. I take her out to the bed, grabbing a towel along the way.

I gently dry her from head to toe as she watches me with clear, pure, vibrantly green eyes that are creased with a smile. I swear to God I can see my future in them.

"Are you okay?" I ask.

"I'm perfect."

A wave of relief resonates through me along with her words. Her smile makes my spirit soar with shameless delight. "I have a feeling we're going to be very fucking clean for a long, long time to come."

She laughs, then her eyes narrow in amusement. "Did we even *use* soap?"

A grin full of hungry anticipation twitches my mouth. "I guess we'll just have to take another one later."

She crawls under the duvet and I wrap my arms around her from behind, warming her further.

"I lied to you, you know," she says.

I feel a deep twist of my heart and a momentary twang of hopelessness in my gut. "Lied?"

"Yeah. I didn't really win that bet." Her transparent voice is thick with emotion and tantalizing with need.

I smile into her neck. "Oh?"

She nods against me, pushing her back even tighter into me. She takes a cleansing breath, a sure sign something wondrous is about to fall from her lips. "I didn't win the bet. You did. I'm moving to New York."

My heart pounds, threatening to penetrate the walls of my chest. Quickly, I climb over her, settling myself on her other side so we are face to face—inches from each other. "Is that a euphemism, sweetheart? Because if you are messing with me, I might just fucking explode."

A brilliant glow spans her beautiful face. "No, I'm not messing with you. And yes, I'm moving to New York."

I take her head, cupping it in my hands. "I need to hear you say it, Piper."

A powerful rush of emotions flood through me, her tear-rimmed eyes mirroring mine when the words I'd only dreamed of spill from her lips. "I love you, Mason Lawrence."

chapter twenty-nine

piper

Champagne is served to us even before the rest of the plane has been boarded. I protested the first-class tickets on principle, but Mason insisted, as these were the only available seats unless we wanted to wait another day. Plus he said I'll have to get used to this sort of thing.

I'm not complaining. I mean, I've lived in some pretty questionable places and resorted to more than my share of flying-by-the-seat-of-my-pants transportation over the years. Still, I'm not sure I could ever get used to this. To being treated like royalty.

Mason reaches over and plucks my untouched drink from my tray, downing the bubbly liquid before calling the attendant over. "She'll have a Jack and Coke. Please do not open them, we'll take care of that."

"Right away, sir," the English-speaking beauty says.

He winks at me and I melt. He could have told me I'm being ridiculous. He could have tried to convince me to quit being suspect of every drink not prepared before me. He could have even said he'd protect me if anything like that were to ever happen again. But he doesn't. He doesn't say any of that. He gets me. And I love him for it.

"So where do you want to go when we land?" he asks.

I've been thinking about that very thing. "Skylar's," I tell him. "I'm going to have my sisters meet me at her townhouse. There are a few things I need to tell them."

He picks up my hand, kissing the back of it; pride seeping from his lips and permeating my skin. "Want me to be there with you?"

I shake my head. "I need to do this alone, Mason. I owe them explanations about my behavior. And I suspect you won't want to be anywhere around when my protective older sisters find out what happened to me. Tears will be shed. Cuss words will be yelled. Shit will get thrown around the room."

"Fair enough." He smiles pensively at my attempt at a joke. "But after that, Piper—where do you want to go after that?" He looks nervously at my hand still enveloped by his. "Will you come back to my place? Will you move in with me?"

My eyes fail to hide my surprise. He might as well have asked if I wanted to meet the Pope. My answer would be the same. I want to, but I'd be nervous as hell and afraid I'd fuck it up.

"I know it may be hard for you at first, when Hailey is around. And I don't expect anything from you—she's *my* responsibility. But you two are the most important people in my life. I want you both with me. Full-time if I have anything to say about it." His deep mesmerizing voice is filled with promise.

My drinks get placed before me and I break the seal on the small liquor bottle, not bothering to mix it with my Coke before I throw my head back and let it burn its way down my throat.

"Just think about it, sweetheart." He puts a hand on my thigh, warming my skin through my jeans as I look out the window, watching as we throttle down the long runway that begins our journey home.

Mason sleeps most of the flight. We didn't get much shut-eye last night. But we did get clean. Several times over. I smile upon the clouds below just thinking about it.

He was so gentle; always making sure it was about me. He didn't need to. After the first time, I knew it would be okay with him. Well, in the shower anyway. It's almost as if I was being cleansed in more ways than one. Every time I stood under the warm water with him, letting it cascade over us, it washed away a little more of the filth I'd kept with me all these years.

My body is still reeling—still aching with the evidence of our love.

Love.

I'm in love with a man. I never thought it would happen. I never thought it *could* happen. He made me say it. He made me say it over and over until we both believed it.

I'm still scared though. Scared of so many things. Not the least of which is being around Hailey. He said it himself, on more than one occasion, that he wants more time with her. If I'm with him—living with him especially—despite what he says there will be certain expectations. I'm no stranger to raising a child. Maddox and I were joined at the hip for a few years. But a little girl?

Mason loves me. I know that. But I'm not naïve enough to think he would ever choose me over her. Nor should it be that way. He and Hailey are a package deal. I do understand that. And I hope like hell my feelings for him will eventually spill over into feelings for her. But what if they don't?

I look over at him. His head is turned to the side, resting comfortably on a plush pillow in his reclining seat. He looks peaceful. The five-day shadow surrounding his sexy, normally well-groomed beard has turned from scruff to fuzz, making him appear older than he is. His eyes twitch in a dream and I think I hear him mumble my name over the thrum of the engines. It hits me square in the heart and I know I never want him to dream of anyone else but me.

"You're beautiful," he says, startling me. I wasn't aware he was even awake as I watched him. He runs a finger across my jawline. "You get more beautiful every time I look at you."

I giggle. "It's the love goggles. My hair is a mess and I've no makeup on. I left it all in New York."

"You mean you left it home," he says, optimism gleaming in his smile.

I look up at him, my throat tightening with emotion. I nod. "Yes. Home."

"Have you decided exactly where that's going to be yet?" His hopeful eyes beg for the answer I'm not ready to give.

"Mason." His name becomes a sigh. "I need some time. I'm still trying to process everything. I want it to happen—us living together—I really do. But I need a minute to catch my breath, okay?"

The strong line of his jaw tightens, and his gaze falls to our entwined hands. "Okay. But can I see you tonight, after you talk to your sisters?"

"Aren't you exhausted?"

His roguish half-smile hypnotizes me with a single upturn of his lips. "I'll never be too tired to see you. It may be a difficult night for you and I want to make sure you're okay."

"Fine." I roll my eyes at his protectiveness. But inwardly, I love it. I love having someone who considers my every need before their own.

My heart sinks a little thinking how that used to be Charlie. I don't even know where she is right now. She said she needed time on her own. Time to not rely on me to justify her very existence. I don't even have a phone on which to stalk her. I wonder if she will ever be lucky enough to find a guy like Mason. Surely more of them exist. My sisters and I couldn't have landed the only three selfless men on the planet. The three of us had to trudge through some deep shit to come out on the other side. Charlie—she's still entrenched in her hell.

My eyes become heavy and I drift off thinking of my best friend.

~ ~ ~

"Thank God."

Mason's words wake me, along with the jolting bumps of the plane's wheels touching the ground.

I look at him with sleepy eyes and laugh. "Not a fan of flying?"

"It's not that," he says, squeezing my hand. "I never thought I'd get you back here. A few days ago, when I found out you left, I thought you'd never come back. I thought you got on that plane and took my fucking heart with you." His icy-blue eyes stare into mine. "So yes—thank God."

My heart surges forward in my chest, clawing its way to him. Still not completely at ease saying those three little words, I tell him, "I'm glad I'm moving to New York."

He nods, his features etched with emotion because he gets me. "I love you too, Piper Mitchell."

He reaches his hand behind my neck and pulls my face to his, kissing me with such intensity and passion that several rows of people around us break out in cheerful applause.

"Sweetheart?" he says, his voice extracting me from my daze.

I look up to see him standing, waiting for me to exit my seat. It appears he kissed me so senseless, I didn't even feel the plane taxi up to the gate.

He grabs our one small bag from the overhead bin, its only contents being my new running shoes and a jacket, along with a few toiletries I'd picked up. We left most of our sweaty, stinky, days-old clothes on the floor of the hotel room.

I smile once again at the shirt he's wearing. It was the only one at the hotel gift shop that fit him. And even at that, his biceps are stretching the material to within an inch of its life. The horizontal red and yellow stripes with the Spanish coat of arms decorate the oh-so-touristy t-shirt.

And knowing he's totally commando under his jeans makes me want to find a shower before he drops me off at Skylar's.

He catches me appraising him. Raising an eyebrow, he says, "Do you think the airport has any showers?"

Yeah. It's creepy how much he gets me.

~ ~ ~

Two pairs of red puffy eyes stare back at me, mirroring my own that are drowning in emotion. Telling my sisters was hard, but just as Mason promised, each time I talk about it, I push the demons further and further away. And the uninhibited cry I shared with them was cathartic.

"I just wish I would have known," Baylor says. "I would have helped you like you helped me."

I shake my head. "You knowing back then would have made it worse. You had a child. You would have tried to talk me out of it. But the circumstances were different, Bay. I just couldn't."

"Cassidy is a flaming bitch," she says. "As if things couldn't get worse for you, she tried to sabotage your relationship by throwing Mason under the bus."

Both of my sisters lunge forward and capture me into the couch with a long hug, muttering apologies along with words of encouragement.

"I knew it," Skylar says, pulling away and wiping her eyes. "I knew all along Mason would be good for you—that he was the one."

Baylor narrows her eyes at her. "Since when did *you* become the romantic sister?"

We all share a much needed laugh.

"So you're staying?" Baylor asks.

My nod is met with shrieks of excitement.

"You can work for me. Be my assistant," Baylor says.

"Oh, no," Skylar protests. "You're not taking my best waitress."

"Better than Mindy?" Baylor asks.

"Mindy's good, but she sleeps with the customers. Sometimes that's not so good for business."

Skylar's comment reminds me of Charlie. I think of my best friend while they continue arguing over who's going to get me to work for them.

"Hold on, guys. I've got a lot to figure out, but none of it will happen tonight. Right now I just want to call my . . . my, uh, boyfriend."

More juvenile squeals come from my sisters.

Boyfriend. It's the first time I've said it out loud. It felt good. Hell, it felt great. Agreeable. Right.

"I need to borrow a phone to call him. As you know, I lost mine."

Skylar shoves hers at me and I tap on the screen until I find his name. It only rings once.

"Skylar, is she okay?" His concern jumps through the phone.

"Not Skylar. Piper. I lost my phone, remember?"

"Right. Are you okay? Can I come over?" he asks.

"Yes. That's why I'm calling. I mean, if you're not too tired."

"Tired?" he asks, his voice laced with maniacal amusement. "Go to the front door, Piper."

"What?"

"Just go, sweetheart."

I walk to the door, my sisters trailing behind me. When I open it, Mason is leaning against the railing, holding out his phone, shrugging.

I look down at my watch. He dropped me off three hours ago. Then I look at the ridiculously tight t-shirt he's still wearing, and I laugh. "You couldn't at least change out of the silly shirt?"

"Silly?" he asks, looking down on it, running a hand over the shirt like it's a fine piece of art. "This is my new favorite shirt. It's a reminder of the day we finally got together. I'm never getting rid of it."

Skylar practically runs me down on her quest to reach Mason. She hugs him hard and he has to catch himself on the railing to keep them from tumbling down the porch steps. "Thank you, Mason. Thank you for bringing her back to us."

They smile and share a look. I know her words run deeper than the obvious meaning.

Baylor pulls Skylar away so she can have her turn at Mason. "And you guys call *me* a romantic?"

When my sisters are done accosting my boyfriend, we go back into the townhouse. Baylor and Skylar both reach for their purses and share another one of their looks. "We're going to Mom's to get the kids," Baylor says. "We'll probably stay for dinner."

"Yeah, and Griffin is out of town on a shoot, so nobody will be home for *hours*," Skylar adds.

Mason laughs, turning to me. "Your sisters are very subtle."

I hand Skylar her phone on their way out. Mason eyeballs the exchange. He pulls his phone out of his pocket and hands it to me. "Here take mine. I don't want you without one. I'll pick you up a new one tomorrow."

I stare at his phone in my hand. Allowing another human to access one's phone is a display of utmost confidence and loyalty. I'm touched that he trusts me with this potentially sensitive information.

"I can get my own phone, Mason."

He pulls me into a hug, smelling my hair as if he hasn't seen me in three months, not three hours. "I know you can. But for once, maybe you could let someone do something for you."

He leans over and sweeps me up into his arms, carrying me over to the stairs. "Like this," he says. "I know you are perfectly capable of climbing these stairs on your own." He walks up the steps with me in his arms, as if my weight is of no more consequence than a pillow—or maybe a football. "But what would be the fun in that?"

I giggle, burying my face in his neck. Even through the lingering scent of the hotel soap, he smells inherently Mason. Manly. Rugged. Spicy.

Heavenly.

chapter thirty

mason

I walk straight through her bedroom into her ensuite bath. "Tell the truth," I say, a sly grin tugging at the corners of my mouth. "You've been fantasizing about ripping this t-shirt right off me since I put it on."

I stand her on the tile and she gives me her best dramatic groupie performance. "Oh. My. God." She fans herself with her hand. "It's Mason Lawrence. You are so hot. Pick me, babe. Please, pick me!"

My eyebrows shoot up and I pull her close. Close enough for her to feel my burgeoning erection. "Call me that again," I insist.

She narrows her eyes at me as she calls me by my full name. "Uh, Mason Lawrence?"

"The *other* name," I utter seductively between gritted teeth.

I watch it dawn on her as she replays her words in her head. Then she blushes. "Babe?"

I nod. "That's the one. Say it again."

Smiling, she rises on her toes and puts her hands behind my neck, pulling my ear down to her mouth. "I want to rip that Spaniard shirt right off your smokin' hot body," —she pauses intentionally as her hot breath flows over my neck— "*babe*."

"Shit," I belt out in passionate desperation. "Shower. Now."

I look around the large bathroom. When Griffin redecorated, he gave the guest room an ensuite almost as ornate and grand as the master. I eye the Jacuzzi tub in the corner and raise a brow at Piper. "Or maybe a bath?"

"Bath?" She glances over at it and then back at me. She shrugs seductively and then nods. "I don't have bad dreams about baths."

I pick her up and she wraps her legs around me. She crushes her mouth on mine, her full sexy lips raw and unapologetic as she forcefully demands more with her hot and hungry tongue. My lips part for her and she moans into my mouth.

I walk backwards, Piper still in my arms, draped over me. When the backs of my legs hit the tub, I sit us down on the edge, reaching over to turn on the water, our mouths never breaking the seal.

When I turn away to plug the tub, she says, "As much as I love this shirt, I'd rather see it on the floor." She traces the outline of the flag, my muscles twitching underneath the cheap cotton.

She's become bold and confident with me in the last twenty-four hours. And it's more than a little sexy. I make quick work of following her directions and deposit my shirt in a crumpled ball at her feet.

Her gaze falls to my tattoo. Her fingers follow the path of her eyes and she touches my still-tender skin. "Did it hurt much?" she asks.

I lift my hand, pulling back her hair before I place a kiss on the rose etched into the skin below her right ear. "Not as much as yours," I whisper.

Her eyes tear up, fully understanding the deeper meaning of my words.

Then she smiles. "You know, if we don't work out, you may have a hard time finding a woman named Roxane. It's not a very popular name. Maybe you should have gotten something more common, say 'Kate' from *The Taming of the Shrew*. I wanted to play her, too."

"Kate, huh?" I laugh. "There isn't a shred of doubt in my mind that I will ever need to find someone else to fit my tattoo. I'm in this for the duration. All four quarters. You are my Super Bowl, sweetheart. As far as I'm concerned I'm your first, your last, and everything in between."

She nods, failing to hold back the tears that have pooled in her gorgeous emerald eyes.

With my thumbs, I wipe the wetness from her cheeks. Then I kiss her. I kiss her like there's no tomorrow. I kiss her like she's the very air I need to breathe. "I love you, sweetheart," I whisper, moving my mouth to her neck. "I love you, my beautiful Roxane." I take her shirt off and lower my lips to her sensuous collar bone. "I love you, Piper Mitchell."

She hastily removes her bra and pulls me up for another kiss. She makes love to my mouth the way I want to make love to her body. "I love you too, babe," she breathes into my mouth.

A groan of approval vibrates through me as my hands seek out her breasts at the same time that she finds the zipper on my jeans.

We swiftly remove each other's jeans. I take a moment to fish a condom out of my pocket. I place it next to us before I step into the tub and turn off the water. Then I offer her my hand.

She carefully steps in beside me, her flesh erupting in goosebumps from the change in temperature. "I want to show you how much, Mason." She looks at me with lidded eyes full of carnal need. Then she takes hold of my hard shaft and lowers herself to her knees in the warm water.

I sigh, victory and caution battling in my head. I sit on the edge of the tub. "You don't have to show me like this, Piper. There are other ways—"

Her lips on my dick shut me up as heated licks of sensation torment me. A ragged gasp of satisfaction coats my throat. I reach down and run my fingers through her hair, being careful not to pull her hard against me.

As she takes me fully into her mouth, my world narrows to nothing but her touch. And when her hand reaches between my legs to cup my balls, I brace myself against the side of the tub as every cell in my body erupts with need. "I'm gonna come, sweetheart."

Her eyes dart up to mine and I detect a fleeting look of unease.

Some girls are simply not comfortable with this. Girls who do this all the time even. Girls who haven't been traumatized. I pull myself back, removing her lips from me. But I'm beyond the point of no return, so I grasp myself in my left hand, pumping a few times until shudders wrack my body. Then the tidal wave of sensation she built within me squirts spectacularly onto her chest and into the water.

With a soft sigh, the edges of her lips curl. "Next time, I'm finishing that," she says.

My eyes close and my languid body slumps back into the wall above the tub. I've never been more content or at ease with a woman in my life. "Next time, I'll let you."

I sink down into the tub, taking much needed air into my lungs. I look at the fruits of her labor still splayed gloriously across her body and I reach for the soap. I squirt some into my hands, getting them lathered up before I lunge forward and clean her body of me.

Her breasts heave into my hands as I wash them. Her rosy nipples are hard under my fingers; her breath hitching when my thumbs rake over them. "My turn," I say with a wry grin.

I pull her against me, and in one swift movement, I reverse our positions and hoist her hips up onto the ledge of the tub. I press her back into the wall before I get up on my knees and worship her breasts with my mouth. I tease and tantalize her stiff peaks while she gazes down on me in appreciation. Pleasuring her while she watches me makes this whole experience better. Hotter. More real.

She spreads her thighs in invitation and my fingers find her sex. She's saturated with both her own juices and the bathwater. I reach a hand around her back, pulling myself close to her as I steady her in place. My mouth follows a seductive trail from her chest down across her taut belly until it joins my fingers at her center.

I'm fully aroused again at the very sight of her—glistening with want of me. My eyes divide their time between watching her face and watching my fingers penetrate her. Her hips rock when I drag my tongue over her quivering clit. Her hands toy with my hair, tugging it furiously when my fingers hit just the right spot inside her. I focus all of my energy on that precise location as my tongue continues to lave her.

Her legs tighten and the tips of her fingers scrape across my back, heightening my arousal with her punishing nails. My groin jerks in greedy expectation when she throws her head back and rides my tongue as she convulses with pleasure around my fingers.

Before her body even finishes shuddering, I've put on the condom and am pulling her down into the water so she's straddling me. We look deep into each other as she sheaths me with her. She gasps as I fill her completely, touching the very end of her. Her mouth comes down hard on mine, joining our bodies in so many places, I can't tell where I end and she begins.

This indescribable kiss. This surreal connection. It's like coming home. It's fucking paradise. I pull back to see that she feels it, too. Tears fill her eyes and I can almost see the light overflowing from her soul.

She's healing. With every kiss we share and every touch she allows, she exorcises more of her demons.

She takes total control, working herself upon me. Her petite, slender body begins to rock back and forth on mine as I thank God that this glorious creature came into my life. My heart thunders and emotions saturate me when I realize this woman is mine.

I want her to feel every single sensation I'm feeling. Inside and out. Spurred by the frantic need building deep inside me, I reach a hand between us and rub slow circles on her sensitive bundle of nerves as she rides me.

Her raspy breathing and strained moans drive me harder as my other hand helps to control her thrusts upon me. I can't stop my long ragged groan of release when I feel her clench and tighten around me. Her orgasm tears through me, plunging us simultaneously into the depths of pleasure as we call out to each other with guttural cries of ecstasy.

black roses

I hold her tightly against me, my body curving protectively around hers, our heartbeats racing as she burrows her head into my neck. We stay like this, flesh on flesh—wet, warm and soft—as we slowly calm our breaths.

A surge of extreme emotion assaults me and I know my life has forever changed because of her presence in it. I never want to be without her—without *this*—ever again.

So I tell her. In every way possible.

Over and over.

chapter thirty-one

piper

I stare down at his phone. The information I have at my fingertips is astounding. It's a window into one's soul.

I fight the urge to pick it up. Look through his pictures. Read his texts. It would be so wrong. But in some way, I feel he expects it of me. Like giving me his phone was an invitation into his deep, dark secrets. Maybe it's his way of telling me how much he trusts me; how much he loves me. Maybe the way I prove the same thing to him is by not letting curiosity get the better of me.

I turn the phone face down on my nightstand and let my mind wander to earlier.

After our bath we laid in bed. He cuddled up behind me as we brainstormed 'safe' places to make love. Pretty much any surface in the bathroom, kitchen or living room made the list.

I can't believe I was talking with a man about sex and smiling about it. Laughing even. How he has truly changed my life is staggering.

I twist the charm on my bracelet—for the first time not out of anxiousness, but in wonder. In hopes that she will one day find a man as incredible as Mason.

My attention is drawn back to the nightstand where his phone vibrates once, indicating a text. It's done this several times since he left earlier.

I know he wanted to stay. I could see it written all over him. But he never asked. And for that I was grateful. I need time and he's giving it to me. Not to mention we're both pretty jet-lagged despite the early hour. After all, it's well past midnight in Barcelona.

When he left, just before seven o'clock, he said he was going for a quick run at the gym before heading home. Then the plan is to meet at Mitchell's NYC for Sunday brunch where he'll bring me a new phone. How he's going to manage purchasing a new one before noon on a Sunday is beyond me. I guess he has connections or something. Maybe this is all part of the stuff he said I would have to get used to if I'm going to be with a famous athlete.

When his cell hums once more, I resist the urge to turn it over and peek at the text. Instead, I head downstairs to get a snack before turning in for some much needed sleep.

On my way, I pass Aaron's nursery. I flick the light on and let my eyes travel around the room. I take in the crib, decorated with muted tones of blue and green; the rocking chair that has a matching blanket carefully laid across the back; the changing table that has tiny outfits of all colors folded on the shelves beneath it. I stare at the collection of family pictures on the wall.

I make a decision right now to hold Aaron the next time I see him. To pick him up and study his little face; smell his sweet baby scent; touch his tiny hands.

Then maybe I can even work my way up to Jordan.

black roses

I look in the mirror over Aaron's dresser and wonder, not for the first time since I've been back, if my baby looks like her. Like Jordan. After all, Baylor and I could sometimes pass for twins if not for our age and slight cosmetic differences. I touch the tiny piercing on my nose and glance at my black hair tips. Of course, Jordan is only eight months old and my daughter is more than five years old. But in my mind, she'll always be the pink and perfect newborn I got to hold for those precious minutes before I gave her away.

I turn around and exit the room, switching off the light on my way out. I need to eat and sleep.

Tomorrow I can take care of the rest.

∼ ∼ ∼

Incessant buzzing wakes me from sleep. Exhausted, I look at the clock, disappointed to see it's half past eight and I've only been sleeping for a few minutes. Someone is calling Mason. I pull the pillow over my head and let it roll to voicemail, not daring to answer his phone.

Seconds later it dances across the bedside table with another call. This time, I pick it up and glance at the screen to see it's not a number from his contacts. I have no idea who's calling him. I put the phone down again and roll back over.

It vibrates again. I sigh, reaching over to shut it off. But I notice it's the same number that has already called twice. Someone really wants to reach him. Maybe it's Janice Greyson. I lazily smile thinking he might not have her saved as a contact.

Then I wonder if it's not Mason who's getting the call—but *me*. Maybe Mason is trying to call me from home. Does he even have a landline there?

With a pang of traitorous guilt, I swipe my finger across the screen to answer. "Hello?"

"Oh, thank God," a young girl's voice belts out nervously. "Is this Mason Lawrence's phone?"

I sit up in bed, protective of my new boyfriend. Some fangirl has gotten his private number. "Who is this and how did you get this number?"

I hear tender cries and squeals of pain coming from her end of the phone. "I need Mr. Lawrence," she begs. "There's been an accident and I can't get a hold of Ms. Whitmeyer."

"Ms. Whitmeyer?" My mind cycles through an index of who I know. "Oh, you mean Cassidy?"

All at once everything clicks together.

Nervous teenager. Wails of a child in pain. Accident.

"What happened? Is Hailey okay? Where are you?" I belt out in panic-driven succession.

"She fell down the stairs. I'm only the sitter. I just got here. I didn't even know the gate was open. I can't reach her mom. Is he there? What do I do? Should I call 911? Can you help me—"

"Stop!" I yell through her frantic ramblings. "What's your name?"

"A-Amanda," she stutters.

"Amanda, you need to calm down or you can't help her. Where are you?"

"At Cassidy's . . . uh, Ms. Whitmeyer's apartment." She rattles off the address of a building I'm familiar with. Skylar lived there when I came back for Baylor's wedding last year. I stayed with her. It's within blocks of a hospital.

I still hear Hailey's cries so I know she's conscious. "Is she bleeding?"

"There's a cut on her head above her eye and she's holding her arm."

In my mind I try to calculate the time it might take for an ambulance to get there. I make a split-second decision. "Amanda, I'm Piper Mitchell, Mason's girlfriend. He's not here right now, but I want you to listen to me. You need to take her to Lenox Hill Hospital. It's only two blocks from where you are. Hang up and take her to their emergency room right now. I'll find Mason and meet you there. Do you understand?"

"O-Okay. I think I can do that," she says tentatively.

"Amanda!" I command her attention. "You just take care of that little girl. I'll find Mason and Cassidy."

"Yes, ma'am," she says, right before I disconnect the call.

I leap out of bed and pull on some clothes that are still neatly folded in my dresser, never having had a chance to pack them in my haste to leave New York. I put my messy hair into a ponytail and pick the phone up off the bed when unease strikes me.

Oh, God. Did I do the right thing? What if she has a neck injury and Amanda moving her is a terrible idea? I take a deep breath and call Baylor as I go downstairs.

"Shouldn't you be otherwise occupied at this hour?" she asks, laughing through her greeting.

"Baylor, you have to go to Mason's apartment and get him." I grab my purse off the table and dart out the front door. I'm surprised to see the sun has just now set, the sky still a purplish hue of brilliant colors. I realize my body clock is still out of whack, having traveled to Spain and back in less than a week.

"Find him? God, Piper—you've been back together for one day and already you're fighting?" She huffs an exasperated big-sister sigh into the phone.

"No, we're fine. He left hours ago, but he left his phone with me. I have no way to contact him." I run out of breath, talking too quickly while my feet propel me as fast as they can towards the subway. "It's Hailey. There's been an accident. She fell down the stairs and the sitter can't reach Cassidy."

Baylor draws in a sharp breath. "Oh my God. What can we do?"

"Go find Mason. He was going for a run at the gym but he should be home by now. Do you know the address?"

I hear her relaying information to others in the background. "Skylar does. We'll call Gavin and leave right now. But, Piper, why aren't *you* going to find him?"

"I'm going to Lenox Hill to meet Hailey and the sitter."

"Good. Good," she says, pride coming through in her voice. "I'll call you when we find him. You're doing the right thing, little sister. You can do this."

It takes me twenty minutes to get to the hospital. Twenty minutes that feels like an eternity. She's not even two years old yet. In fact, I'm pretty sure her birthday is next week. What if she's badly injured? It will devastate Mason.

I call Cassidy from Mason's phone. It rolls to voicemail. I don't tell her who's calling, but it won't take a rocket scientist to figure it out. "Cassidy, get to Lenox Hill Hospital as soon as you get this. Hailey's had a fall." What else could I say? I don't have any more information.

Running into the emergency room, I barrel past people waiting to register. "I need to find a little girl," I say to the nurse behind the glass partition. "Hailey Lawrence. Is she here yet? Is she okay?"

The nurse, who is obviously overwhelmed by this Saturday-night influx of people, gives me an annoyed look.

"Are you Piper?" a voice calls from behind me. I turn around and gasp at what I see. A girl, who can't be more than sixteen, has blood all over her shirt.

"Amanda?" In absolute horror, my wide eyes trace the smeared blood that spans her chest and stains her arm. My hand meets my chest, my heartbeat thundering against my palm. "Oh, God. I thought you said she just had a cut."

"She did. She does." She stares down at her clothes as if just now realizing how bad it looks. "Hailey was scared. She was crying and rubbing her head on my shirt as I carried her here. I think it looks worse than it is. At least I hope so." Her eyes fall to the floor. "I had just arrived at Ms. Whitmeyer's place. I was only there for five minutes. It's my first time sitting for her. I swear I didn't even know there *was* a gate, or that it was open. I went to put my books down and she walked away for a second. *One second.*"

I pat her back. "It's not your fault, Amanda. The gate should have been closed and you should have known about it. Is Hailey okay? Where did they take her and why aren't you with her?"

"They took her back a few minutes ago. They wouldn't let me go with her. Plus, I don't think it would have helped. She doesn't know me. She kept screaming for her Mama and Dada."

I turn around and ask the perturbed nurse at the desk, "Can I please get some information about Hailey Lawrence?"

She shuffles around a few clipboards before turning her attention to me. "That's not my job, Miss. Somebody should be out shortly. But unless you're family, it won't matter anyway. Are you family?"

I ignore her question and point behind me. "I'll be right over here. Please have them come get me."

Nurse Ratched doesn't acknowledge me, going back to handing out forms to the increasingly large line of people before her.

Amanda and I find an empty bench, parking ourselves as close to the front counter as we can get. "We should call Hailey's grandmother," I say, remembering Cassidy once said she would stay with her on occasion. "Do you have her number?"

Amanda gives me a deer-in-headlights look. She shakes her head. "I'm locked out now. All of the emergency numbers were on the refrigerator. Mr. Lawrence was the next one down after Ms. Whitmeyer's number. But the front door locks when you shut it. I forgot about that when we left. All my stuff is still there." She fidgets with the seam on her jeans. "Do you think I'll be in trouble?"

I look at her and see how scared she is. I almost forgot she's just a kid herself. "How old are you, Amanda?"

"I turned fifteen last week."

I remember fifteen. Fifteen was good. Carefree. Fun. And I was babysitting Maddox a lot of the time, who was about as old as Hailey is now. I put a reassuring hand on her knee. "No, you won't be in trouble. It was an accident."

She takes a deep breath, swallowing her relief. Then she narrows her eyes at me. "Don't you have Hailey's grandmother's number? I mean if you're Mr. Lawrence's girlfriend and all."

"Yeah, well that's a fairly new designation." I look down at my phone. Mason's phone. I scroll through the contacts hoping to find another Whitmeyer. No luck.

"I'm looking for the family of Hailey Lawrence."

I spring to my feet at the words, looking over to see they came from an older male doctor. He's got longish hair, like he's not had time for a decent cut lately. Lines that reveal his age dent his forehead, and his white doctor coat sits over a wrinkled t-shirt of a sixties band. Not very professional if you ask me. Maybe he was called in on his night off.

He's not smiling.

Shit.

I almost trample a few people in the waiting area on my way over to him. Amanda follows closely behind me.

"Me," I say, trying to look like I belong here. "I'm with Hailey Lawrence."

He eyeballs me, taking in my nose piercing, my messy ponytail and my clothing that I didn't bother to color-coordinate in my haste to leave the townhouse. "And you are?" he asks with a raised brow.

"Piper Mitchell," I say, leaving it at that.

"Your relationship to the patient?"

I sigh, glancing over at Nurse Ratched. "Um . . . I'm her father's girlfriend."

"Girlfriend," he says flatly. "I'm sorry, young lady. I can't discuss a patient with anyone but family."

I look at the phone in my hand, willing it to ring with news that Mason is on the way—Cassidy even. "I have her dad's phone," I say blindly, as if that somehow qualifies me as family.

He gives me a hard, unwavering stare.

"He gave it to me because I lost mine," I explain desperately. "And now he doesn't have one and I'm trying to find him. I mean, I have sisters who are out looking for him. And Cassidy, uh, Hailey's mom, is out and also can't be reached." I gesture to

Amanda, who is still standing behind me. "Hailey's babysitter brought her in. Please, can you tell us if she's okay?"

He shakes his head and pulls a business card from his coat pocket. "I'm sorry, Piper, is it?" He hands me the card. "Have her mom or dad track me down when they arrive."

Someone comes through the double doors behind him and I hear a child screaming. It's the same gut-wrenching, high-pitched shriek I heard through the phone. I point to where the awful sound is coming from. "That's Hailey," I tell him. "She's back there all alone. Can't you hear her crying?"

"She's not alone," he says coldly. "There's an aide with her."

"An *aide*? You mean a stranger." I raise my voice at him, causing more than a few heads to turn. "She's not even two years old yet and you've got her surrounded by strangers. She's obviously hurt." I motion to Amanda's blood-stained shirt. "She's probably scared to death with all the medical equipment and unfamiliar faces. You have to let me see her."

The doctor holds up a hand as if he knows I'm about to charge past him. "Those are the rules. If her parents don't show up soon, a social worker will be called."

"A social worker?" I shout. "But that would just be another stranger. She must be terrified. Please let me see her."

The door behind him swings open again and Hailey's piercing screams echo through the waiting room. He looks behind him. "I have patients to attend to." He nods at the card in my hand. "Have them find me." Then he walks off through the double doors that require a special badge to open from the outside.

I stand stunned; unable to move. I feel the wetness run down my cheeks as I think of a little helpless girl alone and scared. Does she feel abandoned?

Did my daughter feel that way when I gave her away?

My heart sinks into the pit of my stomach as my back hits the wall and my body slowly slides to the unforgiving concrete floor.

A gentle hand touches my shoulder. I look up to see a nurse who's wearing scrubs with teddy bears on them. Her eyes echo everything I'm feeling. She holds her hand out to help me up. Then she leans in close and whispers, "Come on, honey, some of us know when to break the rules."

My hopeful eyes snap to hers.

"But only one of you," she says, peering around me to Amanda.

"Will you be okay out here?" I ask Amanda.

"Yeah, my mom is on her way. I called her before you got here."

"Good. Thanks, Amanda. You're a good babysitter. You did everything right."

She gives me an apologetic nod as the nurse swipes her card, sneaking me through into the back.

With each step, the traumatic cries become louder. I hear the dull drone of the old doctor talking behind a curtain, and we quickly move past it. The compassionate nurse pulls me through an open door into an actual room with walls. She dismisses the aide who is trying to calm a scared and vulnerable Hailey.

I didn't know what to expect if and when I actually got to her, but when she sees me, her reaction melts me. Her expression changes instantly, as if my walking into the room is the best thing that has ever happened in her entire two years on this earth. "Pie-pie!" she belts out somewhere between a cry and a prayer.

She holds up an arm, the one that's not splinted to her body, rendering it incapable of movement. A bandage spans her forehead, gauze wrapping around her thin tangles of curls to the back of her head. Big, thick balls of tears catch on her lashes before spilling over to her cheeks. She hiccups between her cries, revealing just how long she's been at it.

I try not to gasp as fear grips my throat, overpowering me. Instead, I paste a calming smile on my face and walk over to the hospital bed, that's really more like a crib. "Can I?" I look at the nurse, gesturing to the broken little girl on the bed.

The nurse smiles. "Of course."

Hailey starts climbing over the railing with her good arm to get to me. When I pick her up, she clings to me so hard we practically become the same person. My face falls to the top of her platinum curls and I inhale her sweet angelic scent.

"It's okay, sweet pea," I breathe into her hair, using her father's endearment to help calm her.

"Hailey boo-boo," she whimpers into my shirt.

I nod into her hair, holding back more of my own tears while being careful not to touch the side of her head with the bandage. "Yes. Hailey has a big boo-boo. The doctors will fix you, sweetie. Maybe you'll get a big Band-Aid with a princess on it. Or maybe a pretty pink cast we can decorate with markers and stickers."

I'm not sure how much she understands through her continued tears. But she's not screaming anymore, and for that I'm grateful. I cover her ear with a gentle hand and ask, "They will fix her, right?"

The nurse gives me a reassuring smile. "Crying and screaming—those are actually good signs. It means she most likely doesn't have a brain injury. But she'll probably need a few stitches." She smiles down at Hailey, moving a piece of hair away from her face. "Her gorgeous curls will cover any scar. And she'll need an x-ray of her arm to check for a fracture."

Beeping noises come from outside the door. "Will you be okay in here?" she asks.

I nod, and then through the lump in my throat, I say, "Yes. I think we both will."

Her face bleeds compassion. "I'm Sadie, by the way. Don't let Dr. Warner bully you. You belong here. I'd say her daddy is lucky to have a girlfriend like you."

"Thanks."

She makes her way to the door. "Don't be surprised if she falls asleep from exhaustion. It'll do her some good. When her parents get here, we'll proceed with the tests." She shuts the door quietly on her way out. A window partially covered by blinds remains the only thing separating us from the rest of the emergency room.

I sit down on the chair next to the bed, Hailey still molding her body to mine as her breathing starts to even out. I run soothing strokes down her back and in no time, just like Sadie said, she falls asleep in my arms, hiccupping every so often as her body settles into slumber.

Carefully, I pull Mason's phone out and text Baylor to see what the holdup is. Almost immediately, it vibrates with a call. I answer in barely a whisper. "Baylor, where is he?"

"I can hardly hear you, Piper," she says in a loud voice, as if her volume will make up for mine. "Mason wasn't home so we called the gym and they said he only ran for a short time. Maybe he's on his way home now. Skylar is waiting outside his building and Gavin and I are backtracking to the gym. Maybe he decided to go back to Skylar's after his run. We'll check there, too. What have you found out? Is Hailey okay?"

"She's asleep for now," I whisper, looking down upon her delicate head. "They think she'll be okay, but they can't run tests until a parent is here. Please—find him, Bay."

"You can bet on it, Pipes. You just take care of that sweet girl until he gets there, okay?"

I nod, another viscous knot hitching my voice. "You can bet on it," I say before hanging up.

~ ~ ~

Hailey jolts me awake with her pained cry, the warmth between our bodies confirming we've been like this for some time. A glance at the clock on the wall tells me we both nodded off for a few hours. It's almost midnight. And no Mason. No Cassidy.

I check Mason's phone. It has a few texts from my sisters, who are still looking for my M.I.A. boyfriend. I curse myself for breaking my phone and leaving it on the sidewalk last weekend. If it weren't for that, Mason would already be here and Hailey would be having the test she needs to make her better.

"Shhhh," I breathe into her hair. I rub her back and tell her everything I can remember my mom telling me whenever I would get hurt. I wonder if the pain medication they gave her is wearing off. I wonder why nobody has been by to do anything for her.

"Want Dada," she whimpers into my shoulder.

"Daddy will be here soon. I promise, Hailey."

I look down at Mason's phone again, giving me an idea. I open up his playlist and scroll down until I find it. The song Hailey was humming that day in the park. I press play and turn up the volume, hoping it will distract her from the pain.

She looks up at me and her little lip quivers. Her nose runs and I dab it with the cuff of my sleeve. I start singing along with the song, not caring what my amateur voice sounds like when my only audience is a two-year-old.

One big fat tear rolls down her face, right before her lips turn up into a precious untroubled smile. The smile that sends strong gripping hands through my body, taking a powerful and eternal hold of my heart.

samantha christy

chapter thirty-two

mason

I'm conflicted. I'm awed. I'm speechless.

I want to barge in the room and take my hurt daughter into my arms. The primal need to protect her—protect them—is strong. But what I'm witnessing through the window in Hailey's private room is nothing short of a miracle.

Piper has my daughter in her arms; the type of embrace shared by a mother and child. She is swaying back and forth, rocking Hailey in a gentle calming motion. When Piper turns her body slightly to the side, I can see her mouth moving. It looks like she's singing.

I crack the door slowly and quietly so I don't alarm them. The music hits my ears and I smile. How did she know to play this song? It's not the music that takes my breath away, it's her voice. I haven't heard it since the day I first met her when she was singing in my car. My feet are cemented to the ground as I listen to the love of my life sing and comfort my fragile daughter. I see Hailey's little arm gripping onto her for dear life. My heart is overflowing with joy watching them bond.

The doctor assured me there's no major damage. Maybe some stitches and a splint or cast for her arm. And while the father in me wants to walk over and take Hailey in my arms; the man in me knows this moment is too important for me to interrupt.

When I saw Skylar standing outside my building, running towards me with worry etched on her face, I knew something terrible had happened. I thought maybe it was Piper. Finding out my baby girl was in the emergency room ranked right up there with how I felt after my parents' accident. Flashes of them battered and dying petrified me as Skylar and I raced to the hospital.

This became one of those times being recognized was truly a blessing. The nurse buzzed me back without question and a doctor appeared almost instantly to give me an update before I even made it back to her room. The news was hopeful, and wasn't even cause enough for Skylar or her family to hang around and miss a night of sleep, so I sent them all home to hug their own children, promising to update them if anything changed.

Now, standing here in the doorway, watching the two of them together—I see my whole fucking future in this room.

Hailey shifts in Piper's arms, spotting me leaning against the door frame. "Dada!" she squeals, reaching out to me.

In two swift steps, I'm in front of her, gathering her small, broken body into my arms. After a long embrace, I survey the damage on her battered body. Tears sting my eyes when she starts crying, mumbling indecipherable two-year-old words about her hurt arm and pounding head.

"It will be okay, sweet pea. Daddy's here. The doctor will be in to fix you up soon. Then we can go home. Would you like that?"

She sniffles up at me, nodding her head.

I look over at Piper, who has given us space to share a father-daughter moment. "I can't even begin to thank you for being here. Are you okay?"

Her glossy eyes glance down at Hailey as her hand comes up to cover her heart. She nods, tears spilling from her brilliant green eyes. I swear, beyond the tears, I can see something happening. And I think it's called healing.

There is a bustling in the room behind me. The doctor and nurse have come in wheeling a tray table with blue paper covering it. "Mr. Lawrence, we're here to do Hailey's stitches," Dr. Warner says.

The nurse explains the procedure, telling us the worst part will be the administration of the local anesthetic.

They allow me to hold a screaming Hailey tightly in my arms while they use a needle to numb her forehead. Then they give her a few minutes to calm down and let the drug do its job before putting in the stitches.

I take the time to question Piper about the accident. "Tell me what you know about how this happened."

I listen in horror as she recalls every detail; from the babysitter's frantic call until I walked into this room. I absorb every piece of information, but my mind can't help replaying one bit of it over and over again.

The gate was left open.

I have visions of my baby tumbling helplessly down the stairs. I shake my head in anger, wanting to ring Cassidy's neck for allowing this to happen. "And no word whatsoever from Cassidy?" I ask. "She left my daughter with a brand new sitter and doesn't even bother to answer the goddamn phone?"

Piper looks at me with compassionate eyes. For Cassidy's sake, I hope she's laid up somewhere in this hospital, or I'm liable to kill her with my bare hands.

"We're ready to proceed now, Mr. Lawrence," Dr. Warner says. "You'll need to put her on the bed for this. But you can hold her hand. It looks like she'll need five stitches."

The nurse lowers the tall sides of the bed, allowing me full access to her while they work on her head.

"She's numb," the nurse assures me as they prepare the instruments. "This won't hurt her, but it will probably scare her, so anything you can do to distract her would be beneficial."

Piper steps behind me, holding my phone up for me to see. It has Hailey's favorite song on the screen. "Your turn," she whispers in my ear. I can hear the smile in her voice.

With my left hand, I encompass Hailey's entire forearm. With my right hand, I reach back and lace Piper's fingers with mine. "Together?" I ask?

Then, as Hailey gets stitched up, we sing. Our voices fit together almost as well as our bodies did earlier.

The second time we play it, the nurse joins in, making Hailey smile. The door remains slightly open, and I wonder what passers-by must think about our impromptu performance of the song made famous by a Disney movie.

They finish the stitches, placing a much smaller bandage than before on her forehead. She looks more like my little girl again.

Piper puts a hand on top of the one of mine still covering Hailey's. "You did a great job, sweetie. You are very brave, just like the princess in that song."

Hailey smiles, hearing Piper compare her to a princess. She removes her hand from under ours and her little fingers grab Piper's. "Pitty finners," she says.

Piper proudly displays her deep-blue fingernails as if she's suddenly become a hand model. "Why, thank you, Hailey. Blue is my absolute favoritest color in the whole wide world. Do you want to know why?"

Hailey nods her head in wonder.

"Because it's the color of your eyes," Piper says, smiling at my daughter, then looking at me, her emerald irises speaking all the words her lips are forbidden from saying in present company.

I love you, I mouth to her.

"Yeah, I'm really glad I moved here," she says, with a secret grin only I know the meaning of.

"Oh, you're new to New York?" the nurse asks her.

Piper blushes. "No, I pretty much grew up here, but I didn't move here until recently."

"Okaaaay." The nurse's confused look makes us laugh. "We need to get an x-ray of this little girl's arm. We can bring the equipment in here, but it will take a few minutes and you'll have to wait outside." She gives me a sympathetic look and says quietly, "She'll probably cry and you may not want to see it, so this may be a good time for you to complete the paperwork out front. But don't worry, I promise to take good care of her."

The door swings wide open and a technician wheels in a large machine. I lean down and give Hailey a kiss on her head. "We'll be right outside, sweet pea. They need to take great big pictures of your arm to see your boo-boo." I take Piper's hand and lead her away.

Hailey starts to tear up. The nurse with teddy bears on her scrubs tries to calm her, but the further away we get, the cries turn into screams and my hearts starts breaking.

"Go," Piper says, seeing my face that's swimming in despair. "You don't need to watch this. I'll stay right here. You do what you need to do so we can get her out of here."

"You sure?" I ask, looking at my whimpering baby girl through the window.

Piper's hand touches my arm, sending a warm comforting feeling coursing through me. "I've never been more sure."

My broken heart surges with love for this woman as I kiss her cheek and then walk away, being escorted out front to give them my insurance information.

I'm led through the double doors to the full-on commotion of the crowded ER.

"Ma'am, we can't let you in there like this!" a man yells.

"My baby is back there, you stupid prick. Let me go!"

My head snaps over to the familiar voice. Cassidy is being restrained by a hospital security guard. She looks gorked out, like that night at the movies. I put the clipboard down and rush over to her. "What seems to be the problem here?"

"Mason!" she belts out. "Tell this meathead to let me in."

I look at the guard, who swipes a finger across the tip of his nose several times and then gestures back to Cassidy.

I take a step closer and see it—the faint trace of white power on the edge of her nostrils. "What the fuck, Cass?"

She struggles to free herself from the guard. "My baby is back there. She needs her mama." She barks at him, "Let. Me. Go!"

I shake my head at the guard, letting him know to keep his grip. "Cassidy!" I raise my voice and hold my palm out in front of her to stop her repeated ramblings. "The only reason your baby is here is because you left the goddamn gate open. Were you doped up then, too? How dare you put my daughter in danger like that.

And how could you leave her with a sitter and then go off the fucking grid for *five* hours? What kind of mother does that?"

"How can you be so sure it was me and not, uh . . . Miranda? And what about you?" She maneuvers closer to me with the guard still latched onto her arm. I can smell the rancid mixture of vodka and drugs coming from her every pore. "Your stupid little bitch called me because she couldn't find you. What were *you* doing, Mason? Don't pretend like you're Prince-fucking-Charming when you were off banging some other groupie."

My jaw drops at her hateful, accusing words and I become aware that more than a few people are staring at our exchange. I even see a few phones come out.

Shit.

"Sir," I speak to the guard, "Can we take this somewhere a little more private, please?" I nod at the kid taking video of us as if he's filming the next Emmy-winning documentary.

The security guard looks around the waiting area to see the attention we've managed to draw. "Come on," he says, grabbing Cassidy's arm and parading her through the sea of onlookers as she throws a tantrum that I'm sure will be displayed all over the internet by sunrise.

We're escorted to a private room near the nurses' station. He shuts the door behind us and releases Cassidy, pointing to a chair while staring her down. Like a petulant child, she stomps over to it and sits down melodramatically.

"First off," I tear into her, "the babysitter's name is Amanda, not Miranda. Jesus, Cassidy, do you even know who you are leaving her with?" I shudder to think she's not bothering to screen the people she's entrusting the care of our child to.

"Whatever." She rolls her eyes. "Who cares what her name is. Can we get back to why I can't see my own daughter?"

The guard's eyes ping-pong between us, seeming more interested in our conversation than doing his job.

I step closer to get a good look at her eyes. "You're stoned out of your mind, Cass, and probably drunk, too. You can't see her like this."

The door to our private room swings open with such force, the handle puts a dent in the drywall. A tall man, much too thin for his frame, bursts into the room. Before he even speaks, I take in his bloodshot eyes and the ashy-grey hue of his skin. He looks emaciated, like he belongs in his own hospital bed.

"What the hell is going on?" His eyes dart around the room, and he sniffs incessantly as his gaze settles on Cassidy. "I thought we were here to check on the kid."

"Check on *the kid?*" Rage boils my blood and my hands clench into tight fists as I walk across the room towards him. "Are you referring to my not-even-two-year-old daughter, who was abandoned by her mother and her drug-dealing boyfriend?"

"I suggest you back off, asshole," he says, puffing out his gaunt, skeletal chest to try and make himself look larger. I look him up and down, noting he's a different guy than she was with the night at the movies. But both seeming equally as drugged up as she is.

"How many guys are there, Cassidy? Are you bringing them around my daughter?"

"You chose to walk away, Mason," Cassidy says, defending her actions. "Who I bring around isn't your concern or your problem."

"Not my concern?" A muscle twitches in my jaw as unrelenting fury adds venom to my voice. "She's my daughter, Cass. There *is* no concern greater than her. I didn't walk away from

Hailey. I would never walk away from my child. I walked away from *you*."

Cassidy's nose starts to run and she pulls a tissue from her purse. "What about Snow White? You seem awfully concerned about *her*."

My hard, corded body vibrates with tension as I keep her companion in my periphery. I take a breath to calm myself. The last thing we need here is more of a scene. "Piper is my girlfriend, Cass. Despite your attempts to break us up. That isn't going to change. Well, until she agrees to become my wife."

Cassidy squeals so loud she makes her date jump. "Wife? Are you fucking kidding me?" An icy-cold bitterness contorts her face.

"Is that what this is all about?" I flick my nose. "Me moving on? Because you're delusional if you think I will ever get back with you. And you sealed that deal when you tried to mess with Piper."

She tries to get up, but the security guard puts his hand on her shoulder, forcing her back into the chair.

"Get your hands off her!" her date barks at him, shoving him away from Cassidy and hard against the nearby wall.

Then it all happens in the blink of an eye.

He and the guard start to scuffle and the guy reaches for the guard's gun. Before he gets a finger on it, I tackle him to the floor, pinning him face down with my knee in his back. That's when I notice several small packets of white powder have fallen from his pocket in the time it took me to wrangle him to the floor.

Another guard bursts into the room, pulling his gun on me. I keep my weight on my knee, not letting the prick out from under me, but I hold up my hands in surrender.

"Not him," the first security guard says. He nods to Cassidy's drug-dealing boyfriend on the ground beneath me. "*Him*."

I get up, leaving the dirt-bag to the two guards, one of whom has radioed for the police. I look over at Cassidy whose only concern seems to be the drugs lying on the floor. A trickle of blood trails from her nose as she stares at it.

My stomach clenches when it becomes all too clear. *My kid's mom is a junkie.*

"I have to get back to my daughter," I tell the guards. I grab a piece of paper and pen from the table in the lounge and write my name and number on it, handing it to one of them. "My name is Mason Lawrence. My two-year-old daughter took a fall and is being treated here." I nod to the piece of paper. "That's my private number. If you need me for anything, call me. But you'll have to restrain me, too, if you want to keep me from my family any longer."

The guards look at each other and nod, one of them still keeping the scrawny asshole in a choke hold. "We know who you are, Mr. Lawrence," the guard who saw it all go down says. "You are free to go, but the police will want to get a statement."

"Thank you," I tell them. I turn to Cassidy on my way out. "If you ever want to see Hailey again, you'd better get clean."

She falls to her knees, crying and begging for me to stay. The other guard holds her back as I leave the room and shut the door on her and her pathetic snivels.

My nerves are completely shot as I wade through the people vying for position to see what's going on in the room I just left. My hands are shaking and my heart races a mile a minute. I can't have Hailey see me like this. I make my way out the emergency room doors into the welcoming burst of fresh outdoor air. I race around the corner before anyone can follow me, and then my hands falls to my knees to catch a much needed breath. I stay here for a few minutes, breathing the cool air in and out until my body no longer trembles with anger.

On my way back in, I see an all-night coffee cart and stop to place my order. Piper must be on the brink of collapse. At least I got a few hours' sleep after my run. Exhaustion hit me like a ton of bricks the second I got out of the shower at the gym. I went to lie down for a minute in the owner's office, but I passed out until almost midnight, when I woke up to a massive crick in my neck from the lumpy sofa.

I return to Hailey's room to find the splint removed from her arm; replaced by a small arm brace.

"You okay?" Piper asks, making me realize how wrecked I am by what just happened.

"Will be," I say, putting the two coffees on the bedside tray before I walk over to pick up Hailey. "How's our little angel?"

"She's going to be fine." Piper smiles at our embrace. "It's not broken. Just a contusion, I think they called it. A bone bruise. The brace is so she doesn't hit it on something and hurt herself. She's going to be just fine," she reiterates. "We all are."

With Hailey in my arms, I walk over and pull Piper into our hug. "You were great tonight. A real lifesaver. I don't know what I would do without you."

"Maybe you never need to find out," she says, smiling down at Hailey as her hand traces my shirt over my new tattoo.

"I love you, Piper Mitchell." I lean down to kiss her on the top of her head.

"I love you, too, Mason Lawrence."

Relief rushes through my body; my soul. Relief over Hailey being okay. Over Piper being back where she belongs. Over the three of us standing here like a real family.

I sit down, Hailey now sleeping in my arms, and I reach over and grab a coffee cup from the tray, offering it to Piper. "I brought you a latte. It's been a long night. Thought you could use it."

She looks at the cup, studying it intently before turning her attention back to me.

I give her a reassuring smile. "My eyes never left it, sweetheart. Not even for a second."

Her hand slowly rises to take the cup from me. She opens the lid and pulls it to her lips, taking a drink as her eyes remain locked on mine. Her tired eyes. Her alluring eyes.

Her trusting eyes.

And while she drinks—I breathe. I breathe what I know is the first air of our new life together.

chapter thirty-three

piper

Two things never happened in the past few weeks. I never went back to sleep at Skylar's townhouse. And Hailey never went back to Cassidy's.

I suppose the latter would have been difficult considering Cassidy went right from jail to rehab. She and the guy she was with were arrested on drug charges. Hers was reduced to a misdemeanor because she wasn't carrying much on her, but only if she agreed to an inpatient program.

Mason has since filed for full custody. He's scared to death to even consider the possibility of Hailey going through anything like what Charlie and I endured. He's been more than fair about it, however, taking Hailey to see her mom when visitors are allowed.

Two things that *have* happened are that Mason is now looking for a house just outside the city, and we have been interviewing nannies all week.

His small two-bedroom condo has been pretty crowded since moving all of Hailey's belongings in. I, on the other hand, only took up a couple of drawers and a few inches of closet space. Every day when I come home, I find more clothes; more undergarments; more of my favorite toiletries and cosmetics. He's putting forth a true effort to make it my home as well as his and Hailey's.

I take a peek over at Hailey playing in the corner of the church vestibule as she's supervised by my mother while the rest of us participate in the rehearsal for Skylar and Griffin's wedding.

Baylor nudges my shoulder. "Mom is perfectly capable of watching her for two minutes, Piper."

It's not lost on me that since the night of her accident, I know where Hailey is and what she's doing at all times. My need to protect her is growing stronger each day I spend with her.

She is so much like Mason, not only in looks, but in personality. Even at two years old, she's learning compassion, despite the fact she's got a mother who possesses none. Just last weekend, at her birthday party, a little boy dropped his piece of cake on the ground. Hailey quickly walked over and offered her slice to him. Jaws dropped. People whispered about how cute it was. It didn't even matter that we still had twenty pounds of uneaten cake—her small act of kindness was monumental. And it dawned on me that I was beaming with motherly pride.

"You've really taken to her," Baylor says. It's not a question. It's a statement. A truth. My new reality.

I watch Hailey get down on her knees and try to show nine-month-old Jordan how to crawl. "What's not to love?" I ask, laughing at the adorable little girl's antics.

"Love?" Baylor's voice raises by two octaves.

I give her a confirming nod. "I know she will never replace the little girl I lost. I don't expect her to. And I know I'm not her mother. But, Baylor, she's fantastic. That child is magical. A true gift..." My throat tightens and I can't get any more words out.

Baylor hugs me. "You don't know how glad I am to hear you say that, Piper. It makes all this so much better."

I push her to arm's length. "Makes *what* better?"

She swallows air. "Uh . . . *this*, you know, Skylar and Griffin's wedding. It's just all so romantic and perfect."

I look at Skylar while she and Griffin talk to the pastor as we get ready to practice our walk up the aisle. "Yeah, it is pretty perfect."

I get enveloped in a hug from behind. A hug I've been familiar with since childhood. Although not so much in the past few years.

Dad.

I turn around and let his large arms take me in completely. I'm not sure how many seconds or minutes pass while we share this reuniting embrace. He leans down to place a kiss on the top of my head like he always did when I was little. "I'm sorry, Peanut," he says, using the nickname from my childhood. "I didn't know how to deal with the situation. It threw me. It was more than this stupid father could handle. But that's no excuse for letting you down; for further lowering your expectations of men.

"The day I found out you were raped was the day a part of me died. It will never compare to your own loss, but I let it consume me to the point of alienating you." He pulls back, his wet face breaking into a prideful smile. "I have never been more proud of you. You have grown up to be a wonderful, compassionate woman despite all your hurdles, and I love you more than this old man's words can even express."

I throw my arms back around him. "I love you, too, Daddy."

A small part of me wonders why he chose now to have this special father-daughter moment. Shouldn't he be having a talk like this with Skylar? But I let him hug me as long and hard as he wants to because I know we both need it. And just like that—another piece of my heart falls back into place.

"You guys about ready to start?" Gavin asks. "We've got a seven o'clock reservation for dinner, so can we move this along?" He winks at Baylor and they share a look that makes each of them smile like they're about to burst with a huge secret.

Is this what love looks like after that many years? I mean, they met in college and they're still crazy about each other. Yes, they spent some years apart, but that only seemed to deepen their bond, not break it. When I see them, I wonder if I could be looking at my future with Mason.

It amazes me still, how far we've all come to get to this very point. My sisters and I have all faced very different demons and come out on the other side. Better. Stronger. Tougher.

I can't wait to make my toast tomorrow at the reception. They don't know I know they postponed the wedding for me—so that I would have a fighting chance with Mason. But Mason and I have no secrets from each other anymore. We've spent countless hours lying in bed, talking. Well, more than talking if I'm being totally honest.

I look over to catch him staring at me and I blush. After almost getting caught bare-ass naked by one little Miss Curious on more than one occasion, Mason finally took me to his bed—*our* bed. He reminded me over and over that it was ours and ours alone. That no one else had ever or would ever be there except the two of us. He made love to me so passionately and gently that the rest of the world, along with my nightmares, simply melted away.

black roses

It's not that I don't have them anymore. I do. But now, Mason is there to comfort me every time. Just like I'm there to comfort him when he has his.

We support each other. We love each other.

We get each other.

I can't take my eyes off him as he watches me. He shifts his feet anxiously—something I don't normally see and I wonder if weddings make him nervous.

Baylor pulls me by the elbow. "There's plenty of time to daydream about your hot boyfriend. Come on, we have a job to do."

We all gather in the foyer of the church, just beyond the ornate double doors that lead into the large sanctuary. We line up in order, Maddox leading off the pack carrying a velvety pillow that has a fake ring attached to it.

Next in line are Baylor and Gavin. Then Mason takes his place next to me. I notice beads of sweat dotting his brow. "You okay?" I ask in a whisper, as Skylar barks out orders behind me about how slowly she wants us to walk up the aisle.

"Will be," he says, reminding me of the same words he spoke in the hospital a few weeks ago.

Before I can question him, someone opens the doors and Maddox begins the procession. Music is piped through the sound system so we have an idea how it will be tomorrow with the live organist.

Maddox gets to the altar and moves off to one side. Then Baylor and Gavin reach the front. He kisses her on the cheek before they part, then he takes his place at Griffin's side while she moves off to the left.

Mason's elbow is squeezing my arm tightly, almost painfully, against his body. And even over the soft music, I can hear his deep, labored breathing.

I know Skylar must be about to walk in behind us, but instead of everyone looking at the empty doorway, they are all looking at me, huge grins on their faces. Even Griffin—who put this off for two months because of me—doesn't look for his bride-to-be. In fact, when we make our final approach to the altar, he moves aside and stands closer to Gavin.

Confused, I look back to see that Skylar has raced up the aisle and is coming to stand beside Baylor. And my mom and dad are now sitting with the kids in the first pew. I draw my brows together, looking at Skylar while I try to pull away from Mason so I can take my designated spot. But I'm met with resistance and he won't let me go. When I turn around to see why, my heart plugs up my throat, making it impossible for me to breathe.

Mason has dropped to a knee. He's staring up at me, the expression on his face somewhere between looking ill and wanting to smile.

Oh. My. God.

Flashbacks of the first dream I ever had of Mason flood through me.

My eyes dart around slowly enough to realize that what's happening here is not unexpected—well, except by me.

Maddox walks up to Mason, holding the pillow out to him. My eyes go wide when I see what I thought was a fake ring sitting on top of it. Getting a closer look, I gasp when I see a large sparkly diamond that's casting prisms across the room as it catches the light beaming through a window.

Mason ruffles Maddox's hair. "Not quite yet, buddy. I have to ask her first."

black roses

Laughter from my family echoes through the large room as Maddox takes two bashful steps backwards.

Mason clears his throat and squeezes my hands. "Piper, I know you've been trying to decide what to do with your life—be a waitress, go into publishing, maybe even try your hand at acting again someday. But there is one job I want you to have regardless of what you choose for your profession." Hailey makes a loud squeal and his eyes turn to her as my mom tries to hush her.

He looks back up at me. "Actually, that's not true. I want you to have *two* jobs. If I searched the entire world, I could not have found a better woman—a better role model for my daughter. You've been to hell and back yet you are the strongest person I've ever met. You are fiercely loyal to those worthy of your love. You think you are damaged. I think you are beautiful. You're the most beautiful person, inside and out, that I've ever had the pleasure to know. I want to love you, cherish you, and protect you every day from here on out. I want to be your husband, your best friend, and maybe someday, the father of your children. And I want you to help me raise mine."

Sniffles come from behind me and I know my sisters are both crying. I try to take in everything he has said as my knees attempt to keep me standing. *Husband? Children? Can I do this? Am I even capable?*

"I don't know what the future holds," he says, still looking up at me with pools of hope swimming in his icy-blue eyes. "I can't promise my job won't take us away from here. I can't promise I'll be home for dinner every night. I can't promise I will make every birthday party and holiday celebration. But what I can promise you is my heart. My soul. My devotion. My forever."

He looks over at Maddox. "Now, buddy," he says.

Maddox hurries over and Mason removes the ring from the ties that bind it to the pillow.

"Piper Mitchell, I love you. I love every part of you that I've seen, and every piece of you I've yet to discover." He holds the ring out to me. "So, what do you say, Snow White, will you be my princess, my queen, my one and only wife from now to eternity?"

Big drops of tears fall onto my cheeks as I nod my head over and over. My heart is so full, I'm incapable of speech. I let him slip the ring onto my finger then I fall to my knees, right into his strong arms and welcoming lips.

Applause bounces off the walls around us as we seal the deal with our mouths and then embrace each other like there is no tomorrow. Hailey runs up to us, jumping into our hug as only a two-year-old can do.

Mason laughs, his glistening eyes mirroring mine. "Just to be sure, that was a yes?" he asks.

I nod again as we stand, him holding Hailey as he helps me to my feet. She holds her arms out to me and I take her. "That was a yes," I say. "To everything."

"Everything?" He raises a roguish brow, his face filled with more promises.

"I want it all, Mason. The whole fairy tale. The happily ever after. I'm ready for it now. Thanks to you, I'm ready for it now."

"*We're* ready," he says, putting his arm around the two of us. "Now let's get this party started so I can take my fiancée home."

Fiancée. The word rolls around in my head. Never in a million years did I think I would have someone call me that. But I like it. No, I love it.

He takes my hand and we step off the altar—the first step into our forever.

epilogue

piper

Thirteen years later...

I fiddle with the charm on my bracelet, twisting it around the leather straps that never leave my wrist.

I can't remember ever being so scared and excited at the same time. I try to distract myself with the game Mason and I often play—*guess the body part*. I push into the side of my eight-month belly and see if I can get her to push back.

Griff is getting antsy. His five-year-old body can only sit still for so long, and although it's only been ten minutes, it seems as much of an eternity to me as I'm sure it does to my son. "Tell me again, Daddy," his words, along with his piercing blue eyes beg Mason. "Tell me again about your ring."

Griff, named after Mason's best friend, and one of the two people responsible for getting us together, fingers his father's Super Bowl ring. He twirls it around and around the third finger of Mason's right hand while my gaze becomes affixed on the ring that adorns his left. The ring that makes him mine.

As Mason indulges our son in tales of football for the millionth time, my mind wanders back eighteen years to the day I first met my daughter. The day I said hello and goodbye to her all within an hour. The day I died until Mason brought me back to life.

Eighteen years. Eighteen years, two months and nine days since I've seen her, and she's about to walk through that door any second.

Amber. That's her name. It's the only thing I know about her, other than the fact that she grew up in White Plains, just forty-nine miles from here. Thirty-three minutes away on the express train. So close that we've probably passed on the street. Or eaten in the same restaurant. Or gone to the same movie theater.

My unborn daughter must sense my anxiety as she's doing somersaults in my stomach. I rub my hand across my belly, wondering if she will look like Amber did as a newborn.

I never had a picture. I didn't need one. Even after all these years, her face is still etched into my memory as permanently as the rose is tattooed into my skin.

Then fear grips me and I think, not for the first time, that Amber might not want to know me. She might just want to meet me; getting some kind of closure to whatever story her parents may have told her about me. She may even hate me, especially when she sees I have other children. Children I chose to keep—not give away.

Mason and I debated postponing the meeting until after the baby came. But what it really boiled down to was that we wanted to dive into this head first—the way we've dealt with everything life has thrown at us since the day we got engaged. If it isn't meant to be, we will accept it and move on, just like we did after my multiple miscarriages almost a decade ago.

black roses

I don't know what to expect from this meeting. I've dreamed about this day for years. With Mason's gentle urging, I registered my information on the adoption reunion website the day she turned eighteen. I never imagined she would do the same. But she did, and it only took a few months to get through the red tape and organize a meeting.

Before that, I didn't know if she was even alive. Or if she was living in New York. Or if she had ever been told she was adopted. But whatever happens here, I know Mason has my back. He's had my back since the day I walked off that plane all those years ago.

He encouraged me to get involved in community theater, and after a few years of that, to take some small roles in independent films produced by Gavin's studio. But my heart was always at home with Hailey and Griff.

I look at Mason, in awe of the father he is with our children. He never raises his voice, even when fifteen-year-old Hailey tries to leave the house with a skirt that is three sizes too small. Just as he's always been a leader and motivator on the field, he's handled his kids with respect and grace, making our family cohesive. Significant. Strong.

He slips the chunky Super Bowl ring off his finger and lets Griff play with it as he tells him about the winning touchdown pass he threw to capture the title of MVP.

After eleven years as starting quarterback for the Giants, it was the last game he played before announcing his retirement two seasons ago. Everyone knew he had a good five years left in him, but he didn't want to miss any more birthday parties. He didn't want to hear about Hailey's teenage accomplishments or Griff's first tee-ball game from me. He wanted to live those moments *with* them.

Hailey wanted to be here, but her sophomore class trip to D.C. was this week and we weren't about to let her miss out on that experience. Not even for this. She has always wanted a sister, and now, God willing, she might be able to have two. The fact that they don't share blood has never concerned her. Just as my not being her biological mother has never been an issue. Since she was two years old, I've been *Mom* and Cassidy has been *Mama*. And she is as much my child as Griff and the baby growing inside me.

Mason reaches over to squeeze my hand. "It's going to be okay, sweetheart. We can get through anything, right?"

I nod. "Right, babe."

He smiles and picks up my hand, kissing the back of it when the door to the conference room swings open, causing my heart to smash into the wall of my chest.

She walks through the door and I freeze. Time stands still. Mason leans into me and whispers, "God, Piper, she's *you*."

He's right. It's like looking into a mirror at my eighteen-year-old self, right down to her green eyes. But no way was I this beautiful. Nothing and no one has ever been as beautiful as the creature I see standing before me.

And just like the day I gave birth to her, she instantly works her way into every corner of my being.

With Mason's help, I stand. I remind myself to breathe before I force my legs to walk me across the room.

Amber and I quietly stare at each other with millions of unanswered questions swimming in our identical eyes. As I come around the table and get closer to her, her eyes fall to my stomach. Then they dart over to where Griff has parked himself, staring out the picture window at the tiny cars thirty floors below.

A slow smile creeps up her face, brightening her eyes as they glisten with tears, matching my own. Her smile lights up the room.

It lights up my soul. And for the first time in eighteen years, I feel complete.

"I've always wanted siblings," she says through her smile. Tears of joy roll down my cheeks as the first words I've ever heard her speak wind silken threads around my heart.

She holds her hand out to me. "Hi. I'm Amber," she says, a sweet crest of emotion filling her voice. "Amber Rose Black."

samantha christy

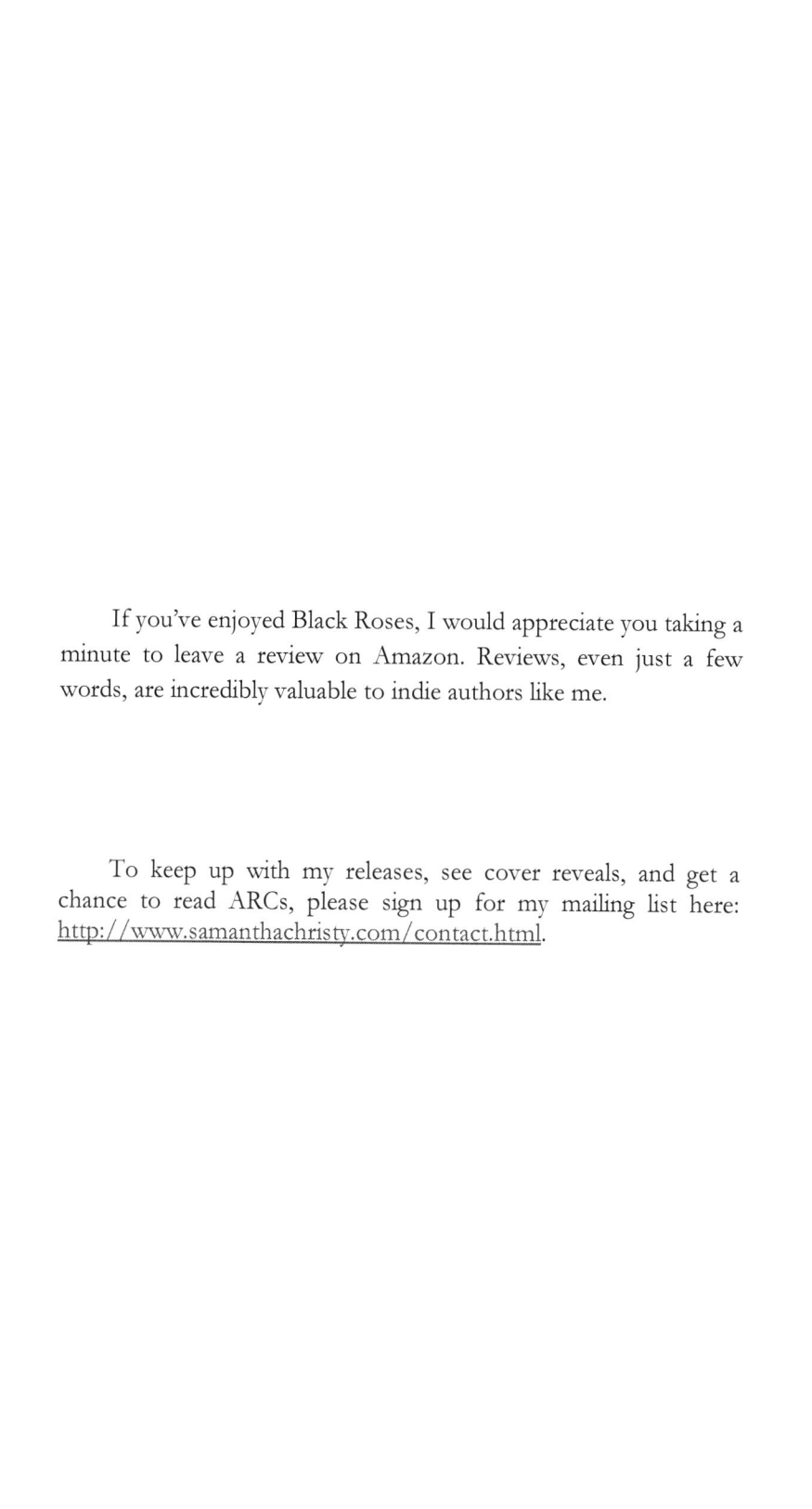

If you've enjoyed Black Roses, I would appreciate you taking a minute to leave a review on Amazon. Reviews, even just a few words, are incredibly valuable to indie authors like me.

To keep up with my releases, see cover reveals, and get a chance to read ARCs, please sign up for my mailing list here: http://www.samanthachristy.com/contact.html.

samantha christy

acknowledgments

It is with both happy and sad tears that I complete this, my first series. Had I known up front how fun it would be, I would have given Baylor, Skylar and Piper three more sisters. However, their legacy will continue with Charlie's story, which will be the first book in my next series following three brothers.

Thank you to my editors, Ann Peters and Jeannie Hinkle. You make me look a lot smarter than I really am. And to my wonderful beta readers, Tammy Dixon, Laura Conley and Angela Marie—your long hours and eyes for detail are appreciated more than you will ever know.

Without the motivation and enthusiasm of my dear friend, April Barnswell, Black Roses would have taken a lot longer for me to write. Her daily emails, bits of encouragement, and friendly competition kept me on track and for that I'm truly grateful.

None of this would be possible without the love and support of my awesome family. Thank you, Bruce, for being not only my husband and best friend, but for being the best damn tech support an author could have.

If someone had told me two years ago that in two years, I'd be publishing my sixth novel, I would have called them crazy. Today, I'm delighted, humbled and honored to be able to call myself a full-time writer.

samantha christy

about the author

Samantha Christy's passion for writing started long before her first novel was published. Graduating from the University of Nebraska with a degree in Criminal Justice, she held the title of Computer Systems Analyst for The Supreme Court of Wisconsin and several major universities around the United States. Raised mainly in Indianapolis, she holds the Midwest and its homegrown values dear to her heart and upon the birth of her third child devoted herself to raising her family full time. While it took time to get from there to here, writing has remained her utmost passion and being a stay-at-home mom facilitated her ability to follow that dream. When she is not writing, she keeps busy cruising to every Caribbean island where ships sail. Samantha Christy currently resides in St. Augustine, Florida with her husband and four children.

You can reach Samantha Christy at any of these wonderful places:

Website: www.samanthachristy.com
Facebook: https://www.facebook.com/SamanthaChristyAuthor
Twitter: @SamLoves2Write
E-mail: samanthachristy@comcast.net